Pariah
Genius

CHEERIO

First published in Great Britain in 2024 by
CHEERIO Publishing
www.cheeriopublishing.com
info@cheeriopublishing.com

Copyright © Iain Sinclair, 2024

Cover design: Tiana Dunlop
Book design: Tiana Dunlop
Cover photograph: *Deakin Drinking* by John Deakin.
Reproduced by kind permission of the John Deakin Estate, 1960s.

Printed and bound in the United Kingdom by Short Run Press Ltd.

A CIP catalogue record for this book is available from the British Library.

ISBN: 9781917283076
eISBN: 9781739440589

Pariah *Genius*

John Deakin
and the Soho Court around Francis Bacon

A PSYCHOBIOGRAPHIC FICTION

Iain Sinclair

CHEERIO

Praise for Iain Sinclair

'It isn't often that one reads a book and is convinced that it's an instant classic, but I'm sure that *London Orbital* will be read 50 years from now.'
– **JG Ballard, author of *Crash*, *High Rise*, and *Empire of the Sun***

'[*Downriver* is one] of those idiosyncratic literary texts that revivify the language, so darn quotable as to be the reader's delight and the reviewer's nightmare.'
– *The Guardian*

'One can only marvel at Sinclair's eye for telling detail and his sense of the subtle ironies of modern London life . . . With its elegantly civilised melancholy for what is lost, neglected or hidden, Sinclair's position is highly seductive.'
– *The Daily Telegraph*

'Sinclair's recent work represents some of the most important in contemporary English letters.'
– *The New Statesman*

'An absolute joy. This unashamedly intellectual traveller uncovers a rich history whose traces are rapidly being wiped from the landscape.'
– *The Times*

'If you are drawn to English that doesn't just sing, but sings the blues and does scat and rocks the joint, try Sinclair. His sentences deliver a rush like no one else's.'
– *The Washington Post*

For Alan Moore, virtuoso of 'Unearthing'

Contents

'Thus electric shock, like Bardo, creates phantoms, it transforms all the pulverised states of the patient, all the facts of his past into phantoms which cannot be utilised for the present and which do not cease to besiege the present.'

– Antonin Artaud, *Artaud le Mômo*

'If Paris is a lovely salon displayed for conversation, London is a lumber-room to be foraged for junk, rubbish, white elephants, treasure. Midsummer is not the time to do it.'

– Mary Butts, *Armed with Madness*

'Generally speaking the dead do not return.'

– Antonin Artaud, *Electroshock*

SAN MICHELE

SAN MICHELE

The shape of the black window, framed by filthy bandages of lace, hanging like perforations on a strip of film, prints in negative across the curdled cream of a descending ceiling. That plaster lid, with its generations of yellowing smoke damage, is far away and hungry to lift into the night, to display cold needles of retreating stars. The ceiling is ironed flat across the candlewick bedspread. The sleeper cannot turn his head. Or close his eyes. He cannot move. Or breathe. He is dead, quite dead, newly dead. The man is unsettled in this novel condition, but he can still hear the steady convulsions of an unforgiving sea: drag and grind, retreat and return. A murmuring mothering sound overwhelms night traffic and the sirens of ambulances ferrying the dying and those caught up, with no way out, in the exultant imminence of childbirth.

The ceiling is a descending floor. A floor in the wrong place. Broken apart. A snowfall of plaster chokes his burning lungs. This is the wrong sea. The wrong time. And there is no time left. Brighton, not Venice. Who dies in Brighton? Apart from campy theatricals. On stage. Matinee for preference. Third encore. Catch the evening headlines. Even poets make it to Hove.

His hands, gripping the sheet, are so white now they are blue. The blue of milk left out in a cracked saucer for a tomcat who is never coming back. He is washed in the lovely thin blue that he favours in his floral paintings, those Edwardian seascapes with serpents. A drop curtain for his fairground strongmen with their mermaid tattoos, their mums and Indian chiefs in turkey cock headdress. Distance is always blue. But he doesn't do distance. Everything is flat. Objects float. He trades on spoiled innocence, drunken cynicism: bitchery as charm. 'I'll be writing your obitchery yet, you old queen,' he tells Dan. When his best chum visits him in the butchers' ward in Hackney, after they stole a substantial chunk of his insides. Dan's great scarlet plank of a face loomed over, fire-breath. To be quite sure that his best pal wasn't faking it. That, this time, he was really done.

The sweetest sleep is on the other side. Before death, death. Before life, a blessed forgetfulness. It was that bird again. Sinking into the pit of the Brighton bed, he heard a sharp bill rapping on the window. The witch's familiar had flown from Venice to take his revenge.

SAN MICHELE

Sloppy avocado mush, drowning under a lingering film of scented oil, did for Max. The jealous painter dipped a finger and teased the bird. The pampered pet fell for the bait with sufficient greed to break the skin. Lifeblood dripped dark and rich in the wet green bowl. The fungicidal toxin, persin, fulfilled its deadly purpose: ruffled feathers, awful wrenching gasps, foul language in dialect. And the merciful relief of apathy that comes just before the end. It was no comedy: the parrot wobbled, tilted forward, crashed from its perch. It is a sorry obitchery when your own funeral is worse attended, and with fewer tears, than that of a vile-tempered bird.

Then there were the other portraits, the photographs he couldn't lose: country house weekends in Hampshire. A society snapper treated almost like a guest and paid to defraud time. The painter plays along, dutiful but unowned. Eyes down. Legs shaved. Painted brows and emphatic lashes. He was a barbered trophy lit from the side like a deposed hopeful from the Rank charm school, put out to rep. A mature juvenile tarting for wartime work when the men were all away. Here was a quite acceptable frontispiece for the promising show of paintings brought back from their travels, the Cork Street exhibition that his wealthy friend was never going to facilitate.

He couldn't forget, in this post-mortem slideshow playing on the ceiling, those other full-figure portraits made in Hampshire. They were studiously composed: painter as woman. All the weekend guests, down from London, were so presented. Their better selves.

In a patterned frock, pearls at the throat, the painter is no flapper, no pastiche. His expression is grave, closer to a guarded truth. Closer to the artist he might have become. Or the working man with proper working hands. With prominent knees and solid thighs above a show of sheer black stockings. There was a lesson to be found in laying down the two commissioned portraits, side by side: revelation through disguise. Masquerade as the only mask that fits. That can never be removed. A revelation of strength he would have to bury. Or delay.

The common mourners, all in cinematic black, dress the deck of the public vaporetto as it glides across the sombre waters of the lagoon, in that special

SAN MICHELE

ambiguity of winter light: anticipation of arty films yet to be made. Of poetry by association. Texts laid over texts. There were so many islands, most of them quite unsuited for the disposal of the dead. You could barely break the first sod with your spade, the stones with your pick, before water flooded from below. But Venice, subject to plague and marsh fevers, had to find a site for human landfill. Or raise its rackety foundations on generations of mortal bones. When nuns gave up their chaste retreat to dereliction and decay, to cats and crows, the Senate sanctioned an ossario, *a decanting of the city's cemeteries.*

The ornate funeral gondola of the collector, keeper of exotic beasts, closed on the landing place at San Michele. Max lay in a gilded glass box, more like a scientific specimen now than a personality with the gift of speaking out of turn, refining insults to a single word. Of those chosen guests, playing their parts in tailored coats and dark glasses, some bareheaded and tawny, some in Russian fur, the late surrealist painter, the primitive with the combed mascara eyelashes, was the most engaged. The only one who, despite himself, was lost in a fugue of empathy for the deceased bird. There is an unbreakable bond, he supposed, between killer and victim.

A good-looking young Italian boy, bribing the gondolier, had been permitted to come aboard. To make a record of the voyage and the ceremony. He was not a Venetian. He came from Sicily and was working hard to establish connections with the magazines. He anticipated the magic of a credited photo essay. Serial compositions telling an honest story made from lies. Local and international celebrities. Let us not dress it up: a freak show.

There was something very wrong in this intrusion. Something in the process of mimed respect: head bowed, camera lifted. Where the others, even the worst of the drunks, settled to silence, arranging themselves as satellites to a genuine loss, the boy in the leather jacket was in constant motion; rocking his head, flicking back his oily hair, trying to anticipate formal patterns; a geometry that would play out as a composition equal to a painting by Giorgio de Chirico. One of those dull and valuable things on the wall of the Palazzo on the Grand Canal. A moulded Renaissance frame on which the parrot would perch and preen. And watch. And wait. And plot his slow revenge.

It was that group on the boat: the woman sitting like a dowager duchess, the bird in its box, the mourners on their feet, holding the rail with expensive leather gloves. And the young hustler nodding and smiling, as if asking for permission he did not require. Here, in a single blinding instant, was the confirmation of the painter's loathing of the whole sorry business of photography. The vile corruption of the class of moral bankrupts who chose to follow this unworthy trade. Stolen images, even when release forms have been signed, victims having no notion of what they are giving up, spoil the natural order. They hinder the mysterious flow of time. Every photograph is a memorial to failure.

And knowing this now, understanding the consequences of the mortal contract, the reforgotten photographer in his anonymous hotel room in Brighton – profession abandoned, paintbrushes reclaimed – smirked in a dying rictus and let it all go. Murderer of parrots. Assassin of reputation. Lover of the loveless. Treasured pariah. Gossip and gutter genius. Soho drudge. Let it all go. It went. And it wasn't coming back.

He should have died in Venice. He did *die in Venice. In that shock of understanding, with the click of the Sicilian's shutter, when he got everything wrong. When he decided that the camera was a weapon for stopping time. And not the reverse. He was self-betrayed. He found his unavoidable calling and he was undone. He waited on the worst.*

EXHIBITIONS

Man and Beast

Memory is contained in architecture: doors, walls, high ceilings. Secret spaces without names. Coming up the wide stone stairs to the vestibule of Burlington House, I began to suspect that my London dream began and ended with major exhibitions by Francis Bacon. The first, in 1962, at the old Tate Gallery on Millbank, was pure shock; a nudge towards a new reality, the revelation of a previously unexplored cultural terrain. The gathered paintings were themselves a journey, an unstable path into a future prophesied in the delirious re-visioning of Vincent van Gogh's *Painter on the Road to Tarascon*. A stalled walker. A pilgrim melting into the dust of his track. The seeker is burdened with implements, policed by a line of cypress trees. And threatened on all sides by spears of southern grass. *Van Gogh, the Man Suicided by Society*. The afternoon of the crows foretells all.

And then, as another kind of provocation, the white bone lantern of Bacon's attack on William Blake's life mask, that intrusive occult procedure committed by the phrenologist J. S. Deville, for exhibition in a shop window on the Strand. There were further masks taken from the original, in anticipation of technologies of reproduction not yet invented. Each version heightened the lineaments of pain, the smothering of the poet's face in plaster. The three-dimensional object, frosted and shining, was later neutralised, thinned by photographic process. It was published in books and magazines. Angled to attract a painter as preternaturally attuned to pictorial subversion as Francis Bacon.

Bacon's Blake in the 1962 exhibition is a carnival mask, a decapitated spectre oddly illuminated in a private hell: hairless, tongueless, hurt by knowledge. The mouth is a surgical slash of agony, cutting through soft tissue, running from cheek to cheek. In company with van Gogh, the man on the road to nowhere, this bridled London icon, embedded in the location where I first witnessed it, became a significant item in my personal mythology. The postcard of *Study for a Portrait II (after the Life Mask of William Blake)* I bought then, and have carried with me ever since, as a bookmark or handy space for notes, differs from later versions. The head is larger, whiter, almost green, and the eternal darkness in which it is suspended is a soupy brown, rather than a rich blue-black. The gouging of the cheeks, the scraped and butchered neck, the scalp raw from clumps of hair torn away in the removal of enveloping plaster: this portrait is a proudly borne assault on mortality. A signature of death in life. Ruined and unyielding.

The years spanning the two exhibitions, the Tate retrospective in 1962 and *Francis Bacon, Man and Beast* in 2022, were an attempt to keep faith with the inspiration of the primal encounter. I tried to maintain a balance between Bacon's van Gogh, the doomed walker on his treadmill of fate, and that animated life mask, the stricken head of the great poet at the mercy of his own vertiginous and unyielding cosmology. The craftsman's pride and courage.

I was a film student, living in the capital for the first time, on the south side of the river. Striking out from Brixton, over Lambeth Bridge, to follow the Thames east towards Westminster, I detoured several times to immerse myself in Bacon's first career survey: a maelstrom of manipulated image-actions. In his introduction to the catalogue for the Tate exhibition, John Rothenstein wrote that Bacon's early paintings had been likened to 'vapours from a magic cauldron, condensing here and there into the wavering likeness of a human form, but about to dissolve and disintegrate again'. Rothenstein could have been describing a primitive response to photography: the alchemical wonder of seeing a face swim out of a dish of developing fluid. The Bacon paintings, in both shows, are most troubling when focus shudders and the layered surface catches the moment of transformation. Oil flatters flesh. Flesh peels to bone. Bone melts to latex. Forensic exposure of nerve and sinew. The carapace of identity is turned inside out. And the results are recorded for catalogues and postcards. But the cards give no accurate sense of that genetic exchange worked by the act of standing and staring, flowing out to meet the projection of the thing that is flowing towards you.

When I met J. G. Ballard, decades later, I learned that he also nominated the Bacon show at Millbank as a moment of revelation, confirming his vision of the contemporary world. He wrote in his 2008 autobiography, *Miracles of Life*, about Bacon as 'the greatest painter of the post-war world'. And about his disappointment, when he finally met the man, in discovering that his hero had no interest in receiving compliments or talking about his own work. Very much like you, I thought. The Shepperton magus was happy to discuss and debate all aspects of our Atrocity Exhibition multiverse. But any mention of his books, published or in progress, was rapidly brushed aside. Ballard found Bacon's interviews 'elliptical and elusive'. They were nothing like his own, which became an art form, conducted in person, out in Shepperton, or over a transatlantic telephone line, as a refreshing break from the solitude of disciplined composition. Nine o'clock start. Lunch break, mid-sentence, for *The World at One*. Bacon, rather like his Tangier friend William Burroughs, was better left as a concept than a collision of personalities.

Ballard, whose stated preference was to have been a painter, should have done the chat for Bacon. 'It was we who sat in those claustrophobic rooms, like TV hospitality suites in need of a coat of paint,' he said, 'under a naked light bulb that might signal the arrival of the dead, the only witnesses at our last interview.' In his later years, Ballard's interrogations were conducted, by choice, in anonymous meeting rooms in the Hilton Hotel, Shepherd's Bush. An area where he knew that he could find a convenient parking bay. Ballard's memorial celebration was held at Tate Modern, Bankside. There were as many artists and filmmakers as writers in attendance.

There is a cleverly composed photograph of Bacon, suited from Harrods, eyes closed, on the steps of the Tate in 1985. It was taken by John Minihan, a working professional who is now based in Ireland, after a long career in Fleet Street and elsewhere. The Minihan portrait, shot by prior arrangement, was used as the cover illustration for *The Visitors' Book*, a twinned biography of Richard Chopping and Denis Wirth-Miller by Jon Lys Turner. The choice of this particular frame from the sequence Minihan snapped was made in order to showcase the warring couple, Dicky and Denis, on the step above Bacon, but looking down at him, one on either side. The attendant lords, approaching the pillared court of culture, have adjusted their expressions for the benefit of the camera. They are seasoned troupers, these men, undeceived and alert to the foibles of their princely friend. Spies as much as courtiers, they keep their own diaries. Wirth-Miller, a specialist in the wavelike rhythms of grass, the dynamics of animals in landscape, is another Bacon collaborator. They shared studio space and wild holidays. Nobody knows quite how much Wirth-Miller contributed to those Bacon exteriors from the Midi and North Africa. Feral dogs are held in common.

I was in London in 1985, working as a bookdealer, but I didn't return to Millbank. The recent paintings were more remote, in their heavy gold frames, safe behind glass. They had lost the appeal of first exposure. The actions were extreme, figures trapped in cycles of theatrical violence. They played out familiar existential horrors against lurid backdrops, reflexes from Bacon's period as an interior decorator in the 1930s. And there must have been sentimental resistance on my part to the biggest horror of all: universal success and adulation of the oligarchs. You could smell the colour of serious money. Or perhaps I was too preoccupied with my own double life, chasing books, selling books, and trying to write.

Fever dreams empty the streets and let the old ghosts out. Early in 2021, I managed the business of booking a ticket when *Man and Beast* was first advertised by the Royal Academy: shortly before the exhibition was lost to Covid. The sense of duty, back then, doing background research for the project on which I was working, was replaced, after months of locked-at-home engagement with the painter and his associates, by a genuine hunger to look again at the paintings that had fired me on my arrival in London.

There is no crush. Most of the figures on the stairs are masked. Here is a convalescent carnival. They are talking very quietly, behind face coverings or raised hands, not quite convinced that permissions will hold up. It is like visiting a rather grand hospital, to witness a virtuoso operation performed by a celebrity neurosurgeon coming out of retirement.

You push through swing doors to enter Gallery One. And you are immediately confronted by the standing figure of Francis Bacon. The professional barker. It is like a return to the days when he rounded up punters for Muriel Belcher. Hair blackened, hands deep in raincoat pockets, the painter is crucified on the cross struts of the wooden panels behind him, a studio wall or studded door. This is an approved brand promotion. Bacon is moody and magnificent, like Jane Russell. The concept is properly credited to a Soho photographer with whom the painter enjoyed a long and complicated relationship: John Deakin. And this is fitting, that the person who contributed so much to a crucial series of Bacon portraits, as something more than a paid facilitator or minor craftsman, should compose the welcoming figure of the artist-doorman at the Royal Academy; the one who invites us to step inside. In many ways, returning to this portrait, after completing my circuit, I felt the obligation to laud Deakin as co-author of Bacon's most obsessive and reworked transformations.

Floating alongside the star's right shoulder in the pristine black-and-white print is a splash of dark red paint. A blood smear. A jammy wound embellished with active scratches from the painter's brush or knife. Submerged within the carmine blot I locate a wolfish outline with snarling mouth, knobbly spine and curved tail. It is not clear if Deakin recovered this image from the floor of Bacon's studio and chose, for his own reasons, to preserve and deface it. Here is proof of collateral damage; legacy archive distressed when Deakin came back, after abandoning a photographic career, to painting. The print must have been salvaged when the Photography Curator Bruce Bernard searched beneath the dead man's bed in his abandoned Berwick Street flat.

The exposed figure, in its own vestibule at the Royal Academy, demonstrated the upgrade in status for the responsible photographer. Deakin's reputation had fallen, then slowly climbed again, when he was rediscovered, in the sixty-year hiatus between the two Bacon exhibitions, as a valued outlier. In changing times, the witness at the window, the clown on the floor, had been promoted to the role of secret sharer: anonymous recorder as equal artist. The Tate catalogue for the 1962 retrospective used a cropped headshot of Bacon, printed in harsh contrast, as its frontispiece. Nowhere in the pages of that publication is the responsible photographer credited. The dramatic portrait, grainy, cinematic, with light bouncing from sweep of hair to glint of leather, was also committed by Deakin. A few crumpled notes in the hand, liquid lunch at Wheeler's if he was lucky, but the jobbing snapper remains invisible. Those who have loaned paintings to the exhibition are dutifully listed. Those who have penned a few words on the painter are honoured. Explainers, granting interviews, are thanked. Deakin's confrontational portrait, we assume, has been self-generated without the technical assistance of the anonymous functionary. The Tate frontispiece has emerged from an obedient mirror manipulated by the narcissism of the subject: the man who has already composed, in the light of a naked bulb, his preferred portrait, layered across his own features in Max Factor, abrasive powder and boot polish.

***

14

In the gallery for Man and Beast, the first partition wall exhibits the looming 1948 Head I as a cinematic dissolve from Deakin's life-sized vision of Bacon to a tormented monster; a hybrid form, animal and human host, devouring and devoured. The elements are locked in an indissoluble Jacobean union, a marriage of opposites. The screaming ape – not screaming but yawning, according to Desmond Morris – emerges from a deleted Pope Innocent. The tassel swings. The armature of the throne is also a punishment cage. An animal sliced from a book by Robert and Ada Yerkes bares its teeth to rip apart this fleshy other; the thing that has summoned it into the throne room, the plush Vatican closet. Positioning the painting in this way colours the relationship of Bacon and Deakin. They need each other but never miss a chance to wound. The lumpen deformity, beast and priest, demonstrated in Head I, subverts the smooth surface of Deakin's portrait of Bacon, in which submerged fits of pique and pride are hidden, before breaking out in a great scarlet shriek.

In the same period as *Head I*, originally exhibited at the Hanover Gallery, Bacon painted *Study from the Human Body*. A muscular male nude, bull-necked and shaven headed, seen from behind, is pushing his way through lead curtains, within the tonal register of that version of man and ape, grisaille on raw canvas. It had never occurred to me before, but this threatening figure is a reverse-angle reprise of Blake's *The Ghost of a Flea*. The sullen weight, the forward-tipping skull, the curtains. Bacon denied all belief systems. He repudiated visions. But he serviced his demons in his own fashion. There are no comets or stars on the far side of Bacon's drapes. He carried Blake's nocturnal intruder into a Turkish bath, a shower stall. The intruders at his midnight studio door are not from the angelic orders, they are solid and biddable. Sometimes, in the boredom of sleepless hours, he welcomes the visitation and puts the ruffian on the stair to service as a model. Just as Blake sketched the prophets and phantoms as they appeared to him.

Early Bacon, whatever his sources, *was* a visionary. I am encouraged to rediscover the force of those post-war paintings, many of which were included in the 1962 retrospective. Now, from the remembered litter of experience, my accidental life in the capital, I looked at Bacon's work in a different way. A slow circuit of the Royal Academy rooms was an appreciative farewell to paintings I knew, and to others passed over in reproduction. Blake's eidetic visions, according to S. Foster Damon, were intensifications of 'normal experience'. From these psychic manifestations, and from his heterodox and wide-ranging scholarship, the poet constructed a mysterious and abiding legend in which historic personages were elevated, to take their place in a cosmic drama. Bacon, using Deakin as one of his evidence-providers, gathered up friends, drinking partners and lovers, before pressing them into a theatre of torture, submission, and suicide. The crew of Soho drinking pals and casual lovers were transformed into other states of being. Into animals, spoiled saints or hungry ghosts. In his ruined, photo-strewn cave, Bacon played at god.

One of the great paintings, status powerfully reasserted here, was known, in 1962, as *The Magdalene*. But Bacon redacted religious implications in later years. His theology was just paint and accident. The cover image from the Tate show was re-christened as *Figure Study II*. It has been positioned in Burlington House as the central panel of an imposing triptych. A figure, probably female, naked, kneeling, draped in a tweed coat that manages to be both heavy and translucent, stretches her mouth in a choreographed howl. Her blue umbrella, primed for Winnie in Beckett's *Happy Days*, is opened against radiation in a pulsing orange room. 'Expanse of scorched grass,' says Beckett's stage direction. And that is here too. A creature gnawing or vomiting up a bouquet of flowers. Thin stalk-legs are trapped in a puddle of African vegetation that looks like a toupee abandoned by Mister Kurtz.

'Where are the flowers?' says Winnie. 'Did you not hear me screaming for you?' Like Winnie's companion, Willie, emerging from his hole, Bacon's beast is crawling out, in an uncanny echo of a play first seen in London at the Royal Court Theatre in the year of the original Tate retrospective.

Moving deeper into the Royal Academy show, Deakin's co-authorship is so much in evidence that you can smell him. He doesn't need to claim credit. He has already plotted his posthumous revenge. The truth is waiting in a box under his abandoned bed. Peter Lacy, nightclub pianist and fighter pilot, Bacon's fiercest lover, the one for whom he brought back twelve rhino hide whips from Africa, is presented as a cornered political prisoner. Or a generic torturer. Sprawled back, taking a break from his labours. The portrait has been lifted, seamlessly, from a set of commissioned Deakin photographs. Skin tight as a stocking mask. Silver hair belligerent in barbered entitlement. Black eyebrows and white face. Black eyes in bruised rims. Lacy could have been the model for that Battle of Britain veteran, short of the readies, rocky with survivor's guilt: the serial-killer suspect adrift in Covent Garden boozers in Alfred Hitchcock's late return to London for *Frenzy*. Both men favoured unbuttoned-at-the-throat officer class shirts. Squadron ties reserved for strangulation parties. The original Deakin print, rescued from archive, is cracked and paint flecked, improved by smudges and fingerprints. Bacon transfused week-old corpse colours onto the naked Lacy. The lower limbs are swallowed in pitch. The male member is rampant, engorged.

Other familiars from the Colony Room, required as Deakin portraits, are present and incorrect. George Dyer. Isabel Rawsthorne. Henrietta Moraes. From poses specified by Bacon, Deakin delivered prints to be cannibalised, time and again. Rawsthorne, a talented painter, is confronted on a Soho street. Moraes, depicted as drowning in the luxuriance of her own flesh, indulged Deakin and inspired Bacon. Sometimes on a sagging mattress. Sometimes on a blue bed. Deakin is ranked, by his patron and the clique of courtiers, as a filthy surgical assistant. A complicit scrubber in some insanitary Victorian operating theatre.

Among the sweepings from Bacon's studio floor, logged, removed, and painstakingly reassembled at the Hugh Lane Gallery in Dublin, was a photograph of Deakin, smoking at the bar, perhaps taken by the painter. At any rate, he kept it. Your man is smartly suited with a crisp white shirt and slim black tie. The bar might be the Golden Lion. Shadows fall across wooden panels. Doors open on fallible memory. Keys turn so slowly in the lock. Drunken evenings are dying in a salt-crusted window.

Heartbreak hotel. Intimations of mortality. Symbols without structure. None of these elements, as yet, cohere or connect. But Deakin is watchful. Primed for the worst.

In our hesitant emergence from a series of coronavirus lockdowns, the traumatised city cakewalked, tempted by a sudden blitz of spaces newly open to advance booking for withheld exhibitions. Londoners stabbed at digital navigation systems like addicts chasing rumours of street drugs being safely landed after a long drought.

All of these group manifestations demanded Francis Bacon as their promotional banker. At the Barbican, for a comprehensive survey of *Postwar Modern: New Art in Britain 1945–65*, an allocated side chapel, labelled 'Cruise', featured a series of sinister Bacon businessmen, solitary at the bar. They were summoned from the Imperial Hotel in Henley-on-Thames. Patrick Hamilton ghosts, marooned in purgatory, threaten violent retribution against the bohemian painter who has dared to expose them. Or so he hopes.

On the upper deck of *A Century of the Artist's Studio: 1920–2020* at the Whitechapel Gallery, there is a reproduction of the reproduction of Bacon's hideaway in Reece Mews, as removed to Dublin. Salvaged detritus, including many photographs, Polaroids, booth strips and pictures cut from magazines, have acquired a quasi-religious status. They have travelled from mess to value. From among a selection of items displayed in a vitrine, I zoomed in on the painter's notes for 18 August 1958. They were scribbled on the flyleaf of V. J. Stanek's *Introducing Monkeys*. The Bacon prompts for the chosen day include: 'Figures on Roads', 'Heads' and 'Figures Staring into Mirrors'.

In my excited examination of the painter's menu of actions, I read the confirmation that I was on the right track. Figures on Roads. Heads. I had no idea where I was going but I think I had got there.

ORIGINS AND ACTIONS

Notorious Jewel

He pranced up the steps, soapy hair watered flat, borrowed jacket brushed. Avoiding the impulse to check his flies, our man clocked the two obvious coppers, the pink one and the old sweat with the tobacco moustache. Lost without their wives, civilians in transit and sad survivors in their itching civvies looked uniformly displaced, not sure if they had the right coins, the right papers. Every person passing through a rail terminal at this ungodly hour qualified as a refugee.

Knees bent, a sailor keeping his foothold in rough sea, the man from Soho scoured the platform, struggling to achieve focus through a blizzard of tiny cerebral hammer blows. He needed to find his way to the concourse, to the newspaper stall and the destination board. Would they have names in English? Underground, among pipes and white tiles, he had managed his old neurosis by jamming the bolt, pushing hard to test resistance. 'I have heard the key turn in the door once and turn once only.' It must always be locked and secured or wide open. He had a terror of the mean crack, the door of destiny left ajar, blowing suddenly shut and trapping him forever.

It was still night, a ridiculous time to be out and about. The thick arms of the station clock were nailed to their glowing lunar dial. Clammy, dripping and poisoned streets had infiltrated the station. Hard to tell if the weather had come inside or if vagrants had torched the bins and benches for a little warmth. Taste the grit of smoke on your black tongue. Taste and relish. This was a sponsored escape. A paid commission. Check the day's standing orders: belt, bracers, bag. And books. All present and correct.

Smog and coal smoke cohabited, stroking the chilled base of the plinth: a possible shot if he'd been in a more receptive mood and not pushed against a timetable. This looming black giant in his winged coat, thick scarf like an ammunition belt, anthracite black and glistening against a sepulchral white arch, was on perpetual guard duty. Flattered by a halo of fogged lamps. The bronze effigy was reading a very thin book. The traveller liked oversize statues. As counterpoint to the vain fools he was obliged to arrange against them. Make a note of this one, perhaps, for another day? Another life. Claim expenses. Unsociable hours. Taxi fare saved by shoe leather. Chitty for lukewarm tea and curling white buffet sandwich. The hope of a brief encounter postponed. Yet again. Duty before pleasure. Thruppeny bit in the chipped saucer. Second thoughts. Take it back.

Head was banging. The crackling announcer's voice sounded as if that monumental scarf had been thrust down the reader's throat. The traveller patted his pockets, loose change, matches, cigarettes. Did you need a passport? The hit was abroad, worse than abroad: it was Wales. It was country, wolves and chapels. And poets!

The ugly dreadlands of the western rail corridor reassured him: warehouses, factories, prisons, parks, and allotments to supply the cabbages and carrots on which we all depend. He got up, for the third time, to slide the door tight shut. A child whimpered and snivelled; his small sandaled foot had been kicking at the gap. It was caught, hurt. Mother enraged. Father conciliatory, pulling out the twist of rationed sweets, the junior crossword he had been saving until they passed Slough or even Swindon. There were servicemen smoking in the corridor, going home with their clap and kitbags. Squaddies and a couple of quite promising sailors. The boy's foot was being massaged by his mother. He was told to be brave, like the soldiers. Nothing would calm him until a group of children who were different, with smoothly ancient faces, like geriatrics trapped in pre-pubertal bodies that were never going to grow, were herded to their prickly seats by a nurse and a sporting man in a dog collar. One of these children came straight across and stood staring at the boy with the hurt foot. And at once he stopped crying, submitted and smiled.

The traveller picked up the books his landlord, his special friend, had sorted for him. One was an entertainment. He'd been told that the person he had to find only read thrillers. He took a stab at it. 'No carefully measured caress would satisfy the approaching dark.' Right there! He tried a few more lines before focus was lost to his thumping headache, then set the orange paperback aside on the brown seat. He couldn't help noticing how every paragraph he sampled seemed to refer directly to his own activities. His mood. Was that a symptom of some weird mental condition?

'A wilderness of allotments opened through the steam, sometimes the monotony broken by tall ugly villas, facing every way, decorated with coloured tiles.'

What he read now was what he saw. The book was a dirty window smeared with language. And what he saw was already in the book, waiting for him. Predicting his fate.

Leave well alone, light up. Try the corridor. Was there a bar? Would it be open when they crossed the border? His story had been written by others and hidden in libraries. 'Stagnant water radiant for a moment with liquid light. Somewhere within the dingy casing lay the ancient city, like a notorious jewel, too stared at, talked of, trafficked over.' A notorious jewel. A murky secret. That was him. All over.

He was supposed to get a signature, an inscription, for the other book. It was worth a few bob, a rarity in its own lifetime. 'I see the boys of summer in their ruin.' The carriage window, greased and dripping with intricate trails of condensation, is changing. 'These boys of light are curdlers in their folly.' Poetry. Money. Madness. Wet English greys and greens fuse and flare. Drowned lands emptied of human traffic are melancholy with huddled cows. The anomie of field after field, tangled copses and thorny earthworks masking the accompanying river, before a sudden skull-splitting vision of brilliant Mediterranean blue, the blue of heaven. He sees what should have been out there, if the train travelled in the right direction, south not west. Fabulous harbours of postponed desire, of crises past and yet to come. Time to ease his restless bowels before Newport?

Disembarked and almost disembowelled by the nag of hunger, soon dismissed, along with a hideous matutinal thirst, a sandpaper-tongued craving, the jaded assassin yawned. He stretched. Army trained, by numbers, he checked again: belt, bag, books. The sprightly, unlanguaged, demob-suited metropolitan on the platform at Carmarthen Town surprised himself: he was quite at home. Comforted to know that this had all happened before, like a play by J. B. Priestley. He had only to impersonate himself and let preordained events unfold. It was like holding a photographic print in your hand and watching it revert to its original purity. To the primal soup.

The man with the motor recognised the alien at once, among the farmers and adventurers who had made a successful return with a cargo of cockles and laverbread from the hazards of Swansea's indoor market. And the Londoner, even without the wink of greeting, never offered, knew his driver. Knew him and liked him. This solid man, up from the estuary village, was drunker than he was. The ripe monologue he delivered – Isn't it, now? – as they swooped down a lovely green tunnel, toy farms, woods, soft hills, confirmed the promise of their initial encounter. Stories of Augustus John and other legends of Fitzrovia tripping towards the hospitality of the old, ivy-swallowed ruin of the castle. The driver was part of the pub, it seemed. Down here they are all related. Incest is a bond best kept in the family, so they say. Cousins to crows and sheep. There might be time, after all, for liquid hospitality, and gossip gathering, before he started work. Call it research. Call it duty. Get a signature for the bar bill. And let the other bugger pay. Cheers, boyo!

1949: From the Graveyard On

The life of the man pressed between pages of the stained magazine is fading fast. Much faster than my recollection of encountering that frequently reproduced image for the first time. I don't remember, in the period when I borrowed the magazine, noticing the discoloration on the paper covers. Coffee or blood? After too many years in the 'used book' trade, the stain made me uncomfortable. This would prove a tricky sale, unless I could assert with confidence that the blood had leaked from somebody of marketable reputation, a suicided painter or reforgotten novelist. A drinking chum from the Soho cellars. Collectors want pristine, *virgo intacta*. Or the illusion of it. Scholars are more tolerant. They know that every scribbled annotation, every doodle, every squashed bug, tells a story. Hip conceptual artists labour to fake creases, spills, neurotic revisions. The portrait of the poet in *Adam International Review* (1953) welcomes the grave. On the hump of gentle hill above a fabled Carmarthenshire village. No sermons. The picture is all there is.

The damp Welsh cemetery was a down-from-the-Smoke gig for a commissioned photographer of growing reputation. The gig being to lay on enough Celtic twilight to suggest, a few months after the illustration appeared in a new American magazine, that the capture demonstrated wizardly prescience. This poet was doomed and New York City was the well-rewarded terminal where he would recognise his destiny at the bottom of a whisky glass.

Photographers are sharks. They circle, picking up the faintest traces of blood. Then reacting in an instant. Always hoping, in those pre-digital days, for a fortunate accident. Botched attempts could be rescued by the magic of the darkroom. Step up the contrast. Some strategic cropping.

Off to the pub by opening time. Negatives and contact sheets in an old shirt box. But honour the superstition, keep the record safe. Just in case. A pension fund. A ribbon of time.

It appears, in the case of the Welsh contract, that the supposed victim was the one who directed the operation. This short, rumpled man was not unhappy to be distracted for a couple of hours from his 'Play for Voices', a work-in-not-much-progress-at-all. Boiled sweets and ciggies in pocket, the poet travelled to London – any excuse – to talk up his project to the usual suspects. The radio commission only moved forward once plot was abandoned. And the author allowed himself to be an auditor of whispers. Limestone and clay voices buried in the rich ground of his fortunate inheritance.

Away from his writing hut, from Brown's Hotel, the restored castle, from Boat House domesticity, the poet controlled the session; as he controlled, with the last of his sweated strength, fired on booze, sleeping pills and cortisone shots, rehearsals for a first staged reading of his play at the Kaufmann Auditorium in New York. Poet guided photographer to the chosen site of conflict: the resting tree-enclosed burial ground parasitical on St Martin's Parish Church.

You can inspect the uncropped version as a frontispiece to *The Life of Dylan Thomas* by Constantine Fitzgibbon, which was originally published in 1965. This cleaner print, with aspects of church wall, ancient yew, tilted crosses, and enveloping flood of leaves, is misdated as 'Dylan in the graveyard at Laugharne, 1952'. The photographer is uncredited. The episode, in fact, occurred three years earlier. Having combed through the seventeen thick black albums of prints made from negatives rescued by Bruce Bernard from a post-mortem flat in Berwick Street, I appreciated that this anonymous professional chose, for commissions like this, to shoot with a degree of promiscuity. He banged away, not particularly concerned about pin-sharp focus. He placed his victim and arranged the pose, before achieving a loose narrative sequence.

In 1952, the same photographer made a series of portraits of Isabel Lambert (later Rawsthorne), a painter of reputation, a designer of opera sets. As with Dylan Thomas, the prevailing mood was theatrical. Lambert is a veiled priestess draped with constellations of excavated coins. She is a revenger from Greek tragedy. Mourning becomes her. She is mourning, not for lost loves or abandoned children, but for the discontinued possibilities of a mislaid career. From being herself an acclaimed artist, the equal of her male peers, she was fated, through the medium of this man's photographs, to become a ghost on a Soho street, best remembered as model or muse to one of the acknowledged masters.

For a time Lambert lived in the same house – 54 Delancey Street, Camden Town – as Dylan Thomas. Margaret Taylor, independently wealthy wife of the historian A. J. P. Taylor, was prepared, with very little return, to find yet another spare property for her unyielding protégé. Dylan enjoyed a gypsy caravan parked in the garden, where he laboured on *Under Milk Wood*. Lambert, from her open window yearned to the nocturnal sounds from London Zoo: the howling of wolves, the bellowing of bison. With austere precision, she sketched the captive animals that called her. The birds and fish of her imagination bled into Dylan's poetry.

Lambert worked on portraits of figures later painted by Bacon from specially commissioned photographs. The Delancey Street artist hoped to sell her own version of Muriel Belcher, the presiding gorgon of the Colony Room Club in Dean Street. The finished work was left at the club and soon disappeared. Lambert also made a small, rather mysterious portrait of Dylan Thomas, which she kept for herself.

Stories are repeated and recorded, paintings given away. There is a single print known to me from the Dylan Thomas session, the one where he is perched, as it appears, alongside his own sepulchre. The portrait was intended for *Flair* and later credited in its many iterations to *Vogue*, where it was featured in March 1950. That photograph is what drew me to Laugharne for the first time. I wanted to make a slow tour, concluding in the cemetery. I did not, back then in my adolescent innocence, consider for one moment the person responsible for making the portrait. I wouldn't have recognised his name, but I appreciated his quality.

The graveyard setting is neo-Romantic, evocative of Bill Brandt's bold-contrast presentations under minatory clouds. But the force in this portrait comes from the conviction that it has no investment in heritage or reputation. Primrose Hill, where the exiled Brandt positioned Francis Bacon, to his discomfort, was the wrong place. It already belonged to another London painter, to Frank Auerbach. Auerbach walked the ground, time and again. He surveyed. He excavated consequences. Brandt's Bacon capture was a striking imposture with no geographic relevance beyond the requirement to make the painter look both trapped and threatening. The Laugharne cemetery, on the other hand, was a valid *temenos*. And the only possible placement for this prodigious and inevitable stare-out between doomed poet and hireling photographer.

Dylan Thomas, in a letter to his friends Helen and Bill McAlpine, dated 'Saturday 12 November 1949', confirms my sense of the cemetery photographer's personality and methods. Both were demonstrated, years later, by the Mediterranean portfolio brought back from a visit to Dylan's widow, Caitlin, in the lustrous entitlement of her score-settling memoir, *Leftover Life to Kill*. She was rid of the thing that was supposed to define her: the impossible genius-child husband. Boozer and adulterer. Her sweet-sucking, easy loving incubus. She started again. She endured. She drank and fought, with renewed vigour. There were children. There was a younger Italian partner. A mortal. New landscapes, new estrangements. Caitlin had a desperate money-spinning catalogue of stories to tell: complaints about vampiric American seducers, false patrons and ratty, betraying photographers. Undeflected, her pale visitor basked in the vitriol.

The episode, when the photographer arrived in Laugharne, was not unwelcome. Dylan, in whimsical flow, always the entertainer, described his encounter with the man from the magazine:

> This morning, a photographer, John Deakin, came down from London to take pictures of me for the new American magazine, terribly tasty, terribly glossy, rich as rich, he says, called *Flair* . . . The cover is by Cocteau. Deakin . . . took

32

pictures of me in a high wind in the church cemetery, one of
them inside the railings of a tomb, my hair, uncut for months,
either completely covering my face (I think he liked that) or
blown up like a great, dancing, mousey busby. I look forward
to the pictures.

Pictures. *Plural*. Where are the others? Who has them now? Can lost
prints emerge from the contact sheet to extend the narrative?

The letter dates and identifies the photograph in the 'Dylan Thomas
Memorial Number' of *Adam*. The one I copied, without wondering who
the photographer was, for my failed seventeen-year-old schoolboy thesis.
The poet's hair is lockdown shaggy – he has been labouring in his hut,
in the pub, for months – but it's a long way from *Struwwelpeter*. Or
a 'mousey busby'. Dylan rises from the bed of the grave like a Stanley
Spencer resurrection with a hangover. Thirsty vegetation claws at his
ankles. Satellite dots from the process of magazine reproduction act as a
filter between poet and camera.

There was no obligation back then, seven years after the death
of Dylan Thomas, with his reputation in eclipse, and poetry politics
dominated by less strident voices, to pay any attention to Deakin, the
unregarded professional who delivered this doleful commission.
I wondered which 'John' was the recipient of the rhyming presentation
inscription on the *Adam* print. 'Love to John, From the graveyard on.'
Was this Dylan's friend, collaborator and radio producer, John
Davenport? Or perhaps Deakin's future publisher, John Lehmann? Years
later, the Swansea-based Thomas scholar Jeff Towns gave his opinion
that it was John Malcolm Brinnin, author of *Dylan Thomas in America*.

Brinnin's lip-smacking horror stories of bad behaviour, fear and
loathing through those four circles of hell, the poetry performances
and death by dinner party in the USA, were anathema to British friends
and to such citizens of Laugharne as bothered to acknowledge them.
Caitlin Thomas told anybody who cared to listen, and many who didn't,
that Brinnin was in love with Dylan and taking his revenge after being
spurned. And here is the curious aspect of the *Adam* illustration: it is the

subject, the victim, who signs the portrait and not the photographer, the artist responsible. Deakin didn't care about any of that. He knew that a good picture, whatever the ostensible subject, is always a self-portrait. A confession. Dylan Thomas took full possession of the Laugharne portrait. And it of him. It would be decades before Deakin and his ilk were puffed and namechecked, curated into reputation and auction value.

Towns had another Dylan Thomas item with a presentation inscription to Brinnin pass through his hands. This was a manuscript of the 'Author's Prologue' to the *Collected Poems 1934–1952*. 'Dear John from Cheap Dylan,' it said. Like Thomas in his graveyard seizure, Brinnin favoured a professorial bow tie and a tweedy weekend jacket. Costume appropriate to braving the truce of polite tea at the Boat House with a warring Dylan and Caitlin: as caught by the respected American photographer Rollie McKenna, shortly before the poet set off for the last trip to America. Caitlin is against it, with good reason. Dylan prevaricates, but decides to go. Brinnin, the reluctant tempter, 'struggles to be objective'.

Disliked by those who didn't know him well, and loathed by those who did (affectionately loathed in some cases), John Deakin made his long and stuttering career into an arc of revenge. He relished, for example, the preordained chaos of bringing Caitlin Thomas, ruinously relaxed after a lunchtime session in Soho's Caves de France, to be interviewed by a panicked and sweating Dan Farson. Under the hot lights of the Associated-Rediffusion studios, Caitlin refused her prepared seat and announced that she would stand up to declaim. Deakin had his tabloid scoop already written. He was on the phone to Fleet Street before they got his drinking partner to her taxi.

Dylan had already encountered the photographer as a minor character in Soho and Fitzrovia, and he tried, whenever possible, to keep him at the far end of the bar. There would be a bibulous street session from 1952, a double portrait with John Davenport, in fisherman's sweater, cigarette holder between strong square teeth, on the day when Thomas was supposed to pick up the Foyle's Prize for his *Collected Poems*. £250 was a decent wedge, rapidly and indecently dissipated. Dylan never actually said it, but he should have changed the title of his orange-covered volume *Deaths and Entrances*, with its wartime London poems, to *Debts and Excuses*.

In the gravity of that afternoon in the Laugharne graveyard, Dylan is solitary and serious. As is his tormentor. Deakin keeps a respectful distance and does not, as in so many Soho portraits, thrust his Rolleiflex hard against his victim. The negative space between the two men is the magic of this engagement. In the uncropped Constantine Fitzgibbon frontispiece, fallen leaves are stacked like pebbles on a winter beach. The sinking sun fires an aureole around the poet's head. All this is lost in the *Adam* version, which isolates the poet against a bleached backdrop. Deakin declines obvious pictorial metaphors. The curve of ornamental ironwork around the cage of the grave does not invoke a crown of thorns.

There was an unacceptable term in that McAlpine letter sent to me by Jeff Towns. Period slang quarantined by square brackets and deemed wholly inappropriate when *The Collected Letters* were published in 1985. 'Deakin, a queer, took pictures of me in a high wind.' Most of Dylan's other prejudices passed unmolested.

The photographer was indeed queer, but rarely gay, unless one of his best friends, inasmuch as he had friends, was having a bad time. The sexual politics of the circles in which Deakin operated were fluid and, in general, non-judgemental. Many of the poets and painters were, by conviction or economic necessity, homosexual. And those who weren't could be woozily compliant when a bed for the night was required. No breakfast, no recriminations. It was the polysexual Dylan, as Brinnin's American report makes clear, who became, in the ugly slang of the next decade, a literal 'shirtlifter'. As a tenured faculty guest on the terrifyingly hospitable academic circuit, Thomas felt entitled to raid well-stocked wardrobes and cupboards.

The queerness Dylan invokes is to do with difference, not sexual orientation. Queer: strange, unconventional, of questionable character, not physically right, counterfeit. Deakin, the barely tolerated photographer, was an alien at the court of Fitzrovia; the undead with their 'well-trodden faces' hovering around Thomas, the prodigal poet, in the Wheatsheaf. And later, in the Colony Room and elsewhere, basking in the nuclear glow of Francis Bacon, hoping for the generosity of vipers: flat fizz with a razor in the glass. Drink up, sham friends, and know when to vanish.

Deakin, who had been around, and who enjoyed (after his own fashion) a good war, was a lightning conductor for insults. The status of the professional photographer was evolving from non-commissioned technician in flying helmet, picking out targets for moustached bombers, to cultural parasite polishing the profiles of promotable artists. Over the next decade, the shift would be extreme: celebrity would migrate to the other side of the camera. And to other districts of London. It was hard work, a career of liver-wrecking dedication, staying drunk in Soho.

But, by that time, Deakin would be bored with the performance and the performers. When he emerged on the scene, in the early Fifties, wits whetted their blades for future biographies. George Melly, jazzman and gallerist, was shrewd enough to link Deakin with his sparring partner and tolerant patron, Dan Farson. Farson was almost a face. He enjoyed temporary exposure as television interviewer, journalist and magazine photographer, before he was obliged to retreat to North Devon, to retrench, and to self-cannibalise in a flurry of scrapbook memoirs. Melly recognised that Farson and Deakin were twinned clowns at the court of successive Colony Room grandees. He said that Deakin was 'Dan's evil genius, a vicious little drunk of such inventive malice and implacable bitchiness that it's surprising he didn't choke on his own venom'.

Hovering in clubland shadows, wine glass raised for a top up, Deakin came out of the war as a scoop of tidewrack in borrowed sheepskin. Farson tagged him, quite nicely, as a rescued merchant mariner. A spluttering convoy survivor dressed in whatever hand-me-downs could be scraped from the bilges. Something like William Golding's Pincher Martin, dead on a rock, but not yet aware of it. Farson said that the fabulously wealthy society matron Barbara Hutton, in forty years of party throwing, on both sides of the Atlantic, found Deakin to be 'the second nastiest little man' she had been unfortunate enough to encounter. The photographer dared to make jokes about her flatulence, while taking the tour of her Tangier palace. Noël Coward, visibly quivering, after an encounter in Brighton, hissed: 'Never let that man near me again.'

A great provoker of wit in others, as well as a master of the acid putdown, this compliant procurer of images was indispensable to those he served and facilitated. Bacon liked him because Deakin did what he was told (when it suited him). He was not only a perceptive portraitist but, in parallel, a subject of portraits; a presence, a thing in constant motion; an intelligence that could not be ignored.

'And yet,' Melly was honest enough to conclude, after his skewering of Deakin, 'such was his vitality, his wit, his delighted relish in his own self-destruction, that, like Farson, we find him irresistible.'

Discoloured rodent teeth, bloodshot eyes, aubergine tongue, the feral Deakin was attractive but unknowable. He made it his business, whenever possible, to only confront victims who possessed the same inner 'daemon'. No fakes need apply, unless they are genuine. He was repeatedly bent, never broken.

I came to Laugharne for the first time because of that Deakin photograph: the poet in the cemetery. Dylan had relocated a few yards, from the vertical pose to a simple white cross banged into the turf. The key locations, church and burial ground, were held back as the climax of a visit begun by identifying, and then peering into, the writer's hut. It looked pretty much as Thomas had left it. The empty wooden chair and plain table against the window. A work-suspending view over the estuary. The postcards pinned to the wall were still postcards, not yet archive. The pictures torn from magazines – Auden, Marianne Moore, Dutch saints and snow – were curling, unloved. The dust was just dust.

The story I did not succeed in extracting began and ended with the man who positioned himself, up to his waist in foliage, in another person's grave. The lazy stroll Dylan Thomas endured on the day the Deakin portrait was made in 1949 was precisely calculated to arrive at the spot where I found myself standing, when I made an expedition, with my own camera, my empty notebook, and the feeling, with no justification whatsoever, that this was a return.

The local anecdotes I gathered were already second-hand, the witnesses bored or suspicious. But I was preparing myself for a belated encounter with the photographer whose name I didn't know and whose part in the shaping of the page in *Adam* I never for a moment considered. There was only one rescued print, both evidence and prophecy. The poet took his fourth and last trip to America. Deakin returned to London.

By the time *Adam* appeared in 1953, the year Dylan died in New York City, the version of Laugharne held within the limits of the magazine page was already fading into legend. There is an editorial gloss to accompany and promote the photograph.

> Poignantly enough, the background to the facing picture, with its strewn leaves and misty evocation of the poet stepping from the tomb, was taken by John Dickin [*sic*] last year in the cemetery at Laugharne where Dylan now lies buried as one 'travelling strange seas of thought alone'.

Poor Deakin! Even his name is botched. Dylan is referenced to Milton, by way of Wordsworth and *The Prelude*. 'Dickin' sounds like a minor comic character from *The Pickwick Papers*. The spiked railings around the chosen grave have morphed into the square brackets in which the photographer's reputation was, for so long, imprisoned.

Many years later, when I had the opportunity to spend time with the seventeen albums from the Deakin archive, getting a sense of how he worked on commission for magazines and publishers, and how he roamed European cities, I became convinced that there must be other shots, still out there, printed from contact sheets, after the day's audience with the poet. I went back to Jeff Towns, the Swansea bookman with the intimate knowledge of whatever had been, or could be, rescued from the shipwreck of those distant lives.

Jeff thought he remembered a number of unattributed captures surfacing alongside newspaper articles; photographs that could be traced, by the clothes and the state of Dylan's hair, to the original Deakin session. In the much-reproduced graveyard portrait, the poet's appearance is buttoned and country neat, and his crop is Welsh curly but combed. And not as wild and woolly as he had implied. Deakin knew what he wanted and he kept snapping until he got it. He stayed with his tried and tested backdrops.

Towns found me another contender. And he located a copy that he'd made. 'It has "FLAIR" stamped on the verso,' he told me. And there it certainly was. *As it had to be.* Same jacket, same bow tie. Cardigan unbuttoned. The poet's tonsure is aspirant Heathcliff, tempest-tossed on Haworth moors. In this new print, Dylan is a scarecrow hanging on the railings around the chosen grave, where Lovecraft vegetation is out to claim him. This is the familiar setting from a different angle. The wall of St Martin's Church is a looming boundary. The poet is giving a standard performance for the camera. A calibrated register of suspicion, scorn, and economic power. Two men of diminutive stature have struck a treaty of acceptance for a brief collision of opposites.

Rollie McKenna, on commission from *Mademoiselle* to illustrate John Malcolm Brinnin's article on Dylan's life in Laugharne, a tease for the fourth reading tour, caught the promoter sitting primly alongside the poet on the terrace outside the Boat House. A study in tweed jackets. Dylan's is borrowed from an earlier self, beyond the reach of steam-pressing. His eyes are hooded against the dazzle of the water, slits in a puffy medicated mask. He is weary of the game. Brinnin is contained, bald and shiny. With the glint of a person from a newer, brighter world, travelling on expenses. He offers a thin smile of strained but still managed forbearance. This is not going to end well.

When the poet was in a seriously bad way, in conflict with his wife who policed him on his second trip to America, he agreed to a photo session with McKenna at her house in Millbrook, New York. The sequence that emerged, Dylan entangled in the bare branches of a tortured tree, is an artful version of the newly recovered Deakin print: arms back against church railings. In both cases, the photographer has allowed the subject to set the terms of engagement. Brinnin explains:

'Sometimes choosing his own settings and almost always "acting" for the camera, Dylan was enough of a professional to want good photographs.'

McKenna's Laugharne, when she made her visit, is more romantic. It has been domesticated. It accurately represents poet and wife and their ordinary extraordinary lives. Caitlin is a handsome, defiant accomplice in mischief. The children are in evidence. A trusted village helper is polishing shoes, outdoors in the sunshine. Here is the enchanted estuary world of late pastoral; spring into summer, herons and fishing boats; the lovely backward-arching poems of yearning and abdication.

But Deakin has no interest in visions of the good life. His sequence, if we reconstruct it from two surviving prints, is about entrapment. The temporary dissolution of the barrier between subject and object. The sequence had to be staged as a way of arriving at a single image that adequately represented a truth that could not be achieved in any other way, at any other time.

And then, yet again, Jeff Towns, master of persistence, came back with another retrieval. 'Just found this buried on my phone.' A very contemporary inhumation. He had successfully rescued a Deakin print from the chaotic souk of eBay. It was identified by another *Flair* studio stamp. Jeff was convinced that this version of Dylan had never been reproduced for print publication.

Deakin worked his magic. He lifted Dylan out of the grave and back to the estuary, the terrace of the Boat House. A door with a glass panel is opening slowly, cornering the doomed poet. Dylan is solemn, tired after his walk. Or bored to death with this nuisance. The yapping London boy. The terrace is enclosed with wire mesh: a chicken coop. The trick Deakin has pulled off, so neatly, is to fix his portrait somewhere between interior and exterior, between private and public spheres. This streak of a man is good at what he does. From a set of mute images he has framed a resistant story.

Was there a history before he attached himself to the court of Francis Bacon? Was there a final act after he laid down his camera? All of those grey places and used up people had to be punished. They kept him away from colour. From the fantasy release he knew that he deserved, Mediterranean light and luxury. Boys in striped jerseys. Shimmering white islands. Sailors and statues good enough to paint.

1942: Malta

The window opens on the resting harbour: a glorious span of history scoured by the strobe of bone-white Mediterranean light. He could smell Africa. Here was a new geology to absorb. A sandstone interval in the uncelebrated, 'cool under fire', period of John Deakin's life.

The drifter has been promoted. He has earned his sergeant's stripes and certain privileges. He's like one of Falstaff's gang of tavern roisterers; those purple-veined, prick-nosed braggarts, brave by default, doomed before battle. The soft sick times of Venice palazzi are done, putative artist and paid companion to a wealthy collector. Gentleman by association. And carrying it off in style. Basking, eyes shut, arms folded, in the 1936 snapshots. The gondolas and parties. The muscular gondoliers in their yellow-and-white liveries. Cocktails with Peggy Guggenheim. Bellinis set out and waiting in Harry's Bar. The island cruises through the Pacific, as the decorative companion of a rich and rootless patron, are so many improved memories. Those vagrant fictions of pre-war Paris when, as Elizabeth Smart claimed, 'hunger brightened his eye', have been endured and enjoyed, polished for future legend. Premature existentialism. Posthumous surrealism. The gleaning of tattoos and trade signs. Despite the elective poverty, the blisters and bandages, Deakin makes fortunate connections. He acquires a decent camera, along with future patrons and subjects for portraits.

Now he experiences reality; another great Siege of Malta, with heavier pounding than the waves of militant Turks offered to the crusading knights of St John. The bombardment of fascist squadrons left an indelible catalogue of ruins, terrific photo opportunities. Deakin is a serving artist attached to the AFPU (Army Film and Photographic

Unit). He is under orders to participate in the action, to witness and record. He does his bit, without fuss. The drinking is a private passion. The sergeant thrives.

A window opens on the future. Wooden shutters obliterate the past. It is all fiction in this cool stone cave. I have no right to describe this country, these actions. They happen an unbridgeable year before, blue in the face and reluctant to draw breath, I enter a world at war.

The photograph of the 'makeshift darkroom' from 1942 is a nominated item in my personal album: prints spread out for a psychobiographical novel to be told in images. Here is a monkish cell burrowed into the thick wall of a harbour fortress waiting for bombardment. The rectangular frame from which strips of film have been hung, flypapers twisting in the breeze, prepares Deakin for the shot of Dylan Thomas by that partly opened door on his Boat House balcony in Laugharne. The weather of war, the nocturnal fury of the bombing raids, and the threatening silence are good tutors in the soldier's discipline of stoic wakefulness.

Portraits made by Deakin in this period are of men in uniform. A certain distance, an ironic dignity, imposed on stiffly formal exchanges, parade grounds and presentation ceremonies. The poet and intelligence officer John Pudney features as a Deakin frontispiece, in company with the photographer's documentation of bomb damage, in a 1943 propagandist effort, *Who Only England Know*. Pudney, stern-visaged, one rogue lock of hair escaping, stands at ease, hands clasped behind back, in front of a baroque frenzy of decoration inside the Co-Cathedral of St John. In his now established style, Deakin arranged his nominated subjects, male or female, against a backdrop chosen for the ability to emphasise mortal pride and tragic insignificance. Living puppets, chests out, stiff backed. And ridiculous, when judged by the stone-faced court of history.

The studio window is open to the day. The husbanded interior of the Maltese cave luxuriates in its subtle darkness. There is a ledge on which to display relevant objects. A manual typewriter: other ranks, permitted clerical use only. Glinting black teeth and splash of white paper. A requisitioned camera. Two bottles of developing fluid. And more bottles: liberated NAAFI stock for those long night hours when harbour bars are locked and shuttered. And aftershave: a desperate temptation for the thirsty ones left on watch above ground, while the local populace is packed away in grain cellars and catacombs.

Deakin had not yet arrived at the reflex elbow jerk of his Soho sabbatical, when he gulped down a finger-printed glass of vintage Parazone: the one that the duty barman, by accident or murderous intent, had substituted for a regular lunchtime dose of white wine. The Golden Lion was a pub Dan Farson characterised as one of the two favoured 'queer' dens of the day. Deakin liked to manifest early, out of nowhere, or Berwick Street, for a swift straightener before the day's cruising began in earnest. Down the hatch, sergeant! That empty wine bottle had been filled with bleach. Farson supported the insulted victim to an obliging quack. The photographer retched up a spray of blood, with some of the gross lees from the previous night's cheap red. Enough to put in a claim. He got his damages, the rest was forgotten and forgiven. You could fire a cigar from petrol breath when he made it back to the French.

The arched frame of that open window is the whole of the waiting world. Church bells, sirens. Voices of fishermen brought across the water on a gentle breeze. Confirmation of naval traffic in the shimmering impermanence of the natural harbour. Deakin was aligned with earlier hermits and bearded saints labouring in solitude over heretical gospels in which demons become capital letters. There are always tempters, beasts or women, sailors and suitors, lurking beyond the door. Auguries mob the window, strange African birds and rays of impregnating light. Those Deakin windows again! Those faces! His dream. His fearful anticipation. A private workspace in wartime Valletta feels both inevitable and loaded with witness. Darkness offset. Distant fortifications unfocused, out of time. The pustular dome of a hilltop church. The turret on a battleship.

Everything about Deakin's studio is ordinary and mysterious. The two bottles on the sill are borrowed from a secret laboratory or bombed bar. Contact strips, blown across each other, make surprising editorial conjunctions. Portraits flap against landscapes. Mouths lick at legs. You can see the upside-down heads of sailor boys in negative. The foredoomed. The perky ghosts. Killed in action before positive prints can be made. This is both a prison cell and a workshop. The military man, under orders, is daily exposed, as in Alcatraz, to an unreachable and forbidden city of pleasure on the far side of dangerous water.

In wartime Malta passing figures can be left out of the picture. Years later, when Deakin achieved his mature style with a dazzling portfolio of Soho portraits, human faces are terrifyingly present: basilisk stares, calculated stubble, cratered pores. Victims freeze in attitudes of defensive magic. It is the city against which they pose that is doomed. The living must secure their allotted space so that architecture is free to crumble.

The year Deakin spent in a heavily besieged Malta, August 1942 to August 1943, was a personal liberation. Under constant bombardment, he was given status by his uniform. With the smell of death so close at hand, and the fortunes of war still unresolved, he was confirmed in the mechanics of a new way of taking on the curse of the world. He carried a camera everywhere. His rosary. He flattered ruins, ancient and very recent. Hollowed churches. Impenetrable thickets of intertwined carvings. Bars for sailors behind the coloured beads of fly curtains. New names twisted his mouth, choking in his dry throat: Muscat and Grech and Zammit. Old buses bouncing and farting over dusty roads policed by goats, sheep and evil-tempered crossbreeds. He was saluted by short stocky herders, old leather-faced men, and strong silent women in black, watchful children.

Deakin luxuriates in the permission to stay inside, in the dark, out of the pulse of late summer heat. He relishes the Precambrian fossils in the stone. Thorn needles and lush pink flowers on cacti. Lizards emerging from cracks, basking on blocks of sandstone. Wandering the port, going with the flow, up narrow steps and through carved arches, is a breathless trial. There are too many compositions begging to be recorded. Through these casual exercises, lifelong obsessions are acquired: nuns, classical statues, graffiti, tradesmen lounging in front of their established enterprises. Valletta is a walking town, blessed by water.

The working citizens rose early, proud of their island past, of

Homeric and Christian legends, cycles of invasion and occupation. And a local cuisine every bit as bad as Deakin would have found in his native Liverpool, in the days of his rapidly dismissed childhood.

I was drawn to this interlude in the photographer's life because the Maltese islands had always been special for me. The harbour, framed by the window in the 1942 documentation of the improvised darkroom, moved me through time. There was a camera click in the head as Deakin's monochrome bled into colour. And a ratio shift from portrait to landscape format as soon as our plane landed at Luqa in October 1967. We were dumped outside the fading colonial glamour of the Phoenicia Hotel, close to the transit point where buses congregated, busy and loud, for all parts of the island. Including the ferry link for the smaller sister island of Gozo, where we had taken, blind, a three-month rental on a house in the village of Munxar owned by the agent of a mute TV glove puppet, Sooty the bear, operated by Harry Corbett.

This gamble made sound economic sense. The house was ours for £3 a week, against £4 for a cupboard room in Hampstead. And the island, with its patchwork of small fields, its megalithic temple complex, older than the pyramids of Egypt, had a magic that captivated us. And which seduced those who paid a visit. Tom Baker, having worked on scripts like *Witchfinder General* with Michael Reeves, spent some of the inheritance the director left him on a basic property, a storage barn with a well. The poet and sculptor Brian Catling was haunted by a setting to which he returned, time and again, until it emerged as a key location, disguised and adapted, in his acclaimed *Vorrh* trilogy. Gozo is revealed as a place of visions, and visitations by strange gods, grounded in a natural order. In sounds and smells. Deakin did not respond to those aspects, that life. He stayed on the larger island. And he was not coming back.

The Grand Harbour, as we sat on the terrace of the hotel, with our bags, books and portable typewriter, for what felt like a breakfast of the elect, was an overwhelming reality. It was obviously intended for somebody else. For Deakin in his earlier life: on cruise liners, in Mayfair, Venice and Mexico. And an entitled, crisp-shirted upper class in wartime, as the photographer sergeant discovered, when he guided his officer-

47

poet, John Pudney, around the fortifications, dowsing for ruins.

'Finally,' Pudney wrote in *Who Only England Know*, 'there is the only hotel, an early Victorian period piece without fuel, food or hot water. The patronage of the Duke of Bronte is still advertised upon the notepaper. Within the sombre shadows, behind pedestals, and cold gilded mirrors, are suites furnished with solid mahogany and Empire rococo . . . Zeppu, the head waiter-hall-porter, mourns the past.'

When we stayed for one night in the Phoenicia, on another trip, after three months sleeping on the stones of Tom Baker's grain store, we couldn't manage the soft bed. We had to throw down our pillows and relocate to the floor. But the Grand Harbour was unchanged. It had outlived apostolic incursions and piratical assaults. Those legends are absorbed into the massive honey-stone ramparts, dancing points of light on the water. 1967 was the right time to be reading Thomas Pynchon's cult novel, *V*.

'Now there was a sun-shower over Valletta, and even a rainbow. Howie Surd the drunken yeoman lay on his stomach under mount 52, head propped on arms, staring at a British landing craft that chugged its way through the rainy Harbour.'

Gun emplacements, barracks, forts and brothels. Ruins built over earlier ruins around preserved megalithic temples. Natural rock formations servicing pre-Christian beliefs that have never faded. Africa is closer than Europe. Sicily is a long swim reserved for local champions like Nicky Farrugia. The Pynchon paperback I'm carrying seems to be dictating the route we have to follow.

'Towered over by ruins, they walked up a hill, around a great curve in the road and through a tunnel. At the other end of the tunnel was a bus stop: threepence into Valletta, as far as the Phoenicia Hotel.'

The light is so old. Deakin had to learn how to take an adopted profession seriously, even in his apprenticeship. Work hours were concentrated. He was rigorous in the discipline of process. The best prints printed themselves.

'The Limeys have a way of getting drunk just before they have to go off and fight,' Pynchon wrote. 'Not like we get drunk . . . the Limeys show imagination.'

Pynchon has a character called Stencil. Valletta might have inspired the author's choice of name. Deakin takes rubbings from stone. He looks for coded messages left on pale walls by faceless others. It is alphabet magic to be collected and filed. He looks for tattoos muscled into shoulders, hidden in the thatch of hairy bellies. He looks for signatures he can stencil onto the graphic masterwork he is beginning to accumulate. Those seventeen thick black albums. A serial autobiography in images. Without a single word of explanation to deface the purity. The yellow boxes that will eventually arrive at my door. 'No time in Valletta. No history, all history at once.'

Repetitions. Returns. Unreliable memories. I am swimming in the flooded salt-pan pools of Sliema, aged eleven. Before the arrival of serious money. Before banks, apartment blocks, tourist hotels. And tax breaks for famous authors. An island that was still, just about, in touch with the Malta Deakin knew. There was a naval parson who took us for afternoon tea to the Phoenicia, a great thing. And later – this man must have been a family friend from Wales – to a sun-hammered parade ground where 42 Commando, Royal Marines, post-Suez, 1954, were striking the flag, pulling out, ending their occupation of the island. And making space for the next round of exploitation: homegrown mafias, passports for sale, church favours and fat euro-finessed contracts. Ominous in-transit luggage was waved through Luqa Airport to deadly resolution over Lockerbie in December 1988.

They say that Sliema got its name from the chapel of Our Lady of Good Voyage, a building that no longer exists. My youthful memories are of heat and dust. The handles on the doors of the hire car are too hot to touch. A first taste of Coca-Cola. The earthy cool of labyrinthine catacombs I was eager to escape.

Deakin is obliged to attend the kind of regimental ceremony I witnessed among the starched wives in their white hats and white gloves. Stiff-backed and patriotic on stone benches, they squirmed to adjust summer dresses. 'Malta Receives the George Cross, 1942.' Sergeant

Deakin takes the official portrait of the exchange: a small box passed between two men in uniform. The print is indistinguishable from the efforts of any other competent journeyman held in the archives of the Imperial War Museum. Field Marshal Sir John Gort, VC, presents a medal-in-a-casket to Sir George Borg, the Maltese Chief Justice and President of the Court of Appeal. September 1942. Alien uniforms on parade among the uncleared detritus of Palace Square.

'Stencil of course didn't see the difference between event and image.'

The anonymous military photographer has that charge. It is his task to convert event into image. And image into the history we choose to preserve. But the immaculate print of Deakin's work cave, with the open window on the Grand Harbour, manages to be both at once, image and event. It means more than it says. Such uncommissioned miracles, moving freely though time, are never less than contemporary.

John Deakin, despite his wealthy patrons and enablers, the tight social circles in which he was a tolerated fixture, was a born again loner. Being so much smarter than the crowd acknowledged was not an advantage. He was a shape-shifter, a chameleon that decided, for strategic reasons, to stick with a single role: pariah, solo artist. A foul-mouthed solitary with a mob of inconvenient acquaintances. A man on his own, prepared to share bed and board, happy to be isolated on the edge of the action, noticing everything. He would invite some of the daily strangers to a bring-your-own-bottle soirée in Berwick Street. That splinter of ice in the soul is no bad qualification for a photographer playing Deakin's long game: perpetual arousal without satisfaction. One more day. One more Soho circuit. Until he was lodged for the last time in Brighton, building up strength for a jolly on a Greek island, after the removal of a cancerous lung. The Maltese window is blacked out. The door creaks. There are no days left.

Like all his favourite artists, Deakin was an elective orphan. He was unparented. He had given birth, fully mature, to himself. His parents, those biological accidents, were unfortunately respectable. His father held a decent clerical position with Lever Brothers. His brother was an accountant. The leper colony he presented as overshadowing his childhood was a hospital founded by monks in 1283. Fabulists know just what to forget. And what to leave out. The biographical morsels this lapsed Catholic offered to the unshockable Colony Room irregulars were Dickensian. And no more fraudulent than the reflex reinventions of other busking drunks. Status was only assured when Deakin upgraded from a facilitator of images for painters to a reluctant model. He became the subject of major portraits by Bacon and Freud. He was in the book. In the catalogue. On the walls of established galleries. His mangled mugshot, scrupulously painted, scraped clean, and painted again, was sold and resold, before picking up a serious auction record.

Lucian Freud purchased many laborious Paddington sessions from a late-rising Deakin with bottles of Pernod. This was worse than paid employment. The head-on confrontation from 1963–64 is a flayed strip of raw flesh with extruded Toby Jug ears. And the world-suffering eyes of an experimental animal. The putty nose has been dragged from a mousetrap. Freud glories in having secured a grotesque worthy of his cruel genius. Deakin, sick on alcohol and morning, acts the part of the battered underdog, knowing that he will have his revenge. He offers a bruised cheek, smirking between slaps. His darkest secrets are being exposed through manipulations of the overworked surface. *But it is still surface.* He is the only one in possession of the untold story. Honed improvisations and revisions weaving around a set of inconvenient and incontrovertible facts.

Fact: John Deakin was born on the Wirral peninsula on 8 May 1912. Fact: here and in London, his path would intersect with that of a noted bohemian artist, Isabel Nicholas. Nicholas – later Lambert, later Rawsthorne – had a double life, as model and drinking companion. Deakin and Rawsthorne rubbed along, good chums when it suited them. In her cups, Isabel admitted to coming into the world in the same year as the photographer. She saw her own life, when she tried to assemble a late autobiography, as a flutter of highlights, with no fallow periods, no drudgery worth recording. She was christened in Hackney. Her father skippered ships out of West India Dock. Force of circumstance beached her on the Wirral. Her family settled in Wallasey, where she put on time, before escaping to London. Famous lovers, brief acclaim and concentrated studio work waited with open arms. London and Paris. And London again. Life to be lived. The curse of Soho. The art is talked and celebrated, but it happens elsewhere. Those Deakin faces pinned up in Bacon's studio, under a bare bulb, take on the characteristics of subterranean stardom. They anticipate the cruel system of exposure and exploitation perfected by Andy Warhol's Factory. The freak show. They start out cancelled. They look forensic. Like murder victims. Like X-rays grown back to dead flesh.

There must have been something salty and prodigiously thirst-inducing about the blunt end of this Cheshire peninsula, between Dee and Mersey. The romance of maritime traffic out of Liverpool. The promise of lost weekends, bars and jazz in New York City. *Lunar Caustic* hallucinations on the road to Bellevue Hospital and the straitjacket. Malcolm Lowry's alcoholic novella has been called a guided tour of 'the Outer Circle of Hell'. Hell as a dimly lit saloon bar in which the dead gather to confess, to husband individual tales of misery. Deakin had a reserved stool waiting for him. Cigarettes were always at the last pull. Glasses never emptied. One lick left.

'But feeling he was being watched, even there, he moved later, drink in hand, to the very obscurest corner of the bar, where, curled up like an embryo, he could not be seen at all,' Lowry wrote.

There is a brotherhood of the damned, the professional drinkers, to which women are freely admitted. Lowry spent time with Dylan Thomas at a small hotel in Vancouver, which he described as 'quite a handsome hellhole'. They got on pretty well. They liked to take their whisky slowly with a view of water.

Three years older than Deakin and Rawsthorne, Malcolm Lowry was born in the Wirral, in New Brighton. The security of the setting – comfortable family circumstances, servants, tennis court and private golf course – provoked a career of restless and thirsty migration. None of the trio of peninsula prodigies could wait to get away. Lowry and

Rawsthorne held on to their fond memories of a sea-shrouded Eden, but Deakin shipped out for Ireland in 1930 with few regrets.

Across the Irish Sea, the future photographer found brief employment as a window dresser in Dublin, before detouring to Spain, where he had an unconvinced punt at landscape painting. He washed up in London, without cash or connections, in 1934. The sprawling metropolis suited him and he stuck. Lowlife and high life. There was room for a fluid career of self-invention: fresh starts, fresh humiliations. Paid commissions that wasted good drinking time.

At this point in the story, verifiable facts run out. Nothing is known until the trial: Deakin was charged with aiding and abetting the accused principals at The Caravan Club in Endell Street, 'London's Greatest Bohemian Rendezvous'. The dive was a lively but short-lived meeting place for gay men, well ahead of its time. Among other attractions, it offered 'lewd and scandalous performances' and a question mark painted on the lavatory door.

This club or another like it is probably where Deakin met the amiable Arthur Jeffress, a wealthy American, born in Acton and educated at Harrow and Pembroke College, Cambridge. For a few years, the two men were travelling companions and intimates. Deakin drifted into lazy weekends in the country house, near Winchester, that Jeffress bought as a venue for entertaining. It was also convenient for Southampton. He preferred the transatlantic sailors to the trade available in Portsmouth.

This period is a dream. Deakin paints and advises Jeffress on which artists to collect. He wears good clothes. He makes intelligent conversation. He travels light, two cases and plenty of exotic labels, against the many trunks his patron requires. Jeffress pays to fix his protégé's rabbity teeth.

They drifted apart shortly before the war, but Deakin's allowance continued. Arthur was a generous man. And, like Deakin, he played his part. He volunteered as an ambulance driver, proud to be photographed in the uniform of a captain. Their paths might have crossed in North Africa but Deakin said that he would never leave Malta while the island was under siege.

War was the condition that made Deakin a documentary photographer. The hobby picked up in Paris, as cover for his compulsive tramping, was given official sanction. He was trained. He was obliged to learn his craft on the move, sometimes under fire. He was useful but totally expendable. Which is a handy definition for the rest of his career. The days with Jeffress were theatre: costume changes, new sets, cruise liners and ritzy hotels. The studio cave in the fortifications of the Grand Harbour was where his journey began.

John Pudney, the intelligence officer, was six years older than Dylan Thomas, the self-satirised 'Rimbaud of Cwmdonkin Drive', but he laboured on for twenty-four years after Thomas was buried. He tasted sporadic popularity, while shifting between fiction, television plays, reportage and country stuff. There was a steady release of occasional verse. Like Dylan, and so many other provincial and suburban neophytes, Pudney frequented David Archer's bookshop in Parton Street. The two poets had something else in common: they liked drink more than drink liked them.

Pudney was educated, alongside Auden and Benjamin Britten, at a mildly progressive institution, Gresham's School in Holt. His first book of poetry was noticed by Lady Ottoline Morrell. The wartime Dylan, from his non-combatant existence in Chelsea and elsewhere, crafted 'A Refusal to Mourn the Death, by Fire, of a Child in London'; an ambitious rhetorical performance ideally suited for public readings and Third Programme radio. Pudney, the serving RAF officer, achieved immediate and lasting acclaim with a single poem, 'For Johnny'. 'Do not despair / For Johnny-head-in-air.'

The poem was not addressed to Deakin. Pudney's 'Johnny' was brave and doomed. He caught the national mood. The Deakin encountered by Pudney in Malta is a different man from the London operator invited to return with a likeness of Dylan Thomas from Laugharne. Liberal but distinctly officer class, of the land, Pudney acknowledged the non-commissioned snapper encountered through the fortunes of war as a useful guide. An interesting little chap worth noticing in a few lines of

Who Only England Know.

'John Deakin, the painter, who is official photographer in Malta and has a surrealist eye for devastation, is leading the way.'

The two men take a *dghaise* across the harbour. The unlikely couple make a survey of bomb damage; one looking for paragraphs of local colour and the other for 'surrealist' imagery. Deakin was still trading on his painter's eye. The camera business was an excuse to inspect ruined churches, the rock burrows and retreats of the starving poor. 'Deakin knows the wife of one of the *dghaise*-men and we see the family rations.'

'When you have seen Senglea,' Deakin told him, 'you have seen the cruellest ruins in Malta.' The connoisseur of ruins chose to retreat, as often as he could, to his private cave within the outer shell of the defensive labyrinth. The only consummated silence.

Deakin's Maltese prints, illustrations for *Who Only England Know*, are given no special prominence. They sit, unheralded, alongside shots credited to Woodbine and Palmer. The other photographs in the book are stock footage from anonymous journeymen covered by Crown Copyright.

In rumpled battledress, emerging from a 'riot of primitive baroque' inside the Co-Cathedral of St John, Pudney poses for Deakin. He has been turned a little, so that a becoming shadow teases his left profile. Deakin identified the approach he will favour for the rest of his career: strong character, male or female, at variable distance from statuary or wall hanging or antique painting. Hands behind back, like royalty on tour, Pudney avoids the photographer's challenging gaze. One of the cathedral gargoyles is grinning down at him, at the absurdity of yet another invader having his miserable trespass recorded. Men in ill-fitting uniforms borrowed from the dead. Vertical targets with service ribbons and swagger sticks.

The flamboyance of Deakin's military portfolio, male on male, contrasts with another published portrait: the Honourable Mabel Strickland, island grandee, proprietor and editor-in-chief of her own daily newspaper, *The Times of Malta*. Here is a formidable personality given her due. When critics interpreted Deakin's boredom with routine fashion shoots for *Vogue* as a disinclination to photograph women, they were quite wrong. This conflicted man, watcher and witness, understood the spell that women cast. At Marwell House, the high camp Jeffress weekend retreat, men dressed as women. And women dressed as men dressing as women. Barbara Ker-Seymer took the photographs. Deakin, off duty, lounged back, basking in calibrations of difference, in permitted display. Jeffress kept the crested albums against the day when a biography would be written.

Years later, offering historic gossip to the painter Beryl Cook, Ker-Seymer boasted that she was the one who taught Deakin. 'A very apt pupil,' she said. And trusted him with her Rolleiflex. 'But too much of a drunk and a dilettante.' Ker-Seymer made the publicity shots for Deakin's first exhibition. Before any of the other Soho snappers, she successfully presented a divided personality: confrontational and butch, a big glass in a big hand. And then, as if on the reverse of a mirror, with downcast eyes, mascara and lipstick, the leading boy at the stage door, in tailored jacket and silk tie.

Pudney saw the Honourable Mabel as 'imperiously feminine'. But confessed that 'her deep voice belongs to a man'. He thought that she looked, in her tweeds, 'like a woman you might meet at a Horse Show in Ireland'. Deakin presents Strickland scowling against statuary in her garden, in dialogue with a stone warrior in swishing skirt. Addressing him like an under-gardener. She is square-shouldered, colder and stiffer than the effigy. Her left hand grips her right thumb, in a protective gesture, against the opened legs of the classical demigod. The tight lips are scornful. The hair is cropped. Mabel has Deakin's number. His admiration. But he doesn't back off. He is learning the tricks of his future trade.

The only other Deakin image in the Pudney book confesses his recent Maltese obsession, ruins. The staircase of the Grand Masters at Valletta is a twisting slice of dream, with scale established by the diminutive figure of a man in uniform supported against a bombed column. The surrealist ambiance that intrigued Pudney is confirmed in yet another open door, going nowhere, at the head of a slanted and hollowed pillar. Painterly light and shade. Arches and entrances. This is an active mapping of the resting silence that follows aftershock.

'The sad brocades of history flutter,' said Pudney, 'and the painted woodwork creaks . . . the thunder of gun and fume of petrol . . . that sombre Mediterranean devotion which outlasts any war.'

A change in the passage of war took Deakin to Egypt, where he was attached to the 8th Army. Having experienced one of Montgomery's lisping no-nonsense, rocking-on-the-toes briefings, he wondered if he was fighting on the right side. But he survived, did his duty, went on gunboat patrols. He was posted to Syria and the Lebanon. He was promoted to Second Lieutenant. A rank which didn't prevent him, according to legend, from being unceremoniously ejected from the Army and Navy Club, on his return to Blighty, for impersonating an officer. Perhaps he was insufficiently drunk that day? Rude in the wrong way, his sour wit unconvincing among the usual bluster of vein-popping entitlement. Deakin was always the wrong size, even in the officer's overcoat, a British Warm, given to him by Lucian Freud.

After inspecting available scraps from the archive of Deakin's wartime credits, all the stiff portraits, the military ceremonies, the shattered citadels, I return to the Grand Harbour studio. The print of this alchemist's workshop reads like the manifesto for a new life. The Maltese cell predicts everything that is to come. In the cave within a cave that the photographer established for himself, by arranging his instruments and possessions against the frame of the open window, against a clarity of light, he found no way to look back into a future he wanted to avoid. He was initiated. He would grow into his myth.

1945: Africa Speaks in Manchester

In the depths of the third Covid-19 lockdown, when London was in brain-dead hibernation, and all projects launched before this time were suspended or abandoned, the messenger from Arnold Circus came to my Hackney door with two enormous yellow boxes. Like cardboard coffins on special offer from Ikea. The boxes contained seventeen albums of John Deakin's photographs, fresh prints made from recovered negatives and contact sheets; a substantial history of his labours, a flickbook parade of the stunned and waxy faces of his place and time. This momentous gift, a short-term loan, was both a blessing and a curse. I had to extract life – and a measure of coherence – out of these beautifully presented retrievals. They were not the physical materials handled by the artist, handled and junked. But glossed and preserved artefacts lifted out of the recent past and asked to explain themselves. No Deakin DNA, no psychic contamination. The Soho photographer, always alert, skewed and swaying, pre-drunk, post-drunk, pretend-drunk, had landed me, at one remove, with the resurrected eidolons of a story that was his to tell. And only his. A story in pictures. A story he preferred to bury. This was his last joke, after naming Francis Bacon as next of kin, and ensuring that the hermit of Reece Mews would have to make a dire trip to Brighton to acknowledge a corpse.

The delivery of albums felt a legal obligation out of a Victorian novel. Unappeased voices were screaming out of the hairballs and cobwebs of the photographer's last perch in Berwick Street. And from the layered, paint-spattered filth on the floor of Bacon's studio. His retreat. His man-cave. Now shipped to Dublin.

We inhabit an amnesiac era when the past has to be constantly rebranded. Re-curated. Redacted and improved. Arnold Circus, on the cusp of Shoreditch, had a noble pedigree. Out of extreme poverty – the poster venue for historic blight – came solid municipal dwellings, built to be occupied by obedient families in regular employment. And came too, within a hundred years, a bucolic oasis noticed and celebrated by Patrick Keiller: a site of transcendent stillness and meditation, of *listening*. At the cinema's golden hour, when leaves take flame, the Circus claimed its place among the three pilgrimages of Keiller's influential 1994 film *London*. The bandstand mound, with its ambulatory paths, its Panopticon summit offering views down seven roads, is a borderland between past and future, between remembered horrors and coming dread. A modestly rewilded toy town replica of Pieter Bruegel the Elder's *Tower of Babel*.

Dappled in dancing shadows from established plane trees, and lavished with birdsong, the Circus solicits movement: the impulse to circle, postponing a slow release of breath, before taking measure of what it means to live on ground where 'deep topography' has not yet been extinguished. Arnold Circus invites the overlap of many languages, not as a signature of alienation, but as a human resource. Migrants pause in their migrations. In shady courtyards, observed from open windows, children of different ethnicities play among the conceptual plantings of their triumphantly realised locality.

At the time of the Olympics in 2012, as if to escape noise and fuss, the great London painter Leon Kossoff came here from suburban migration, back to his childhood landscape, the family baker's shop, in order to make a series of elegiac perambulations. To sketch. To catch at fleeting impressions, where he no longer had the strength to undertake large-scale oil paintings. He left his equipment overnight in what had once been the neighbourhood school.

I knew that Boundary Estate school, Rochelle, from Sunday mornings in the 1970s. I recognised the way that a solid redbrick structure complemented the blocks of improved late-Victorian tenements. Starting early, I made my way to Cheshire Street, to scavenge for unsuspecting books. All the trophies of a vanishing world, barely sorted and displayed for negotiated sale, seemed to be within tantalising reach. For four or five fortunate years there were sufficient finds to keep hope alive, to fill my sacks. And my Camden Passage bookstall. The shelves never grew lighter no matter how many volumes I shifted. A heritage of uncatalogued lumber for someone else to clear. When, out of nowhere, the hour came.

The Shoreditch demographic adapted as the rage and ruckus of tribal race wars faded. Premature Brexiteers with shaven heads, and revivalist Mosleyites tapping into echoes of hate crime, confronted slogan-emblazoned righteous opponents, defenders of diversity, at the head of Brick Lane, before retreating into Essex. There were deaths. There were petrol bombs for emerging convenience stores. Outrage and physical challenge morphed into property speculation, style tourism and communal weekend derangement. Deakin's dungeons, and private clubs where it was always the yellow hour, started to leak out from Soho into Shoreditch. Laughing gas in parks, glittering silver cylinders dressing gutters. White powder in revamped tea warehouses now occupied by dedicated bohemians and trustafarians. It was the twilight of art slackers and genius retailers. And the art colonised the walls.

All I know is that place dictates the story. The petty interventions of humans are of no account. We raid the past to make the present bearable. *But there is no present.* Just images, scratches, blood colours. Chalk, oil, aerosol: legacy. And outliers to record it.

There is a neighbourhood restaurant, tagged with the required artisan flourish as 'The Canteen'. By repute, it serves recommended lunches for practising artists. And money artists. The fiscally enlightened. And those who buy into the semi-collegiate, enclosed ambience. The venue, booked in advance, offers respite from the fitness clubs and yoga brands. Rochelle is no longer a school. It does not educate or coerce. It is an oasis for those in need of such a thing. The secure redoubt has been re-visioned into workshops for architects, designers, producers and publishers. And anyone capable of acknowledging the troubling residue of dark history as a resource. Done with and fit for translation. With light and space. Aerobic fixtures and fittings. A converted gymnasium for the hatching of a brave new world. And for serious archival storage.

One meaningful tranche of the past, symbol of cultural drift,

Soho to Shoreditch, was the rescued collection of John Deakin prints and negatives dragged from under the bed in his final flat by the picture editor Bruce Bernard and acquired by the artist James Moores, the founding father of the Rochelle project. The one who arranged for those two storage boxes to be delivered to my home.

There are so many holes in the fever dream. In the official story as it can be teased out from archive. After the initiation of the stone cave in Malta, it was impossible to return to the scrabbling nightlife of London, a city in shock. Deakin resigned his commission and got himself transferred to the Ministry of Information. How? How does the naïf painter, the documentary photographer, become an agent? There are connections in the homosexual underworld with the Secret State, but most of them are spying for Russia. From The Caravan Club to White's is quite a step, but many made it. Like Graham Greene, Deakin, this double man of all the talents, all the flaws, was sent to West Africa. Whatever magic he was now pursuing, it is not in the record. A few paper traces, without images, from travels in Nigeria, can be found by fanatically diligent researchers in obscure Californian archives. He would never forget the ripeness of that first evening, the heat, the physical excitement. England faded fast.

How can new prints, made from rescued negatives, weigh so much? It takes two of us to wrestle the yellow boxes through my door. The courier, gracious enough to make the cargo transfer from Arnold Circus, in the days of facemasks and universal pestilence, stopped at the gate to chat. He hovered for a moment, respecting social distance. It was strange, after so many months, to be talking to a person and not a Zoom spectre.

He told me about the Deakin manifestation that had really grabbed his attention, an exhibition held in Rivington Place, just a short stroll across Shoreditch High Street from Arnold Circus. I knew something of the countercultural experiment that happened here in the dog days of the late 1960s, the Anti-University of the Camden anti-psychiatrists. The ones who were also acquiring Hackney properties for voyages through madness. But I'd missed this 2015 photography show, running from July to September. It was called *Black Chronicles III: The Fifth Pan-African Congress*. Deakin was the permitted outsider, the witness despatched by *Picture Post*. The quirky, mock-primitive painter had successfully traded up as a magazine professional: a person trusted to come back with the story. Pictorial evidence to be splashed across a double-page spread of thrusting journalism. A newsreel, with brisk prose, on paper.

The Manchester Congress, an event of consequence, was held five months after the end of the Second World War in Europe. Among stated aims was the demand 'that European powers liberate hundreds of millions of Africans living under colonial rule'. As might be expected, there were ringing condemnations of imperialism, racial discrimination, and the whole crumbling facade of Anglo-American capitalism. There were eighty-seven delegates representing fifty organisations. Future presidents Jomo Kenyatta and Kwame Nkrumah were present, along with a number of Black activists living in Manchester. The venue was the municipal Town Hall at Chorlton-on-Medlock.

The mainstream British press offered minimal coverage. This was Deakin's first and only assignment for *Picture Post*. He accompanied the writer Hilde Marchant. Their report, from 10 November 1945, was flagged as 'Africa Speaks in Manchester'. Marchant was a pioneering war correspondent sent by Arthur Christiansen of the *Express* to cover the Siege of Madrid in 1936, where she would have been in company, and in competition, with Martha Gellhorn. Returned home, Marchant reported on 'the greatest bombing tragedy of the whole of London': a direct hit on a block of nineteenth-century flats in Coronation Avenue, Stoke Newington, on 13 October 1940. One hundred and fifty-four tenants, and others taking shelter, were killed; many being Jews who had escaped the tightening horrors of Hitler's Germany. A memorial can be found in Abney Park Cemetery.

How was Deakin chosen for this prestigious assignation? And never used again. Was there a clue to be found in his Nigerian experience? It could be the Alice in Wonderland *logic of the Secret State, but I couldn't help imagining the photographer reporting back to his masters in Curzon Street.*

Doing the sort of job he liked best and being paid twice. The camera was a weapon in plain sight. He was an officer who had given up his status. The Jeffress allowance was no longer reliable. There was open warfare at the Hanover Gallery. It was impractical to owe allegiance to his former patron and to Bacon, the coming man. Their dislike was mutual and permanent. It hissed acid. The liquid on which Deakin traded.

In Chorlton-on-Medlock, Deakin was a bag carrier, a technician on sufferance. Marchant was the adequately rewarded star. But I didn't find her anywhere among the Deakin portraits in the seventeen albums deposited in my house. Chain-smoking through a stylish black holder, eyebrows arched in perpetual disbelief, Marchant radiated character: watch out! For her *Picture Post* commissions, this woman certainly covered the waterfront. After the politics and speechifying of Manchester, she found herself obliged to deliver 'The Truth About Teddy Boys – and Teddy Girls'. And later, in a lavish expense-account Paris hotel room, she posed with a celebrity chimpanzee from an American TV show. She manages to keep her professional cool as the beast shoves a speculative finger into her painted mouth. She got the 'interview'. And wrote it up. Classic journalistic ventriloquism.

In 1956, now accompanied by Haywood Magee, she travelled to Southampton to witness the arrival of Caribbean immigrants. 'Thirty Thousand Colour Problems': a tabloid strapline for an article later critiqued by the sociologist Stuart Hall for presenting immigration as 'a universal, ubiquitous "problem" for British society'. Displayed alongside Magee's photograph of a young woman in a summer hat, isolated in the crush of the disembarking crowd, Marchant writes of her 'bewilderment'. She describes the hopeful new arrivals as 'cargo'. Her report has the required apocalyptic undertow. It nudges towards the fictions of that hipped cultural commentator, Colin MacInnes. *City of Spades* appeared in 1957. And *Absolute Beginners*, featuring the Notting Hill race riots, in 1959. Deakin would take a number of the best-known and most frequently reproduced portraits of MacInnes: jaw-jutting, disabused, stroppy. Sometimes alone. Always on guard. Sometimes in company with a Black friend, protégé or lover.

'West Indian immigrants are now arriving in Britain at the rate of 3,000 a month,' Marchant warned. 'This year 30,000 are expected. All seek work and homes. Both are becoming difficult to find. Trouble and disaster are brewing.'

The story breaks eleven years after Marchant's visit to Manchester, on duty with Deakin. This was a period when only a few Black activists living in the city, men like Len Johnson (Communist Party member and former boxer), were able to participate in the conference. The hard-bitten former war correspondent, now representing the interests of her editor and her proprietor, adopts the persona of an ordinary citizen, fearful of disruption to the status quo. And fearful of perceived threats to future employment – especially those jobs that were too dirty or difficult for locals to undertake. It was frictionless to denounce imperialism and colonialism, but more challenging to adequately excavate the reasons behind the hard decisions taken by those who risked everything to move to a strange cold land.

As a woman who had to fight every yard of the way for status and remuneration, Marchant tailored her opinions to the mood of the moment. Celebrity and commissions vanished with the magazines that employed her. Rumour says that Marchant's career tanked. There was no biographer to rescue her reputation. Deakin could be resurrected by way of the prints he left behind. The star journalist ghosted into the shadowland of microfilm loops nobody was cranking. Lost to the record after a period of assumed vagrancy, Marchant was last noticed, a statistic without obituary, slumped in unremarkable death under a railway arch.

The 2015 'recovery' of Deakin's Manchester report, and the exhibition based on the Fifth Pan-African Congress in a fashionable Shoreditch gallery, arrived with all kinds of qualifications. Mixed-use territory on the border of the old City of London had made its adjustments as it slipped through the decades. Reproduction furniture and tailoring sweatshops had never, in their recorded histories, their poverty mappings, registered a significant Black population on census forms. But the man who transported my giant yellow boxes was inspired by the accident of locality. It was a five-minute walk from Arnold Circus to the previously unseen Deakin prints displayed on the walls at Rivington Place.

Two of the *Picture Post* captures, on their own, justified this exhibition. 'John McNair, General Secretary of the Independent Labour Party, addresses the Fifth Pan-African Congress in Manchester. Also on the stage is Amy Jacques Garvey, the second wife of Marcus Garvey.' 'Concilio et Labore,' says the heraldic Town Hall shield. The lighting is so dim, a trio of hanging bell shapes glowing through the fug of cigarettes and steaming overcoats like dying stars. The hall is strident with posters. ARABS AND JEWS UNITE! AGAINST BRITISH IMPERIALISM. OPPRESSED PEOPLES OF THE EARTH UNITE. DOWN WITH TRUSTEESHIP. The established white politician, hands clasped, is bareheaded. Amy Jacques Garvey, seated behind a table on the stage, wears a sporty hat. Below the stage, three white women, reporters or record keepers, scribble away at another table. It feels almost like a socially distanced Covid-19 audience, seen from behind, delegates in white collars, suits and raincoats. A chill leaks into the building.

The head-on Deakin confrontation with 'Kenyan statesman Jomo Kenyatta' is unforgiving, remorseless as a prison passport. This is the portrait I would nominate to set alongside the doomed Dylan Thomas in my own phantom exhibition. The directness of the engagement between anti-colonial activist and London photographer anticipates the series of searching Soho portraits that followed Deakin's employment with *Vogue*. But there are telling differences. The backdrop is the wrinkled curtain dropping from the high stage. He occupies a place at its approximate centre. Was the position chosen by subject or photographer? Kenyatta's powerful head, tilting to the right, partly masks one of the posters: ETHIOPIA WANTS EXIT TO THE SEA.

The Kikuyu strategist, a former student at Moscow's Communist University of the Toilers and the London School of Economics, returned to his country within a year of the Manchester Congress. As President of the Kenya African Union, he continued his assault on British colonialism. And he faced arrest as one of 'the Kapenguria Six', charged with being the inspiration behind the Mau Mau uprising. He endured seven years of political imprisonment and two years of exile in Lodwar.

In Manchester, Kenyatta's steady stare outlives its immediate occasion. Right eye narrowed, left eye stretched wide: here is a premonition of security files, identity parades. Of a state instrument pronouncing sentence on a nominated suspect. Deakin, alert but politically neutral, also catches the activist's proud self-confidence. The grudging tolerance of the lowly functionary with the lifted camera, the one serving his propaganda purpose.

Armoured against northern weather in bearskin coat, and displaying a generous expanse of buttoned cuffs with his striped shirt, Kenyatta is a considerable presence. One large hand encloses the other. The heavy signet ring is the size of an Olympic medal. After acclaim as 'Father of the Nation', after Premiership and Presidency, the growing charges of 'dictatorship', 'neo-colonialism' and unmerited tribal favours were inevitable. Deakin, indifferent to hindsight, caught it all.

When he photographs the painter Hussein Shariffe, twenty years after the Manchester Congress, Deakin references the portrait of Kenyatta. Shariffe is posed against a wall, mid-shot, head tilted to his right. He is sharply presented in coat, striped shirt. The eyes are slits, closed against the light. Shariffe questions Deakin's legitimacy, his dubious intentions. It's a suitably moody capture for a style magazine. But austere. What Deakin likes, or what he tries to provoke in his victim, is that stare of unbridled suspicion.

Among the detritus salvaged by Bruce Bernard from Deakin's Berwick Street flat was a yellow packet of negatives with a typewritten list of capitalised names. An inventory of achieved or potential victims. Future subjects to be backed against white-tiled Piccadilly walls. Compliant figures to be sprawled on Chelsea beds. A quorum of exploitable friends and not-yet-confirmed enemies. Casual drinking pals, stepped over but not intimate, are given approximate versions of their full names: Ralph Romney [*sic*], Humphrey Lytteton [*sic*], Richard Burton, William Walton. Others, with shared history, are on first name terms: Dylan,

Caitlin, 'Francis & Tim at Limehouse'. 'Bill' Empson, poet and patron, is granted an ambiguous status, both chummy and formal. The Black painter, the one posed against the Soho wall with the white rectangle, is listed as 'Hussein'. But the social critic and trend spotter, Colin MacInnes, gets his full entitlement. As Dan Farson said, this man took no prisoners. He treated the door of the Colony Room 'as if it had done him an injustice'. But still he was tolerated, even welcomed, by Muriel Belcher. Colin was officer class with a famous mother he dutifully despised. He was often in funds. He was also a tinderbox liability, capable of kicking off after a single misplaced compliment from one of the thirsty peasants on the cadge.

Deakin took some trouble over his portraits of MacInnes: stiff-backed, laying down the law, on a narrow single bed. And then, in the same flat, a young Black man, finger against cheek, identified as 'Unknown Sitter'. The photographer has pulled off the trick of implying a drama, brought about by his presence, without his actually being there. The couple are together but in separate frames. They do not look at each other and they do not look at Deakin. Tension is expressed through the furnishings, the skewed painting, the peeling and unimproved wall. The props in this cramped unit have been accumulated but not chosen. The room, for gentlemen sharing, is one of those minimal spaces rented to a faceless population of urban drifters, occupied but not inhabited. The Deakin portraits propose a Royal Court drama that has not yet been written.

Close-cropped and belligerent, MacInnes glowers, patrolling his chosen environment like a game warden, dowsing for copy. Son of the popular novelist Angela Thirkell, he courted danger: in the clubs he patronised, and in his voyeuristic compulsion to hang out with visiting dance companies. He was frequently mistaken for Old Bill. In a habitual duffel coat, he stamped the Soho decks like a face from the bridge of a corvette in *The Cruel Sea*. He channelled his inner Jack Hawkins. It was inevitable that this posh trade was going to invite close personal acquaintance with bent coppers from West End Central and Notting Hill. As a predatory bisexual man, preferring Black partners, and a mouthy defender of lovers met in a subterranean milieu, MacInnes would very soon gather material for his novel of immigrant life, *City of Spades*. And for his fiction of law and disorder, of judicial malpractice, *Mr Love and Justice*.

Being fitted up and comprehensively worked over was a rite of passage. It went with the turf. The police, with their not so free masonry and their undeclared pension funds, preferred the company of professionals. Gangsters and compliant pornographers appreciating the culture and tradition of the 'little drink'. The wrong kind of foreigners were not welcome on our streets. MacInnes dramatises these 'misunderstandings' at the heart of his novels.

Placed in the angle between two impressive Arts and Crafts windows, for another portrait, MacInnes has to admit that Deakin has his number. The writer is in his pomp, hands in pockets of coat, eyebrows raised. A missionary priest with history. An educated outsider preaching to the unconverted. The churchy grid of shield-shaped windows floods the trapped martyr in white light. But there is no escape. For either man. For portraitist or portrait.

I asked the London memory man, Michael Moorcock, who started editing and publishing in his teens, and who met everybody of consequence at one time or another, what he made of MacInnes. He pointed out that the Notting Hill novelist, compelled to chase the coming story, was an early immigrant into a still uncolonised East End. You could hide but you couldn't run.

'He lived in Bow,' Moorcock said, 'when it still had bombsites. He was maybe the first writer I knew. He was unlikeable.'

Unlikeable but available, MacInnes offered gruff hospitality to young hopefuls. He took up, for example, with Teddy Taylor, author of the cult novel *Baron's Court, All Change*. His interest derived from the discovery that Taylor was a new thing. He was into the latest scam for sharp operators on the make: photography. This young man from the suburbs would become one of the key inspirations for the protagonist of *Absolute Beginners*.

Deakin was around, but he was street furniture, bar furniture. A skeletal hand holding an empty glass. Colin never appreciated the skill with which that knotty little nuisance operated. Taylor had the speed and attitude the cruising author needed for his most famous fiction. Photography was a racket for failed hairdressers, kids who wanted to get close to girls chasing bands. In *Absolute Beginners*, MacInnes dismisses the salvage of Deakin's psychogeographic rambles, the art stuff shown at the gallery in David Archer's bookshop. Portfolios brought back from abroad, from days drifting with intent through Rome and Paris and Athens. Portfolios ambitious of becoming books.

Teddy Taylor was in agreement. 'It was like a photograph by one of those arty photographers who have a ball with nuns and dirty washing and have their snaps covered in grain and not too well in focus. Sort of romantic and dramatic, if you know what I mean,' he wrote in *Baron's Court, All Change*.

Taylor, a quick study, was always in tight focus. He processed passports in Wardour Street. Strips of cameo portraits intentionally drained of character. Stamp-sized representations made to look as if they were authored by a machine. According to Tony Gould, the MacInnes biographer, Teddy got off on 'jazz, soft drugs and hustling'. He helped out at Victor Musgrave's Gallery One, where he soon took up residence; first as an assistant, and then a lover, to Musgrave's partner, Ida Kar. It was the era, Taylor said, when 'all the women seemed as if they hadn't had a bit for a year and all the men couldn't make up their mind if they were queer or not'. Ida Kar, like Deakin, took portraits of the circle around Francis Bacon. She had style and was a good tutor.

The cover of *Absolute Beginners*, projected to catch the teen zeitgeist before it disappeared, was a Notting Dale, mid-action freeze-frame by Roger Mayne, a talented photographer who built his reputation around the life of Southam Street. He lifted its feral vitality, the children at play. He also noticed youths experimenting with attitude, women on doorsteps: the mysteries of the mundane. Everything that was ripe to be swept away. Southam Street was demolished in 1969 to make room for Ernő Goldfinger's brutalist Trellick Tower.

The modish youth with his slouching back to Mayne's camera and the girl with windblown hair and white raincoat, gazing modestly down at her white shoes, could be accidental models or just another combative couple caught during one of Mayne's prospecting walks. Research reveals that this encounter was set up, a commission from Colin MacInnes. A commission that became a production still for nostalgia. And a film by Julien Temple, with David Bowie, that could not be shot for another thirty years. A product doomed to choke on its own hype, it was as fated as the street itself. Mayne's intense regard for locality, his chosen terrace fading as it recedes into white, like a fog of advancing dementia, was upbeat under the grime of disregard, the promise of compulsory purchase and rehousing in one of those nicely appointed tower blocks with the asbestos cladding. The parked cars from Mayne's documentation could have been abandoned some time before the last war.

These were the years when photographers photographed photographers. The Oxford-educated Mayne, a Balliol man, and a contributor to *Picture Post*, decided that he would pay a fellow practitioner to track his every move, as he tracked Southam Street. London was becoming as visually clotted and multi-referenced as Antonioni's *Blow-Up*. While Mayne, in stalker disguise, in long gaberdine raincoat, rubs against walls chalked with childish cartoons and teenage invocations of Elvis, he is himself stalked by his hired shadow: John Deakin. Deakin seemed like the right choice. He had a reputation among his peers. He delivered a modicum of reality for the glossy magazines. It didn't signify. Mayne became another Deakin victim. A capture by the spy's spy. An unlabelled character in a black album assembled for the hidden masters. What he wanted from Deakin was to understand how the trick was worked. 'He learnt,' *Vogue* picture editor Robin Muir reported, 'almost nothing at all.' Deakin was not a sharer. What he did, in terms of technique, felt like nothing. It happened fast. And it looked like an accident, a nervous twitch. But somehow, miraculously, more often than not, it registered. It is still there.

What Mayne did learn, without appreciating it, was that his own way was the only way. Trust your obsessions. The *Absolute Beginners* cover is a direct invocation of the promotional gig Deakin contracted for the John Player Cigarette Company. Advertising photography was every opportunist's second or third career of choice. Many of the coming names picked up the basics in the military, war or National Service. By the end of the decade, ambitious lads, proud to assert their working-class credentials, tried crimping, graphic design, copywriting, pop management and kitchen business. Or one-off novels doomed to be rediscovered every ten years, and rapidly reforgotten, like *Baron's Court, All Change*.

Deakin's unique attempt at storyboarding a photo romance for cigarettes involved railway stations and an outing to Hastings pier. The result twinned neatly with Mayne's cover. Deakin's choice of model was Virginia Slater. The boy was Josh Avery. The episode was lightly mythologised in *Dog Days in Soho: One Man's Adventures in 1950s Bohemia*, a hybrid novel by Nigel Richardson. Established boundaries between disciplines, between reportage and fantasy, were porous. A book jacket could be a grab from a film.

Virginia Slater is featured in the Michael Andrews paintings of the Colony Room. Along with Bacon and Deakin. 'I've seen a lot of Deakin portraits and the subjects never smile,' Richardson wrote. 'Even Francis Bacon looks a bit bloody scared of Deakin's lens. Not that it was a cruel lens, according to Deakin anyway. He said he didn't victimise his sitters, he just exposed in them what they were usually too clever to reveal: the terror and melancholy and so on.'

And yet the man himself, the artist called John Deakin, remains a cipher. His surface is explored in portraits by the best of them: Bacon, Freud, Andrews. They are fascinated by the texture of skin, the flaws, bumps, corrupted colours. They want the surface to be realised so completely that it will crack the secret and hint at what is always withheld, inside. This Deakin, in the oil paintings, in the photographs of a solitary figure, glass raised, smoking in a crowded bar, is both exposed and private. Perhaps we approach him in the wrong way? We need the journals. We need access to his letters, to every word this man wrote. We need to understand the warring intimacy with Dan Farson. Deakin can feel like a Farson invention, like his other self. His motor spirit. The artist Farson wants to become. But Deakin also needs Farson. As unsanctioned biographer. The embellishments, the lies, they are all true. The wilder the better. This odd couple, bitching and sniping, stay close. To the end.

Farson was an exemplary revealer and improver. If he couldn't actually *be* there, he made it up, and made it better. He had the terrifying carcinogenic glow of studio lights. He could illuminate a dark cellar. The cathode ray enhancement of a permanently flushed complexion. Coming through a door on Dean Street, he always looked as if he was just back from a weekend in Miami. Booze gave him the metallic sheen that costs Donald Trump a fortune in cosmetics. Dan knew that he was rushing towards a fall. He knew fame was a snare. He cultivated it: TV star, showbiz publican, celebrity gossip. Party boy. Reprobate betrayer. And decent journalist/photographer. If he didn't get the shot he wanted to confirm a story, he could always finesse the anecdote. Farson claimed that Deakin's excursion for Player's was an utter fiasco, because the photographer used the wrong brand of prop cigarettes. Nigel Richardson refutes the canard, saying that he owned 'three out-takes from the shoot' and 'a cardboard point-of-sale display with a triangular flap at the back'.

The Deakin picture from Hastings pier, used in Richardson's book, has the same English weather as Mayne's cover for *Absolute Beginners*. Unruly hair, tight flannels creased against chapped calves. Cold hands thrust deep in pockets to discipline flapping coats. 'Josh and Virginia are both wearing macs and these ripple and ruck like Renaissance marble in a stiff offshore breeze.'

There is a considerable socio-cultural lurch from the paid witness of the ex-soldier, John Deakin, at the Fifth Pan-African Congress in Manchester, to the post-colonial predations of Colin MacInnes, hitting clubs in search of partners prepared to accept his angry patronage. When the job description changed, and there was a new role to keep him in the thick of the action, Deakin found ways to be at the back of the room, as watcher and recorder. He shot so promiscuously that there were always spare contact sheets for the clerks at the ministry. The ones charged with filing and ignoring evidence from paid informants. Those boxes left under the bed of his abandoned Berwick Street flat were an alternative legend willed to posterity. 'Invent me again. Invent me better.' MacInnes, more visible, but more graciously received by contemporary critics, died with his books. His flaws unexposed. Unforgotten.

'What had attracted him to blacks in the first place was their *un*acceptability,' wrote the biographer Tony Gould. 'To put it crudely, what he wanted was to be raped by a big black, a "primitive", or – better still – by several.'

'Hence,' Gould concluded, 'his preference for Africans over either West Indians or black Americans – they were "more authentic"; they were the real thing.'

Choosing to live in rented rooms in old working-class districts, in Spitalfields and Cable Street, MacInnes was putting himself at the risk of arrest. He was duly picked up by the police at a Whitechapel gambling den, processed and routinely assaulted in the local nick. Result! Excellent copy. Swallow it all. MacInnes set off on marathon walks across London in company with the writer Francis Wyndham. 'Colin had a provincial's – not to say, colonial's – curiosity about the metropolis,' Gould wrote.

A major influence on *City of Spades* was *The Lonely Londoners*, the 1956 novel by Samuel Selvon. Selvon drew on remembered specifics of Black immigrant experience in a depressed decade. MacInnes proposed a series of programmes to the BBC. He wanted to track the lives of Londoners newly arrived from Africa. They turned him down. Until, in the media buzz of his fashionable novels, he was invited back, to take part in a discussion on 'immigration': meaning West Indian immigration.

Tone and attitude in *City of Spades* belong firmly in 1957. 'Sitting on the bed, dressed in a pair of underpants decorated with palm leaves, was a stocky youth topped by an immense gollywog fuzz of hair.' Reading this prose, it is not difficult to see what fired the Manchester Congress.

The contracted researcher, not knowing quite who had hired him, nor how he was going to be paid, if anyone survived this plague, built a nest of books. They told the same stories in so many different voices. More and more, he felt that the only way out of this lay with the photographs. Mercifully bereft of explanation or justification. When, after many months, perhaps years, a postcard dropped on his mat, it said: 'Never forget. You are writing a novel, not literary criticism.' It was unsigned.

In the fourth of the black albums, among highbred horses and fancy-dress huntsmen, among vampires of the Soho night, opera divas and Medusa-mask hostesses crippled by wealth, Deakin arrives at Colin MacInnes. Twenty-one exposures of the cornered bruiser: staring, standing, smoking. In his cardigan. In his party suit and tie. Against high-lit windows. Only two images on the contact strip have been wasted on arty or incompetent double exposures. Trickery is not required. Deakin is not Man Ray. Or Alvin Langdon Coburn. He is a realist. The collision is beautifully balanced: Deakin and MacInnes are both active, both engaged with the matter of London. Both lost. MacInnes thinks he can romance the culture of the moment like another Dickens. He's wrong. Deakin is less deceived and therefore more contemporary. He has been to Paris. He slipstreams existential fatalism. Twenty-one exposures for Colin MacInnes. Which left just a single shot for the author's current partner. An unidentified young Black man gazing out of frame. He has been squeezed into the corner of a grubby bedsitter, drapes over sagging couch, cracks in the plaster. Deakin's camera is still there, but the man himself, as heat and smell and touch, has vanished. The door creaks. Drinkers close up in a tighter huddle, elbows out, as he makes his entry into the Golden Lion.

1947: Stag Fashion

These were the high days of taxis and expenses. Of having places to go, appointments to keep. Of being in drink and invited to overdressed gatherings of the great and good where he was never welcome. But where he could be relied on to deliver quality scandal. To abuse monsters everybody else wanted to abuse, but didn't dare. Next day the whole office would be talking. The worse he behaved, the more equipment he lost or smashed, the more secure their own contracts.

And taxis were great at absorbing nuisance tripods and light meters. Deakin was an artist, not a bearer on a game reserve. Fat black cabs were leathery wombs with a view. He drew thin knees against his chest. He gripped a heaving stomach, his trembling hands a cincture. Deakin was foetal and wrecked. He knew the reassuring throb of the engine like a mother's heart. His lids were sticky. His nose dripped. His tongue looked as if he had been licking ashtrays after hours in the Caves de France. London taxis were reliable as death. Every Loughton cabbie a ferryman. They got him there. He kept his duty dates. And he filed his expenses. These were the lost years of an accidental career.

But the human geometry was all wrong. The models were badly assembled. They were like silk scarves draped over Scandinavian light fittings. They had the self-serving instincts of birds. Flamingos. The cold intelligence. Peck or be pecked. He was both attracted and repelled by their difference. Their *indifference* to his boorish performance, his sexual neutrality. They had words, if pressed, complaints, but no conversation. They had no daemons worth exorcising by torchlight. They could be brave or brazen, but never wild. They were too well schooled, too disciplined in movement. They were putting on time, waiting for a connection. They were frigid, stiff with hunger for approval. But not from *him*.

He was inducted into the wrong London. The Mall. Palaces. Parks. Sober, Deakin did his best to get rid of equipment for which he had to sign a chit. It was premature to dump the camera. Without it, he would make astonishing images by psychic means, printing the heat of his lifelong hurt directly onto the emulsion. He would dispense with commissions, faces, needy performers, waxwork models. Horrible sets, dead theatre. Promotions for shopkeepers. Bring on the girls. A breeding directory for aristocrats.

He had no lust for the wrappings of these women, their *smell*. They were as hard as he was, more professional. He did his job.

Lucian Freud, with some reluctance, booked Deakin as a sitter, when he wearied of the perpetual rabbit of that other photographer and embattled model, Harry Diamond. Harry was short but feisty. The lengthy sessions Freud demanded interrupted his eternal stamping across London. He found employment as a casual stagehand but came to life as a compulsive pedestrian. Harry had no use for taxis. He knew that blisters were the surest route to enlightenment. Foreshortened, squashed down by imposed gravity in a Paddington interior, Harry's visions and resentments were only kept in check by the dubious protection of an all-seasons gaberdine raincoat. A meteor out of the east, Harry was the original diamond geezer with the smeared spectacles. And now he was being replaced by that iffy military man and failed primitive, John Deakin. No recriminations. They were in the same game, recording London. Taking the dictation of happenstance. To keep Deakin in character, back on the street, climbing the stairs to the Colony Room, Freud presented him with a camelhair overcoat. The painter had an infallible eye for fashion. For himself and for his models. He knew how to make an instant impression at a society ball or a breakfast table under Smithfield Market. He combined quality Savile Row tailoring with charity surplus, begged, borrowed or stolen.

'Very maudlin and self-pitying in the transition between pretty boy and monster.'

That was how Freud, in conversation with William Feaver, summed up the Deakin of this post-war era. The blotchy face declines to come into focus. There seem to be two or three other faces hidden beneath it. But there is still a serviceable suit bearing rather too much evidence of service. And there is employment, as a freelance and then as a once-renewed, twice-curtailed contractee with prestigious British *Vogue*. Deakin resisted his talent. He could no longer trade on youthful looks and promise as a coming painter, a thing to be patronised. So he put in the necessary hours. He took taxis and trains. He refined his special gift for biting the hand that fed him.

In Paris, he associated with (and photographed) Christian Bérard, painter and opium addict. Bérard introduced him to Michel de Brunhoff, editor of French *Vogue*, and brother to Jean de Brunhoff, creator of Babar, the politically incorrect African elephant. The Condé Nast publishing empire spread across many borders. De Brunhoff recommended Deakin to Audrey Withers at *Vogue* in London.

In 1947, Somerville-educated Withers, having little interest in fashion, beyond hats, turned Deakin loose on the *Vogue* stable of mock haughty and genuinely affronted models. Young women, schooled to behave a decade beyond their years, mimed respect for the fabulous frivolity in which they were costumed. And imprisoned by merciless gay designers and demi-artists. They had to look mature enough, disciplined enough, to be serious about the business of acquiring a wealthy and preferably titled husband.

Withers later asserted that Deakin was constitutionally incapable of making any woman look good. It is true that he was never at his most engaged with the parade ring of high-bred fashion in fancy dress. He despised the Cecil Beaton combination of affectless hauteur and scenic bombsite: the wounded rubble of the City. Deakin's models were briskly manoeuvred but otherwise free of predation. They were unmolested. The expensive photographic equipment, leased by *Vogue*, was always unsafe in a Deakin taxi. If he couldn't mislay a necessary piece of kit, then he'd find a way to drop it, sit on it, or crush it underfoot. Withers was obliged to let him go within a year of the original appointment.

Propped against a pillar of Kensington Church Street tat, best-quality architectural salvage, and white-shirted with a mortician's black tie, Deakin directs a self-portrait as *Vogue* professional. This is a calling card and also a plea: *get me out of this madness*. Bat ears twitch. Cheeks are shadow-bruised and abraded. Eyes are pitted, unblinking, lacking pupils. The man has been excavated and warmed up with neat spirits. A convalescent revenant, dragged from the sleep of ages, and pushed into the cruel light of day for a second life.

It's like the army, with frocks and taxis. Deakin does his duty. He endured more than five hundred of these *Vogue* 'sittings', while the jealous sorority of hired performers made angular shapes against backdrops from a surrealist nightmare. When he was released from the iron lung of the studio, he could draw breath and block his models into scenarios for unrealised films. They dressed location hunts: royal parks and empty palaces, fur coats and smoke-fouled stucco alongside dunes of uncleared rubble. Celebrity wives, fit to be profiled in the glossies, treated modelling as a paying hobby. It conferred status, before early retirement to the shires.

'Mrs. Charles Johnson, formerly Princess Natasha Bagration, is related to the famous General Bagration of Tolstoy's "War and Peace".

Her husband is at the Foreign Office, writes poetry.' Mrs Johnson rests a white gloved hand, diffidently, on the trunk of a dirty London tree. She plays demure.

'Mrs. Christopher Sykes is a daughter of Sir Thomas Russell Pasha, who was for many years Commandant of the Egyptian Police. Her husband, the well-known author.' Deakin's society portraits are careful not to outrank the outrageously sycophantic copywriting that accompanies them in weighty but frivolous magazines. Wives and daughters. Putting on time. Postponing release into a worse prison, wealth by association. Motherhood. Breeding stock. Status.

The quiddity of a special talent subverts the stifling conventions of the period, conventions flattered by the accomplished whimsy of Norman Parkinson and Cecil Beaton. Even when going through the motions, Deakin manages to deliver something more ambitious than its immediate occasion. His 'Out in the Afternoon' promotion for fur coats, published by *Vogue* in November 1947, has a formalism that anticipates *I vinti*, Michelangelo Antonioni's first London-based feature film, released in 1952. Deakin was regarded as a tolerated mercenary, Antonioni lauded as a significant artist. The director's European sensibility flirted with decadence as social critique: disengaged figures validate architecture. Somnambulist performers are in dialogue with, and oppressed by, industrial buildings, terminal suburbs, private hospitals, golf courses. They behave with the last-breath anomie of fashion models – until the moment of crisis is achieved, with *Blow-Up* in 1966. Now actors, photographers, painters, vagrants and students, compete in a treasure hunt for junk-shop salvage and unclaimed locations. They drift across London, Woolwich to Kennington. Places where Deakin, too drunk to remember, lodged and partied.

The 'Out in the Afternoon' print is about a city emerging from war, about seductive luxury and conspicuous consumption in a time of shortages and rationing. It's about organising disillusion to mimic neo-realism. It's about smuggling a scenario of alienation into a fashion shoot published on glossy paper. Transitory immortality.

To achieve the shot, Deakin is down on the pavement, in the dirt, on his knees. The angle dramatises the sauntering approach of the woman in her three-quarter-length fur. She sways on high heels. Downcast eyes are locked in impenetrable reverie. A hatless man in a business suit, papers in left hand, moves towards a parked car. Other vehicles, at the edge of the frame, hint at a taxi rank. At watchers behind unmoving newspapers. In the distance, another woman, in a white coat, has paused to follow the unfolding action: aftermath of crime or feature film with unrecognised foreign stars?

It was happening again. The conviction that the watcher is always watched. The little scenes Deakin directed confessed his paranoia. He couldn't walk away. If he is the third man, who are the other two? That woman has a gun concealed in her Russian cuffs. If she looks up, he's dead. They are going to kill him for a secret he doesn't possess. He makes painters look like assassins. London is Vienna. All the players are on something. There are more buyers than secrets.

This image, reproduced in a magazine, is generically promiscuous: fashion, true crime, thriller. That slice of wall, serving as backdrop, becomes an open-air screen from which one of the principal actors has escaped into the city. She will be pursued, kidnapped, drugged. Raped or rewarded with a passport. Courses of exposed brickwork are sprocket holes. The streets without obvious bomb damage have survived from an older newsreel. From the time when Graham Greene and Eric Ambler loaded their transcontinental romances with rumours of war. With women who could not be trusted. With dealers in arms. Stolen cameras and lost negatives hold the plans for submarine pens. Instructions for political murders.

The woman in fur has arrived by car, there is no dust on her polished shoes. The man with his back to her, in unflurried retreat, could be a dismissed chauffeur, an afternoon lover or current husband. The star has been integrated into the pictorial event in a way Deakin rarely attempted in his fashion jobs. He liked to pick up the arbitrary momentum of the streets, even if inconvenient pedestrians got in the way. He liked street furniture, things that didn't move: shop windows, advertisements, trade signs, anonymous public statues, monuments to the forgotten in city cemeteries.

Accepting a photo shoot with Wenda Rogerson, model wife of his *Vogue* rival, Norman Parkinson, was a trial run for the career-defining portraits he took when Audrey Withers, seduced by gallery manifestations, hired him for an unprecedented second time in 1951. Free from the grim ballet of commodity promotion, Deakin came back refreshed, skills sharpened and trigger finger still itchy. These prints, from the second stint with the glossy magazine, would establish his status. He liked to work fast and to get in close. Appointments would have to be arranged between the fixed points of his day: a liquid lunch and a long evening's trawl towards some borrowed bed. He already knew most of the victims suitable for preferment in *Vogue*. Under pressure, he delivered the defining portfolio of the period. And the place: Soho. Big faces in high contrast. Thieves of time forced to pay their dues. Quality passports for the Styx made by one of the damned.

Rogerson, drink untouched on the round table, and protected by a flawlessly applied cosmetic mask, plays real at the Fine Arts Club in Savile Row. She is scribbling a shopping list, or improving a claim for expenses, making an entry in a posh notebook of the kind promoted by the creative consultancy of Samantha Cameron. She's smiling, but she's not amused. Deakin's focus is tactful. But it's not the tact of inebriation or incompetence, not this time. Mr Deakin is just beginning to enjoy himself. On retainer, liberated into portraiture, the photographer can challenge Bacon and Freud. He can hit the town and be well rewarded for it. When he isn't pimping Bacon-commissioned muff shots to sailors in bars, he is on call. When he moonlights as a male model for the best of the painters, he is also drinking at their expense. And swallowing oysters at Wheeler's in Old Compton Street. Muriel will tolerate him at the Colony Room. Finally, all the barriers are down. This will be the time of his time.

SEA OF BOILING BLOOD

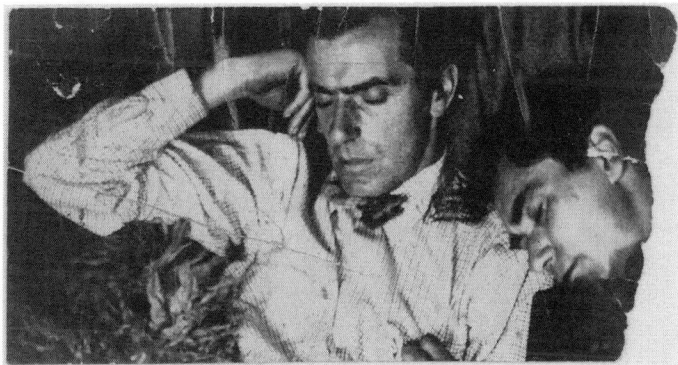

Art Crap, Poetry Crap

Deakin must have had profound respect for the craft of poetry to give it such high praise. 'Art crap, poetry crap,' he spat at George Barker. Work and relaxation were strictly segregated. Joining the Essex party at Tilty Mill in Dunmow, the commissioned photographer struggled to detach the poet from a boozy threesome with the twinned Scottish painters (and unlikely child carers) Robert Colquhoun and Robert MacBryde. Two warring, loving Glasgow headcases on a single set of shoulders. The Roberts refused to perform for the camera. Or anyone else. They occupied their space, fought their battles, and faded into legend, without too much complaint, when that indulgent and romantic era was over. Colquhoun, working on a comeback show, from territory where there is no return, died in MacBryde's arms in 1962. His partner left for Dublin. Dancing outside a pub, he was run down by a car and killed, four years after his friend.

The reluctant weekender was one of the few to grant equal status to poets and painters. At that time, during the Second War and its grudging aftermath, they were all professionally skint. It was a career choice: learning to beg, charm, blackmail, pimp and whore for a dole of cash. For a spare farm cottage. A borrowed couch. A floor. Competitive notoriety. Francis Bacon and Dylan Thomas. Lucian Freud and W. S. Graham. Frank Auerbach and George Barker. Johnny Minton and John Heath-Stubbs. John Craxton and David Gascoyne. Michael Andrews and Dom Moraes. Men. Names. On the make. Work before everything. Most, but not all, were dedicated alcoholics. Some preferred amphetamines. They rushed and twitched, sweating to fix their legacy, before moving on to a better place: oblivion.

In the 1960s, Robin Cook lived hard and wrote fast. Back from another life, another suspended sentence as a vineyard labourer, he metamorphosed into Derek Raymond, night-poet of bleak memory, of unspeakable crimes and burnt-out detectives. Cook was revealed as a beret-topped Coach and Horses philosopher quoting Eliot. Fingers fluent on the keys, back on the last tube to his West Hampstead pit, Cook disinterred psychopathic slaughter, rotting meat under the floorboards, upright sex in rats' alley, and the compulsion to blend Série noire pulp with Keats. In extremity, he channelled Bacon: he lifted the leaking cadavers, the suited businessmen at the bar, the Greek Furies. He borrowed Bacon's interior hells in order to craft fictions from paintings that became storyboards. He rubbed shoulders, for all the hours of hidden daylight, with the best and worst of the shiftless Soho crowd. *Cook was another one damned by early praise: novelist! The dead wouldn't back off.*

Painters and poets. Wilfred Owen is acknowledged as one of the secret heroes of *The Hidden Files*, a Derek Raymond memoir. 'It is not necessary to die in order to understand death.' Cook quotes Eliot. In the lost years of his lifelong literary apprenticeship, Cook was in danger of giving Old Etonians a good name. He hated the establishment public school, a conveyor belt of privilege, and got out as soon as he could. But Eton marked him in two ways: unforced affability and an address book of wealthy chancers with cash to burn.

The filmmaker and novelist Chris Petit, a perceptive collector of lowlife London literature, employed a diluted version of Robin Cook in his cult Soho novel *Robinson*. 'I came to enjoy his company. He was entirely oblivious to his own failure.'

Poetry in the end was about failure; failure achieved, with a good grace, through self-sacrifice. Failure was an entitlement. And it had a specific location, somewhere like North Soho. Flatter it with a branded coinage, Fitzrovia. Mother of biographies. A limbo of cheap restaurants and pubs in which poets could hone their grievances, away from the film hustlers, the brooding villains and spoiled trash in Soho improper, south of Oxford Street. A poet would have to leave the party early, in as committed a style as Dylan Thomas, to become part of the mythos of place. The fortunate, or the most driven, the most disciplined of the painters, would become rich and notorious: Midas-cursed and hounded by a train of parasites wanting the touch. John Deakin, the outsider, former future painter, deserves to be valued as the truest witness to the drama of reputation. He surveyed the devastated continents of those Soho faces, weathered by cigarette smoke and disappointment. He pressed close to catch one spark that could be connected to other sparks in a tapestry of record.

And he was tolerated. Despite everything, he was tolerated. When he wasn't there, something vital was missing from the action.

'Soho was largely inhabited by failures, the ruined men of the forties, whom the war had somehow confirmed in a natural dislike for the mere struggle for circumstantial success,' Anthony Cronin wrote in *Dead as Doornails*. Like the narrator of Petit's *Robinson*, like Julian Maclaren-Ross with his gold-topped stick and green glasses, like Ivan Ginsberg's survivalist grubbing in Roland Camberton's *Scamp*, Cronin felt that the ultimate refuge for the lost was only to be found on the wrong side of Oxford Street.

This is the optimum moment for a collaboration of equals, the loudest voices at the bar. The elbow room for party-piece stories and obscene limericks is shared between poets and painters, avid for patronage from Cyril Connolly at *Horizon*, Tambimuttu at *Poetry London*, or independent publishers of means, such as John Lehmann. There is a general recognition, at closing time, of political crisis, of operating at the end of things. Thirst and delirium conjoin to summon apocalypse, angelic visitations. Blake rises over the river. Language takes flight. Cosmic messages are picked out of salvaged tatters of invoices and racing papers: *Man's Life Is This Meat*. Images fragment. But bad behaviour – *hommage* to Artaud and Rimbaud – is still in vogue. Scrounging is the third art. Keeping journals as a pension plan. Some of the crowd hoarded and polished anecdotes to cash in when the inevitable flood of biographies would creep over the horizon, after a decent interval of thirty to fifty years. When most of the principal actors would be dead or too far gone to afford libel lawyers. For the others, and for Deakin most of all, as participant and accredited documentarist, there were specific photographs of record. Future illustrations, future cover designs. Future retrospective exhibitions: present penury.

Robert Fraser, tracking George Barker for *The Chameleon Poet*, a biography published in 2001, noticed the way Deakin's spectral presence was required – barely noticed, always there – to validate any episode of note in Soho, Fitzrovia or rural Essex. He was a necessary shadow at every wake, every weekend orgy. Without his witness, the unsuspecting host would crumble into dust. Stalker. Provocateur. Conductor of chaos. 'John Deakin,' Fraser said, 'artist and reluctant photographer of genius'. Pariah genius. The man you do not notice on the stair. The smell that arrives first and leaves last.

Fraser claimed that Deakin abetted the painters and the poets in their cult of personality. He colluded. He made the men craggier, more bruised and awkward than they were in life. He loved their flaws. He pimped them for his own predilections. For his solitary custom. He granted the women on the scene room in which to experiment with other versions of themselves. And he was fly enough to catch the moment of revelation, of challenge or submission. The look. The heartbreaking glance.

The Deakin Rolleiflex, familiarly handled, was an instrument of fate. On that evening at Tilty Mill, with the boisterous weekend menagerie of children and Soho casualties indulged by Elizabeth Smart, who had inherited use of the farmhouse property from Ruthven Todd, George Barker strenuously resisted Deakin's attempts to terminate his monologue, and to yank the poet away from the double jeopardy of the drunk Scottish painters, before it kicked off.

'My dear Deakin,' Barker said, 'life is a sea of boiling blood. If I on my island and Colquhoun on his island may not be permitted to wave to one another across the ensanguined flood, it is a pretty sorry state of affairs?'

Who was taking down this dialogue for posterity? Deakin was exasperated. He could not compose the shot he wanted. 'Art crap! Poetry crap!' he shouted. And they all laughed.

David Archer and the Poets

David Archer was a mild man who kept a collection of whips. He befriended and supported a procession of difficult poets before they majored in that topic. Before difficulty became a defensive posture. Before the world hammered them with intimations of virtual success and actual poverty. Archer was a modest Soho godfather with the eccentricities required of any self-respecting bookseller. He *hated* to part with stock and tried to redirect customers, away from Greek Street to Foyles on Charing Cross Road. He looked, in Deakin's portraits, like a bank manager up on a charge. Like a regretful sex criminal. This was a kind of revenge for Archer's continued generosity and support: the forensic interrogation of surface. Truth behind truth, fictional truth etched into exposed flesh. If anybody in those turbulent times could claim a defining quality, Archer was that person: innocence. He was a good man. A mendicant saint dedicated to squandering his inheritance on poets, on unworthy young men and reliable quantities of drink. And as fast as possible. So that he could achieve the higher state of destitution in a charity barracks.

The bookseller found Deakin in the same way that he found his poets. His pulse raced when he closed on genius. He offered two exhibitions in the gallery at the bookshop. He offered exposure to the praise and cynicism of collectors and critics. He launched Deakin in a new direction and he gave him somewhere to live. They were, for a time, a kind of unaligned and combative couple flirting with the domesticity of dominance and submission.

Sanity was located in the Serpentine. Archer swam early and often, spectacles on, head tilted back, under that sky, those trees: London! The ruffled waters of oblivion. With the athletes and the suicides. With the lost rivers. Away from Soho and Deakin and books. The photographer was reliable, he never missed a chance to snipe at his benefactor. He denied him, several times, when Archer was broken and reduced to begging back a few coins from the bounty he had handed over, asked or unasked, in the good days.

Before the final plunge into the abyss, the patron of poets liked to dance barefoot and unpartnered across the West End in a tragic tarantella. He stamped on the imaginary spiders of delirium, before they could bite back. They had already eaten his lost shoes. His socks. It was all over. And it was glorious. He could, at last, come down from those high bookshop ladders where supercilious poets were always positioning him in their amusing anecdotes. The labouring toff with his one good hand stretched out for a hammer, like a relay baton in the race for fame. Drop it and you pay with another vanity tribute.

Pressed by dozens of convalescent volumes, a library of stiff spines mocking the nation's sickness, the hireling researcher crumbled. His target was a man of paper swinging in the wind. Biographers cornered their prey without landing a fatal blow. Shoulder to the wall, after the exit was sealed with useless stacks of pulp, he found that the only door was lost. The man of the margins stayed in the margins. When the scholars tell you too much, learn to lie. Let the ghost talk to ghosts.

'Unenergetically homosexual,' said Robert Fraser. 'Stiff as a Prussian.' In the shadows but of central importance to the recovered history of the period, Archer owned and operated a series of bookshops that were never to be found in the same location twice. He offered the prize of publication in book form to the riskiest talents. The bright boys who drifted, yawning with nerves or beer, into his shop. His parting Masonic handshake might pass on a matchbox with a banknote folded inside. For a few months, this man was permitted to be the lover and provider for Deakin in a comfortable Bayswater flat. George Barker wrote to his brother Kit that the ambiance of a gallery show at Archer's bookshop could be delightful: 'if only people would refrain from sprinkling broken glass on the floor'.

From the classic Deakin portrait of Archer you would never guess that these men were intimate, lovers even. The marmoreal expression is stern or brave, according to taste. Pinprick patterns of grey on grey. Striations, across a cold concrete wall, bleeding into the harshly lit pallor of dead skin. State interrogator or state victim? An obedient officer betrayed by his affections? Disguised as a frigid establishment figure, Archer is an agent of modernist revolution. George Smiley despatching poets across the border from his office near Cambridge Circus. A reserved man of sensibility undone in bed. The shop in Greek Street was always a front, a honeytrap for poets, conveniently close to the Coach and Horses. Archer saw his primary role as keeping the ordinary punters out, repelling footfall. Dan Farson said that there was always a certain welcome, if you could get through a door that had been wedged tight with a wooden block.

Late-afternoon bristles give texture to Archer's grey mask. Frown lines on the lengthening brow are deeply scored. The silvering at the temples chimes with thatched eyebrows. The living man behind the authoritarian spectacles is conventionally barbered; managed tufts from ears and nose, and a clump of stray hair to distinguish well-bred cheekbones. White shirt, dark tie. Brushed shoulders of a good country jacket. But there is something senatorial in the pose, reminiscent of the way Deakin favoured busts of Roman gods and heroes as a heritage backdrop.

Without being an overt predator, Archer had an uncanny knack for discovering combative poetry by young men who had not yet celebrated their majority. He made his original Bloomsbury shop at 4 Parton Street, a now demolished tunnel between Southampton Row and Red Lion Square, the place where confident but undiscovered talents, arriving from the provinces or the other side of town, could march in and allow him the privilege of paying for their first books of verse. This was the most significant aspect of Archer's career as a tweeded, left-leaning and benevolent revolutionary. He was such an unobtrusive commissar. He brought out *Thirty Preliminary Poems* by the twenty-year-old George Barker in 1933. And *18 Poems* by Barker's jealous rival, another twenty-year-old, Dylan Thomas, in 1934. And then in 1936, to round off this miraculous set, a triptych with not a single dud, *Man's Life Is This Meat*, by the third twenty-year-old, David Gascoyne. The precocious Gascoyne had already published *Roman Balcony and Other Poems*, along with an apprentice novel, *Opening Day*.

It was a time of fortunate transactions between voice and image, painting and photograph. Negative capabilities. 'Unspoken is unseen / Until unknown,' Gascoyne wrote. 'Recurrent words / Slipping between the cracks.'

Never settling for anything but the best, the most stridently recalcitrant voices, Archer's Parton Press, having migrated in wartime to 23 Windsor Terrace in Glasgow, released *Cage Without Grievance* by W. S. Graham. Graham was judged to be still under the sway of the intoxicating rhetoric of Dylan Thomas. Barker and Gascoyne met and bonded. They saw each other in London and in the country. They wrote poems about their unexpected alliance. In 1943, Sydney Graham was a mature starter for The Parton Press: he was already twenty-four-years-old.

Archer's last flush, in the third decade of the fading romance of poetic patronage (without reward or gratitude), came when he encountered the handsome Bombay-born Dom Moraes. Moraes met and married – providing the surname she stuck with for her later career – the life-affirming young woman who ran the coffee counter in the basement of the Greek Street bookshop. Henrietta Abbott, an ebullient presence, was known to favoured customers as 'Fuck off darling'. She was a gift to mythmakers, herself included. Deakin, as ever, responded with an unavoidable portrait of the reckless beauty, a blow-up placed in a suitable alcove. The Archer enterprise, in its infancy, was turning into a museum of its own future history. Conversations between consenting adults and contender celebrities sounded like an anthology of quotations. With Deakin as the secret and unacknowledged recorder. The man with the camera. The spook. It is hard to know, at this juncture, if he reported to Archer as his handler, controller of the whole circus. Or if he was waiting for a chance to pass on irrefutable evidence to the court of fate.

Everything Deakin attempted in his Soho portraits is about forcing victims to recognise and accept the intrusion of the camera. Archer, with his walk-on role in biographies of the poets, is otherworldly and myopic, staring off into the wings. Waiting for the next rogue angel, the next bailiff with a writ. The biographers want him as a melancholy monk, ripe for a fall. They want him trapped on that swaying bookshop ladder, reaching for a hammer with which to nail his own hand to the shelf. The Catholic poet George Barker, a committed heretic, presented his publisher as a self-conscious martyr. A fond and foolish benefactor leaking coins. Archer's other arm was withered from birth, like something left too long in the womb. He covered this minor distinguishing feature by never being caught without a bouquet of books, manuscripts and newspapers.

The Archer expression Deakin crafts for his photographic portrait is not merely affronted, it flinches from the surrounding darkness, from the condition of mortality. A crippling rigidity trembles with the effort of giving nothing away under interrogation, the close scrutiny of the camera. Polyfilled ridges in ruled hair. A strobing weave in the lapel of the tweed jacket. Grey abstractions against the complicated essence of the trapped man. The publisher is not a bank manager. He is not peddling insurance. Nothing so perverse, so banal. Archer is more like one of the filmmakers Deakin shot on commission for the magazines. Even his surname invokes the production company run by Michael Powell and Emeric Pressburger: The Archers. The twinned writer/directors wanted to call up William Blake and his 'bow of burning gold', his 'arrows of desire'. They wanted that imagined and eternal England. Unlike any banker or reputable film producer, Archer was using his own money.

As Deakin depicts him, Archer seems to belong in the portfolio alongside the frowning film producer Michael Truman. Alongside Robert Hamer's pickled pose. Alongside David Lean, Michael Balcon and Michael Relph. He belongs with Wardour Street businessmen and not with Greek Street poets. He belongs with incontinent ambition and managed debt. And no promise of great expectations.

Take note of how the smart curators of archive read it. In the 2002 collection *A Maverick Eye*, Robin Muir positions the 1952 portrait of Archer opposite a capture of Elizabeth Smart: novelist, editor, muse and hostess. An unlikely blind date that works pretty well, a paper marriage of opposites. The couple could be meeting for the first time at the registry office, exchanging an envelope of banknotes for a passport. Both of them have taken their bruises from engagement with George Barker. Both, in their day, were embedded in the matter of Soho: twin spectres of the Colony Room. They exchanged loving insults with Muriel Belcher. In Muir's alignment of the two Deakin portraits, this man and this woman become duke and duchess of a doomed court. Smart is backed by creased linen, not concrete. She is fierce, proud, and driven. Hair swept back, nose tilted, full lips reduced to an ever-tighter ring. And the knowledge in those eyes! She was the pursuer caught by her prey, by George Barker. The couple loved and wounded in competitive fictions. Smart got her retaliation in first with *By Grand Central Station I Sat Down and Wept* in 1945. Barker responded with *The Dead Seagull* in 1950. Smart was one of the den mothers of George's tribe of children. And the reason for his late-life moustache and beard. After a lively domestic dispute, she bit through the fleshy parts beneath his nose and tore away his upper lip.

There is another Deakin photograph of Archer from 1958. He is now in company with Dan Farson. Nothing much has changed. The frown lines are deeper. The suit must have aged. Three men are present, at a bar or hospitality suite, somewhere in permanent remission like a television studio. Or like Sartre's *Huis clos*: Soho purgatory, anteroom of hell. The cigarette that never goes out. Dissatisfied glances that refuse to meet. Men without women. Women without drinks. Hanging out. Hanging on. Waiting to turn the latest treachery to profit. Waiting to see who comes through the door.

When Muir shuffled the pack and laid out his chosen prints in a different order for *John Deakin: Photographs* (1996), the book is prefaced by a quote from Elizabeth Smart. 'Who is John Deakin? He is a photographer with extraordinary eyes.' The claim is proved by the self-portrait that accompanies it. The tumble-dried Deakin, a warned-off Irish jockey who has lost his horse, leans on an insecure plinth. His eyes are bullet holes scooped out by a ricochet. He is the most deeply wounded of all the sitters. For this selection, the Archer portrait lifted from the contact sheet of *A Maverick Eye* comes with harsher contrast and deeper abrasions in the concrete. It feels very much like a page torn in anger from a notebook, before being pasted to backing card. It has been signed: 'DAVID ARCHER by John Deakin'.

No Man's Land

Deakin's portraits of the poets of those years, the ones coddled by David Archer, remind me of the housebound and warring characters in Harold Pinter's 1975 play *No Man's Land*. Figures banished to a limbo of dust and furniture and treacherous memory. In a punctured Hampstead of the soul. And proud of it. Spooner, the invader poet, 'dressed in a very old and shabby suit', has inveigled his way into the spacious home of Hirst, a person of presumed wealth and status, a published author. It is a pickup of sorts. 'I often hang about Hampstead Heath myself,' Spooner improvises, 'expecting nothing.' His greasy pinstripe, an autobiography in fag ash and prostate miscalculations, is borrowed from Deakin's frequently reproduced portrait of George Barker, trapped against a cliff of white tiles, between binges, in the gents at Piccadilly Circus. A cruising pit stop on the long road to Hampstead, this popular facility offered better access to overnight chemists.

Everything about that Deakin capture invokes Spooner in Pinter's play. The Hackney-born playwright never quite shook himself free from the irritation of poetry. That life, its recklessness, its poverty, haunted him to the end. He delivered verse units susceptible to public performance, but he reserved his real craft, sharp and shining, for the stage. He knew and satirised, with affection, the grubby world of the peer group readings by confessional verse-makers and unstoppable outpatients in rooms above pubs in Holborn and Hammersmith. The generosity Pinter showed to the poets Deakin photographed underwrote reforgotten publications. He helped to burnish reputations soured by years of neglect. In this, the begetter of *No Man's Land* was surgically spliced between his two characters: the successful man of letters, costive with entitlement, and the ingratiating weasel poet, protected by a carapace of well-deserved obscurity. The invisibly published enjoy a great privilege, they are beyond the reach of criticism.

But Deakin notices. That is why he is employed by faceless controllers. He notices every wart, scar, smirk. Every wayward shirt button. He presents Barker as Spooner, years before Pinter séanced his mysterious play from echoes of T. S. Eliot. The milky glare that can never blink. One of the terrible afflictions of leprosy is signalled when an inability to close the lids leads to blindness. Poets train themselves to see everything that isn't there. And they suffer for it. Deakin limits himself to surfaces. He drinks to kill conclusions. His cornered Barker, up against the tiles, summons Spooner from the Heath. To a roofless house where heavy curtains refuse any hint of daylight.

Barker's flat cap is tilted to disguise creeping hair loss. He models an experimental combination of wedding suit in broad stripes accompanied by a checked shirt. A borrowed club tie and a wink of pocket handkerchief. No visible cuffs, sleeves drawn over manual labourer's reliable hands. The poet is standing, as instructed, against a cold wall. A man guilty of so many innocent trespasses is waiting, without blindfold or cigar, for a drunken firing squad.

George is between engagements, between boltholes. Between wives. He was a prodigious sire. He fathered almost as many children as Lucian Freud, but he shared them out between fewer partners. He was sexually polymorphous and open to suggestion. Unlike Spooner, he took patronage as his due. He worked, without sabbaticals, at his life's task: the mining and setting of words.

Harold Pinter visited sites associated with the poets in company with Elspeth Barker, George's widow. And he recorded Barker's poem 'At Thurgarton Church' for a television film on Elspeth's life. The Barkers dined with Pinter and Lady Antonia Fraser at the Caprice, where the poet played his required role, as Spooner's avatar, by misbehaving and putting himself to the business of composing a publishable letter of apology. Something of a speciality for Dylan Thomas and most of Archer's boys.

The engagement was even closer with Sydney Graham. Pinter had a practitioner's appreciation of Graham's innovation, his philosophical 'slipperiness'. The Scottish poet was an extreme model for what the playwright wanted to achieve, through repeated revisions and risks, in his more public sphere of operation. Graham, the man, demanded financial and critical support.

The favoured Deakin portrait of Graham has the huge face of the freckled Clydeside poet cupped by stubby ringed fingers. Honest dirt in broken nails. The eyes are not so much bloodshot as blood-burst, flooded. Powerful paws squeeze the violated mask. This is the same formal device Deakin adopted for painters, for John Minton and William Scott. And for the sculptor Eduardo Paolozzi. Minton's fingers are longer than Graham's. The kiss curl is too calculated. The once fashionable artist and illustrator has been spoiled by inherited money and the wrong sort of success. Nothing can save him now. Graham escaped the fatal moment of Soho celebrity, without suicide. He hunkered down at the end of the land in Cornwall. He socialised with the St Ives painters, the drinkers and talkers. The doomed glider pilots. Taking no prisoners, he waited on his muse.

It would be nice if, in the context of Pinter's ghost play, the smell of the poets, the footprints they leave in the dust of the stage, a working acquaintance with Deakin's portraits could be proved. But there is no hard evidence. These are parallel worlds. *No Man's Land* has been conjured from a collection of family photographs, authentic, or salvaged from a junk shop. Can the critical momentum of a life be found in images that provoke unreliable Pinter monologues? The playwright worked through a long list of alternative titles: *Faces in Shadow, A Sidelong Glance, The Previous Subject*. 'They reek of desolation or mortality,' Michael Billington wrote in his Pinter biography. Without question, the rejected title coming closest to the heart of the matter was: *The Photograph Album*.

The private conflict in the transactions between Deakin and David Archer, facilitator of poets, in their shared Bayswater accommodation, was re-enacted in power plays given public exposure by Pinter. Dominance through servitude. The cruelty of the supplicant. The grim busking, every yellow evening, for booze and sexual favours. Deadly games enlivened by honed insults. A place on the shelf for what Archer, the mildest of men, referred to as his 'favourite whip'. This could, out of nowhere, erupt into sudden and violent rages. Before the issuing of an abject apology.

Where is the landscape of the past without images of record? The wealthy Hampstead author, Hirst, announces that he contemplates showing the potman poet his photograph album. 'You might even see a face in it which might remind you of your own, of what you once were. You might see faces of others, in shadow, or cheeks of others, turning, or jaws, or backs of necks, or eyes, dark under hats, which might remind you of others, whom once you knew, whom you thought long dead, but from whom you will still receive a sidelong glance, if you can face the good ghost.'

This shadow play is a manifesto for the posthumous resurrection of the Deakin albums. The blistering stare of those chosen revenants. Pinter sees the production of the photo album as an experiment, a test for his victim. And himself. Exposure to long dead emotions, love trapped on a slide. The subjects of these photographs are imprisoned. 'I say to you,' Hirst concludes, 'tender the dead, as you would yourself be tendered, now, in what you would describe as your life.'

Poetic for sure. But an illusion. 'They're blank, mate, blank,' retorts the dominant manservant. All the Pinter characters are prepared to interrogate fixed fragments of a past that might never have happened. Nobody asks the key question: *who was the photographer?* What was his story? Who is paying?

Spooner, the deflated poet, registers the horror of stasis. Faces that can never break their smile, never grow older. Photographs are 'icy and silent'. That silence is absolute. Beyond remission. The best of Deakin's portraits catch it, existential dread. One indrawn breath that lasts forever.

'What is this?' The postcard from the Circus, Arnold Circus, challenged the researcher. He had delivered the first tranche of papers. 'What do fashionable plays have to do with the story?' He composed a defence. And sat on it. The photographer, he said, could not be recovered from a quarantined city, from

books or the yarns of other drunks. If the man of myth existed anywhere – as
a living entity – *it was in some parallel world. Empty rooms in cobwebbed
mansions where the undead repeat their actions on a nightly basis. Beyond
that, he confessed, he had nothing to offer. Unsourced quotations on file cards.*

When Deakin was ratted out with Soho, the vitriol coming his way from
Muriel Belcher for, among lesser crimes, his denial of David Archer, the
photographer made his escape to Hampstead. To better air and taller
houses. Village life among the enlightened. Hospitality was on offer from
the Cambridge poet and literary theorist William Empson, and his wife,
Hetta. A complicated couple. It wasn't exactly restful, but Empson's beard
elevated Deakin's portraits in the way that Lord Tennyson's face foliage
worked for Julia Margaret Cameron. Poets and their patrons. Spooner
got his revenge, for the meagre charity he had endured, by insulting
Hirst with the offer of a poetry reading in the squalid room above a pub.
'Perhaps you might agree to half a dozen photographs or so, no more.'

They agree. Without counting the cost. The poets always submit
to readings, to the stable above the pub. To the camera. It's part of the
general contract: if they want to live on beyond their brief moment of
illumination, if they want their scatter of words to be remembered. They
must submit to stillness and silence, seizures factored by John Deakin.
That lowlife scrounger. The self-cashiered officer who has taken over the
instrument of fate, the Rolleiflex.

John Heath-Stubbs submits, pirate patch over dud right eye. He
chews on the blackened ivory of a cigarette holder. Low angle. Night.
Trade signs. A comprehensively 'danced' print (as the curators call it). A
line running down the middle. The politics of anxiety. Like something
out of Fritz Lang and his silent-screen nightmares, tapping the zeitgeist,
ahead of flight to Paris.

Dylan Thomas is flirting with an ivy-choked grave, yards from where
his own husk will be interred. With Deakin in attendance, gravedigger
and witness. Up in town, after another Paddington rattle, the Welsh poet
is puffy and surfeit swollen, sulky about being paused somewhere between
liquid appointments and purgatory. Between Chelsea and World's End.

Sydney Graham is trapped in the frame of his own hands. The brow is not so much furrowed as trenched with a spade. There is no yolk left in the blooded pebbles of his eyes. The prisoner-poet realises that he is staring into a mirror of no return.

Louis MacNeice is undeceived. He is Anglo-Irish, long-faced, properly suspicious. The tweed of his jacket is an ancient landscape. This is a job interview Deakin has failed. He'll go thirsty tonight.

George Barker, player and prophet, is an understudy to his suit. He hangs around in a white-tiled den until Pinter writes his portrait back to life in *No Man's Land*.

Oliver Bernard is handsome, the oldest of three brothers, active on the scene. The one stuck with being an acknowledged poet. Brothers are less useful in the arts than in crime. Dark hair, cheekbones: it's impossible. Under orders, Oliver has not shaved. In recompense, Deakin will shoot the cover for his book of poems.

William Empson, magus of a Haverstock Hill ménage in a large house owned and directed by his wife, is the subject of a notable Deakin sequence, most of the frames never reproduced. Hetta let rooms to *émigrés* of interest and to previous, current or future lovers. There were many of these. Elias Canetti, as he confesses in his memoir, *Party in the Blitz*, was a regular visitor. And the kind of reporter you have to search at the door for a contraband notebook. Nobel Prize still some distance over the horizon, the great man was merciless to those who did not fully and immediately recognise his worth. Empson, he said, 'spoke incessantly, at an extremely high intellectual level, and never listened to anyone'. Canetti characterised him, in balance to his active wife, as 'completely asexual'.

Poets performed in the basement: Eliot, Dylan Thomas, Kathleen Raine. Canetti, sketching as rapidly and effectively as Deakin, skewered them all. Before being caught unawares by the photographer Cornelius Meffert, as he stepped out of the Hampstead underground station in three-piece suit, scarf, raincoat. A short and sturdy alien debating if he is Hirst or Spooner that day. 'Detached memories that need to be re-animated,' Canetti wrote. He did not register the presence of Deakin lurking in the social shallows.

Friends brought friends they barely knew from the pub to literary parties at the Empson house. Deakin was admitted for a while. He photographed the metaphysical essayist in a mandarin smock. Like a Chinese conjuror in a pantomime. Empson's magnificent beard doesn't belong with the bespectacled face. Worn like a thick dog-hair scarf, this chin topiary protects a vulnerable throat in winter. Deakin is hiding out. He places Empson against wall hangings brought back from academic stints in the Far East. He has him sprawl on an elbow. He messes about with focus. There are twelve attempts and the poet's expression never changes. Deakin is not the registered keeper of this bear. When you stop the poet talking, on and on, he's not really there.

The most striking Empson print from the Deakin sequence has a seminal smear, an accidental intervention, running across the mouth. The poet could be wheezing out a bubble of creamy ectoplasm to feed his abundant beard. Somebody, perhaps Deakin, has added a black beauty spot in the shape of a heart.

Confined in the Covid lockdowns to a limited territory, and unable to strike out in pursuit of survivors to interview, I started to re-read all the poets Deakin photographed. I opened his black albums to the relevant portraits and kept them alongside the poetry books published by David Archer. David Gascoyne was the only one with whom I shared some personal experience: long phone calls about London and Rimbaud, on Sunday evenings, when the poet's wife, Judy, was in church. There were occasional performances on both sides of the Solent and excursions to the Isle of Wight. Deakin treated Gascoyne with a degree of formality, as if they had just been introduced. He placed him somewhere between poet and leading man in repertory theatre. He noted the bow ties Gascoyne shared with Sydney Graham. He was aware of the poet's friendship with George Barker. There are five Gascoyne prints in the black albums. They come directly before a run featuring Bacon's lover and victim: George Dyer. George is immaculate, brutally coiffed and bracered. He has arranged large hands in some coded way over his groin.

A poet's poet, Gascoyne was an amphetamine-fuelled, border-hopping European afflicted by visionary seizures. A night-stalker of unfrequented river paths thrust into messianic overdrive by Dr Karl Theodor Bluth with his infamous ox-blood and methedrine cocktails. Bluth also supplied Anna Kavan, George Barker and many others from the Notting Hill interface of art and society. He kept his valued clients wolf-eyed and speeding, while he hammered away on a grand piano. Like Laird Cregar in John Brahm's outré film version of Patrick Hamilton's *Hangover Square*. Bohemia looks backwards with a sentimental sniff, those were the daze. Deakin's cynical witness permitted no such indulgence. He exposed surfaces, boosted flaws.

Titular spirits recur, male and female: David Archer and Elizabeth Smart. Archer with his migrating shops, his publications, and those matchboxes of folded pound notes. Elizabeth Smart, sculpted by circumstance, was a rapturous and wounded author. House mother to the serially homeless Gascoyne when he washed up in London. And to most of the floating detritus of Soho. Smart signed Barker into the Colony Room as her guest. She had a brief and tempestuous affair with Graham.

Deakin kept the pictorial record, but Pinter's Spooner, busking for patronage, has the last word: 'My career, I admit it freely, has been chequered. I was one of the golden of my generation. Something happened. I don't know what it was.'

Everything now is building towards the decline and fall of David Archer. And, as a consequence, the disappearance of the youthful meteors he published and supported. In Archer's place, a new figure emerges to dominate the rest of the unwritten graphic novel: Francis Bacon. The past doesn't swim back from smell or taste, a chocolate digestive melting in builder's tea. It lives on, out of time, in rescued photographs. Bacon is Deakin's Baron Palamède de Charlus. Painted cheeks and teeth scoured by abrasive powders. Hair blackened with shoe polish. Leather jacket bouncing borrowed light. The master manipulator conducts his swarming court. He would like to channel Velázquez and prophesy the downfall of kings through an arrangement of mirrors and easels and open doors. But his talents are of a different order and the Colony Room is a fetid tank. A Turkish bath that doesn't serve water, bottled or tap. Upstairs on Dean Street, it is a Labour Exchange for the electively unemployed.

It can feel as if all Deakin's preliminary sniffing and circling has been about preparing himself for the arrival of Bacon. Where court painters found their necessary patronage in portraits of princes and popes, the stalking photographer identified this painter as the bright star around which the peripheral figures would play.

Everything has been contrived to prepare for the final drama: David Archer, released from the indignity of performing as stiffly as a marble bust, is brought to life in a two-shot Deakin composition. He is lined up in a bar with a long mirror and a picture gallery of rippling half-stripped boxers. He is in studied conversation with a willowy Indian student in tweed jacket: Dom Moraes. Empty cocktail glass. Cigarette stub about to be crushed in the Ricard ashtray. Archer is balancing a white manuscript across his lap. His collar is askew. These men won't look at each other or the camera. A slice of Archer's professorial head burnishes the mirror.

Deakin makes a spy shot of the covert couple as they broker a poetry deal. There are two abandoned newspapers in evidence. How long was Archer kept waiting? Maurice Chevalier winks from the wall. An offer has been made. 1957: The Parton Press will publish the first Dom Moraes book, *A Beginning*. It will be Archer's last substantial venture. And Deakin is there to catch, or stage, this moment.

The independent publisher fades into the shadows. Moraes takes his prizes. He marries Henrietta (née Audrey Wendy Abbott). She keeps his surname through many liaisons, many falls. Including the literal kind, down from a drainpipe, during her brief apprenticeship as an amateur cat burglar. But 1957 is too late for poetry. The golden era has been foreclosed. This will be no juicy biopic for Dom and Hen. They are caught in the fallow period between Dylan and Caitlin, Ted and Sylvia. There will be no breakfast caravans on location in Victoria Park.

When the opportunity arose for published confessions, Henrietta Moraes recalled Archer and Deakin as a single unit, a warring couple.

'I had spent my early youth drinking in the same places as they did and this bond, once forged, is impossible to overlook.' Deakin, as we know, enlarged a Moraes portrait to nine feet by seven, and hung it in an alcove at the back of Archer's shop, close to the coffee counter. Henrietta characterised her employer as 'gently born, eccentrically orientated, altruistically minded, hysterically tempered, kind, perceptive, a left-wing Fascist and patron saint of the Forties and Fifties poets'. She thought he behaved like a jump jockey with a great nose for a winner.

The proprietor of The Parton Press worked miracles in getting through the burden of his inheritance. Shucking off the bad karma of wealth and family, military adventurism and inappropriate territorial exploitation, Archer tried to borrow back a coin or two from those he had supported. But he wasn't a natural beggar. You have to be trained, like Deakin or Dylan Thomas, over many years. And many bars. You have to be acknowledged (and avoided) in the purlieus of Soho and Fitzrovia. You have to be recognised as a potential genius, reliably unreliable in the way of broken promises and forgotten debts. You must be known to all by your Christian name. You are a person without shame. When you aren't around, you will be the principal topic of conversation. They give you radio gigs. And holiday cottages. It's almost like being a politician.

Punctured below the waterline and sinking fast, Archer accepted that penance in the basement of an Oxford Street department store. There was one last desperate punt. He summoned the nice young Mr Moraes, a poet who would very soon be going up to Jesus College in Oxford, and he gave him a diplomatic task. Dom was despatched to the countryside, to Castle Eaton in Wiltshire, in order to put the bite, with proper deference, on Archer's old man, the retired officer adrift in a melancholy English landscape.

Here was a scene begging to be adapted into a television drama by Stephen Poliakoff or Sir David Hare: the disappointed aristo – Bill Nighy, Michael Gambon, Charles Dance – at the window of the big house, staring out at an inherited park, the woods and lake no longer under his custodianship. Weeds in the unraked gravel. Bentley up on bricks in the stables. The young Indian of good family, a poet influenced by

European modernists, will flag up understated ironies among borrowed family portraits and elephant-hoof holders for assorted walking sticks. Someone will massacre a pheasant.

It was left to Moraes to organise a trust fund for the major's son, busted publisher and bookseller. And it was Moraes who invited Allen Ginsberg and Gregory Corso to shock literary Oxford into the contemporary world. They were orthodox Beats on the grand tour, taking photographs, clocking the sites and stripping at parties. They tried to kiss Auden's well-tramped carpet slippers. They met Archer on the streets of Soho but missed Deakin, the photographer Ginsberg would collect, a few years later, in Tangier.

The decent old military man, David Archer's father, gestures with a weary arm. 'Do you see those three hills? The first paid for the Welshman's book. The next for Barker. The last for the Scottish fellow. There are no hills left.'

It could be that Deakin's composition in the Soho bar, Archer and Moraes smoking and scheming together, was about the plot to squeeze a few pounds out of the Wiltshire estate. But Archer was too broken in spirit to travel. It was all for nothing now. There was no inherited ground left to sell.

Deakin moved on. He delivered a set of promotional portraits of Moraes as the coming man. Unlike the more confrontational displays of the earlier poets, it feels as if the poet is in charge of his own performance. He poses against mosaics, against veins in marble, against the arched roof of a railway station. Dom is a romantic figure from a period novel coloured by Evelyn Waugh, not Kingsley Amis. He is leaving Soho and catching a train for Oxford. With Deakin in determined pursuit. He stalks Moraes through the night: a tidy flat where the smoking poet toys with a white pad of paper, waiting for inspiration. On and on it goes, shot after shot. Rooms and streets. A Colin Wilson rollneck is matched with a good tweed jacket. England is so cold. Back to the bar. Back to the museum. Back to the flat.

The discarded landlord and lover, patron of poets, has no place in the new story. No longer a subject worthy to be photographed, Archer's physical presence diminishes. He can't sustain his dismal role among the electrical appliances. Georgina Barker, handsome daughter of George, told Elizabeth Smart that Archer was dead. Socially, this was true. But the bankrupt publisher still had a few months left on the streets, a ghost traumatised by the catalogue prices now achieved for fine copies of Dylan Thomas's *18 Poems*. The ones he preferred to give away, or reluctantly let go at 3/6d a unit. In October 1971, the former bookman washed up in the Swiss Pub on Old Compton Street, clutching a jumbo-sized aspirin bottle. 'Do you think these will do the trick?'

Back at the Salvation Army hostel, Archer laboured to compose a collectable set of last letters. Next morning, the cleaner found his body. And the excuse for another Colony Room wake. Muriel Belcher blamed Deakin. But the stain of shame, for Soho's failure to support one of its own, spread far wider than any one person. In truth, the best account we have of this kindly, complicated man are the sequences achieved by Deakin's camera. The groups of portraits scattered in clusters through the seventeen thick albums.

Old money never quite vanishes. A decent tranche was waiting for Archer, but he'd gone to ground, no fixed address, and it never reached him. He was interred in 1971. And then, a year later, as if in sympathy, Deakin joined him. After which, they both enjoyed a decade or so of respectful silence before the rescuers, the salvage artists and avid collectors, launched the inevitable process of resurrection. Before the exhibitions and memoirs and packed gatherings of literary romantics in Soho pubs. Jeff Towns, one of the great enthusiasts, a determined archaeologist of scraps and fragments, sent me a letter he had found buried somewhere among his computer files.

'I did know John Deakin and remember his photographs,' John Heath-Stubbs typed from 22 Artesian Road, W2, in 1994. 'I don't think I have much to say about him. To be frank I didn't really like him very much – although he was always friendly to me. I expect you know the tragic comic story of his death.'

And then Heath-Stubbs, with justified poetic licence, revises the famous tale, from years before Deakin's actual Brighton finale: the swallowing of cleaning fluid instead of wine at the Golden Lion. The hospital, the stomach pump, the rapid return to action. A couple of stiff ones to cleanse the palate. The episode was very much part of the Deakin myth, but it wasn't the end. The real event was kinder; a convalescent bed at the seaside, paid for by Francis Bacon, and a good night out in an excursion town that knew how to party.

'Is it true?' Jeff asked.

Poet true, I thought. There was another ephemeral item of interest in the Towns package. A photocopy of the cover of that Parton Press book by Dom Moraes, *A Beginning*. By our covers shall we be remembered. Even when all the pages of all the books are innocent of text, phantom covers designed by Deakin and his ilk will be preserved by archivists in white gloves. Stephen Spender, a rival verse-maker who never really got along with David Gascoyne, supplied a characteristically feline quote for the Moraes publication, invoking the earlier Parton Press surrealist. 'A quite peculiar tenderness and loneliness, reminiscent of David Gascoyne.' Sad words that could have been applied to Archer himself: tender, lonely, peculiar. A facilitator of originality in others.

A London bookdealer from Charing Cross Road, now based in Suffolk, sold 'an album of Deakin prints' to Towns in 1996. Deakin, by that time, was a solid commodity, an investment. The bookman had regular dealings with George Barker; poets in their twilight days, if they outlive early celebrity, must learn to cultivate the market. 'I bought quite a bit from Barker and sold most of it. Interesting guy but slightly nasty when drunk.'

Nightfish, a collection of forty-three 'original photographs by the Soho photographer John Deakin', was dated from 1987. The prints came to Sebastian Barker, the poet's son, by way of *Vogue*, where his mother, Elizabeth Smart, had worked as an editor and writer. 'Published by Sebastian Barker in an edition of one,' said the London dealer's catalogue. There were twelve portraits of Smart, five of George Barker, one of Dylan Thomas with John Davenport six of W. S. Graham, four of Paul Potts, one of Lucian Freud, two of Francis Bacon, and six of the painters Robert

Colquhoun and Robert MacBryde. 'Cloth bound, in excellent condition throughout.' The asking price for this unique item was £1,800. Sold! To Mr Towns.

Jeff told me that he believed that the album had been originally assembled by Sebastian as a gift to his mother. Deakin, even beyond his connection with Dylan Thomas, was a subject of considerable interest for the Swansea collector. Jeff asked his friend, the novelist Max Porter, about the Deakin cameo in *The Death of Francis Bacon*. This was basically one line in the book, remarking on Deakin's peculiar odour. And, yes, Max, that corpse smell, once it has become established, cannot be shifted. And its name is anger.

Still haunted by the mysteries of the moment of death, an irreversible accident always intended, I mentioned Bacon's Spanish exit to a researcher based in Madrid. How could this awful thing be permitted without Deakin's witness? Without the painter's faithful shadow being in attendance.

The email response was prompt:

I'm enclosing several items. In one of these (Image Number 1) you will see something curious: a photo of Bacon's corpse in the morgue, where he appears with a kind of visor masking his eyes. At his funeral there was only a bouquet of flowers and very few people. It took place at the crematorium of La Almundena cemetery.

HIGH SALVAGE IN SOHO

At the Purple Court of Bacon

Lives mesh and tangle. Doors are neither open nor shut now. It all depends, he hazards, on which side you find yourself standing. Sometimes rectangular panels are wooden mirrors like unprimed canvases, sometimes crucifixions. There are muffled voices upstairs. Rats scratching behind the skirting. A glass shatters. Is that wine or blood running down your leg? Malevolent shadows, with no visible host, flow out from under the mattress. Man-shaped puddles.

I am no closer to the heart of the mystery. But it doesn't belong in Brighton. The faces I circled have developed beaks. Bat teeth. Wings retract into the leather of the curtains. Kill the borrowed light.

Alternative biographies are as valid as documented history. Out of social accidents – school, university, sexual inclination – treaties of influence come together: in the way your lifeblood will settle, post-mortem, in the lower back. Careers are forged. And lost. Out of drinking clubs and afternoon affairs, courts form. Popes are chosen.

John Deakin and Patrick White, both tricky, both cursed with the nag of uncommon gifts, were born in May 1912. White felt much older from the start; sheep-station tan, of the land, privately schooled and funded. Whatever was out there, he was against it. Deakin, the elective orphan, weakened as he aged, but played young: he shed inhibitions he'd never really had. He spiked any notion of husbanding a reputation. Both men served in the Middle East during the Second World War. They inhabited intersecting circles of a primarily homosexual London art world: Chelsea, Belgravia, Soho. Both men had their dealings with Francis Bacon. Bacon was mentored, in the early days, by an Australian modernist painter, Roy de Maistre. White began writing under the influence of a fellow countryman already established on the London scene. He dedicated his first novel, Happy Valley, *to de Maistre.*

Bacon took what he wanted from this fortunate immigrant, a man whose influence was strongest in the early phase as an interior designer. He grafted aspects of Graham Sutherland on his Midi landscapes. Despite a changing cast of patrons, associates, lovers, Bacon was solitary: he knew how it had to be done and how it must be lived. He would never be part of anyone's court. Others would pay their respects. They would flatter his performance with myths and lies. And loud lunches.

Sucked in by the centripetal force of Bacon's aura, Deakin maintained his integrity through acid wit and bad behaviour. Patrick White was always secure in his uncomfortable genius: he watched painters, he cultivated suspicious friendships. He collected paintings. With acquaintances and locations in common, Deakin and White, never colliding, moved through parallel worlds. The Australian novelist shared the photographer's existential horror at the implications of doors. They are a repeated motif in the hallucinatory aspects of The Aunt's Story, *published in 1948. 'But there are occasions on which you cannot stop the closing of the door . . . It would happen. It would be like this in time.' And again. 'A reflection walking through mirrors, towards the door which had always been more mirror than door.'*

White is on one side. Deakin on the other. The phantom door swivels and spins. The jacket design for The Aunt's Story *is a photographic theft from a painting by Roy de Maistre.* Figure in a Garden (The Aunt) *is an ambiguous tailor's dummy, costume protected and long skirted. A gloved hand clutches a wilted daisy-flower. The set is a post-Cubist nightmare, a threatening stack of floating doors and window frames.*

'She closed doors, and he was left standing in his handsome mahogany interior, which was external, fatally external, outside . . .'

The fictional Deakin I tried to recover from books and photo albums, during the submerged interval of lockdown paranoia, was another species of de Maistre abstraction. This projection was being assembled from second-generation prints. When, with detail swimming before my eyes, I dropped my guard, it felt as if the novel was being posthumously dictated by Dan Farson. I shuffled my file cards. 'There was only the primitive raving of pariah dogs.'

***

The position of sanctioned fool, at any court, is one of privilege and obligation. One moment you are up on the table in a paper crown and the next in chains, sleeping with swine. No king worth the title maintains his status without a dwarf, jester, ape; something smaller, leaner, smellier. And more grounded. Open to insult or to striking back under the covering laughter of the mob. The official clown is a hardened victim of regal tantrums, swallowing the spittle of scorn in order to secure regular patronage: shelter in a kitchen corner, cakes and bones, leftover dregs at the bottom of the lipsticked glass. Access to the reflected nimbus of fame. To be always of the court and its migrations. To have elbow room in the drunken taxi. To be ticked off on the guest list. In position on the steps of the Tate Gallery at Millbank, snapping away at preening fortunates ascending in triumph to the private view. On the train for Paris. For Venice. A fetch-and-carry member of the entourage. Heading east, downriver, after the event. Locked in with the select coven of inebriates after closing time. With or without a camera. Most alert when most lost in fug of gossip and man-sweat and smoke.

The London of myth, stitched from a web of repeated or contradictory memoirs, interviews and retrievals, is mapped by overlapping courts; courts dominated by figures who seem, in retrospect, to represent the spirit of their time. Francis Bacon and Lucian Freud loom large. They accumulate legends, which they also shape and improve. They provoke, play up, and tease their tolerated confidants. Before withdrawing into secure properties.

Nightgames in gambling clubs and convivial cellars put them into direct competition with rival and more obviously savage courts. With the Krays. Those sculpted Easter Island heads in shiny suits, muscling in from the east with others of their ilk. The boys from Bethnal Green relied on family: strong mum, absent dad, brother. Occulted twins. As house photographer, the Krays employed David Bailey, whose portraits owed a debt to Deakin, because they had a superstitious faith in the voodoo of images. The Twins went to church (when they needed favours, a court reference from the priest, promise of a top dollar send-off funeral). The Soho fraternity of artists bonded as a family through fear of solitude. The terror of the studio. They were loyal to their drinking holes. But from those first pale flickers of burgeoning post-war reputation, the first proper sales, unlikely alliances were forged between painters, punters, thugs, smart Irish bookies and landowning aristocrats. Ronnie and Reggie considered Bacon's portraits decadent and distasteful, but like any good judge of horseflesh, they sniffed a winner. And invited the bent artist to contribute to their collection. Freud cultivated glamorous, bone-breaking debts that made him invaluable to free-market businessmen with equine and property interests. Favours were solicited and returned. Every court had its shadowy double. Every court revolved around a dominant figure. A screaming pope in mufti.

Graham Sutherland, who had strong support, before Bacon, as the rising man, never established a satellite court of explainers, flatterers and thirsty supplicants. He liked Venice. Its light and its airless society. He suffered the drudgery of commissioned portraiture. The kind of well-rewarded work that killed his reputation. Arthur Jeffress, Deakin's old lover, hung his Sutherland in a place of honour. Man-spread around a curlicued garden chair, the victim's laboured pose anticipates Christine Keeler. Jeffress is bottle bronzed, well fed, and fading fast, from the legs up. With no soulmate in occupation since the departure of Deakin, he was a suicide in remission. Sutherland's crowning public glory, his Churchill presentation, ended in the furnace at Chartwell. Instead of cultivating a court of his own, a cult of risk and mystery, Sutherland appeared to be a man in search of the sort of aristocrats who might appreciate his talent.

When Deakin confronted Sutherland in 1948, at the apex of the painter's fame, it was for an unused Vogue illustration. A respectful but disengaged mid-shot in the neutral space of a West End gallery. Sutherland is crisply presented: well-behaved hair, lightweight jacket, pocket handkerchief and button-down shirt. The expat who has not yet cleared his tax status. But who knows that London is another country. A slightly soured stare into the wings. The balance is off. Here is an official portrait, made without fire or consequence. The painters who knew Deakin as a fellow toper, a face at the end of the bar, glare right back, allowing him, as he later confessed, to superimpose the sketch in his head on the reality of the reflex twitch when the shutter clicks. Sutherland does not want to think about why he is there. Some unspoken horror is creeping towards him from afar. Even in his coolest captures, Deakin tries to nail character through strict geometry. He doesn't need to say: 'Hold that.' He doesn't say anything. He is the supreme confessor of accidental encounters. Get it done and move on. Before they call time. On sitter and image thief.

What is today's quotation on the file card? 'Photography was unmasked, and shown not to be a faithful witness but an interpreter. The subject would now tend to become not the reason for the picture, but its pretext; the picture's first function was to reveal the photographer.'

Last Supper at Lunchtime

All too often the least competent and most suspect compositions, a burden to sitters and photographer alike, are the ones that are best remembered; retrievals from chaos illuminate subsequent histories. Paid commissions charged with tension become fictional improvisations around a time that never was. In the accepted gospel of Soho, this oyster bar lunch at Wheeler's, with empty glasses and no food, was Deakin's great moment: his punt at a blasphemous Last Supper. Reproductions multiply, even as those manipulated participants, the great ones, succumb to age and neglect. They fade and flake like Leonardo's noble wall at the Dominican convent of Santa Maria delle Grazie at Milan. Dust on studio floor.

Dan Farson appreciated Deakin's brief period of success: top-end magazine gigs and handy locations. Farson's 1987 memoir, *Soho in the Fifties*, has a summary of the invariable routine.

> At that time John Deakin worked for *Vogue*, where he had the perfect set-up. The offices were conveniently close to the French, around the corner in Shaftesbury Avenue where Deakin's backcloth was available and quickly lit by such talented assistants as Tom Hawkyard. When there was a photo-call, Deakin would make his appearance, take several full-face and profile shots, and hurry back to Gaston.

This outline of a well-lived life is given emphasis in Farson's book by the author's own triumphantly pissed bodge shot of Deakin, jowled and grinning in the French, congratulating himself on another nicely managed scam. The Farson portrait does its job pretty well: Deakin's nose is flattened by the sweaty intimacy of the pub. He looks like a waking corpse out of Edgar Allan Poe pushing against the misted porthole of a coffin. Harsh cropping cuts him off above the eyebrows, but indulges a flabby concertina of gecko skin beneath the exaggerated chin. 'Deakin's sitters became his victims,' Farson wrote. And confirmed his thesis by portraying the smashed photographer as a subterranean grotesque, a character assassin acid-scorched by his own 'caustic wit'.

Chased by his demons, Deakin scuttled around the labyrinth, from studio to pub, always on the move, trying to remember the places from which, just yesterday, he had been barred. And always with one bleary eye open for a pal in funds, a one-night patron. As registered artisans, photographers like Deakin must have noticed how their Soho trajectories intersected with girls clipping along on brave heels, faces a bright mask, make-up boxes swinging like Geiger counters, as they rushed from club to club, the working strippers. *With nobody after him, he was on the run. A fugitive. The camera was his weapon, his disguise. Without faith, he had to confess.*

The photographer never let go of the germ of a proper historic sense, his unspoken belief that all this fuss, the suicides, the sudden and unwelcome gush of fame or money to be burnt, was worth recording. When there was no poet or personality available, he sacrificed himself, by directing Farson or some fellow inebriate, one of the brotherhood, in how to make the shot. There is a cracking Deakin self-portrait (taken by other hands), at the bar of the 'queer pub', the Golden Lion. Deakin is peering over his shoulder, eyebrows raised like Tower Bridge, tight lips spitting to get his retribution in first. Farson says that a mystery surrounds this capture. 'Both Francis Bacon and Frank Auerbach believe that they operated the camera on Deakin's instructions.'

It was when Farson realised that a temporary career pause in Soho had become a permanent stranding, from which there was no way out, that he latched on to Bacon, a lunchtime enabler in a 'well-cut grey suit and open-neck shirt'. The new friend offered a free drink, but did not introduce himself by name. Introductions were bad form. 'Shall we go on to Wheeler's for something to eat?'

The date of the Wheeler's group portrait is as uncertain as the focus in most of the Deakin shots. Some say it happened in 1962, and others, going with the holograph inscription on a print in the archive, opt for 'March 1963'. Whenever the dyspeptic gathering occurred, John Deakin – through the good offices of Elizabeth Smart, then employed by a glossy called *About Town* – was the one invited by Francis Wyndham to come up with a fix on the painters of the old guard. These incorrigibles were still working in oil, still trowelling away at portraiture and landscape, still arguing with the accepted masters of the canon. They were not yet, not quite, branded as 'School of London'. But that was the implication: that individualists, sometimes allied, sometimes squabbling, were a functioning collective engaged in investigating and expressing the spirit of the city. Leon Kossoff, the one painter whose essential subject matter was indeed London, its railways, excavations, transients, was not invited. Leon was never a Colony Room barnacle. He was probably labouring in his studio. Or inspecting holes in the ground somewhere around Bishopsgate.

Francis Wyndham, writer, editor, patron of photojournalists, appreciated the flow and flux of London as a shaken tapestry of scribblers and visual artists, snappers and scoundrels. Stories he commissioned were often picture led. He gave space and decent design to Don McCullin, Bailey, Donovan and Duffy. He also visited, in company with their redoubtable mother, Violet, whichever Kray happened to be in Parkhurst at the time. It is appropriate that the editor of colour supplements laid out like storyboards for unmade documentaries should also be the advocate of photographer as director: as actor, player and significant personality in a hyped culture stew. The time demanded an image. The image a signature.

A single shot by Deakin taken late morning at Wheeler's had a shelf life very much like certain films to which social historians keep returning, convinced that close study of the accidents of a commercial enterprise will somehow reveal secrets of former times in London. John MacKenzie's *The Long Good Friday*, completed in 1979, drawing on the local newspaper experience of Barrie Keeffe in Stratford, anticipated the exploitation of old docklands by politicians and money-laundering bullion thieves, in the vacuum between the Krays and Margaret Thatcher. With the spectre of the great Olympic circus coming over the horizon. *Performance*, a collaboration between Donald Cammell and Nicolas Roeg, was drawn from urban myths and soused in bad magic. The film proved to be a source of endless rumour and misinterpretation. *Blow-Up* initiated the genre: fictions warped from journalism warped from life.

The psychogeography of Antonioni's 1966 London essay owed much of its gestation to Wyndham's personal guidance through locations and sub-cultures. The central character, a fashion photographer sniffing after traces of poverty and dereliction, before embarking on a spectacular *dérive* in his Rolls-Royce convertible, acknowledges the status of craftsman as celebrity. The photographer is now a bigger star than those he photographs. Antonioni takes Julio Cortázar's Paris-based story of an amateur on the prowl, witnessing and recording a suspicious encounter. He promotes this photographer-as-detective into a person worthy of hire by Wyndham and the colour supplements. Into a brand name with assistants and a desirable West London studio. Here is the man with the camera, an author-without-words, lunching in a fashionable South Kensington trattoria, sampling sauces in the kitchen, before choosing the prints for a glossy book of the city, of Swinging London: the sort produced by David Bailey. And texted by a hired journeyman.

When this restless and exhausting character, played by David Hemmings, encounters a painter, he is not of the school of Bacon or Freud or Auerbach. He is a tormented soul agonising over enigmatic abstracts. They look like photographic negatives not yet brought into resolution. Antonioni says that he only made sense of his own paintings when he isolated certain details and enlarged them. So that they were no longer his own. They were a distillation of the matter of the universe. Mysteries of being and essence.

What Wyndham commissioned from Deakin, three years before *Blow-Up*, was a scenario for something that he himself might have composed, around the palpable tensions among a group of painters, as revealed through a single photographic tableau. Not so much a Renaissance Last Supper as a blasphemous parody, after the fashion of misbehaving beggars, at their banquet in *Viridiana*, a Luis Buñuel film which had appeared two years earlier. Bacon, for obvious reasons – razored eyeball, priests dragging dead donkeys on a piano, a woman fellating the marble toe of a statue – was a Buñuel enthusiast. He would have been well aware of the game Deakin was playing in the deserted fish restaurant. The photographer spent time in smoky afternoon cinemas, often shooting from the screen, stealing. It was much less nuisance than dealing with live performers.

Viridiana is the story of a former nun, drugged and violated by an old landowner, a relative, before she decides to practise her unyielding charity on a troop of sullen and mock-humble mendicants. 'I thought that I'd enjoy seeing the beggars dine in the manor dining-room, on a great table covered with an embroidered cloth and candles,' Buñuel said. 'Suddenly I realised that they were in the position of a picture, evoking Leonardo da Vinci's *Last Supper*. Finally, I linked Handel's *Messiah* with the beggars' dance and orgy.'

According to Frank Auerbach, the participants in the parodic tableau at Wheeler's oyster bar were grumpy and out of sorts. They had been convened too early in the day. The guests at this banquet of future millionaires, actors without scripts, were in a Buñuel scenario: aspects of *Viridiana* fading into the purgatory of *El ángel exterminador*, when the guests find themselves unable to leave the party. This is a Soho banquet without food. Without drink. Without Handel. Invitation only. A famous group portrait never used in its own time. A decommissioned commission, with a sturdy afterlife, surviving well beyond its originating circumstance.

Eleven a.m. and it is *la mala hora*, the evil hour, between a good session of work for the early starters, heads ringing, and the opening of the pubs. Freud has been up all night. Bacon and Auerbach begrudge the lost hours of studio time. But Deakin has assembled three of the acknowledged giants of the scene, gold chip future investments. Along with Michael Andrews, the respected but still undervalued master of group portraiture. The best recorder of the Colony Room. And of cult faces pressed to service for painterly conclaves based on Norman Mailer's reforgotten 1955 novel, *The Deer Park*.

'The bars, cocktail lounges, and night clubs were made to look like a jungle, an underwater grotto, or the lounge of a modern movie theater,' Mailer wrote. 'Drinking in that atmosphere, I never knew whether it was night or day, and I think that kind of uncertainty got into everybody's conversation.'

And then there was Timothy Behrens, dishevelled, strung out, isolated in evident inadequacy at the end of the table. He is hunched over an empty glass and contemptuously ignored by Freud. Whose disciple is he? Leonardo places Bartholomew, one of the first flayed martyrs, in this position. The portrait Andrews painted of Behrens, the year before the Wheeler's gathering, is about surprise. Questionable identity. Confusion. Caged by a series of vertical lines, and dressed in subdued autumnal colours, the ginger Behrens, dead faced and pre-traumatic, hobbles towards us like a reluctant revenant. His large hands, forks or claws, are unoccupied appendages. Auerbach remarked on how useless this young man had been when working alongside him as a temporary postman on Paddington Station. Behrens did nothing but strike attitudes and pose on mailbags. Not a bad preparation for the role Freud would give him as a contingent model.

Interviewed, years later, for Darren Coffield's *Tales from the Colony Room*, Behrens said: 'The School of London never existed . . . We were just a group of guys who got together in Wheeler's or the Colony Room to drink . . . Lucian wasn't good and he knew himself he was a pedantic painter. I detested the way he painted . . . I always preferred Bacon, and especially Michael Andrews.'

At that terrible foodless feast, tables pushed together, Deakin balancing on the bar to get the best angle, the cowed Behrens contemplates a pepper grinder. He wants the status of eager attendee, but the others are jealous of awarding it. When he was involved with some sporadic teaching assignments at the Slade – beautifully suited in grey, white shirt unbuttoned, flicking a lighter to better examine pubic hair and get it right – Freud took up with this young man. Behrens was serious money, his father was oil. The awkward student was an old Etonian on the bum, caravanning through the usual boho properties, houses gifted by John Minton and then sold on. And it is Behrens, outlier, supplicant, who makes the Wheeler's parody bite. He confirms the atmosphere of yawning boredom. He hosts the suspicion of his peers, the established artists, the final starburst of a great tradition.

When this gruesome business is done and they are about to disperse, rushing off to their various fates, Behrens is the one who tries to keep the party going. Who asks if that virgin bottle of Moët in its ice bucket, a prop, can be broached. Bacon agrees, without enthusiasm: he will be paying.

The alpha painters, Freud and Bacon, have accumulated such history, so many scrapes, conversations, pre-sexual and post-coital postures: competitive spasms of portrait making, with role reversal. Nights that happen before fame, and the wealth that fame brings, can heat and crack the varnish of strategic friendship. We steal energy from those who are closest to us. And blame them for it.

Freud held on to *Two Figures*, the 1953 Bacon painting of two men wrestling on a wrecked bed in a black cell, the one he called 'The Buggers'. Lucian was always reluctant to let it out for exhibitions. In later years, he built up a discerning collection of Auerbachs. Without question, as the curators confirm, these paintings were among the best of their time. Despite emerging from the required level of monastic concentration delivered by Freud, they were far enough away, in subject and technique, to avoid direct competition. And they could, eventually, be set against death duties on the Freud estate. Lucian gambled, shrewdly, that Auerbach was the one who would last. He was dismissive of the reflex gestures, the burnt orange, the space-filling of Bacon's last years.

But here they all are, at the behest of this person, this painter's dummy, failed painter, nuisance, pander on genius: John Deakin. Deakin is the director of the scene, issuing terse instructions from the top of the bar. The shot is taken. And taken again. And again. It's a concept and not a realisation. It's the prompt for another potential group painting, should Michael Andrews feel a twitch of interest. He doesn't. The Deakin print is a potential rival to the measured philosophical séance by Helen Lessore, *Symposium I* (1974–77): a garden room with a slightly different cast. Bacon, Freud, Andrews and Auerbach are present. Joined by Kossoff, Craigie Aitchison and Euan Uglow. Unlike the cryogenic Deakin wake at Wheeler's, these artists are talking and drinking. They could almost be enjoying themselves.

No joy for Deakin. His laboriously contrived group portrait was spiked by Wyndham, in favour of a single headshot of Freud. Everything was wrong with this faked occasion, but the photographs worked. Success was not achieved in the teeth of the obvious unease between the assembled characters, but because of it. The lighting is mean. Furniture, napkins and cutlery have been borrowed from a touring production. The most popular shot for future biographers is the one where Bacon holds an empty glass to his chin and whispers a bitchy quip at Freud. Michael Andrews, scratching his head, feints to share a laugh with Auerbach. There are too many ugly plates on the wall. Too many ceramic fish and miniature brandy barrels. The composition is a mess. It's not a standard Bacon lunch. It's not a private view. Flaws are the only truth.

The favoured Deakin trophy from Wheeler's is a mounted print, signed by the photographer and all the artists. The group have been squeezed, shoulder to shoulder, behind two small tables, with Bacon as the dominant figure. It looks as if he isn't sure how long he'll stay. He hasn't taken off his mac. Freud is placed at his right hand: John or Judas? Auerbach is solid and driven: Peter the rock. There are plenty of other unexhibited shots in the Deakin albums. With good reason.

The tone throughout is subdued, a drowned Soho. Some of the prints have been flipped, so that Behrens now appears on the right. And the ceramic turbot, plaice or brill, is swimming against the tide. Clinical depression deepens like a continental shelf. Like mid-morning radio on the ward. Then, suddenly, Deakin clears his head and focus sharpens. Conversation, or even the pretence of it, dries up entirely. Andrews laughs like a patient told the worst. Auerbach is a gamekeeper invited into the kitchen. He really is Georges Géret, stubbled and corduroyed, in Buñuel's *The Diary of a Chambermaid*. Freud frowns. And seethes. He kettles spite.

Cigarettes come and go, a nightmare for continuity. Twenty-four prints. There is no decisive moment. A flipbook of indecision. Photographer crushed by weight of opposition. Focus slips again. At one point, bread appears, a small French loaf, looking as if it has been cast in plaster of Paris. Freud reaches out. Before something very interesting in the meniscus of a fingernail takes his attention. Auerbach cups a hand to fire Bacon's cigarette. You can hear them pushing the tables back.

Decades later, this momentous non-event is rescued, when somebody smart at the official Deakin Archive decides to compile 'an animated sequence of the best negatives'. The conceit is a success. It does indeed 'bring the occasion back to life . . . exposing mini-narratives and new insights'. The original contact sheet has been treated like a set of consecutive frames from a newsreel that was never made, but which has been transported, intact, into the present moment. The painters interact. They joke, sulk, snarl: *they live.*

One minute and fifty seconds of magic as the proof of an unwritten Deakin thesis. The black albums have become a novel of incident, of persons and places. Deakin, keeping his balance on the bar, faces the camera with the grin of a solemn, all-knowing clown. The botched negatives from the Wheeler's lunch achieve their deserved resolution: as cinema.

The living dead are back among us. Auerbach, the only certified survivor at the moment of writing, anchors the tableau with his scepticism, his justified retreat from such demeaning promotion. The animation reveals certain involuntary movements of shoulders and wrists. The tilting of heads. Wisps of cigarette smoke. Here is a small miracle of resurrection.

Michael Andrews giggles and flaps. The camera zooms in on the actors with a series of jumps and shudders, like paddles being applied to a stopped heart. Auerbach and Andrews are pilots in a Biggin Hill hut, keeping up their spirits, waiting for the siren. Behrens has been catting on the tiles, he has a chipped tooth. Bacon sways, infallibly, at the centre of everything. And Freud produces – you only catch this in the animation – his trademark glare of foxy astonishment. At the effrontery. No still image, no print by Deakin, traps that defining *tic douloureux*, the phantom trigeminal neuralgia. The habit was as much part of Freud's social persona as Labour lion Gordon Brown's slightly hesitating creak of jaw, his rictal snarl in television interviews. The fishless feast is a revelation.

Nothing recovers the spark and spirit of these Soho painters in quite this way, until you encounter the 'lost' films of a young Italian-Jewish artist and author, Lorenza Mazzetti. During an adventurous exile in London, Lorenza filmed, on scavenged art-school cameras, two unapproved Kafka adaptations and one miraculous progress through bomb-damaged Thames reaches, drifting from shared lodgings through warehouses, working docks and partying pubs. Together, produced as part of the Free Cinema movement, featured Michael Andrews and Eduardo Paolozzi. When he dances with his umbrella across Whitechapel roofs in

Mazzetti's *K*, Andrews is so young, and so much present, that it hurts. No flickering resurrection of Deakin stills from Wheeler's can achieve the time-travelling magic of the Italian woman's documentation.

As an old lady, fizzing with performative vim, when interviewed in Rome, Mazzetti conjures Michael Andrews as a lover of effortless charm. And imperishable innocence. She also recalls, with a slight shudder, the unblinking ice-chip glare of the blue-eyed Freud. In a few words of strategically improved English those personalities and eternal moments are ours. We are invited to share something of Mazzetti's amusement, her pride.

In the same fashion, through the never intended animation of Deakin's sequence at the lunch table, we are granted access to an occasion the glossy magazine spiked ... When the Gagosian staged an exhibition called *Friends and Relations: Lucian Freud, Francis Bacon, Frank Auerbach, Michael Andrews* in November 2022, the entry to the show was dominated by a huge blow-up of Deakin's photograph of the Wheeler's lunch. You would need sharp eyes to find his credit. Although, in supporting promotional notes, it is said that the show 'takes its inspiration' from the famous image. We can imagine how the painters would howl, so many years after that dire session, when they discovered that Deakin's impertinent snapshot was being branded as the instigator of a major exhibition: manipulated reproduction, yet again, taking precedence over reality. Alongside a collection of highlights from the named artists, a substantial group of photographs was also featured. Sharp, nicely managed reportage by Bruce Bernard. Classic photojournalism. Studio visits. Benevolent exchanges. Bernard is praised for his particular gift in bringing photographs together with paintings.

The Folk Upstairs

Another room. Playroom for the big boys. Rogues and gentlemen by invitation only. Officers' mess with covert title: the Thursday Club. While the rackety court of Francis Bacon, with Deakin as sanctioned photographer, picked at their catch of the day and slurped Chablis at street level in Wheeler's, established upper-crust bohemians – naval queens, celebrity crims, housetrained comics, obliging osteopaths and custodians of English acres – met in a private dining room on the second floor, once a week. Lunches with indifferent food and a shuttle of acceptable wines, chased with brandy, port, cigars. Gold-braid sailors on shore leave. With off-colour chappish jokes. Before going on for an early evening of extracurricular indulgence at David Mountbatten's flat in Grosvenor Square. Mountbatten, 3rd Marquess of Milford Haven, introduced his cousin, Prince Philip, to the set. The photographer in residence upstairs was Sterling Henry Nahum, who traded as Baron. Baron had royal connections – he did Philip's wedding to Princess Elizabeth in 1947 – but was knocked back for the Coronation gig. The Queen Mother favoured that arch flatterer, Cecil Beaton: Deakin's nemesis. Cecil was another Thomas Lawrence, a Gainsborough. An artist with drapes and fabrics and statuary.

The Krays, as ever, were social accessories, putting in appearances upstairs and downstairs, shouldering into the shot. Another one for Vi and the post-trial memoirs. But Deakin was canny enough to keep his distance. There were elements he needed for his great graphic novel of Soho. Vice and virtue. The black diaries of the period, evidence for the prosecution, included one notable capture: Dr Stephen Ward.

What was most troubling now was not the inability to command his limbs, he was used to that. He had carried a folded suicide permit for years, calling it 'the Saviour in my pocket'. And it was not the way that his redundant physical being lifted off in layers, flat as a series of prints, skin by skin; lifted off and floated clear to heaven. What pained the dead man on the Brighton bed were those lurid representations of karma and revenge. In the terrible dreams of the bardo, versions of his own past melded with films and poems and stories told when his defences were down, pillow talk. Vivid hallucinations from a bleak desert landscape. He saw a small withered and humped version of the childhood of John Deakin, in fancy dress, black velvet and knee britches, trapped in a net. On the way to punishment. Swung over a bubbling cauldron. Judged without trial. He saw the abuse of abusers. He saw torture and its instruments. He had been, so he thought, in his own fashion, a kind man. Charitable in his scorn. Friend to the friendless. He saw hell. The men around the table, their chests heaving with medals, laid out his pictures.

I read somewhere, or perhaps dreamed it, that Ward's trademark dark glasses, as modelled by an enervated Marcello Mastroianni sleepwalking through Italian decadence, or adopted against the vulgarity of daylight by 'three-in-a-bed' politicians like Lord Lambton, turned up in a jar of crushed bones and ashes. The heavy black shades were all that remained of the medical masseur after a poorly attended cremation ceremony at Mortlake, once the stamping ground of another doctor of dubious reputation, the Elizabethan magus John Dee. Indestructible plastic crinkled in the fire, lenses shattered into a spider's web. Ward's sorry spectacles manifested like a potent symbol for an impossibly tangled episode in an era when political incompetence was exposed, thanks to a warped set of values, through a social pantomime of lacklustre sexual dalliance. The anger of tabloid editors was finally aroused by the revelation that young Christine Keeler, trailer trash from upstream (as she was presented in awful scapegoating shorthand), had a number of intimate relationships with Black men in Notting Hill. And that Ward, a person of no particular family, acted as the slippery conduit to high society. He took on his dark glasses, prematurely, as a shield against the coming blizzard of popping bulbs when the paparazzi pack was sent out baying for his blood.

Figures on the private stairs in good suits bear traces of having left their dress uniforms at home. A stew of conspiracy punctuated by the stamping of handmade shoes, cobbled from individual lasts. The laughter of wolves circling for a kill. Security on the door.

Downstairs, behind mullioned windows but still connected to the traffic of the street, painters slump and yawn. The Thursday Club is all rumour. The fish restaurant is an open secret and Francis will, as ever, once he's copped for a decent sale, be clearing the slate.

Upstairs, Beaton is welcome at the private table. Baron is one of the founding fathers. The Club was established to cope with the inevitable tedium – rationing coupons, for some – that follows a good war. There will be no freelance photo opportunities. No record beyond what is commissioned for bribery and coercion. Men with bulges under their tight jackets are lurking in plain sight. Royalty has been piped aboard.

Miles Kington, a person of family, slumming as a journalist, came away with sanctioned gossip. Who was at table? Lord Louis Mountbatten. Prince Philip. John Betjeman. The Kray Twins. Arthur Koestler. And a quorum of reliable showbiz faces with polished anecdotes: Larry Adler,

Peter Ustinov, David Niven, James Robertson Justice. Kim Philby. And Dr Stephen Ward. What you have, on the second floor of Wheeler's, beyond future dramas for Netflix, is the ultimate rootball of conspiracy theories. Most are true, all are fiction. You have reputed spies, agents and double agents, royalty (legit and criminal). And superior sailors: Admiralty Arch or yachting with Uffa Fox at Cowes. And a brace of tame newspaper editors charged with suppressing news. Ward, the 'society osteopath', is a tolerated sketcher of portraits. A gifted amateur open to trade. His diligent sketches are designed to sit on pianos. To hide a damp spot. To disappear. There are drawings of Philip. Intimations of potential blackmail. Everything is scripted, nothing confirmed: Ward, as a Soviet asset, is rumoured to be employing Keeler to use pre-arranged sexual assignations to milk the information that everybody already knows from war minister John Profumo. Information that will be passed on, in bed or out, to Yevgeni Mikhailovitch Ivanov.

The carousel spins. Spooks are unbuttoned at the private lunch table. Is the restaurant bugged? Scandal behind closed doors in Mayfair. Sir Anthony Blunt is brought in from the cold to acquire sensitive artworks. Ward will be played, when they come to sift this tacky heritage, by John Hurt. Francis Bacon will be impersonated by Derek Jacobi for John Maybury's *Love Is the Devil*. The resurrected James Bond, Daniel Craig, will have a sweaty shot at poor George Dyer. Deakin, caught in the vortex of these events, happening overhead without bringing down the plaster, is impersonated by the Welsh actor Karl Johnson. The man who played Wittgenstein for Derek Jarman. Dylan Thomas, inevitably, was in the mix. Johnson had a role in Lyndsey Turner's production of *Under Milk Wood* at the National Theatre.

Six Mortlake mourners sniffing the sour river, floodwater sewage on a rising tide. A solitary wreath of white carnations sent by Kenneth Tynan. With inscribed card: 'To Stephen Ward, Victim of Hypocrisy'. A pair of melted spectacles shaken onto the grass. A lumpy grit of ashes scattered among the roses. Or blown into the air by the sirocco of ceaseless traffic on Upper Richmond Road.

In that final flash of drugged consciousness, before the lights go out, Ward confuses the mechanics of portraiture with the subtle manipulation of stiff male backs. He was always a person of interest to that great oxymoron, British Intelligence. Convicted pimp and suicide. Self-murder, he recalled, was once a crime punishable by death. If you look a little closer into archival records, Ward emerges with a career résumé shamelessly lifted from John le Carré. Ill-deserved punishment at minor public school festers social resentment. Carpet salesman in Houndsditch. Translator for Shell Oil in Hamburg. Questionable American qualification in osteopathy. Undistinguished army service when posted to India. Psychiatric hospital, discharge. And a life of modest reinvention behind fashionable vampire shades. Like Deakin, he watched and waited. While they watched him. He found a court. Like Deakin he made portraits. But they didn't last. Operatives cleaned up the traces. There were no pictures left under the bed.

In the end, it is all television. With manipulated images and internet facts, you can connect anything with anything. Stephen Ward treats the American ambassador W. Averell Harriman. Harriman, a banker with railway interests, was formerly Ambassador to the Soviet Union. He was sanctioned, in wartime, for looking after the Wall Street interests of Fritz Thyssen, a significant industrial and financial backer of the National Socialists, the Nazi gang. Ward treats Duncan Sandys, Churchill's son-in-law. Sandys is the cabinet minister tabloids nominate as the 'headless man' being orally pleasured in the notorious Polaroid from the Duchess of Argyll's divorce case. Harriman owns the Polaroid Corporation.

Personally recommended, word of mouth, and moving up fast, the osteopath is security vetted. He is declared a suitable person to treat Churchill in his creaking senility. With shades of that web of coincidences knitted around Lee Harvey Oswald, Ward applies for a visa to visit the Soviet Union. He wants to make portraits of granite-faced political bosses for *The Illustrated London News*. Reputation secure, the society bone-tweaker is exploited, by way of Ivanov, as a backchannel for the Foreign Office. But when he becomes too visible in the wrong company, Ward is sacrificed. Conspiracy theorists have him taken out by a named

MI6 operative. A man who persuades him, now sloppy with drink, to down the necessary quantity of barbiturates. Such theatrics were hardly necessary. Ward was already a broken man. He understood all too well the price he would have to pay for consorting with the great and good.

The sixth of the Deakin albums from Arnold Circus is a rich chapter, made from apparently disconnected mugshots. They slide inexorably towards the spectre of Dr Stephen Ward: a drained husk in black funeral suit and dark glasses. A willing victim trapped in a bare room, a studio or a Secret State cell. There is a spray of portrait drawings scattered across a table. An autopsy on vanished fame about which he will be interrogated. A person of undefined sex or status is skulking at the door. A woman's bulging handbag, visible on the floor, hints at some unseen presence. The one who must not be shown.

These photographs, in the Deakin album, are the only record of the occasion when the photographer from the downstairs oyster bar was permitted a brief audience with the figure from the second floor chosen to take the fall for the indulgences of his time and place.

Landowners are running for cover, back to their secure estates. To Tuscany. To tax havens. An insignificant commission acquires traction as two men, players in overlapping Soho scenes, meet on the cusp of eternity.

Shuffle and cut this Arnold Circus album and you appreciate the experiments of William Burroughs, J. G. Ballard and B. S. Johnson. Use Deakin as raw material for a storyboard. First shot: low-angle interior. Male in corduroy bomber jacket. Moulded ceiling. A bar. Reluctant hitman brought back from retirement? Saturnine. Brooding. He grips a rolled newspaper like a truncheon. It's Frank Auerbach. Who is reputed to spend every living breathing hour of his existence in his Mornington Crescent studio. Deakin is on his best behaviour here, every frame is in focus. Flick the page.

A barman with folded arms. Another man, lateral scar across

unshaven chin, balances a huge, wrapped block of ice on his shoulder. Nobody laughs. The subjects challenge the intruder.

Soho. Opening time. The hour before punters, before painters are on the prowl. Before monkish boozers scuttle to the call of Sext, their favoured canonical hour, at the Coach and Horses. We are still in Deakin's bardo dreamtime, but feelers are already reaching out across the decades to John Maybury and *Love Is the Devil*. To improved versions of themselves.

Another venue, an unidentified woman. Imagine Deakin's terse instructions about the required pose, the position of the head. Who passed on those instructions? One of the painters? One of the spooks? In a better book all these characters would be given properly researched and approved biographies. They would acquire story arcs with beginnings and conclusions. But I don't have the time. These are years of approaching catastrophe. You can smell it in the streets. Feel it in the parks. The dogs are circling and snarling. The people are mesmerised by their screens. I could lose myself for years, decades, in thickets of insecure facts and seductive misappropriations.

Deakin's faces. His portfolio. I have other and pressing assignments. It's evening, night in London. The lights are coming on. This woman is dressed to go out, a PVC raincoat, her right hand raised in a coincidentally Maoist salute of departure. A last cigarette. Eyes closed, a conceded smile. As instructed. As recorded. As forgotten. Every shot in Deakin's album is arranged in expectation of something else, something off-screen: a mistaken fuck, an assault, a quarrel that changed history. The black album is a London love story, a spy story. A romance, dictated over the phone, changing direction with every new paragraph. Do the facts stand up? You're not composing a biography. You are writing a novel where anything goes. No more postcards. The backers are backing off. Uncut paranoia is better than Viagra.

With the introduction of a suspect pair, both of them clammy with crime and awaiting retribution, Deakin's story takes a darker turn. Expressionist lighting: hot lamps flaring behind frosted glass. The chopping blades of an overhead fan. An involuntary discharge of soft white wax around the neck of a fat-bellied Italian wine bottle. *Mr Norris Changes Trains.* A Soho waiting room: clap clinic or benefits office? Massage parlour or clip joint? Gerald Hamilton, 'conman and masochist', is discovered, in awkward two-shot, with his incorruptible interrogator, Dan Farson. Debriefing as a form of popular television. Shot from a safe distance by Deakin.

Hamilton eked out a career, in a show of perceived wickedness, with the amiability of Sydney Greenstreet, hat in hands, as he delivers sibilant threats with Edwardian courtesy. A man of uncertain heritage, by way of the Balkans or Beirut, and a nip of Sligo. Christopher Isherwood flattered the Hamilton myth, placing him at the heart of a literary fiction, and providing his portly model with enough cover to launch memoirs of his own, each one contradicting the last. Hamilton liked to pretend that he had known Roger Casement, the Anglo-Irish diplomat, compiler of government reports and black diaries; the one hanged as a traitor in Pentonville. After yet another of his scrapes, Hamilton said that he'd taken the boat to Ireland disguised as a Mother Superior. He shared a flat for a time with Aleister Crowley, from whom he inherited the shopsoiled title of 'the wickedest man in Europe'.

Hamilton and Farson are not in a film studio. And even with a supporting cast of border jumpers, creeps and informers, this is not *Casablanca*. It is the heart of the island that is Soho: the Caves de France. Hamilton, long nosed, bald as marble, pouts. He is Mr Norris. He channels Robert Morley (another portrait in the Deakin file). This man has the size and shiftiness, but not the bumbling charm, of Peter Ustinov in *Topkapi*, that screen adaptation of Eric Ambler's *The Light of Day*. Ustinov was upstairs, a member of the Thursday Club in good standing. Deakin collected him, illegitimately, for the sixth volume.

The theft was well ahead of its time, before screen grabs and the digital age when every tedious frame ever shot would be subject to cannibalisation and recomposition. Deakin snapped away, in the West End dark, in cinemas close to his studio. Close to his favoured drinking holes. He made portraits of portraits. He raided television interviews and feature films. And let it be thought that he'd been closeted with Brando, with Arthur Miller and a compliant Tennessee Williams. He stole Groucho Marx in Puritan's hat. Harpo with mouth agape. There are even photographs in which he gives the game away by including subtitles: 'I was just thinking . . . I'm afraid it isn't possible just now.' Deakin believed that he'd waited around in Claridge's. He believed that he'd doorstepped Hollywood in the Savoy.

On a wavering TV screen in a betting shop, Ustinov is mid-anecdote. Fingers interlocked, fat watch on the wrist, he is beginning to enjoy his own performance. He looks like the Russian spy George Blake delivering a propaganda recital for the benefit of state media, after escaping from the Scrubs. Medal and promotion assured.

Deakin's prints expose the crimes of others, while concealing his own. His gift came at a cost. Recording everything, he was obliged to eat the sins he depicted. His true confession was never heard.

The Caves de France was an ideal rendezvous for the joust between Farson and Hamilton. Everything would be admitted, nothing believed. None of it mattered. Aleister Crowley, taking a break from satanic rituals on Chancery Lane, reported back to Special Branch on the activities of Hamilton, his flatmate: the suspect Comintern agent. Hamilton reported to anyone with spare cash. He masqueraded as a foreign correspondent for *The Times* and a close associate of Willi Münzenberg, Moscow's man in Berlin. It was Deakin who suggested the Caves de France. He did the casting, he found the location. He was disciplined. He had stopped drinking between pubs.

Pendulous lower lip quivering like a starving man licking a menu, large hands masking the crook of his walking stick, ready to talk for hours and not deliver one word of truth, Hamilton deflects the gaze of his befuddled interrogator. Half-cut and slobbering, he is an unfrocked bishop. He stares at (and through) his tormentor. Hot light bounces from a polished tortoise skull. With shots to spare on his last roll of film, Deakin messes about with superimposition: Hamilton doubled, Hamilton sitting on his own face. There are too many masks to be caught in a single print. The photographer tries another run at Farson, but Hamilton is primed to leave. He wants to cash the promised cheque right away, before the banks close. And the police arrive.

Everything leads back to the confrontation between Deakin and Stephen Ward. The man from the Thursday Club is safe behind dark glasses. The long finger of ash on the stub of his cigarette is about to detach. The osteopath is stroking loose sheets of portraiture laid out on the table. If he had been hired to impersonate a society pimp, this is how he might dress, how he might behave.

The cigarette grows its ash again. The doomed society portraitist signs a sketch. The black ladder against the wall looks like a resting bier. Somebody official, and keen to keep his face out of shot, flits across an open door. A suspect cab is heavy-breathing outside. On the clock. See you in Mortlake, John. Good luck. Goodbye.

Job done, Deakin scuttles to the Colony Room. Muriel Belcher is etched in her dislike of the crumpled man on the stair. 'You're barred, cunty.' And this time, there is no reprieve. Not for the photographs of Stephen Ward. Or the guilty photographer.

Man on the Bed

'I think there is death after death,' said the painter, favouring one of his scribes, a breakfast companion who knew how to obey the rules. Shafts of Germanic profundity among the English teacups and the wounding gossip. Acolytes orbit the enchanter. A warmed pot of Earl Grey on Kensington Church Street. Scrambled egg moist on crisp toast. A razored sliver of nougat to take home, wrapped in a starched napkin. And a reliable man, unafraid of exposing his love, his naked self, to carry the newspapers. The Bentley, restored after this week's shunt, is lodged in its secure bay. That skewering hawkish glare. More penetrating than his bearded grandfather.

Recycled myths of the bohemian city choke us. Images gain consequence in reproduction. They acquire significance like an implanted patina of scars and bruises on the mortal map of a pressed sitter. Old leaking bodies, bones poking through flesh, are striated by experience. Tables turned, artist as model: Lucian Freud is photographed by Deakin in an unequal exchange. According to the catalogue, there were eighteen portraits of Freud undertaken by Bacon and two of Bacon released and admitted by his great friend and rival. One of these was stolen in Berlin and lost to rumour. Making Freud the winner of an undeclared competition, that particular vision of Bacon can never be challenged. For a person so suspicious of photographers as a class – he allowed some merit to Deakin and Cartier-Bresson – Lucian offered himself, many times, to exposure by amateurs and chosen professionals. He was caught in restaurants, at society balls, in the studio. Like Picasso, he developed the 'look' as an affront; a challenge, a reflex performance. That twitch again.

And here he is now, as a contender, a young meteor, in the first of Deakin's black albums. Freud has agreed to face the camera as necessary penance, in avoidance of awkward face-to-face confrontation, for a group of Bacon paintings. The sequence on the brass bed parallels the Deakin session with Henrietta Moraes. To complicate this perverse threesome, with its repeatedly exchanged roles, Freud also painted Moraes when she was still Wendy Abbott. She lived with him for a time in Delamere Terrace, Paddington.

'I was in Lucian's power, like a mesmerised rabbit,' she said. 'But being in a trance doesn't stop pain and after I discovered somebody else's menstrual fluid in what I thought of as my bed I decided that I could take no more.'

It feels right that the graphic novel emerging from Deakin's seventeen albums opens with Freud's piercing stare of avoidance. He bristles: arms folded, cuffs unbuttoned, sleeveless sweater. The hair is meticulously disarranged. The slender body quivers on an item of rescued furniture with a leatherette finish. The wall behind the spongy and buttoned sofa is a migraine of gestural paint marks. From the beginning, Freud sets the terms for everything that follows in the confession extracted from Deakin's abandoned negatives. The albums laid out by anonymous editors treat the photographer's work with respect. They choose to begin with the person who is most suspicious of the pitch. And of the blindfolded dance that follows, the interactions between portraitists and models, hustlers and patrons. The flux of sexuality and power. Of bitchy lunches, drunken afternoons and taxis to Limehouse.

There are twelve prints. Freud is experimenting with ways of delivering himself, before he climbs on the bed. He does his copyright I-can't-believe-this-is-happening stare of dismissal. He does eyes-down contemplation. He does hands-in-pockets, back to mirror, barely confessing the easel at the edge of frame. There are stuffed monkeys on a mantelpiece. There is a wide shot revealing the length of the puckered whorehouse sofa. It is no longer leatherette, it is velour and bumpy. There are a number of reversed canvases stashed against the wall. And a spindly period chair on which Freud performs his party trick, standing on his head.

Then there is the undeniable fact of the brass bed. Which is fated to become an artwork, first by Bacon and later by Jasper Johns. In some way, with the passage of time, Deakin's photographs have taken on more historic drag than the paintings: a portrait sequence by an acknowledged master. With Bacon, you have a secondary energy, the stretch into another dimension. And, almost in opposition, you have the raw immediacy of Deakin's audience with Freud, convened at Bacon's instruction, on this particular bed. Freud, as model, is accepting and resenting. Delivering his own yoga of graceful embarrassment. He is not required to remove his clothes. But there are elements of an unconsummated seduction.

The first Deakin bed shot is pristine. Nothing has intervened, so it is not art: it is staged accident. No need to pop a vein, *click click*, we are just starting. Here is a bed that, by implication, has seen plenty of action. But it is a long way from the sentiment of salvaged autobiography, from Tracey Emin and the institutional collectors. It's closer to Mary Poppins or Habitat. You wouldn't be surprised if this bed levitated towards Julie Andrews.

It is a bright new day: Freud is in his alternative outfit, the cook's striped trousers that some high-toned London restaurants are obliged to wave through. The privileges of cash and celebrity. A white shirt with rolled sleeves, ready for anything. Lucian is perched on the edge, fists knotted. By the time the original prints have been doctored for a Christie's catalogue and primped for gallery exposure, they have lived for years in the chaos of Bacon's studio. They are smeared, crumpled, torn. *But they have been activated.* You notice newspapers on the floor beside the brass bed. The studio where Deakin operates, once fit for a lifestyle feature in the supplements, has become a squat, a Chatterton garret. The catalogue print belongs to Bacon. It solicits the always alert engagement of Jasper Johns. A man with a line in masterpiece erasure. He rubbed out a drawing by Willem de Kooning, making the loud absence his own. Who better to find the hidden skull in the fold of an auction house reproduction of the gelatin silver print – with paper clips – of the man on the bed? Lucian Freud is scratching his scalp. He wants us to know that he is in pain. In a ratty bolthole with old newspapers.

Consider the quilt. By the time you reach the danced Bacon print, sifted through so many technologies of reproduction, the quilt is barely visible. Diamond patterns look like blood stains running from Freud's wrists. In the Deakin original, that quilt is craftwork, collectible. Such a quilt should be a palimpsest of family memories; generations of worn-out coverings, rags, shirts, stitched together, around the guidelines of the diamond pattern, by a circle of initiated women of all generations. This is a magic carpet. Mother of stories. Birth rug. Corpse blanket. Dream quilt woven from fables.

Freud reverts to a man-spread sprawl, legs wide apart and cook's trousers smeared with grease or worse. He employs sharp elbows to keep his physical integrity at one remove from the prophylaxis of the borrowed quilt. Newspapers, signalling a terrible boredom between shots, are slipping from the bed.

The key Deakin capture, and the one that engaged Jasper Johns, has Freud acting, striking a Rodin pose, hiding his face. You can make out the headline in the floored newspaper: SPARE FILLY . . . The rest is lost. The racing papers have not been kind. Freud is miming *despair*. There is an unopened envelope on the floor, perhaps a bill.

And so the session continues, as both men weary. As usual, Deakin lets focus drift: that's probably how the world looks to him by mid-afternoon, the dead hours. In the print where Freud is inspecting something – postcard, final demand, or horoscope – the photographer has developed terminal shakes and the painter is halfway towards his reappearance as pastiche Bacon. Wet pink and grey pigment: flesh wounds of velocity.

Abruptly, on the turn of a page, it's over. And Freud is back out on the street: eyes closed, eyes down. White shirt, lightweight suit. Deakin's prints are flecked and dashed with an anxiety of black paint splodges. The improving damage lifts documentation to another level. To narrative. To a record of man and place and occasion. Never to be re-lived, but frequently reproduced.

Somebody somewhere has commissioned all this. To be sure that it is never made public. To be certain that the key images are safely buried among inconsequential and justly forgotten faces. Deakin knows just how to do it. But he doesn't know why. He is the loneliest man in London. He follows the crowd, hiding his gifts, his intelligence.

Bacon opens the large brown envelope. He fans out the Deakin prints. They serve a purpose. He can clamp hard on Freud. Who is fated to become one of the repeat presences in the painter's claustrophobic chamber theatre. Some of Bacon's victims were lovers, paid tormentors. Bullies from upstream hotels in chalkstripe suits. Post-traumatic sadists. Gentle villains with broken knuckles. Some were drinking pals, sparring partners at the bar. There are lying figures and reclining figures and figures splayed on a dais or slumped boneless in purple silk on a papal throne. The triptych, *Study for Portrait of Lucian Freud* (1964), would seem to emerge directly from the sequence taken by Deakin. The three gold-framed panels were soon disassembled by the Marlborough Gallery, separated into individual items for swifter and more rewarding sale.

Shoes like melting hooves. Like skin and leather married on a flaming pavement. Bacon admires Freud's highly polished black numbers with their red-brown soles. He tears open his model's white shirt. He inserts a naked light bulb, a regular motif, from his own studio. He sets the clock to midnight. He floods the wintery monochrome of Deakin's sofa with a sickly limegreen wash. He makes a Monet swamp of the floor, a stagnant pond with torn underwear in place of water lilies. The defensive gesture of the man on the bed is emphasised. A hand is raised to touch the wounded head, to cup a missing ear. To draw us deeper into a sound-proof cell.

There are associated sketches, further assaults on chairs, with Freud's piercing spite manifested in the grimaces of martial art. He is an acrobat, a grounded equestrian. But still he is trapped in the unbearable tedium of sitting for this portrait. He crosses and uncrosses his legs. He squeezes a wrist, checking his racing pulse.

In time, all Bacon's sitters, male and female, bleed into one another. They ferment. Freud holds a pose that Bacon will later attempt in a self-portrait. As a mere model, Lucian must give up his clothes, his belt, his precious shoes. In a painting from 1967, George Dyer, Bacon's lover, is 'coupled' with Freud. There is a pink ashtray and an ornamental cat. Two men, on a curved bench, waiting for their euthanasia certificates. Clients and strangers in a house of pleasure. Between hell and the Colony Room. The third party from this tragic play, unseen and uncredited, is the man with the camera. Deakin, as directed, directs the production. He wears blame as a battle honour.

On the ornamental quilt, Freud twists against the burden of the great name imposed on him at birth. The dying grandfather with a cigar addict's cancerous jaw attracting flies. The sweetness of decay in a darkened Hampstead consulting room, heavy with figurines of old gods. The painter is in a double bind, choked by what must be killed so that he can live and breathe, and what must be accepted: contingent funds arriving from the shared royalties on his grandfather's publications.

Any form of self-analysis – for which photography is a useful tool – is anathema to Lucian. He is his own inquisitor and supreme fiction. The necessary engagement with such creatures as Deakin must be justified, at minimal cost, by the production of a magnificent portrait. If Bacon paints Dyer, then Freud will borrow the model and better him. Revenge before crime. Retaliation anticipating insult. A whoring of talent in the game of fate. The stakes could not be higher. Lucian, the middle son, remembers. He boasts: 'I am the thief who stole my grandfather's gold coins from my father's desk.'

The Deakin session in 1964, recording Freud's argument with the brass bed, is a pivotal moment in establishing the status of photography for the School of London painters. Prints are handed over to Bacon. He treats them with no particular respect. He folds, splashes, cuts. He pins them to the wall. Or lets them float to the floor as part of a carpet of rip-outs, postcards, pornography and high art reproductions. The works that emerge, paintings of which he is not ashamed, like *Study for Portrait of Lucian Freud* and *Three Studies for a Portrait of Lucian Freud*, are, at least in part, about shifting and dragging the figure from a fixed geometric space into a landscape of domination and personal nightmare. The armature of the face collapses and is re-set as a death mask. Identity is provisional and insecure.

Love turns against the object of obsession. In *Francis Bacon: The Logic of Sensation*, Gilles Deleuze asserts that the painter demonstrates 'a radical hostility to photography'. Not as a rival technology, but as a more limited and constricting truth. The word 'hostility' contains *host*, a role that Bacon liked to play; out on the town or in his studio with its mulch of secondary images. Freud entertained on his own terms. He kept his lovers, children, friends and patrons apart. He was always more of a guest than a host. He charmed landed families, seducing wives and daughters and sketching the livestock. In private, he relished living with certain paintings, with Bacons and Auerbachs; in order to probe them at leisure, to dowse for their secrets. Bacon eviscerated magazines, film stills, medical reports and source books for art, architecture, and anthropology. He spoke of the essential bond between photography and painting as an 'engendering'. The subject of the predatory masculine gaze would become something much richer and harder to explain. It would be disgendered, unsexed: silk stockings, suspenders and a butch leather jacket.

When forced to talk about his family, Lucian said that they were unknown to him: a set of ghostly photographs of relatives who disappeared into the industrial horror of the German death machine. And there was the implication too, in the last period of their intimacy, that Bacon had been driven mad by the trash of images with which he had walled himself into his Reece Mews den. Dirty blankets were nailed across the windows. He locked the door. He wouldn't allow his former friend inside. Freud said that Bacon's workplace had become 'real Eumenides'. The Furies had broken free of the prints in which Deakin had imprisoned them. And there was no strength left with which to perform an exorcism in paint.

Tormented by the demands of daily performance, regular but resented acts of generosity in clubs and drinking holes, Bacon was no longer manipulating the visionary aftershock of delirium tremens, he was reflecting it back into the world. Behind that foul blanket, there really was an unknown man perched on the sill, waiting for access. To neutralise the power of the vision, Bacon painted himself holding a camera. He obliterated the debt to Deakin. He cut him loose.

Almost fifty years after the Deakin photographs were taken of the man on the brass bed, that chilled contemporary artist, Jasper Johns, inspected his catalogue from the London auction house. Deakin's prints had an established value. There were interested parties entrusted with keeping prices at an acceptable level. And clever critics were beginning to see that the assumed hierarchy of master painter to subservient image provider did not hold: this was a very unstable collaboration. The Deakin photographs, in all their iterations, had their own dynamic. They were unappeased.

Johns got that. And took it as the starting point for something new, a ritual through which the established pyramid of painter and model and photographer would be interrogated. Johns was a philosopher, a conceptualist; an eloquent advocate for the mundane. He read Wittgenstein. And said that his own work was best described as 'a constant negation of impulse'. Johns didn't covet an original Deakin print: the reproduction, glorying in flaws of touch and authenticity, was more appealing.

The glamour of this item, offered in the Christie's sale, was that it had been 'rescued' from the floor of Bacon's studio. Which was now itself a reproduction. The mess of dead life, confabulated from rearranged detritus, was safe in its reflective cage. The once shocking Grand Guignol figures, groping and submitting and screaming, contained in this way, were neutralised. They were now fit for export, quotations of themselves. And fit for the casual crowd.

Lovers died. Circumstances changed. Fashion was fallible. It is never easy in New York City. Major artists have to make a fresh start every decade or so. They have to find ways to repeat themselves as a resurrected novelty. Johns was touched by intimations of mortality. The Deakin print from a vanished London could be occulted into a memento mori. Something amazing happened. Placing a photocopy against the published print, Johns created a mirror image. Where the two drawings met, a phantom emerged, as in the portrait of *The Ambassadors* by Hans Holbein the Younger: a prophetic skull. Each succeeding reproduction was more real than the last. Closer to transcendence, further from source.

Initially, Johns was unaware that the man on the bed was Lucian Freud. Working in pencil, pastel, watercolour, charcoal, ink on mylar, Johns extracted more versions of the Deakin print than Bacon ever managed. And there were numerous etchings proofed in all their stages. Bacon had torn the original photograph of Freud clutching his head, in order to source it as *Study for Self-Portrait*. That was the ultimate insult to the integrity of the original documentation. To the man. The brass bed. The witness with the camera. Deakin knew that he was never more, in this context, than a procurer of possibilities. Every element in the process he initiated, the interactions between formality, fame and market value, affected the others. The artworks by Bacon and Johns were invisibly co-signed by Deakin, first as an uncredited source of supply and then as a figure of interest.

When the dust is settled and all the studios are redeveloped or transferred to museums, the surest pathways to an unreachable past will be auction catalogues and wordless black albums freighted with Deakin's cleaned-up, second-generation prints.

But who made them? And why? Who authored this retrospective editing of time? On one of his unaccompanied rambles through Paris, Deakin picked up a pamphlet called The Nerve Meter. *'Everything depends on a certain flocculation of things, on the clustering of all these mental gems around a point which has yet to be found.' Now he had found his task, his justification. The missing point of it all, the misery.*

Broken Doll

A very different commission this time, with no borrowed studio, no neutral space permitting nakedness in the service of art. This was a private house, an occupied bedroom, and a vivid personality. One of the Soho fellowship in good standing. An honorary chap and a woman of character. A Colony Room regular willing to oblige Francis. And prepared to tolerate Deakin. To call him friend. Or friend of a friend – David Archer – from way back, in the what's-yours-is-mine sessions at the Coach and Horses. One of the inner kissing and killing circle. Deakin was established in his questionable pomp: a slightly foxed member of a pickled court. Painted by Freud and Andrews. Procurer of images by appointment to Bacon. And still wounded, nursing bruised ribs, solitary in the mob, going with the flow. Willingly cursed. Blessed with infamy. Carrying the camera like a security-tagged bracelet. See it and know where Deakin is hiding.

Days of privilege. And modest payment. The best of London at the best of times. 9 Apollo Place, hidden down a cul-de-sac behind the King's Arms, just off Cheyne Walk in Chelsea, was a gift from Johnny Minton. A timely inheritance for a woman with a complicated life. You could smell the river. Catch the leaf-dance in that privileged light. The script was good: days drifted, obscurely moneyed, a party for improper people, high and low, without bailiffs and urgent bills. Husbands came and went. One of them, Dom, the handsome Indian poet, stepped out for cigarettes and never came back. Henrietta understood. She had already passed, as she said in her memoir, through all the stages of anger and madness. And hearing the creak of an inhuman tread on the stairs at night. That was before she noticed Dom's doppelgänger cruising on King's Road. A ghost so persistent that its outline hardened into the actual man. Henrietta followed this pale shade to a house in Wellington Square. After a previous disappearance and fugue, Moraes was so fragile that he had to be helped into a taxi, where it was discovered that 'his thick black hair was lousy, hundreds of tiny white eggs showed up clearly'.

Through Dom Moraes, Henrietta encountered Allen Ginsberg and Gregory Corso. She visited the Beat Hotel at rue Gît-le-Cœur in Paris and attended readings in London. Reputations flare and burn out. The characters seem to be proving each other, borrowing and betraying: whatever it takes to spice the legend.

Those are the stories that are always told. And none of them are irrefutable. Deeper fictions are embedded in photographs. Deakin got around. He was everywhere. He constructed stories without words. What do we learn from the sets ordained by Francis Bacon, the physical arrangements specifically requested and paid for in cash? Qualities not to be found, for example, in production stills taken by Jorge Leon for John Maybury's Bacon feature, *Love Is the Devil*. Leon locates his version of reality in the time-travelling artifice of the film. He is delivering portraits of actors who are themselves portraits of personalities, living or dead; personalities who were, in their turn, adept at playing projections of themselves. The difference is in endured experience, in scars proudly worn, in established defence mechanisms. As Borges said: 'It is that other one with the same name to whom things happen.' The world shifts when actors fake it and act the acting. Even when the duplicate shares the tastes of the entity he (or she) is attempting to replicate. Personality is finite. The duplicate lives on: in book, film or photograph. 'I do not know which of us has written this page,' Borges concludes.

Jorge Leon, commissioned to make black-and-white portraits of deceased Soho players, pastiches Deakin. The resulting prints, even with harsh contrast, cannot successfully channel the Londoner's sense of witness. Of being an implicated accomplice in the framing of an unstable and unauthored narrative. Maybury wanted Leon to concentrate on the future Bond, Daniel Craig, in his agonised impersonation of George Dyer. The resulting production stills come closer to the grandiose rhetoric of Bacon's paintings than to undeceived reports by Deakin. With his cynicism, his chip of ice.

Henrietta Moraes is played in the film by Annabel Brooks, who later diversified, very sensibly, into money. She owns and operates Avenue Property: 'Luxury Home Rentals and Escapes'. A better option than continuing in the sort of art cinema that gets approved by the British Film Institute production board. *Love Is the Devil* is a nightmare collision of Bacon-infected imagery – direct quotation was forbidden – and retooled myths promoted by Dan Farson, especially in *The Gilded Gutter Life of Francis Bacon*.

The supporting faces from the Bacon court – Isabel Rawsthorne, Henrietta Moraes – did not make it into Leon's promotional portfolio. The waspish Deakin of Karl Johnson was set aside when the crew moved east, with the tide of fashion, to 3 Mills Studios, near Bow Lock on the River Lea. Maybury's drama was concerned with masculinity: stripped, posturing, preening and doomed. Leon was encouraged to summon from the darkness the magic of Deakin's photographs. But it was far too late. The new man owed his allegiance to a hipper technology: he favoured a Hasselblad 6 x 6 camera over Deakin's trusty Rolleiflex.

In a production note by Nigel Arthur, a curator at the BFI, it was suggested that Deakin's archive was not lost but wilfully destroyed: 'due to the status of photography at this time'.

He destroyed nothing, any more than Bacon did. The trash, the slashed canvases, they fed into the myth. To be disappeared is to be safe. Deakin never gave a bugger for the 'status of photography'. Or Britain. Or time. It's still there if you know where to look. He weighs nothing now but the Brighton mattress is as ripe and heavy as Henrietta. Though not as loud or kind. The feathers want to envelop him. To wear him like a new coat wears a woman. To absorb his heat and his lies.

Within the black albums there are numerous portraits of women, young and mature, standing out from the battery of affronted or affected male gaze. There are Sirens and raven-beaked Furies and ingénues designated as 'unknown'; randomly beautiful faces smoking or playing their part as extras in the film of the city. Production stills for a story that was never to be developed. Deakin squared up to women of character, the ones who barely tolerated his nuisance: Caitlin Thomas (hand on hips), Elizabeth Smart, Isabel Rawsthorne. And Muriel Belcher with her corvine death-stare and that white claw of a hand resting on a dark table. Venom is a value Deakin can appreciate, even when it is coming straight back at him. He does well to hold his nerve and not to melt into a puddle at her polished feet.

Jackie Ellis, a pert Canadian-born actress working in London, could be the Jean Seberg of Godard's *Breathless*. Deakin's wide-eyed gamine reflects a fashionable Nouvelle Vague independence: cropped hair, plain dark sweater. The portrait is an instant of small perfection. Ellis was the second wife of Jeffrey Bernard, a working stagehand when she was appearing at the Old Vic. Another set of images, photographer unknown, fleshes out the context: Bernard, quiffed, tweed coat, collar up, like a crooner from the Larry Parnes stable, and Jackie Ellis. They are pressing close together for a double portrait at the Hampstead Registry Office. Happy days!

And there were so many others, caught in passing: noted and filed. In the album of strategic innocence and redeemable rapture. Lost but never quite forgotten. Unidentified: 'Girl in Soho'. Some welcomed the tribute of the camera. Some scarcely noticed. Some composed themselves in the comfortable darkness of an afternoon bar. Georgina Barker, who had been snapped in the past as a playful child, in Deakin's homage to George, her poet-father, reappeared now as a moody young woman in a Germanic leather coat, trapped in the corner against a painted brick wall.

Rising writers, some of whom never received the credit they were due, were noticed (and collected) by Deakin. Laura Del-Rivo, author of *The Furnished Room*, was also photographed by Ida Kar; alone, brooding on a bed. An image fashioned in such a way as to make her fiction appear autobiographical. In her novel, Del-Rivo depicts a scene in a hangout bohemian café where a hustler tries to sell a camera. 'His manner was generally rude and offensive . . . They accepted his rudeness as a peculiarity of speech, like a foreign accent. He was now examining the camera closely, without speaking.'

The writer gets the last word. Deakin was written into a life he never lived, but he still managed to snare his prey. To make the shot in which Del-Rivo is definitively fixed. As she stares back. As she contemplates her revenge, the way she will recalibrate this brief encounter. A duel of equal antagonists. Del-Rivo catches the ambience in which Deakin operated, as he manoeuvred to compose her portrait. They both trawled for telling details, for atmosphere. 'She posed for a moment in front of the Woodbine mirror, then immediately started to greet people.'

Telling her own version of the Deakin encounter in 1963, Henrietta Moraes is very direct. She positions her fiction of memory somewhere between tabloid journalism and a lowlife novelist of the period. She has a lively prose style and dramatic things happen without dreary moralising. She is as jaunty (and brave) as her pal, that other Soho irregular, old Etonian 'morrie' of Chelsea and the French, Robin Cook. *Bombe Surprise. The Legacy of the Stiff Upper Lip. Private Parts and Public Places.* Cook lived the writing and wrote the life, while managing to avoid becoming trapped in the treacle of anecdotage leaking from Dan Farson, George Melly and other spectres of the Colony Room. Cook flowed like a mercury spill, keeping a yard to two ahead of retribution. He knew when to disappear and when to come back as another man. As Derek Raymond: night-driver and sleep-defying typist. He processed those purple hours with Henrietta Moraes and the others. *How the Dead Live. He Died with His Eyes Open. The Devil's Home on Leave.* 'I have no human passion except on paper.'

Before Notting Hill, long before Hackney, Chelsea had its moment. With his first novel, *The Crust on Its Uppers*, Cook bore witness. 'Well, one way and another, there's Chelsea for you. It won't win a prize . . . *la vie artistique* . . . I think it's a crying shame, myself. Because it's nothing but slag, come to a rub, moody old nymphos . . . morries and aged queans beating each other black and blue.'

It is June 1962. *The Crust on Its Uppers* has been out and about for two months. Smart critics applaud his inventive use of slang, the picaresque doings and undoings of upper-class wasters and genial conmen. The publishing money has gone. Robin stands at his window: 'a limp, lovely green Chelsea evening'. He needs to get out, to circulate, to glean fresh material. In his 1992 autobiography, *The Hidden Files*, he recalls that moment.

'Ah, I know what I'll do. I'll go straight round and see Henrietta Moraes over at Apollo Place.'

Cook makes the call. She's at home.

'Hello darling, how nice to see you.'

Henrietta warns that 'a poisonous-looking person bundled up in a suit' is already in residence. A hack scratching a living by peddling gossip to the Sunday linens. A generic figure smelling something like Deakin and behaving like Dan Farson. Moraes is a useful conduit with a nice house, unspoiled by forgotten Minton parties and remembered suicides. Cook, the bent toff, is fluent in faux Cockney and invented criminal argot. Jonathan Meades reckoned that Eric Partridge called *The Crust on Its Uppers* 'the greatest source of slang in quarter of a century'. Henrietta Moraes and Jeffrey Bernard are in there. With the conmen and party folk. But not Deakin.

They drink, choice of poison unspecified. And it's going well. 'In fact I could feel the fun boiling up in me,' Cook said. When Henrietta decides to push him out, he understands the urgency: another woman is about to arrive. 'You are the epitome of everything Veronica loathes and detests.'

Cook is intrigued. Apollo Place is like that. The new arrival has been taking elocution lessons from Muriel Belcher. 'Who, is, *this*? It looks very much to me as if you were a cunt.'

That was the conversational style. Among those folk. In their gathering places. Their pits and clubs. In this Chelsea house. Cook and Veronica Hull become great friends. He was an admirer of her only novel, *The Monkey Puzzle*, a headlong account of existential disenchantment, from academia to Soho labyrinth to asylum. A book good enough to excite a fellow writer, and then, almost immediately, to fade from sight. No Deakin portrait, no entry in the catalogue.

The photo shoot with Moraes feels like a preordained drift from the bar at the French to the property in Apollo Place. Bacon says that he's contemplating a series of paintings of his friends and he wants to send Deakin round to take snaps from which he can work. Getting naked for a suspect gay man is no problem.

'You are beautiful, darling, and you always will be, you mustn't worry about that,' the painter said.

Deakin duly presents himself in Chelsea.

'We had some drinks and a little later retired to my bedroom.' Moraes confessed to feeling shy about stripping in front of a person incapable of fancying her – and who, like John Ruskin, so she believed, had never seen a female body in its hirsute 'entirety'. A wild enough surmise to explain the awkwardness, the twice-removed distance between the obliging woman on the bed and the masochistic painter waiting in his bolthole studio. With Deakin as unreliable go-between.

The session is heavily documented. It's chamber theatre. Future art. And it is pornography too: when Deakin hawks prints to sailors in Soho pubs. The story is pulp fiction, even as it happens.

The initial engagement is full on, gynaecological; both parties under instruction from Bacon, the remote viewer.

'I had a couple more drinks and gave in,' said Henrietta. But that might have been Deakin, voicing his disinclination to drudge indoors in a supporting role, instead of wandering the streets like one of those Paris snoops. An artist with light.

The procession of Moraes nudes, as arranged in the black albums, seems to advance from autopsy to obstetric examination. From death to life. Eyes clamped, the willing but amateur model lies back, arm across head, legs wide apart. Henrietta can't believe Bacon is plotting a Courbet, *The Origin of the World*. Deakin reassures her and she gives way. 'It's only images, after all.' She chooses two of them to illustrate her own memoir. Along with the dogs, children, Marianne Faithfull, John Michell and hippie caravans.

It takes two sessions to produce what Bacon needs, an arranged sprawl preordaining a sensationalised future: the hypodermic needle in the arm. The painter identifies a potentiality, a chemical need that Moraes had not yet recognised, throbbing in her nerves and cells. Addiction obeyed the improvised image.

Bacon was dismayed. He did not want this 'herculean' and womanly figure rudely splayed out by Deakin. There was far too much of the wrong sort of reality. The painter promoted himself to the company of T. S. Eliot: 'You tossed a blanket from the bed, / You lay upon your back, and waited.' The Deakin prints from the first Moraes session were useless. The bored model fiddled compulsively with the dial of a small portable radio.

Unlike the jaded neutrality of a St Anne's Court pin-up shoot of the period, in some claustrophobic pit with bamboo backdrop and prison lighting, this bedroom is ripe with evidence of an actual woman's life. Furniture, mirrors, cups, books, photographs; choice of coverings brought back from travels: they are not a distraction. They are the story. Moraes sits up, hands clasping feet. She smiles. 'We're done.' And that is one of the illustrations she selects for her memoir. 'A more informal Deakin photograph.'

There is not much formality on offer in the repeat session. The second print Moraes deploys in her book – reverse angle, head to camera, arms spread, knees bent – is directly related to the Bacon painting with the syringe embedded in her flesh. Henrietta is very decent about it when she comes across Deakin flogging these prints for 'ten bob a time'. She asks him to fetch her a drink on his takings. 'His leathery face grinning, he bought me several.'

Dates are fluid here. Bacon's *Crouching Nude* (1961) appears to derive from the way Moraes positioned herself on the bed, leaning on an elbow. A photograph that Deakin was commanded to execute two years later. Time is a casualty of binge drinking, of Colony Room monologues that circle back on themselves. *Lying Figure with Hypodermic Syringe* (1963) is a revision of the earlier Moraes nude. But where is the lie, before, after or always? He prevaricates. She *lies* on a bed: a pun. Is the big needle wedged in her arm, or the chi-chi grape colours of the painted backdrop, the real falsehood?

Henrietta Moraes is named and acknowledged by Bacon. Deakin remains anonymous, his collaboration an open secret. The painter works with the reflexes of a cosmetic surgeon. He sculpts the prow of the Moraes nose and chisels away the haughty tilt that had Farson naming her 'Lady Brett', after the Hemingway character in *The Sun Also Rises*. Against his usual practice, Bacon chose to make some of the preliminary Moraes studies from life. He wanted her there, gifting him a direct energy transfer. Heat. He needed to be reassured of a vulnerability that was always attractive. It was honest.

By 1969, the painter was merging the archetypal Moraes from the Apollo Place session with stills of Emmanuelle Riva sharing a shower in the Alain Resnais film *Hiroshima mon amour*. The painting, *Study of Henrietta Moraes*, is then photographed, to become a full-page illustration, with provenance, in the *Catalogue Raisonné*: a solid-gold guarantee of authenticity and value.

By the time of the 1962 Tate Gallery retrospective, Francis Bacon was being acknowledged as a contemporary great. 'This is the black night of the twentieth-century soul,' wrote the anonymous critic from *The Times*. 'Flashed on the canvas, like one of the startling news-photos or cinematic images from which the paintings often derive, is the cry of agony of our own age, an age which has lost its faith.'

How curious that a personality once regarded as a renegade should be canonised, draped in purple, and led from the gutter – in Farson's garish phrase – to a papal throne. Bacon came through muck and fire to be welcomed by the establishment. While, just two years earlier, Michael Powell, a recognised master of English cinema, was being anathematised, savaged by tabloids and weekend heavies alike, his career in ruins, for the crime of trespassing in the purlieus of Bacon's Soho. *Peeping Tom* dabbled in the unstable colour field of the acclaimed painter's Sadean world. Eastmancolor flooding in a lurid sodium spill across hosed cobbles and neon signage in Fitzrovia.

Powell operated in the wrong medium. Cinema provoked delinquency, rapes and moral turpitude. Bacon was congratulated for his courage in cannibalising film and photography at the moment when Powell, elevating similar themes and obsessions to operatic heights, was treated as a monster. And expelled from polite society. *Peeping Tom* and its pencil-moustached gentleman director were definitively cancelled many decades before social media lynch mobs trawled ancient tweets and ruled by fear. Before the tearful non-apologies of politicians moved from suburban doorsteps to presidential lecterns draped with ugly flags.

The exteriors for Powell's film were shot in Fitzrovia and Soho. Newman Passage, a sinister gash in the fabric of time, is a bent alley skulking between pubs favoured by the likes of Julian Maclaren-Ross and Dylan Thomas. The passage is the director's shorthand for a dark Hogarthian past of stock prostitutes and ritual slaughter. Colours inside this nightmare topography are sickly sour. The principal character, the I-am-a-camera scoptophile psychopath in the duffel coat, played very effectively by a softly spoken German, has been so damaged by his scientist father that he can only experience life by filming it. A pathology Deakin understood all too well. In Powell's conceit, reality is a lurid wine-stained cartoon. His film-within-a-film, shot on a clockwork 16mm camera by a compulsive voyeur, is monochrome. A found-footage animation from a set of Deakin photographs. Powell's protagonist, an Oedipal victim, recorded from childhood by his own father (played by the director), an experiment in terror, is never without a camera. He occupies the same streets as Deakin, but he is solitary, a stalking eye. The fictional Mark Lewis is complicit in his own madness.

While Bacon is praised, like Walter Sickert before him, for making use of the dot matrix of newspaper reproduction, and celebrated for lifting details from crimes and massacres, Powell is damned for trespassing in pornography, and for exploiting aberrant psychosexual behaviour. High art asset strips cinema with no moral repercussions.

Peeping Tom was conceived and written by Leo Marks, a wartime cryptographer, son of the bookseller who owned 84 Charing Cross Road. Extreme acts, involving cameras, mirrors, and tripods with bayonet blades, made no direct reference to the vision of Francis Bacon. That would have to wait for *Performance* in 1970. Donald Cammell drew on Bacon as much as on Borges. The bulky Kray-cloned bookmaker played by Johnny Shannon is like one of those unlikely patrons of Lucian Freud; red-knuckled, thick-wristed men fortunate enough to take valuable paintings in lieu of gambling debts. The schizophrenic splittings and doublings of drug-induced occult ceremonies dissolve the interface between thug and rock performer, bookmaker and art collector. Soft cell interiors, lit and photographed by Nicolas Roeg, directly reference Bacon paintings.

And behind Bacon, Deakin. Always Deakin. It can feel, to the conspiracy obsessive, initiated by the tarot of the albums, that the stalking photographer lurks somewhere at the back of all the cultural manifestations. He served, he provoked. He kept the record.

James Fox, gangland enforcer on the run, is like a stock figure from earlier British cinema, from the era of *Peeping Tom*, trapped in the wrong part of town, Powis Square, and finding himself swallowed into a Bacon memoir composed by Dan Farson. Like Bacon, the Fox character is beaten with a buckled belt. His 'performance' is a trance of sadism and masochism, assault and submission. The fortuitous intrusion into the communal house of Mick Jagger's faded rock star parallels, very neatly, the psychic absorption of well-hung minor criminals like George Dyer into the life and legend of Francis Bacon. Such socio-sexual entanglements were a theme of the period, reprised in Harold Pinter's screenplay from Robin Maugham's novel *The Servant*, for the film by Joseph Losey. Another Chelsea property, not too far from Henrietta Moraes. Another viperish class argument. James Fox, this time, is the connected toff, undone by pre-coital languor.

The scenes where the fiction of Mark Lewis, the Powell character played by Karlheinz Böhm, invade the psychodrama of John Deakin and Henrietta Moraes come early in *Peeping Tom*. The Lewis snuff documentary is shot in black and white, while the city containing it is ripe with nightmare colour. Fulfilling a posthumous commission from his scientist father, Lewis advances with his camera on the paid woman, performed by Brenda Bruce, who is arranging herself on a brass bed. He solicits the unreachable gaze of the moment of extinction; the look that Henrietta Moraes is never going to offer, as she plays along, making all the required shapes, from parodies of the cellophane-wrapped pin-up genre to unfeigned boredom.

When Lewis, in a makeshift studio above a Soho tobacconist's shop selling dirty pictures to *Telegraph* readers, shoots a session with contemporary glamour model Pamela Green, we have a crude sketch of the séance Deakin conducted in Apollo Place. One of the other girls, pricking his pretensions, even asks Lewis if he's trying to do a Cecil Beaton. Both projects, Deakin's and Powell's, are about the status of the gaze. And both projects – *Peeping Tom* overtly and Deakin covertly – are about the reach and condition of pain.

Deakin works close. He sniffs for weakness. Leo Marks, the former spook, layered his script for *Peeping Tom* with teasing detail. The underlying thesis was about the nature of suffering, physical and moral. Marks said that he learned to calibrate the precise temperature of fear – cold sweat dripping down the spine in certain knowledge of coming torture and probable death – by watching SOE agents when they were waiting to be dropped behind enemy lines. He made pain his special subject. Aspects of pain and the foreknowledge of pain were coded as plot points at prearranged moments in the structure of Powell's film. Pain trapped but accessible in the frozen time of a preserved childhood snapshot.

Powell dressed his sets with mirrors. With reflections of divided selves. 'I am photographing you photographing me,' says the victim; the one who is allowed to play behind the camera, before her actions become a terrible conclusion. There are so many films within this film: faked documentaries, parodied studio productions. The feature on which Lewis is drudging as focus-puller is called *The Walls Are Closing In*. In a cruel Powell joke, the role of the pretend director is performed by a blind actor, Esmond Knight. Maxine Audley, the suspicious, whisky-swilling mother of the killer's girlfriend, is played as a blind woman, threatened by the bayonet-tripod as she staggers against a home movie screen. That humble role of 'focus-puller' is a coded nudge from Marks, an onanistic insert. When Deakin lost sharpness in his portraits, he was bored. Blood sugar levels were dipping between drinks. Irritation became incompetence.

If the whole Deakin sequence with Henrietta Moraes, naked on the bed, flickered like that short film made from photographs of the Wheeler's lunch, then the natural climax would arrive when Moraes sits up, stares straight at the photographer, and smiles. Here is a conclusion of sorts and a signal that the performance is over.

We cut, immediately, to the model in everyday surroundings. Moraes, clothed in a scoop-necked summer dress, is returned to her natural habitat, the bar. The glance at Deakin is shared knowledge: the little man is a pest again, wasting good drinking time. Henrietta, as requested, turns her head, strikes a pose, but the effect is awkward. Her eyes are tired. Deakin moves on to Michael Andrews.

Within this maelstrom of cultural interconnections and references, the painter, Francis Bacon, becomes a director; dressing, undressing and manipulating his creatures across a closed set, while lifting frames from Eisenstein or Buñuel, and pouring acid over the features of characters in promotional stills and movie magazines. The process wins the approval of critics. It rehabilitates, or makes glamorous, a previously questionable reputation.

Meanwhile, Michael Powell, a professional director in good standing, indulges, for his own private pleasure, that dot or splash or accidental smear of colour. He knows that that commentators will never notice. His High Tory persona, with its love of landscape and tradition, has made him a 1961 pariah. And now, after the fiasco of *Peeping Tom*, a calculating pornographer.

Bacon operates, successfully, on his own terms. He poses as a risk-taker, another Artaud or Genet; a gambler absorbed in classical literature. A poet in another medium. Powell paints with light. Witness the confident detail of that discarded yellow film package dropped in the waste bin at the entrance to Newman Passage. A small bright flare among the wet cobbles and dull grey-brown detritus of the city. Bacon's *Lying Figure* (1969), his final version of Deakin's upside-down Moraes, spiked on the bed, has an unexpected yellow disc. It is egg-shaped and floats across the mauve wall, behind the rumpled sheets. We can believe, if we so choose, that the cinema-literate painter wanted to summon, if not the weather of *Peeping Tom*, then, at least, the strident yellow carton in Newman Passage.

Exiled, driven out of England, Powell made two films in Australia. *They're a Weird Mob*, which sounds like an alternate title for a history of the Colony Room, and *Age of Consent*. The second film, based on a semi-autobiographical novel by Norman Lindsay, gave Powell permission to contemplate a better life in the freedom of the open air, toshing paintings of a young and feral Helen Mirren, naked on a Great Barrier Reef island. *Age of Consent* starred, and was co-produced by, James Mason. Mason's reputation had, narrowly, survived Kubrick's *Lolita*, released two years after *Peeping Tom*. The Bacon/Moraes melodrama – flagging artist, 'jaded by success', finds inspiration rekindled by naked muse – is spun into Powell's penultimate feature film. After that, there was only *The Boy Who Turned Yellow*, for the Children's Film Foundation.

By 1966, round about the time when the Sixties were actually becoming the Sixties, the figure of photographer as celebrity achieved resolution in *Blow-Up*. The original inspiration for the film came from Paris, not London. From *Las babas del diablo*, the Julio Cortázar story about an encounter between a young boy and an older woman; an encounter caught on camera by an exiled man drifting listlessly through an alien city. Another witness, a man in a grey hat, tries to take possession of the film. The truth about what the photographer has captured by accident will only be revealed when the image is enlarged and fixed to a wall.

'But in all ways when one is walking about with a camera, one has almost a duty to be attentive, to not lose that abrupt and happy rebound of sun's rays off an old stone,' Cortázar wrote, setting the agenda for Deakin, at a loose end, coming away from Bacon's property in Narrow Street, Limehouse.

With the advent of Cortázar in our chain of connections, the detour is complete. The final twist comes when Deakin's sequence, achieved in collaboration with Henrietta Moraes, returns as the unacknowledged in-spiration for a literary experiment by Cortázar. In the collection *Around the Day in Eighty Worlds*, there is a short piece called 'The Broken Doll'. It is illustrated by consecutive frames from a run of photographs shot by the author himself. The images are as much part of the essay as the words. Cortázar has defined a period in which fiction and documentation have an equal value. Distinctions are meaningless. It feels as if the great pictorial novel, hinted at in Deakin's wordless album, has found its moment.

Cortázar talks about reaching an unexpected destination by 'navigating crosscurrents'. 'Merely by concentrating on something,' he says, 'one causes endless analogies to collect around it, even to penetrate the boundaries of the subject itself.'

There is always, outside the author and his or her imagined topic, a duplicate reality stitched from references, a 'meteor shower' of sudden inspirations. Cortázar calls this pathology 'the other'. The story on which he is labouring has already been written. And written better because it has never been spoiled by publication. In reading, we rewrite, in order to reforget. 'Not text but texture,' Cortázar quotes Nabokov. He finds what he needs by dipping, at random, into the books by Gaston Bachelard, Adorno, Rimbaud, that come to hand.

And where is the 'broken doll' of his title? It is hidden among those vertical strips of film at the margins of his page. The pictorial narrative takes place on a rumbled bed. The doll is arranged in a series of provocative poses. Here is a replay, or precise memory (without previous knowledge), of the Deakin shoot with Henrietta Moraes. A quotation from an album that has not yet been assembled. The broken doll of Cortázar is the storyboard for Deakin. Evidence waiting to be processed by Bacon. Here is a spectacular 'othering' of the Chelsea drama. A premature afterlife. Cortázar quotes Bachelard: 'All duration is essentially polymorphic; the true action of time reclaims the richness of coincidences.'

MABUSE IN MEXICO

When at last there was nothing to be witnessed and the night sky was darker than the sea, voices of future crimes came to him in a chorus of static. Recordings that seethed and hissed like a bag of snakes. Quotations with no identifiable source.

'I don't want to die,' he wrote in one of his poems, 'till I've known the black dogs of Mexico who sleep without dreams. I don't want to die till I've savoured the taste of death.'

Posthumous dreams were supernova interference. He blocked his ears with candle wax and welcomed the husks of creatures making their nests in his bed of sand. The parasite was wriggling in his spinal cord. Terror peeled his senses.

With the chair dragged from its corner and wedged across the door, tilted to balance under the handle, and with the key turning, turned, removed, hidden under the pillow, the hotel window was the only possible point of access. Unless the thing was already in the room! Curled and waiting in or under the bed. Something held him fast. Something like broad leather straps around the chest. Like a rubber bridle, an alien tongue thickened to fill his mouth. Muffling the words he couldn't find. Blocking his throat. Stifling language. He could not utter a squeak of protest. Some entity, some force of nature, on this windless, waveless, starless night, ruffled the muslin curtains. And gave authority to the black rectangle. The point of entry to the dark regions.

Mexico City: Jeffress in his pomp, hanging out with film people, Hollywood trash, border jumpers, druggies, Stalinists, conscription dodgers, sex criminals, runaway English aristos, Jewish poets, Spanish Republicans, all of them wanting a new mark to pay the mordida. To bankroll insane movie projects for bar girls and pimps and blacklisted hacks. That lost year in Mexico, the one nobody ever talks about.

The spittle of the rasp. The cinder of the coal without teeth. Was that when the evil spirit took possession? Was that when the slow, lifelong suicide the old ones demanded began to foul his breath?

In those fathom-deep hours at the seaside hotel, when the dead man couldn't close his eyes, couldn't see anything move beyond the frame of teasing *light, beyond shadows sourced from nowhere on the cracked ceiling, he found himself returning, again and again, to the last days with Arturo, two intimate strangers, irregularly coupling in a foreign land. Never settling, always on the run. Heading for the coast. Coming ashore from the liner at Vera Cruz, flying out from Mazatlán. That's where the Californians hung out. Too soon for Mitchum and Jane Russell and Vincent Price. Arturo knew how to dress the part. He had form with The Footlights in Cambridge. He played a sailor boy for the Sitwells. He was a talker, a traveller. A collector with impeccable taste – when he took the right advice. Bosom chums with Zachary Scott and Ruth Ford, but that was much later? Back in New York? Before or after the catastrophe? There is no such distinction now. Before the meeting with the old pervert, the Spaniard? Did he give Arturo a bit in a crowd scene? In drag? In white silk? Walking a blind dog into a church wedding?* The Criminal Life of . . . Somebody or Other.

That sadist helped to find the house. Now with every last breath that cannot be drawn, blocked nose, mouth wedged with locusts, he sees those red steel gates, that high white wall. The gates open slowly, the building is faced with volcanic stone, a dry pink. But he never penetrates. The gates open wide. He drags his knuckles over the walls, leaving behind a little skin. He takes a step or two, levitating, but he does not advance. Then he is naked in the snow on a railway platform.

Cerrada de Félix Cuevas in Colonia del Valle was a good address, between the sprawl of the spider city, its parasitical shacks and slums, and the film studios. He rode in an American car. Arturo took photographs in the garden, on picnics in the mountains, with Indians, on a private beach. What happened to that album? When a camera is passed around to just anybody – bellboy, barman, woman – it loses potency, but the results can be magical. It's like paintings by children, lunatics. There is no nonsense about art and significance, no self-censorship. Those accidental instantaneous laughing snapshots have a truth the professionals can't match.

When Arturo took himself off for cocktails with the film people at the Ultramar offices on Avenida Paseo de la Reforma, that diagonal thrust across the heart of Mexico City, his travelling companion, the dead man in remission, spent his afternoons in the little cinema he found on the same block. He walked. He would have walked all day. The city resisted. The heat. The hustle. It was too picturesque. Men dragging blocks of ice. Men on benches. He went into the dark. He found a season of those silent films he liked, the German things with mad doctors, conspiracies, an underworld in parallel with authority. And there was that scene when the great secret, the general theory of everything, was about to be revealed, when a curtain was pulled back. The voice of a controlling intelligence at the centre of the electronic web.

Finish it. Kill yourself now. Dumb advice to a dead man. The delicate bones of the inner ear have fused. But his hearing has never been so acute. Death to van Gogh's ear! Fragments of stupid conversations in the bar below. Catching every nuance, like a lip reader, from the mimed dialogue of a silent film. Identifying with absolute precision the crisis of the turning of the tide. Advancing steps on the carpeted stairs. Shamanic sacrifice. With no reward. The spittle of the rasp running down his cold cheek. Cinders from the coal in the socket of his eye.

Something was sealing him in this sheath of the spirit, this body bag. Pulling the zip. The Indians said that whites were the ones the spirits had abandoned. The red gates are opening. He draws his knuckles along the white wall. Mexico was the revelation that never happened. It was when, among all those competing surrealists, the jealousy, the backbiting, the ice picks, he knew that painting was over. He accepted initiation into the greater task. And the price demanded. Form is nothing. Images are always exaggerated. An atmosphere of madness must be established in which the rational mind loses its footing and the spirit advances without check.

The curtains draw back. There is nothing there. Nobody. A camera on a table. A glass of water. A certain agency. Nobody is coming to get him. Nobody cares. The official magicians are all tricksters for hire. He is alone. Quite alone now. And glad of it.

DEAKIN AS PSYCHOGEOGRAPHER

'Well, it's not like I knew he was there!
He was lurking. He was low profile.'
'Of course he bloody was. He's a fucking pariah.'

– Mick Herron, *Slow Horses*

Narrow Street

The stained group photograph, heavy with the implications of a shift to the east, the afterhours taxi out of Dean Street, was not committed by John Deakin. He features in the centre of the composition, thinly smirking, confident in his role as the provocateur around which all the chaos and darkness of the period must spin.

Francis Bacon, no longer able to pursue his private horrors in comparative obscurity, had succumbed. He followed Farson and Andrew Sinclair, his future biographers, and he acquired a riverside property at 80 Narrow Street. Dan had located an enviable hideaway above a working barge-yard, twelve years earlier, when nobody from the Colony Room clan was looking. And he boasted, as did so many others, ahead of the colonisation by celebrity: 'I moved into Limehouse before it was fashionable.'

But this stretch of the river had always been fashionable: with ocean-going mariners, with traders and publicans living on their custom. Popular with seafaring men of all nations. The ones who decided to come ashore and settle. And with authors, journalists, amateur topographers, evangelists, and charitable politicians attracted by rumours of poverty, crime and disease. Outsiders made their expeditions, drunk on the drench of sour hops, the choking dust of lime kilns, the sweet stink of spice warehouses. There were quality copywriters preparing the ground for Farson: Thomas De Quincey, Charles Dickens, Oscar Wilde and Conan Doyle. The father of the *fin-de-siècle* poet Ernest Dowson had a business in Narrow Street. Dowson lived for a time in Limehouse. He was a friend of Wilde and introduced him to the romance of these reaches. There were exploiters of the opium myths of the Pennyfields Chinese quarter: the benevolent Thomas Burke and Sax Rohmer, puppeteer of Dr Fu Manchu and the Yellow Peril.

The group photograph from Farson's archive, either remotely triggered, or snapped by some obliging punter, was taken in Charlie Brown's (as the Railway Tavern, on the corner of Garford Street and West India Dock Road, was commonly known). The place reeked of suspended history. The intruders from Soho sucked in their bellies and posed. Another memento. An obituary. Behind the bar, like a voodoo of colourful cigarette packets left by sailors, criminous mugshots and faraway postcards were nailed to the wall.

Bacon is chubbier and happier than he generally permitted himself to appear, however drunk, in portraits by Deakin or Farson. There are chemical or seminal smears all over him. A congealed white blob is crawling across his lower abdomen. A loosely knotted woollen scarf protects his throat. His sparkling eyes are lost in the fat of laughing cheeks. His arm is snaking around the more suspicious docker; the one with his pint, his check shirt, rolled sleeves, work trousers. The man has dropped in to Charlie Brown's on the way home from a day's labours in or around the dying deepwater docks. Bacon is pleased with the innocence of the company, with the masculine aroma. Testosterone and larded hair. Cheap cigars and wet dog. He fingers his glass like a spare ear left in an ashtray.

Calm and collected, debonair, as if he had personally arranged the whole thing, Deakin flouts a distressed corduroy suit. There is no trace of his habitual venom. He is shorter than the others and could be a visiting academic leading a successful tour of the lowlife. Farson, oiled hair shining, leather jacket challenged by increasing girth, eyes his docker like a tasty morsel. He knows that the black door has the capitalised word GENTLEMEN on show. A dribble from Deakin's shoulder spreads across the print from Farson's leather to the younger of the working men.

'A funny night out.' The phrase Tony Lambrianou, an obliging associate of the Krays, employed for the regular courts held by the Twins at the Carpenters Arms in Cheshire Street. Anything could happen and frequently did. That was the point of these gatherings. 'Ronnie had his own sense of humour.' As did Bacon.

For a time, Francis enjoyed the local cruising scene but he couldn't settle into the house in Narrow Street. He might entertain, in suitably formal surroundings, serious French visitors, such as Michel Leiris, or family members from South Africa. Or he might give the place over to his accommodator at the Marlborough Gallery, Miss Valerie Beston. There was so much money now, rolls of fifties hot to be dispersed, that it spoiled the hang of his leather blouson.

Narrow Street, Bacon decided, was no longer a place where 'one could reasonably hope to be murdered'. It never was, despite the intricately woven mysteries of *Our Mutual Friend* and the sensationalist speculations of De Quincey in his essay *On Murder Considered as One of the Fine Arts*. Violence was sudden, unexplained and ordinary. It lived in the stones and was not to be summoned at will as a sexual refinement for slumming aesthetes.

The latest iteration of Deakin's recorded but enigmatic life placed him in Charlie Brown's, at the heart of a group of five men: two working dockers, a rich and famous painter, and two competitive and occasionally talented photographers. He is almost at ease, a talisman with jug-handle ears. The venerable Poplar boozer was lurid with atmosphere it didn't have to promote. The guv'nor who gave his name to the place died in 1932. He worked hard to cultivate the legends: Burke's Chinatown and an eccentric collection of curiosities brought in on the tide. In the seventeenth century, this impressive trawl of glass-cabinet junk could, like Elias Ashmole's canny pillage, have founded a museum in Oxford. Charlie was described in a report by the American journalist Wentworth Day as 'friend of cabinet ministers and able seamen alike'. This was the social interface that Dan Farson revived, many years later, at the Waterman's Arms. Charlie Brown's was demolished in 1989 to prepare the ground for the construction of the Limehouse Link tunnel, smooth passage between old and new financial centres.

If Bacon, undone by river light, couldn't paint here, an incomer from a later, overlapping generation could. Jock McFadyen, perching for a time in Turner's Road, enjoyed the camaraderie of a number of pubs within the gravitational pull of St Anne's, Nicholas Hawksmoor's Limehouse church. On his bike, McFadyen got around the territory, recording provisional architecture and clients of bus halts, such as the one favoured by Bacon. The McFadyen paintings were of real cartoon humans and their Cortinas frozen in proud entropy. Curs on string and derelicts with bent spines. The Portland stone blocks of the church were awarded no more significance than the blue plastic bags from a Tesco supermarket blown against razor wire. Misassembled calamine-lotion faces appeared to have been sculpted by a baseball bat on their way to Dr David Widgery's clinic.

Bacon was a privileged colonist, while Jock was embedded in the muck and drift. McFadyen's paintings were made somewhere between the stick-person mappings of L. S. Lowry, whose work he admired (and who looked, on his rent-collecting rounds, very much like a character McFadyen might have included in one of his canvases), and the flesh-splash gestures of Bacon. In the excitement of his Limehouse days, Jock peppered the autobiographical mix with the knock-off swagger of early Hockney. His paintings danced. His characters threatened to kick their way out of the frame.

Jock gleaned, bringing home photographs of street signs, concrete cancers; urban blight of just the sort Deakin looked to catalogue on his own downriver expeditions. The Soho visitor gathered a rich haul that he failed to convert into a successful book or exhibition. There was never an accompanying text. This territory wrote itself. Artistic tourists might be permitted to make some small contribution, but there was no question of ownership.

I visited McFadyen's studio, his factory at the back of London Fields in Hackney. I admired research snapshots from the times when Jock investigated streets that had once seduced Deakin. Evidence was paint-flecked, creased, torn, and taped to other prints. There were portraits of Jock himself in his leathers, rough riding with his painter pals. And of his wife, the musician Susie Honeyman. Otherwise, the provisional paper-bound album was void of human figures: elevated railways, snooker clubs, dumped cars, A13 tower blocks, the rank canal. Nothing was fixed, everything was wide open, ripe for exploitation.

Harry Diamond, labourer in a brake factory, jobbing stagehand, and reluctant model for Lucian Freud, dropped in on McFadyen in his Turner's Road hideaway. Coming late to photography, Harry was, in his own fashion, Jock's Deakin. He kept a record of the action, while being himself the inspiration for new work. The Scottish painter rewarded his new chum with a 1984 painting: *Harry Diamond Dancing in Paul Tonkin's Prefab*. Harry: life-enhancer. Unaccompanied dad dancer. Model. Epic pedestrian. And a bit of a pest.

Deakin enters the stories by way of the pub. Harry was more of a café man, a regular at Coffee An', which was where he met Freud for the first time. Diamond was short, stocky, belligerent and very definitely not the butt for anyone's philanthropy. Freud reckoned when Harry took up a camera, it was a Damascene conversion. 'Like someone finding Jesus.' Things were never the same again. Photographers began photographing photographers. Artists posed for their models. Roles were exchanged like borrowed coats. Nobody wanted Harry's rainwear (except Freud, for whom it had an almost religious aura, independent of its host). Diamond stomped for miles across town, holes in his boots. When he was not sustaining a pose and kvetching about Freud making his legs too short, he was dancing. He was talking, steaming, conducting with yellow fingers.

With an introduction from Freud, Diamond was commissioned to make portraits of painters. Inevitably there was a dispute over ownership.

Harry threatened to smash up the gallery. Freud, provocative as ever, hoped to position him as being more capable than Deakin of factoring a *comédie humaine*, a Balzacian panorama of persons, high and low. The novel in pictures, project of a lifetime, imposed by secret masters in Mexico, was in danger of being stolen.

When Freud's portrait of Diamond, who felt himself spiritually drained by their daily sessions, was photographed for a catalogue, the painter was excited by the fact that a shadow had been excised. Something happened between the mechanical reproduction and the painting as it appeared on the wall of the gallery. Meanwhile, the yucca tree in the Paddington interior had withered to a stump. And died. The truths of photography are the lies that survive. What Freud discovered was that certain parts of the guilty photographer also decay through some sort of mysterious Dorian Gray symbiosis with the stolen image.

Bacon followed Farson to Narrow Street, a very desirable stretch of the river for later incomers. Freud kept a bolthole in Leman Street, in old Whitechapel, in a period when much of the established Jewish population was being nudged out or swept into social care and the asylums of Epsom. But Harry resisted, he would not travel with the tide. As a tenant or sharer of Freud's space, he was a barnacle. *He belonged here.* Leman Street was where new arrivals from Poland and Russia were sheltered and processed. The epic duel, between painter and parasite, became another Pinter drama; another mouthy caretaker quivering with righteous indignation.

When Diamond was out and about, he walked. *He marched.* He saved the bus fare and hammered across town, that classic east/west Jewish treadmill described by Bernard Kops, when he shuttled from Stepney to Soho. Family home to book barrow. Harry pushed it, Leman Street to Harrow Road. Different countries, different tribes. And everything in-between. There is an embattled accumulation of particulars in the standing figure confronting Freud in his studio.

Harry Diamond came alive in the stories Jock McFadyen had to tell. Jock's conversations always started with the same challenge.

'How old are you now?'

Jock liked to satisfy himself that I was still a few years closer to deliquescence and dribbling senility, before moving on to art business, property and gossip. Mention of Harry Diamond brings a twinkle to the eye. He recalls in particular Harry's costume: stackheel shoes and an Irish tweed jacket from a charity shop. The man loved the stamp of rhythm, the automated shrug of shoulders. Dancing and shadowboxing. Giving no quarter to obstacles, the clutter of the streets. Taking no prisoners. Camera secure in pocket.

When Jock's mother came to Turner's Road, to the smashed windows and National Front graffiti, to corrugated fences tipped over by weight of buddleia and the thrust of sparrow bushes, to bomb damage and light industrial failures, she ran into Harry, punting the pavements on his stick. She went home with a Diamond photo of Jock and his son to put in a frame. The London stories enchanted her.

One evening in town, Jock found Harry ripping down flypitched posters promoting his own show at a gallery run by Michael Parkin. Diamond was worried about word getting out and reaching the paymasters of National Assistance. He carried his camera everywhere. And he directed his sitters: 'Move yer bonce closer to the light.' A merciless eye with which to retaliate against insults, real or imagined: *Gotcha!*

Jock dragged himself upstairs to the Colony Room a couple of times, but he preferred to shoot back east, after an opening, to the Five Bells & Blade Bone in Three Colt Street, another lock-in.

'Harry would tramp to Streatham to buy five fags for a few pence less.'

Diamond achieved one of the best portraits of Deakin; a non-judgemental account of a fellow professional. It is summer in Soho and Deakin has tilted his head, in thoughtful conversation. He has paused for a moment in the doorway, alongside the guardian of the bar. It might be the French House. The letters on the awning, directly above Deakin's head, spell out: WINES. It is the kind of morning when he imagines himself back in Rome. On the loose, empty diary. The freelance photographer is comfortable in lightweight clothes, his veined hand clutching newspaper. Cigarette unfired. Glasses and pens in pocket. This a composition made without hidden agenda. Two contrasting figures and the head of another, in profile, in motion, on the far side of the street. Two consenting photographers doing what they do, getting through another day.

The Deakin Archive in the seventeen albums hints at the potential for a number of stalled books, left in limbo: more from Rome, a Genoa factory, Moroccan tourism, tattoo parlours and street art. *London Walls* and *Paris Walls* were made into files without achieving resolution. There should have been an ideal version that could only come into existence when Deakin stopped adding to it. Before he died in Brighton, dreaming of a ferry across the Sea of Crete.

Prints recovered from the unrealised *London Walls* sequence of the 1960s position Deakin firmly in the tradition of the urban stalker. He claims his spot in the Brotherhood alongside Robert Frank (in the City of London and Bethnal Green) and Eugène Atget (in early-morning Paris). He found the subjects that he knew were waiting for him. He found the hidden places his controller told him to visit. He took down evidence and kicked it under the bed, while he waited for the man who was never coming. There was a message to be found among spectral trade signs, faded traces of immigrant lives. He did not have the madness to excavate everything the wounded ground wanted to give back. Deakin was still in hock to the court of Bacon. He was impatient to recognise the accidents that can lift a project to another dimension. It takes a total surrender of the rational to catch what isn't quite there and to make it manifest.

There is an unconscious psychogeographical bias in the route taken. Deakin has left clues from which his *dérive* can be spooled back towards vestiges of Chinese life around Pennyfields, and along Limehouse Causeway to the properties occupied by Farson, Bacon and Andrew Sinclair in Narrow Street. It feels as if Deakin struck out on his own, from rooms he had already visited, in the general direction of Charlie Brown's pub; then pushed on to the tight nest of Poplar streets, squeezed between major highways, where Chinese immigrants had been permitted to settle.

In pride of place, upstairs at 90 Narrow Street – before the economic catastrophe of Farson's purchase of the Waterman's Arms – was the Lucian Freud portrait of Deakin. It was more comfortable than having the man himself in residence. Farson also squirrelled away an Auerbach and a Bacon portrait of a surgeon, one that he 'rescued' from imminent destruction. In *Limehouse Days*, Farson writes well about his technique for identifying the place where he wanted to live. He embarked on a series of downriver walks, undertaken in parallel with earlier accounts by Charles Dickens, Jack London, William Fishman and other established authorities.

Photographs were made. Modest records of river frontage. Narrow Street in its last working days. The Christ statue with the raised arm in the grounds of Limehouse Church. Then, out of nowhere, Farson comes to a thing not to be found anywhere in Deakin's compulsive survey of Poplar walls and windows: a face transcending occasion. A face outside time. Stricken. Without illusions. An unyielding somnambulist from Edgar Allan Poe's *The Man of the Crowd*. A living spectre doomed to tramp, forever, from suburb to centre; contemplating crime, assured of damnation.

Farson's survey, by way of river and Whitechapel labyrinth, drew him to Narrow Street, and allowed him, before his retreat to North Devon, to experience those submerged lines of desire. Like so many others, he quotes from Jack London's *The People of the Abyss*, from *Our Mutual Friend* (a primer of pedestrianism and pursuit), and from Conrad. He hesitates beside the Hawksmoor church. And he finds himself, not knowing how or why, on Brick Lane, where his only possible subject, the Beckettian figure with the 'stained bowler and frayed collar', is waiting. This man will never be there again. He is a contemporary of the lost generations: Victorians, Edwardians, damaged survivors of wars. A faded elegance: black melon of the bowler, striped suit, striped tie, round collar. Hollowed cheeks and a frost of stubble. And the eyes! The foreknowledge!

'The photograph has haunted me since I took it,' Farson wrote. 'It shows quite clearly a man who has come face to face with death.'

The portraits Deakin made with artists and poets, with girls in cafés and waiters outside Italian restaurants, were collaborative. The subjects were willing, obeying basic instructions. The personality of the photographer provoked an immediate reaction. Results could be dramatic. But the only works delivered with something approaching the authenticity of Farson's encounter on Brick Lane are self-portraits, often made in drink. Using a delayed-action setting (or passing the camera over to a fellow toper), Deakin offered himself up for the kind of horrified revelation achieved by Freud and Bacon. Gritted teeth. Pitted skin. Half naked and half peeled, the skewed Soho prisoner raises a huge glass. A man in duress. Last cigarette fisted in yellow claw. Arms folded. The photographer confronts the terrible truth of a record that must be kept.

Caught close by Farson in the York Minster, 'circa 1953', in the early days in their friendship, with an ear like the residue of an exit wound, another Deakin is exposed. Farson has been manipulated to achieve the version that Deakin needs to confess. The coming triumphs and disasters of the two men would never be untangled. They were now roped together, socially and professionally, over a yawning chasm. Farson drew Deakin to Narrow Street. And Deakin struck out along Limehouse Causeway for his unrealised project, *London Walls*. He had no other choice. Place insisted.

'It is a tale of lovers that they tell in the low-lit Causeway that slinks from West India Dock Road to the dark waste of waters beyond. In Pennyfields, too, you may hear it,' begins *Limehouse Nights* (1916), the set of picaresque tales by the author (and journalist) Thomas Burke. Deakin's expedition tracked an established but unfashionable model: myths of opium dens and interracial liaisons and working people with exotic customs embedded in alien territory. Territory that teased and destroyed unwary outsiders.

With images collected as the memory prompts by which to navigate, Deakin parsed poetic excesses. He stripped his narrative to bare brickwork, signs left on dead walls. There are the partial names of forgotten traders and graphic obituaries for failed promotions; a silent cinema witnessed only by serial sentimentalists and topographical bloggers. SAU-SAGES (BEEF). Price tickets for marine outfitters. 'Rebuffs before secrets,' Deakin said. With the voice of experience. Murder sites and wooden doors turned into facemasks by the addition of a chalked mouth. De-commissioned toilets with broken stalls and tin commandments: DO NOT SPIT ON THE FLOOR.

'You need to be a futurist to discover ecstatic beauty in the torn wastes of tiles, the groupings of iron and stone, and the nightmare of chimney-stacks and gas-works,' Burke warned. 'These crazy things touch only those who do not live among them.'

Deakin walks and walks again. There are no faces. He is on his own with the recalcitrant buildings. The Causeway is a saturnine reef heaped against the implication of the river. Deakin is a futurist walking back-wards, erasing by recording, making destruction inevitable by the act of cataloguing the ultimate traces of the city of memory. *London Walls* was not a history of ruins but an ignored primer for highway planners and deep excavators. In attempting to fix the future, developers only succeed-ed in shaming the past. Deakin lost himself between worlds. The great Soho portraits were made by a man in drink. Reaching out, through ardent spirits, to the *loups-garous*, diabolic familiars flitting through the night, zombies on the treadmill of deadening employment. The walls of Poplar were recorded by a man in denial; drying out, fugue walking as therapy.

But before he can stride off, looking for breakfast cafés and Chinese calligraphy on the pompous Corinthian pillars of municipal offices, he is obliged to shadow Bacon on his invariable route from Narrow Street to the bus stop on Commercial Road: the turkey-stepping, hands-in-pockets morning transit across the grounds of St Anne's. The path the painter follows without once looking up to acknowledge church, relocated gravestones or resting vagrants.

Deakin circles: a lone wolf. Photographs he takes are without signature. They could have been taken by anybody. He notices the old memorials stacked against the brick wall. He likes the curves, the sharp lines. The names recovered and the names obliterated. His prints are unstable. It's hard to tell if a clammy mist is rising from the ground or from a misapplied development process. The stones are aborted missives from another time, tolerated in parks, standing proud against ivy-covered buildings with dark windows. *The beast is untethered now. But it has no name.*

The Wisdom of Solomon pyramid, drawn by Hablot Browne, illustrator of novels by Dickens, was produced in a popular engraving. It enjoyed a status equal to the Hawksmoor church. A burial party gathers in the foreground. Any photograph of the pyramid is a rite of passage, a challenge Deakin underplays. He manages to divorce pyramid from church. He frames it among summer trees, as if he had come across this teasing object – part sculpture, part tomb, part building – on a walk through the forest. Light, which might have been generated by the shifting sails of the trees, the clotted ground, or invisible Swedenborgian forces, leaks through Deakin's rescued print, spoiling its potential for reproduction. None of the words left on the surface of the Portland stone of the pyramid can be recovered. The panelled pages are not blank. Leaded alphabets have been licked and eaten.

After this necessary detour, part of a required Narrow Street ritual, Deakin concentrates on signage. He comes to the end of Limehouse Causeway, crosses West India Dock Road and launches his search for traces of Thomas Burke's Chinatown. BEST PRICES GIVEN FOR RAGS. Pennyfields permits broken glass along the lip of a brick course, in order to deter anyone tempted into climbing an antique lighting pole from stealing the bulb. The Chinese Seamen's Union is a wreck with wooden shutters. New bureaucratic rules and regulations have done for that trade. There is a nice print of Old Friends Restaurant in Mandarin Street: narrow doorway, Chinese script and high window packed with provisions. Shattered roofs, corrugated iron sheets. Abandoned shells dedicated to GENTS HAIRCUTTING. The shaving of bloodless ghosts. Dockers treating themselves before weekend parties in suits returned from the pawnbroker. Skeleton bridges across fouled canals. The sign for Ming Street is capped by a musical score knitted from barbed wire.

Deakin appreciates the decorative art of discontinued Chinese restaurants. Secret alleyways leading nowhere. Portals to opium dens that only exist in fiction. But which you can still smell, pungent and provocative, from contemporary pavements. Salvationist shelters have been cancelled, leaving nothing behind but their bannered commandments. Limehouse freeholds are offered at auction, two properties in Three Colt Street for £141 per annum in 1955. A thriving tobacconist, clean window thick with product, is loud with carcinogenic seductions: *The tipped cigarette you can taste!*

Pasted announcements have been around so long they appear to be holding up the buildings. Boxing bills, of course, as homage to Burke's *Limehouse Nights* and 'Battling Burrows, the lightning welterweight of Shadwell'. Burke pegs his man as a sentimentalist. The boxer takes a girl with a bundle of rags into his Pekin Street home. The story became a film. The film a memory. Bills for silent cinema, bills for music hall. Bills for murders, real and fictional.

Shirts, pyjamas, Merchant Marine caps in the window. Like dry-cleaned racks rescued from the drowned. Ex-Government Leather Knee Boots for twenty shillings: recommended for Sewermen. Sack Merchants. Funeral parlours barely distinguishable from Charlie Brown's pub. And a notice from the Port of London Authority to Lightermen about 'Queen's Birthday Arrangements' for 1958. More *breakfast's* with rogue apostrophes. More cigarettes and 'Castle Brand Lettered Rock'. More Broken Cream Bars at discount prices.

Deakin kept walking. He recorded messages in stone. He was absorbed into monochrome, trying to keep a pace or two ahead of the creeping mist, the river flux. He liked the incised glass panels outside bright pubs. But he didn't push through the door. He stayed with the borrowed aesthetics of Burke: 'In the Chinatown Causeway, too, were half-tones of rose and silver . . . Cinnamon and aconite, betel and bhang hung on the air.'

What is less evident, unless the story is taken back to the period when Bacon experimented as an interior decorator, is the way the painter *anticipated* Deakin in this fascination with occulted signs and scratches, with reading London like the Rosetta Stone.

In his 1981 autobiography, *Flaws in the Glass*, Patrick White recalled an encounter with Bacon.

> I like to remember his beautiful pansy-shaped face, sometimes with too much lipstick on it. He opened my eyes to a thing or two. One afternoon at Battersea, crossing the river together by a temporary footbridge while the permanent structure was under repair, he became entranced by the abstract graffiti scribbled in pencil on the timbered sides. Alone, I don't expect I would have noticed the effortless convolutions of line he pointed out for me to admire . . . In those days Francis was living at the end of Ebury Street . . . He had an old nanny who used to go out shoplifting whenever they were hard up, and as lover there was an alderman.

Deakin followed Bacon's bohemian template. He catalogued the signs, he was open to patronage from the rich and famous, from respectable lovers eager to be exploited. He warped time, leaving graphic evidence from which future journeys of discovery would be launched, travelling backwards into nowhere.

Deakin's Soho was outside my knowledge. In recent times, the ground of his most celebrated achievements had been islanded by enclosures and the deep tunnelling of a promised Crossrail system that remained subject to infinite postponement. I had never been much drawn to a place I experienced, on rare occasions, for social reasons and the business of film. Now, with the Covid plague, it was done. But Narrow Street still felt like a possible point of access for tracking Deakin's desire lines by way of the photographic prints he left us. All I had learned from my walks and my Limehouse workdays was that the past shrugs, settles itself, and clots. And that I would never be more than an uninvited tourist bleating about places in which I had no earned investment.

A route, pre-tested by Deakin, through buildings on the cusp of disappearance, struck me as the only way to initiate a dialogue with a photographer who was eager to junk failed projects and move on to the last act. I came to Narrow Street on the day of the winter solstice in the dreadful year of 2021, when even the most resistant of ghosts had decamped. Enveloping wraiths around the stacked graves of St Paul's in Shadwell were enlivened by a harvest of glittering blue and silver mirror balls hanging from bare trees by ropes of red bulbs. A knot of the faithful waited for redemption within the open doors of the church, where, many years ago, I witnessed a strange palm-waving, chanting and drumming voodoo ceremony. Or where I conjured one up, out of an ordinary riverside afternoon.

I talked to a man raking leaves, keeping the field of the dead respectable. He was, as so often, a guardian of the legends, historian of his own small patch, generous with information. I looked closely at scars in the brickwork, empty alcoves. I tried to anticipate the photographs that Deakin might have made. I was prepared to taste the rim of nautical gravestones in order to acquire the patina of his aubergine tongue. To experience the neurotic impulses running through his deadly sober veins when he tried to obey the lessons of a Mexican initiation: 'witness demonic reality as a "spectacle" by submitting to the spiritual power embodied in landscape'. The stones are no more than portraits of the peoples that obey them.

Deakin walked. Alone. Uncommissioned. His patrons, the indulgent editors, had no part in this. If anything, he was waiting for the signs on half-demolished buildings to communicate, to accept his intrusion. If it worked, he would remain anonymous. But any backward step, however well intended, is doomed. What the Deakin portfolio of drift does reveal, *through the photographs he did not make*, through the faces and the shuffling walks and the sweat of fear, was a lacuna from which news would eventually emerge: brazen, wealthy and swaggering with entitlement. Tattered remnants of locality would be reduced to decor for persistent stalkers.

There are no welcoming shadows in Narrow Street. These are the lost hours of a dying year. I know how it feels to become the walk and not the walker. To live in the risk of a magnesium flash when a photographic assault dies with its instant. And only then. In the foolish theft of an image out of time, snatched from the stream. With no ground left between camera and shadow.

I stood at the window of Bacon's old Narrow Street house and scanned the illuminated interior with considerable envy. A woman was working at a partners' desk with a panoramic river view. The extended living space was lined with books, spines basking in a soft and subtle glow. Was this the recently retired literary agent Deborah Owen, who represented Delia Smith, Lord Archer and Amos Oz? Testing a Smith recipe, Owen served up a 'companionable' macaroni cheese dish, gritted with breadcrumbs, for the lunch attended by the four founding conspirators of the Social Democratic Party. An agreeably democratic feast washed down – for the benefit of Roy Jenkins – by a decent bottle or two of undemocratic Château Lafite. High times by the river. Grim days for politics.

When Dan Farson made his own Limehouse return, pricking fallible memory for the books of legend that would have to be produced in North Devon, he was comforted to see that his old nest above the pub carried a plaque referencing his pioneering tenancy. But now, as I discover, pub and plaque are gone. Plenty of the music hall performers Farson championed have their residences recorded in Hoxton and De Beauvoir Town and Brixton, but Dan has been struck from the Narrow Street register. Perhaps for the crime of pointing out, with some evidence, that the famous riverside hostelry The Grapes, co-owned by Sir Ian McKellen, was *not* the inspiration for the Six Jolly Fellowship Porters in *Our Mutual Friend*. Farson decided that the original was the Two Brewers, on the other side of his own property. It had what The Grapes lacked: 'a crazy wooden verandah impending over the water'.

The Limehouse Causeway followed by Deakin now disappears into overarching railways, frenzied road systems and complicated approaches to Canary Wharf ramps: further pedestrianism is folly. Charlie Brown's salvaged gimcracks, the old Railway Tavern, are dust and grit. It has gone with the steam trains, sailors and dockers.

After crossing Westferry Road, only slightly skinned of former lives and pretensions, faint imprints of Deakin's anxious survey can still be located: Pennyfields, Ming Street, Pekin Street, Canton Street. Chinese signage memorialising a vanished population. The romances of Thomas Burke replaced by the migration of Sax Rohmer's 'Yellow Peril' fantasies into Canary Wharf's version of Hong Kong or Shanghai. Into rapacious and successful Chinese property speculation along the river from the Isle of Dogs to Silvertown, to Custom House and the Royal Albert and Royal Victoria Docks. The gigantic hangar of the ExCel conference centre could easily stand as the secret redoubt of Dr Fu Manchu. It is tempting to picture Christopher Lee's bootlace-moustached doctor ghosting through arms fairs and fingering instruments of enhanced interrogation.

I photographed the signs. LAST WATCH. NOODLES. The only viable Chinese restaurant was open, dimly lit and innocent of customers. My unreturning made a critical shift. When I washed against the railings of the sombre plantation of Pennyfields Park and looked up at the coloured lights burning in the adjacent tower block, I was jolted away from Deakin and into my own past. Place is more potent than the images that represent it. The scruffy patches of grass I mowed in the Seventies, even in their improved state, activated sluggish neural channels. The challenge of my original trespass, among the community of urban gardeners, was renewed. It had been a privilege to tend these schools and churches, to be a minor element in an active and available civic history. Cyril Jackson Primary. Pennyfields Park. Trinity Gardens. Upper North Street. Even the gesture of trying, in the doorway of a block of flats, to write those names in my notebook took me back to the days of scribbling, while the real gardeners enjoyed a roll-up break, a few prompts for the notes that became *Lud Heat*, a book I self-published in 1975.

In that all-enveloping Poplar twilight, I felt the vibrations of my mower grinding against tough grass, tangling with bicycle chains, shit-covered sticks, rags, stones. I smelt the burn of the Old Holborn tobacco. *And heard nothing.* No human voice under the tidal surge of traffic, the electronic hiss and hum of devices in tower block hives.

My expedition had to finish on a site that resisted, or even resented, its present status: Limehouse Church. And the Wisdom of Solomon pyramid. Deakin must have detoured. He doubled back on himself. The pyramid was a portrait of something he did not want to reproduce. His seemingly casual print was about the mysterious transmission of light between leaf and stone. It was about flaw not resolution. The softness of Deakin's images of exploration around the grounds of St Anne's cancelled the harsher focus of his photographs of surviving trade signs, the accidental memorabilia of Pennyfields.

Stone speaks to stone. There is a form of communication like the telepathy of trees in urban parks and forests at the outer limits of London. After sharing this ground with Deakin, I developed an unproven hunch about how we find ourselves carried forward on walks that become a sequence of pictures. 'Lines of force' linking buildings and earthworks, or violent incidents to which we grant some peculiar significance, have less conviction than the subterranean networks of fungi, unseen roots and filaments tracing out their own essential maps. The pyramid, as a visible obstacle, was the *omphalos* around which, and from which, stone-fed mycelia ventured. Why else would so many displaced photographers, with no shared heritage, no connections one to another, find their way to this church, to these streets, to the same monuments in the same wilderness cemeteries?

The longer I looked at the pyramid, the more convinced I became that Deakin requires us to make a new judgement about the definition of competence. He delivered the photographs necessary for an essay on London walls, but his story was spiked. The captures complemented disappearance, leaving the Soho photographer stranded on his return to Narrow Street. He had to pass the pyramid. He had to make the shot, but he had no ambition to achieve a poetic effect. Deakin's pyramid suggests an interrupted journey. That is the beauty of the thing: stone yielding to vegetation.

In the intimacy of the portraits of painters and poets – Bacon, Freud, Auerbach, Dylan Thomas, George Barker, David Gascoyne – the subjects are both revealed and diminished. They give so generously of themselves that the human donors fade. Biographies are buried in books, in theses and monographs. Masterpieces are explained through accidents of life. These men will never again be quite so *present* as they are in Deakin's portraiture. But that 'failed' photograph of the pyramid allows the thing itself, the obstacle in the church grounds, to continue unmolested. To exist on its own terms. In its own place. While the image thief is diminished, put on trial by history. And required to respond. To defend an indefensible legacy.

Waterman's Arms

The culture stew of this much-maligned period, the years of drift from west to east, moved further downriver, to the pub where Dan Farson hosted a party at the end of the world. Here was a feverish celebration in keeping with those funny nights out at the Carpenters Arms in Cheshire Street. Everything from Ronnie Kray's ventriloquist act with a midget on his knee to berserk butchery in Shacklewell. An informal knees-up with strict rules: sharp suits, razor-cut barnets, a bit of business. Questionable comedy, a rash of visiting celebrities: mayhem. Dan Farson was the enabler, go-between by appointment to studio tans, to the ring-kissed cardinals of local crime and the court of Francis Bacon. He was also fixer, PR man and location scout for Joan Littlewood's feature film, *Sparrows Can't Sing*. He had them shooting sequences at the mouth of Narrow Street.

Deakin, after his lonely survey of the vanished Chinese quarter of Limehouse, was still close to his old colleague and sparring partner, but this was not his turf. He wanted to travel again, trains, fabulous harbours. He wanted abroad. He wanted sunshine. He wanted Rome. A better class of ruin. At the very end, before Brighton, there were holidays planned in company with Dan.

The Waterman's Arms on Glenaffric Avenue, Isle of Dogs, had been such a seething roaring floor-shuddering success that Farson was comprehensively busted, flush out, and the party with him. He sold up, left London and tried his luck as a writer, a memory man cashing in anecdotes of high times and the dead who are beyond litigation. Seductive fables backed by the documentary evidence of photographs that might have been taken by Deakin on an off day. And righteous files of persons and places: the famous, the infamous, and the fading life of the river. His projected post-expulsion pension was being there, as witness and participant, and having the willpower, when crawling to the bucket, to lift a camera. To secure and preserve the prints. Keep them in another place.

Dan Farson, at a distance, in a property inherited from Negley Farson, his writer father, cooked the story. And Deakin became a major part of it: a character, a minor grotesque, the best sort of pariah. The Soho photographer was a scapegoat trading failure against future market value. While Deakin grumbled in hospital, after having his ribs split and a cancerous lung removed, Farson was in Romania, ostensibly carrying out research into Count Dracula. It was almost like a return to the glory days of television celebrity, the magazine assignments on expenses. He wanted exploitable colour for his biography of Bram Stoker, his granduncle. He was in the wrong place. The real vampires, sex predators, money launderers and property speculators, had followed the Count into downriver London. If all went well, Farson and Deakin, comrades in booze, voyagers in hallucination, would meet for their hard-earned rest and recreation on the island of Poros. Hello sailor!

The Thames cancels more projects than it permits to surface and secure landfall. The Narrow Street incomers of the Sixties faced the same choices as those who came before and after them: they must know when to sell up and return to wherever they came from, taking a grudging profit. Or they could, like Farson, drift further from old centres of wealth and civilisation, and try again.

Dan was sensitive to the shift of tectonic plates. As if, in harvesting the dazzle of the great, he would somehow be tolerated in their company. He took his brief moment of national exposure – well-oiled public conversations, primitive game shows – before, in 1962, trading a measure of inherited liquidity for a failing pub called the Newcastle Arms. He did well to keep it afloat for two years. From the other side of the river, a vantage point in Greenwich, this loomed like a tempting proposition. The dispirited terraces of dockworkers stayed tactfully out of sight. The alignment was perfect: a riverside hostelry at the end of a slipway. An obliging clump of trees topped by the spire of Christ Church. The whole prospect masqueraded as a country village; shore leave for fishermen, smugglers and thirsty tourists.

Flashy renovations were initiated. Farson put in the money. He commissioned a smart architect, Roddy Gradidge. A dividing wall was replaced. There was an upper level for the regulars who would surely appear one day. And the rest tricked out like a Camden Passage boutique, with caryatids, vintage posters, Victorian and Edwardian song sheets, and a murder of blood-red paint. A wet dream of music hall with customised vices. The doors opened at the lunch hour, nobody came. Then, in the evening, the party began.

You can see how it looked by digging out a DVD of *London in the Raw*, a 1964 clubland tasting menu by Arnold L. Miller and Stanley Long. This brisk exercise in cynicism is a flaccid sermon sponsored by the pre-coital weariness of venues set up to be denounced in the voice of Sunday morning journalism. What the film proves, with its *Look at Life* celebration of form over function, is how grim were London's available pleasures. What a penance, for performers and punters alike: old men, tired men, veined and knotted men, suited and chain-smoking, in close proximity with young girls painted and powdered, lacquered and sprayed, frozen in the tedium of witnessing a robotic cabaret of mimed onanism. Or dancing as if they were geriatric carers shaking breath into a succession of living corpses, their silent and sweating benefactors.

The segment shot at the Waterman's Arms, paying its dues to Farson, and offering a brief glimpse at a place of consequence, almost justifies this exploitative travelogue. The atmosphere feels more authentic than the youth club pieties sampled by Tony Richardson and the moralists of the Free Cinema movement in the late Fifties. The pub is so rammed that nobody can get to the bar. The crowd, as witnessed here, are quite different from the stories told in posthumous histories. They are not all slummers and reforgotten faces. They are grafting Islanders, lads from Dagenham, smart Stepney girls. There are hardmen armoured in Italian tailoring. They are generously cologne-splashed and meanly barbered. This is no last-gasp bohemia. There are no duffel coats or sandals, no folk singers. Steady booze, pints and chasers, amphetamines and cigarettes.

Gangsters put in a duty appearance. The old Colony gang – Bacon, Freud, Deakin – show willing and give it a try. Pub acts are introduced by the vivacious Kim Cordell. And complemented by a cameo number from a pregnant Shirley Bassey. Stars pay for free drinks with rictal smiles for the house photographer, a florid tribute in the visitors' book: Tony Bennett, Clint Eastwood, Groucho Marx, Kim Philby, Judy Garland, Trevor Howard. And the old surrealist George Melly, who was always good for a bluesy turn.

Chokingly suited and close shaven, Farson was snapped behind the bar, leaning towards a couple of characters who look like they've come around for protection money. Tutored as a publican by the blues singer Queenie Watts from the Ironbridge, Dan did his best to play host. He basked in the bounce of studio lights, grinned in the teeth of an encroaching nightmare. For these raucous party nights, the resurrection of music hall in its original public house setting, the imported faces enjoyed being a part of the crowd. They clapped Irish baritones and roared at the comic songs of Tommy Pudding with his orthodontically challenged leer and his smirking innuendo: mouth like a man trying to swallow a saucer of bent forks.

It felt as if that group photograph from Charlie Brown's – Farson,

Bacon, Deakin and their docker pals – had been computer-generated into a seething mob of multiples, rebranded and made over by fashionable crimpers with two Christian names. But Deakin was off duty. He was only there for the booze, the bitching and the birching: he took no photographs. Farson bottled the zeitgeist. He had finally cracked it: £3,000 in the hole with his bankers and blood favours owed to the sort of businessmen who charge a Shylock premium. He was in serious hock to brewers who had stitched him up with a punitive contract. Happy days!

It was sneaky how *London in the Raw* cut straight from the Waterman's Arms to another kind of drinking school: methsmen deranged on blue, squatting in rubble, dribbling threats. Arnold L. Miller wanted that Hogarthian contrast, descent of the rake. The implication lurks: Farson and Deakin are one step from the gutter.

They were all in one place at one time, all the faces with files in Secret State basements, all the ones collected by the National Portrait Gallery. All the overlapping half-lives required for a big fat conspiracy. For fiction as psychobiography. Stephen Ward. Guy Burgess. George Raft. Ronnie Kray. Lord Boothby. William Burroughs. Francis Bacon. Film directors. Playwrights. Architects. And Deakin, the man with the camera, does not take a single photograph.

I've always been intrigued by Dan's rapid capitulation and how the whole scene – criminals, showbiz, politicians, hairdressers, music hall comedians, figurative painters – went down with him. Only to resurface, the fortunate few, in future memoirs. How could the comprehensively documented success of the nights at the Waterman's Arms turn, on a beat, into exile from London?

Deakin was right to throw his boxes of negatives under the bed. The risks are too high. Prints demand stories. Roberto Bolaño, talking about a collection of London photographs by his fellow countryman, Sergio Larraín, said: 'The killer sleeps as the victim photographs him.' This sentence, delivered with chilling calm in a throaty whisper, has been haunting me for years. The killer sleeps. The victim takes pictures. And someone is hired to bend the story.

I never knowingly set eyes on Deakin. And whatever I imagined that I knew about him came from the portraits he made of others and the stories told by Farson. By close inspection of the Freud painting. The Soho photographer was dead and buried before I paid him the attention he deserved. It is relatively easy now to manufacture a simulacrum of the man, the pariah. It is impossible to understand the discriminations of solitude, the lingering wounds.

There was a partial solution to the mystery of Farson's disappearance in the first volume of William Feaver's biography of Freud. Feaver traces a line of fate from the publican's rushed sale of Freud's Deakin portrait, outside the reach of the gallery system, in a desperate punt at raising the readies.

'When he went down to Limehouse to reclaim the picture,' Feaver wrote, 'Freud bumped into Teddy Smith. It was a doorstep encounter best avoided. Teddy worked for the Krays as a debt collector. Wrote poems.'

Taking a profitable entertainment venue in the wrong territory comes with certain non-negotiable add-ons. 'Dan Farson had no idea about people at all,' Feaver said. 'The Krays got hold of him and took the pub he ran.' The Twins kept the celebrity publican under observation by way of his drivers. Farson didn't have a car but they supplied him with four nicely appointed chauffeurs.

Feaver develops his metaphor of control and coercion: from East End protection rackets and homoerotic byplay to the rivalry between Bacon and Freud over the use of Deakin's photographs. The power struggle between photography and painting. 'Deakin . . . was acceptable to Bacon because generally he did what he was told. Even his most contrived photographs, such as the one of Dylan Thomas waist deep in a grave and those he took for *Vogue* in 1954 of Bacon stripped to the waist and beset with beef carcasses, were tolerable in that they catered to the sitters' fancies.'

The real Deakin was far out of reach, but I did witness the late Farson, back in Soho, on leave from his Devon retreat, and showing his face: flushed, beet-red, slack-skinned. A portrait sketched in lipstick on a bank robber's nylon mask. Dan swayed, glass in hand, gathering a few acolytes, while he spoke to the dead. He was a presence at Maxim Jakubowski's Charing Cross Road shop, Murder One. He turned out for a book launch, which happened to be a Penguin series of Sherlock Holmes novels with new introductions.

'What you do in the world is a matter of no consequence. The question is, what can you make people believe that you have done.'

Or so I remember. I *saw* Farson, heard him launching into a recycled Deakin anecdote, when a youth in a black vest asked about the story of Henrietta Moraes, up on a table in Ireland, legs spread, no knickers. All wrong: it must have been another gathering in the same shop. With the same groupies. Farson died in 1997. Which does not altogether disqualify him; half the Murder One mob were undecided, hovering between delirium and termination, between Harrow Road and Kensal Green Cemetery. Maybe it was a more suspect publication to which Farson had contributed: *Who Was Jack the Ripper?* That one was back in 1995. Dan was cranking out waxwork conspiracies. 'I believe that as he walked onto the cold void of dawn, satiated yet empty, his brain trembled for a moment and he realised what he had done . . . and then took his own appalled and appalling life.'

I did witness Farson's relatively subdued comeback to a pub from which he had been banned, the French in Dean Street. Among the inebriates and revenants of all generations drifting in to pay their respects at the wake for Robin Cook in 1994, Farson's ravaged features made no special impact. He was far gone and quite at home. It was through Cook, post-mortem, that I grasped how it worked for Farson and Deakin, and how the legend might be fixed.

What purported to be a final interview with Cook (in his 'Derek Raymond' persona) turned up, as a 'loosely inserted' typescript, in a copy I found of his dystopian novel, *A State of Denmark*. 'My waking thought is a stream of figures that I have been adding and subtracting all night in my sleep.'

This mesmerising Cook confession to an unknown interrogator, spilling over from pub to Chinese restaurant, and back to pub, demonstrates an effortless ability to pick up on yarns belonging to other people and to make them his own. That's how he worked the novels, translating days in Soho into dictation, through the hours of darkness, in West Hampstead. In episodes where I *had* been present – such as the shooting of a Channel 4 film at the City Airport in Silvertown – Cook inducted characters he met for the first time into lifetime buddies, nascent hitmen, visionaries. There was an infinitely adaptable Cookian version of the world as a multiverse: new faces could be instantly recognised in places they had never been.

As the interview grinds on, Cook's monologue, prompted by questions which are not recorded, becomes as poetic as *Krapp's Last Tape*, as stone-cold weird as *The Last Words of Dutch Schultz*, as captured by William Burroughs. Like a dying man (which, by then, he was), Cook flashes from adventure to adventure, country to country. He is with Bacon in Tangier. 'So I thought . . . *abroad*, that was the answer . . . Car theft. I did a lot of motors. Smuggling from Gibraltar to Spain . . . Just check with the barman at the Coach and Horses. Bacon was after boys, I was after women. Did some notes for Bruce Bernard, turned into a story. Slid past each other tangentially.'

A lot of slipping and sliding. A great many tangents. Before his liver was shot, and he was given five years by the quack. A generous overestimate, unfortunately.

> Dom Moraes? Still alive? Henrietta, absolute knockout. Johnny Minton . . . Where was I? Cheers. Oh Bacon, that's right. Dan Farson, very nice writer. Waterman's Arms, good god that was a pub! That was sheer mania land. Far as I know, Dan drinks literally anything . . . I've always been a drinker. O god yes. My generation . . . The tricky thing about the liver is that it doesn't hurt, doesn't let you know when it's in distress . . . I turned white like that tablecloth. Five years. Won't get my bus pass . . . Just back from Afghanistan, haven't seen anything quite as bad on the battlefields.

He begins, in this beautiful free-associating ramble, to call up books he read in hospital, at the wheel of the cab, waiting for his customer to emerge from an industrial unit in Lewisham. Books he thinks he wrote. Edmund Wilson. Lorca. *The Monkey Puzzle* by Veronica Hull. *It's A Battlefield* by Graham Greene. 'There was always a punter at Muriel's you could chat up for a gin and tonic ... I wonder what that loo in the Colony Club hasn't seen. It was slightly smaller than Christie's burial cupboard at Rillington Place.'

The ruined Cook faces were fading fast. Already, his references meant nothing to his youthful interrogators. But abroad sounded good. Cook got away when things were catching up with him in the Sixties: Italy, Spain, North Africa, and hard years in France, labouring in a vineyard. Great copy. *Abroad*. Farson gave his passport a good bashing in the television days. He plotted that reconnection with Deakin, a house on the harbour, waiting in Poros. It would be like winding the clock back and falling into a painting by John Craxton.

I wish I had pressed in closer that Soho evening, rather than getting away, as soon as possible, from the Murder One launch – whatever the book in question. Farson was running wild with his grand theory of everything. He yapped about 'the basic slate, the universal hue'. While his own hue lurched with every swallow from purple to grey. 'There is a substance in us that prevails.' He beat his hollow chest. I thought about how interactions between Deakin and the painters who commissioned him bred heresies for future explainers. Lucian, Farson said, was good enough in his pomp to stop time. Good enough, after all those sessions, night into day, cold game and decent wine, door half-open between bathroom and cupboard, to produce portraits worthy of representing the hours of the driven and unyielding life that he had dedicated to them.

But Bacon, whose calculated front was nibbled at by Deakin, a goblin he had summoned to his court, finished up, god help him, iced in mid-performance like a tragic mask. He was paralysed by his failure to exorcise demons raised through the shamanic act of splashing paint on canvas. And the knowledge that he had so nearly touched it, held it. And lost it. The quantum of immortality.

Farson spilled a full glass over a book that a boy was holding out for signature. He steadied himself. In trying to describe the mechanics of that moment, I can almost believe it happened.

ABROAD

Paris to Athens

There is no adequate chronology for the fiction of 'abroad'. Deakin came and went at the whim of unreliable patrons. Before the war and in the immediate aftermath, he applied the same dreams of escape to different cities. There were sudden disappearances and unheralded returns. An empty space at the bar of the Golden Lion. For a time, Soho was like methadone: a substitute for the real thing, Europe by proxy. Ground coffee and garlic bulbs. Cigars and cologne. Chianti and sugared cakes. German newspapers and French films. But it was not enough. Deakin was barred from so many establishments that regulars were never sure when he would manifest, mid-sentence, with the gossip of the night. The man was a recurring nightmare.

Projects were talked up and set aside as soon as interest was expressed. Most of them involved fantasies of cities where the photographer had submerged, dodging assignments and creditors, for a few days or a few months: Paris, Athens, Rome, Tangier. Sullen dawn streets anticipating the next invasion. Tattered posters from disgraced regimes. Archaeological ruins. Cemeteries where women released from unnamed films waited to be noticed on damp tombs. Crowds frozen in prophetic patterns in public squares. Artists striking a pose against more art in white-walled studios. The wealthy, interrupted at table in their palaces, tolerate the temporary intrusion of a person without pedigree. Statues die of boredom in gardens. Statues are lost in sheds. Broken-nosed classical busts in deserted museums: with special reference to stance and musculature. Without means or preordained plan, *what was Deakin chasing?* A different life. A life closer to the version of himself that he kept well hidden from the Colony coterie, the faces that made his reputation. A version he would never adequately inhabit or sustain.

'The future is unavoidable,' Borges wrote, 'but it may not happen.' Deakin's future was already overdrawn. His past, or those snippets we can access from his travel photographs, continues to happen: again and again. Abroad is about experimenting with a new identity by following the example of Patricia Highsmith's character Ripley, and borrowing a pre-used life. Something closer to the status of the painter he had been in the days of leisurely expeditions with Arthur Jeffress. Now Deakin struggled to remember those lies about failing to find tubes of paint on Tahiti and travelling onwards to Fiji, to the New Hebrides; a two-thousand-mile voyage before locating the right Chinese chemist, a phantom out of De Quincey. That Ripley role, amusing a rich patron by playing a part somewhere between protégé and lover, bred valuable resentments. It fired the venom of his true art: revenge.

Arturo in Mexico. If that album can't be found, did it happen? And was he there? In the mountains? He had arrived at that stage of drunkenness where it becomes necessary to shake hands with everyone.

In the spirit of the Thirties – of poets like David Gascoyne, who flitted back and forth between London and Paris, high times and the pinch of poverty – Deakin cultivated his disguise as a pariah figure. He boasted that he preferred to consort with lepers in Cairo than society dowagers in European mansions. In his more Catholic moods, chasing priests in Rome, he saw himself as one of Graham Greene's burnt-out cases. Scabby Deakin. Scobie. Querry. Homonyms. Husks.

Elizabeth Smart flattered the conceit and lavished praise on the prints shown in the *John Deakin's Paris* exhibition of July 1956. She said that they belonged in the company of Rimbaud, Villon and the fellowship of the arches. Deakin had been tramping, she said. He was a solitary pilgrim engaging with other outcasts, wearing holes in his boots as he covered the city, Père Lachaise to Les Halles.

It is not clear how the walks began. The story is that Deakin picked up 'a cheap camera' after a party, took a number of exposures, as much blackmail as future art, lost them and started from there. But there is solid evidence to suggest that he made social contact with the gallerist André Ostier, who introduced him to Christian Bérard, a painter, illustrator and set designer. Deakin caught Bérard leaning from a balcony window in crumpled velour dressing gown, squinting against the morning light. And he is asking, through the muff of his knotted, insect-harbouring beard, what the pesky photographer thinks he's about, wandering abroad before the hour of coffee.

Bérard introduced Deakin to French *Vogue*. And then, by way of Audrey Withers, to the English version. His own life, via opium addiction, ended in 1949. A heart attack on stage. As the dedicatee of his friend Jean Cocteau's film *Orphée*, Bérard was primed to act as conduit to the nightworld on the other side of a gilded mirror. He was the chosen guide through the labyrinth of wartime collaboration, poetry and gay politics. The illustrator knew everybody. Poulenc composed *Stabat Mater* in his memory. And he was the subject of a poem by Gertrude Stein, in which she talked about the 'preamble to restitution'. A restitution Deakin was primed to launch, absorbing Bérard's prompts and keeping a record of the Paris streets to stand alongside Cocteau's film.

It would be too facile to suggest that Deakin's portraits carried the imprint of fate. But the Bérard capture, a man exposed on his balcony, neither inside nor outside, says everything that needs to be known. The open relationship with Boris Kochno of the Ballets Russes. The fashion illustrations for Coco Chanel and Schiaparelli. The designs for Cocteau's *La Belle et la Bête*. The encounter with Deakin and the realisation that this snapshot marked the beginning of the end. For himself, for the milieu, and even for Deakin. The only possible advance in Paris was by absorbing the street plan of the past. Posthumously, Bérard found a place in the collection of the National Portrait Gallery in London. The portrait was taken by Cecil Beaton, not Deakin, and it was accepted in lieu of death duties. A tactfully composed image of a younger man, with moderate beard, in repose, arm stretched out, playing the game.

Deakin enjoyed the company of another guide to the streets, Paul Dieu, 'a threadbare aristocrat with sharp eyes . . . who slept in the gutter with the grace of a Renaissance angel'. Dieu, who obligingly fades from the story after this single act, leads Deakin to Bérard and Michel de Brunhoff at *Vogue*. But none of this name-dropping gossip diminishes what Deakin delivers in his second home, Paris. The city where his dawn wanderings belonged in a respected tradition. And where his pictorial gleanings could have built a bankable reputation. He took magazine portraits of Sartre and Ionesco, but he was never sufficiently embedded in the subsoil to produce anything to equal the fervid intimacy of his portfolio of Soho celebrities.

Fifty-five of Deakin's Paris prints were hung by Bruce Bernard in the gallery space of David Archer's bookshop at 34 Greek Street. In handling them, Bernard responded to their openness and immediacy. Glimpses of one city, with its margins available again after the years of German occupation, were transported to the walls of another grime-encrusted capital still recovering from bombs and fire. The show was praised by Colin MacInnes, who detected strains of 'affection' and 'pity' in Deakin's predatory gaze. Bacon's most visible explainer and intermediary, David Sylvester, supplied a positive review in *The Listener*. Deakin came close, at this point, to securing a reputation as an approved trans-European figure. But high-minded aesthetic tourism remained a jealously preserved privilege of wealth and class. The Sitwells. Oxbridge dilettantes. Vestiges of the grand tour. Deakin didn't have the Latin. Or embossed letters to diplomats and minor aristocrats with whom he'd shared a desk. Snappers were still expected, like Beaton, to play the game and not to relish the retelling of the infamous episode when Bacon catcalled the Cole Porter numbers mangled by Princess Margaret.

Deakin rose early on innocent Paris days when he went out hunting with his camera. When he hunted alone. Prints in the black albums support the selection made for the Archer show. The face of the guilty man, the *flâneur*, is never seen; except as a spectral reflection in frosted windows, where the photographer's looming shape is dark enough to bring out flaws in the glass. There is a clouded membrane, rubbed and smeared, between stalker and public street. The laid-out sequence of the Paris prints confides, through a mass of barely registered detail, the precise itinerary of the epic walks. Nameplates for certain streets offer posthumous surveillance. But they are only admitted when they add exoticism to the casual composition.

Paris flatters the itinerant photographer in ways London never could. Which was one of the difficulties for Deakin. He thrived on resistance. On his status as pariah or outlier. Although the projection of a new life, a new character, is no guarantee of achieved art, there is a genuine and quantifiable achievement in the surviving record of Deakin's Paris portfolio. As the walker tires and lets go of London's conditioned reflexes, the new place begins to reveal itself in new ways. Deakin's manifest *dérives* were made in the period when the Paris Lettrists were defining and testing the philosophical propositions that emerged as psychogeography.

Deakin's natural bias was towards the form of safe surrealism already making an impact in England through magazine journalism and advertising illustrations inspired by émigrés. In our contemporary digital world we are addicted to copying the copyists. And keeping a mobile phone record of the ever-changing tide of graffiti; walls loud with upper-case politics, retrospective subversion, and spray-can auditions for a brilliant career in a Hoxton gallery. In Paris and in London, Deakin was gathering found material for a book without words. Even in 1956 this was a doomed endeavour. The exercise belonged with the time when he first picked up a camera in the 1930s. Romantic storyboards of café life, market life, bars and brothels, were being extracted from a city soon to be lost to invaders. Unauthorised street photography could be punished by imprisonment and execution. Slogan painting carried real danger. Many artists and intellectuals were rounded up for transportation. Others vanished underground. A darkroom of the kind available to Deakin in Malta would be a confession of resistance, a crime.

According to Elizabeth Smart's introduction to the exhibition in David Archer's Greek Street gallery, Deakin sweated and suffered as he tramped. He aligned himself with *clochards*, with the hungry and dispossessed, with the crazy ones. The prints in the black albums flatter that reading. They also confess to sidelong glances, meditative halts, sudden epiphanies that require him to swivel on his heels, to stop and stare directly at some fragment of the city that has caught his camera eye. After a few hours, the instrument dictates the terms.

The most endearing presence burning out from Deakin's Paris pedestrianism is a woman with plaits. She is handsome and androgynous, something like a Native American, a Plains Indian. A circus barker or music hall performer. Deakin is in thrall to the uncanny potential of this transaction. The woman becomes his angel of the city, in just the way that the final plate of Gustave Doré's illustrations for *London: A Pilgrimage*, his 1872 collaboration with William Blanchard Jerrold, shows a 'New Zealander', a tribal figure sitting on a boulder inspecting the apocalyptic ruins of imperial pomp and vanity. The emblematic Paris woman is like Farson's old man in Brick Lane, an inevitability. A collision waiting to happen. A recorded confrontation in which the photographer is of no consequence.

The self-imposed duty of achieving prints worthy of exhibition, significant moments, breaks down into a procession of classified files that could be shuffled in any order. Deakin loves displays of printed matter: *tabac* kiosks, muscle magazines, official notices. He likes random figures in the street, especially geometric groupings offering visible social contrasts:

the squat working woman with a bucket, for example, positioned on the diagonal against a soft-focus Parisienne in a light coat, hovering beside the arches of an arcade. He likes all varieties of accidental surrealism. A stag's great horned head, thrusting out from a ruff of corn sheaves, framed between tall Corinthian columns. A caped boulevardier with his arm resting on the lacrimal punctum of a carnival giant's eye. A graphic invocation of somewhere like Aragon's Parc des Buttes-Chaumont. An empty birdcage big enough for a kettle of vultures. Flea circuses. Sensational film posters, frequently ripped to reveal the numerous layers beneath. Complicated palimpsests of engraved information, ready for Max Ernst. Voyeuristic séances. A woman inside a bistro applying make-up, as witnessed through a polished window reflecting lime trees and the scattered action of the street. Evidence for his own prosecution. Evidence of his exclusion from the crowd.

In this entire exercise, Deakin remains the elective pariah: he does not step inside. He is a phantom of the camera. An unpaid spy. A recorder of brick courses and decorative grilles. Mannequins and window displays. Jumbles of amatory initials carved in plaster or stone. Overloaded bookshops and *bibliothèques* with flapping postcards and sepia portraits of dead writers. Political and racist interventions treated as auditioning artworks. Street children posed against distressed walls and dark metal doors. The borrowed sentiment of boneless Simenon drinkers slumped on hard benches, on cobbles by the Seine. Images made from memory of images.

Neighbourhoods. Courtyards. Other walkers paused to inspect other photographs. That man in the black beret mesmerised by a grid of exotic dancers in Pigalle. The dusty connoisseur, in homburg, funeral coat and rolled umbrella, stroking his chin while he contemplates an arrangement of art reproductions.

DÉFENSE D'AFFICHER.

Regiments of engaged couples, rosaries of public affection, displayed at a kiosk. Nuns, eyes averted, passing a bar. A sister of mercy pushing a market trolley across the street from Café de Flore. Père Lachaise with its own brand of baroque necro-surrealism: arms reaching out of tombs;

sculpted lovers embracing, chatting again, after waking from death's brief sleep.

Catacombs. Manhole covers. Fortune tellers. Flea markets. Carts and carriers.

There is such *energy* in Deakin's engagement. The walks made, in order to gather material suitable for exhibition or publication, become more than themselves. The photographer rubs his cheek against the fabric of the city. He celebrates and he compiles. He is poet and actuary. Paris is the life he has chosen not to live. A way of working and walking that could never be translated into London. In Soho, he staggered home from bars and clubs. He knew the gatekeepers and the shopkeepers, villains and slummers. He had his own space, his studio. In Paris, he is out on the street, in motion. His captures are a diary of lostness, like the file cards of Walter Benjamin. Notes and prompts for a book with no end and infinite potential.

The coded marks on Paris walls are a chapter all to themselves: scars, symbols, occult instructions. Published timetables for buses become prophetic charts diagnosing the health of the city. A panel of brass entry bells has been framed like a display of curated nipples. Invocations everywhere of Breton and Duchamp. Exploded alphabets. *Calligrammes* of Apollinaire resurrected from chalked graffiti. (Oliver Bernard, brother of Bruce, subject of a brooding Deakin portrait, translated and introduced Apollinaire's *Selected Poems* for Penguin. He dedicated the book to other Deakin faces, the two Roberts, Colquhoun and MacBryde. Deakin's Paris was a bridge between cultures, a mingling of ghosts and influences.)

PAIX EN ALGÉRIE. CHANTIER INTERDIT AU PUBLIC. VIVE LE ROI.

Rust-locked rivets. Diamond-pattern tiles. The miraculous psycho-pathology of lichen dressings. SAINT MICHEL ASCENSEUR. MAGGIE. MONIQUE. TINY BOOBS. MIKE. JERRY. Words are prison-gouged with blunt nails, with stolen kitchen knives. VIVE FLN.

And then Deakin, coming out of reverie, back to art, collects a free exhibition of anonymous Art Brut figuration; a pantheon of Oceanic masks, voodoo gods, and electro-convulsive ideograms. His photographs try to paraphrase the visionary madness of Artaud.

The spittle of the rasp . . . The cinder of the coal without teeth . . . Bardo is the pang of death into which the self falls with a splash, and there is in electric shock a splash state through which every traumatised person passes . . . A white page to separate the text of the book, which is finished, from all the swarming of Bardo.

But Deakin, alone, on the tramp, does not qualify for the benediction of Rodez, for drugs and lightning shocks, for heretical sainthood. He remains on the wrong side of the wall, the wrong side of history. He can't shake free from stone-cold sanity. From London. He is photographed by Harry Diamond and Dan Farson, not Dreyer and Abel Gance. He does not hear the confession of the martyred Joan, as played by Falconetti, before burning.

Outlines of chthonic entities crouch in caves without roofs. Owl-headed angels. Frenetic copulation with beasts. Hydrocephalic monsters. Swirling female spirits escaping from a swamp of scratched crosses. Edible ghosts. Egyptian eyes. Third Eyes. Eyes in bottles. Snakes emerging from mouths. Mediterranean yachts. Flags. Numbers. Letters. None of it makes sense. Nothing to explain, everything to be logged and abandoned.

John Deakin is released from his demons. John Deakin is walking with Atget, with Brassaï and Cartier-Bresson. John Deakin is nominating fifty-five items from so many possibles, to arrange on the walls of David Archer's Parton Gallery. He is leading the much shorter walk that visitors to Greek Street will have to make as they perambulate, discussing the romance of a fabulous transit, Paris into London. Meticulous captures captured and given away.

The exhibition was a critical success, it was talked about. And followed, two months later, by *John Deakin's Rome*. The photographer enjoyed his time in Italy. He could have stayed and let our cold damp island become the new abroad. He could have moved on from his parasitical reliance on the circle around Francis Bacon. As with Paris, Deakin knew Rome from his wanderings with Arthur Jeffress in the 1930s and his time with the military in the war. After being let go by *Vogue* for the second (and final) time, he settled in the via dei Greci. For the Parton Gallery exhibition, he drew on all those experiences, as well as a commission to illustrate Christopher Kininmonth's travel book *Rome Alive* (1951).

The Roman photographs, made with a square-format Rolleiflex, employed the tried and tested psychogeographic methods developed in Deakin's exploration of Paris. In Rome there were more priests and many more nuns. He tracked them with the relish of Fellini. The city, with its immortal light, felt more like a fashion show. It was so confident in its glories, its bloody legends, and quite indifferent to the presence of the migrant photographer. The journeyman. Outsider.

Popes replace cinema stars on the postcards. There are the same references to process: soldiers watching a street photographer. While Deakin watches them. More cellars, catacombs, ruins. More street kids. Classical statues instead of the wax mannequins of Paris. Rome feels like a neo-realist project that never quite took fire. Deakin seems to be the inspiration for Colin MacInnes in *Absolute Beginners*. 'So there was I, in fact, crossing it in my new Roman suit . . . And around my neck hung my Rolleiflex, which I always keep at the ready, night and day, because you never know, a disaster might occur.'

It never did. No eruptions, no plagues. No visitations from patronising demons and kiss-curl incubi. And without them, and without the blessing of madness, Deakin was obliged to ship out. Athens, as represented in the black albums, is a record of inauthentic tourism. Of hanging around waiting for an invitation to the islands. Deakin gathered his prints into folders of acceptable categories: walls, windows, priests, sailors, sculpture, ruined temples. With the occasional artist portrait. With groups of unexplained males lurking with intent on stone stairs. He encountered Giannis Moralis, a celebrated member of the brotherhood known as 'The Thirties' Generation'. Painters, poets, writers and intellectuals. Men. Always men. Athenian light is seductive. Clarity of outline is extreme.

The Deakin prints reference a man on the prowl. Greece is a good place for a holiday. For putting meat on stories of Lucian Freud and John Craxton in their youth, behaving badly together on a garrisoned island. Sharing a room, incubating future rivalry. Greece is time out. Athens, for Deakin, is not much more than a parade of handsome soldier boys in costume.

I show the relevant Athens albums to a contemporary Greek photographer, Effie Paleologou. Effie spent much of her youth in the family home on Poros: the house on the harbour where Freud stayed with Craxton. Where Patrick Leigh Fermor and Margot Fonteyn, Henry Miller and Lawrence Durrell paid their respects. Later, Effie lived with her mother and sister in an Athens apartment.

She looks very closely at the prints made from Deakin's originals. She spends an afternoon with the albums. She relays to me her amused sense of this man, as a visitor, making all the obvious moves, seeing the obvious people. She tracks his footsteps and says that he did not stay long enough in Athens to break through to a deeper engagement. There are more human presences than he allows in the Paris compositions. The story comes indoors. It is more social. Men gather, where no women are permitted, at round tables in high-ceilinged restaurants, in tavernas and bars. The crisp uniforms of the military replace the black of the Roman nuns.

Paleologou, escaping the constricted life, her always-watched existence on Poros, began a lifelong photographic project in Athens: a project of unbelonging, making art from the places to which she was attracted, but in which she was never quite able to settle. There is a city that is all cities, Effie believed. A city of colours and contrasts where we are doomed to be 'homeless at home'. Homeric wanderers, in a fugue or dream, return as dislocated strangers. They yearn for a past that never happened, for a redacted future. For trying yet again to map the precise limits of the topography of alienation.

Looking at prints from Paleologou's Athens, and how they bleed quite seamlessly into an exile's London, I appreciate the chasm between Deakin's liberated saunter, the sexual permissions of being 'abroad', and

Effie's exacting solitude. She is a woman alone, at night, walking fast, hugging walls and perimeter fences; her weaponised camera protects her, like a charm, from the deepest fears. She is not complicit at any level with journalism. She is a pilgrim who understands that *making* a photograph might also be the unmaking of the thing it labours to represent.

Deakin is tolerated wherever he goes, but he is always the unwelcome guest, the thirsty supplicant. He depends on his contacts, his patrons. For Paleologou, home is the other place. The country of memory. She predicts a universal digital metropolis in which the standard cultural markers promoted by Deakin are already chipped and debased. Swamped in neon. Wrapped in empty hoardings.

There are many cities in Deakin's albums. He doesn't belong in any of them. He doesn't kill or steal or rage. The graphic record he has left behind is the fiction of a man in perpetual transit. A man without family or significant attachments. He is free to make his fugitive escape, for a few weeks, from the claustrophobic choke of Soho and the Colony Room, but he always creeps back before anyone notices that he has gone anywhere further than the Gents.

Continued attendance at the court of Bacon, in the spin of later years, cancers blooming in a carcinogenic haze, offers diminishing returns. Life does not collude with the Deakin portraits that represent it. The ritual of photography implies stasis. For subject and perpetrator. The favoured vehicles for Effie Paleologou are stalled buses and missed trains. There are contrails from doomed aircraft in a lowering sky. Streaks of dazzling pollution advertise the flux of unceasing commuters, rushing between nowhere and nowhere.

Julio Cortázar ends a memoir of Greece written in Paris with a bus and a story borrowed from someone else: 'The ones I sought and knew in Athens no longer exist for me, they have been dislodged, disproved by these phantasms that are stronger than the world they invent only to destroy in the end, in the false citadel of memory.'

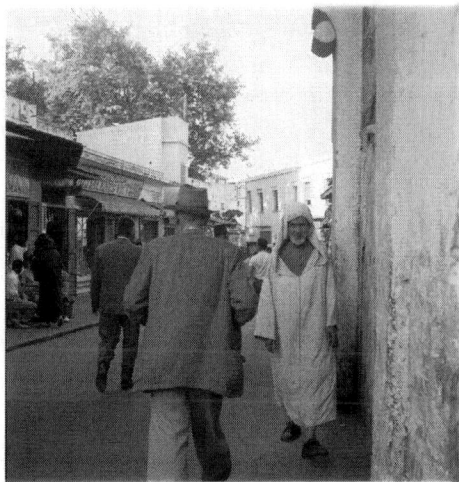

Interzone Tangier

I was stopped in my shuffling of the Deakin prints by that back view, the mark snagged somewhere in the Socco Chico, in the medina quarter of Tangier: the scurrying and furtive man in a hat, the one who was not William Burroughs. *El hombre invisible.* Shape-shifter. Alien. Addict. Author. The Deakin sneak-shot looked so much like Burroughs, in his spectral photo-negative persona, that I had to check my impressions with two Burroughs scholars, his biographer Barry Miles and the publisher/ collector Jim Pennington. What hooked me, beyond legends of spirit doubles, junk doppelgängers, surgical clones produced by Dr Benway – and replicants hauled by junk fever into an independent existence – was the walkabout *reality* of this North African set as recorded and filed by John Deakin.

After living for so many months with the seventeen black albums, I concluded that Deakin, like Burroughs, worked to establish a series of psychogeographical and psychosexual locations: Soho, Wapping, Malta, Mexico, Brighton. And Tangier. Game reserves. Cruising grounds. Once the backdrop is comprehensively mapped – smells, tastes, action – fully fledged characters will emerge from the developing fluid. They will be born to flight, ready to walk away, as fast and as far as possible, from the clutch of their putative 'creators'.

You can't photograph ghosts. But you are free to try. Deakin's Tangier was a spirit trap to position alongside his translation of Paris. Beyond the standard cast of hooded Kasbah figures, street traders, suspects in European tailoring, identifiable human personalities with passports and histories were required. The Beat Generation, fervent tourists and 'lonesome travellers', felt a compulsion to photograph each other at every pit stop. Burroughs plastered the walls of his rented cave, Dutch Tony's flop, with taped grids of snapshots. Friends, lovers, potential sets. Image dictates script. In his reliance on the temporal permeability of postcards, he followed the practice of Francis Bacon. The two men got along pretty well, after their fashion. The quiet American trust fund oddball and the risk-everything gambler, the disappointed Soho masochist. Hiding out in London, taking Dr Dent's apomorphine cure, Burroughs never found his ideal bar. He went to the Colony Room with Bacon, but it was much too tight a fit. It was too self-conscious in its watch-the-door decadence. Bill liked to have clear space in which to sit down. With close acquaintances. Watching the moves, spinning tales. He liked the Café Central in Tangier. 'His world model,' wrote James Grauerholz, editor and keeper of the Burroughs legend, 'is that of an indeterminate universe of endless permutation and recombination.'

Tangier was prime interspecies slippage, it was where substantial characters turned up on the wrong stages, like some cynical superhero branding exercise by DC Comics. You don't want to come across Bradley Martin being channelled by Ronnie and Reggie Kray. They were all there, the faces of the moment, but Deakin did not confirm it in his albums. He was too busy cultivating his own form of anonymity: a Burroughs centipede too jaded to find an obliging host. He hung on the wire like forgotten laundry.

Ronnie Kray bought flowers by the cart when he was socialising. He called on Bacon. They dined together. Bacon offered Ron a painting; he wouldn't touch it. It was like being gifted a free dose of the clap. Monstrous things with no sense of Bethnal Green decorum. And, in the worst of his dry-retch psychotic night sweats, when the slithering messengers of hell called, much too close to home. Later, when he heard what these terrible visions were fetching, Ron changed his mind. In the leisured asylum years, in Broadmoor, he produced his own poems and therapeutic artworks. They had no technical merit, but enjoyed a certain prestige in the burgeoning true crime heritage market. He returned the favour and sent prime madhouse samples to Bacon.

At that time, 1957, when Bacon tried the life for fourteen months, and then again for a few years into the Sixties, Tangier was the holding pen of convenience for male sex tourists, car smugglers, kief smokers, remittance men, society queens and elective exiles of every stripe. It was *Casablanca* by the Hungarian in Hollywood, Michael Curtiz, lifted out of the studio and dropped into a terminal café: Dean's Bar instead of Rick's, Burroughs for Bogart. And Bacon's violent lover, Peter Lacy, tinkling the ivories instead of Sam, but not always capable of playing it for the first time, let alone again.

Tangier, according to Burroughs, had good restaurants with modest prices, cheap rooms and even houses to rent. Deakin's obsessive record of movement against and across wildly ecumenical architecture, his eye for the salient detail, mirrored the brief descriptive text Burroughs published as 'International Zone'. The psychic divination of the Burroughs method for fixing a map is duplicated in Deakin's peripatetic captures. His illustrations for the unwritten black book. They navigated by dark stars.

'After four months, I still find my way in the Medina by a system of moving from one landmark to another,' Burroughs wrote. 'The smell is almost incredible, and it is difficult to identify all the ingredients. Hashish, seared meat and sewage are well represented. You see filth, poverty, disease, all endured with a curiously apathetic indifference.'

This was the famed Interzone, conquered, reconquered, but never submitting: a city without a nation. The comfortable vagueness over passports and regulations was the big attraction. Time was smoke. They were here, the future ghosts (and their ghostwriters); passing through, even when release was impossible. Tennessee Williams and Kenneth Williams. Truman Capote and Joe Orton. And up in the mountains, in their palaces: David Herbert, second son of the Earl of Pembroke, and Barbara Hutton, second wife of Cary Grant. Paul Bowles and Jane Bowles. In theoretical residence. With their local protégés. Not quite well, under attack from sorcery, obliged to entertain all comers. Hacks. Trust fund dopers. Memoir pimps. A countercultural rite of passage. William Burroughs and Brion Gysin.

Many of the temporary *colons* met with indifference, if not active dislike, from the earlier settlers. Over time, they subsided into shows of intimacy or even, as with Burroughs and Gysin, genuine friendship. They made the best of being suspended in the same purgatory. Robin Cook checked in, after his smuggling runs from Gibraltar, and polished stories of Francis Bacon and Peter Lacy for future interviews. He said that everybody told Lacy that he should have been a pianist. 'With the difference that he was one.'

From the overlapping and contradictory accounts in the biographies of the writers, painters and retired criminals who lived in the zone, or made repeated visits, Tangier emerges as a secular monastery or brothel for believers of no faith, a cold-turkey gentleman's club. It handed out faked gold membership cards to all the characters from all the books and papers that I sampled by way of research. The Socco Chico was like being permanently trapped, glass half-raised, in one of those seductive Michael Andrews group paintings, *The Colony Room* and *The Deer Park*.

It was inevitable, given their shared interests, their impulsive migrations, that Bacon and Burroughs would chum up: the two most provocative conversationalists on a landlocked ocean voyage. Bacon couldn't endure boredom: he required constant alarms, violence (under coercion) in his lovers. Bruises like a sunrise by Monet. A fresh tooth in the butter. He also liked clean linen, decent table manners, and properties in which he could talk about the potential for getting himself murdered. Burroughs took intravenous ennui as his special inheritance: he measured out his life in cooking spoons. Boredom was his element. He absorbed it through his gills. And made the grey fog of his invented worlds shine like silver. He lived in squalor and regarded it as having no importance, when set against the hunger to transcribe scripts dictated by merciless Mayan gods. It was Bacon who brought Burroughs downriver: to Limehouse and Poplar, queer bars, Chinatown. He ferried him to the Waterman's Arms, Dan Farson's own version of the Interzone. Here was Tangier's Café Central translated into the Isle of Dogs.

'Where's Philby?'

Where indeed? Where's Ron? Where's Tony Snowdon? Terry Southern? Where's Judy Garland? Hip to microclimate, Bacon asked Burroughs the right question. Out loud. Under an imaginary spotlight. With an asthmatic wheeze and a death rattle in the throat, he was performing for his coterie and a mob of river-rat inebriates innocent of his fame. Death wish. And death was off duty. Out of town. The great painter tried his voluble best to make public the identity of the fourth man in the Philby case. He trilled out, for the benefit of the party crowd, the whole ongoing conspiracy of establishment spooks, drinkers and lovers. And traitors. The soundtrack in Farson's convivial pub was a paranoid Burroughs cut-up with music hall songs and bawdy comics. The grey man made mental notes.

Bill registered Tangier and the short crossing to Spain by way of Graham Greene and Joseph Conrad. Bacon quoted, with appropriate gestures, from Greek tragedy, from the lucid smog of Eliot's breakdown. Robin Cook, on the night shift as a minicabber, used the prick of a sharp blade in the back of his neck as a memory prompt: he listened to the chat of punters he was running out east. He finessed their slurred monologues into bleak noir fictions.

At the lock-in on the Isle of Dogs, that 'elegant-looking middle-aged chap in a blazer and dark glasses' is Stephen Ward. Not yet dead or not quite. Or back from the dead. Michael Peppiatt, in his memoir,

Francis Bacon in Your Blood, describes his first run to the Waterman's Arms. He cabbed out from Soho with Bacon and Deakin. This party is infinitely transferrable. It will reconvene in Tangier. Someone asks Peppiatt, the fresh-faced Cambridge ingénue, if he would like to go on to another party, where he will have to stand naked and be paid a guinea a stroke to be whipped. The suited criminals, the obligated old bill, the bribed journalists, the honest villains, the bent spies, and the resurrected nut-brown entertainers: they are all there. All primed to take a strategic break in the Kasbah. That is, the ones who are not already doomed, not going down, taking a scapegoat's fall: prison, madhouse, suicide.

News of the World. Flashbulbs. Barbiturates. Deakin has covered the entire cast list. He's bagged the troop in their studios and on the street. He has kicked them under the bed. The caravan lurches towards Brighton. Endgame. While Deakin glories in his difference, his solitude. The others knew he was there, wanted him there: his rancid suits, his sandpaper tongue. No need to ask where Deakin was. Just where you didn't need him. Stirring. Snapping. They did not appreciate that, like them, he was on a quest. They thought he was the odd man out, but all the time he was nailing his own gallery of freaks. 'Pariahs adorned the walk,' he said when he got back to the hotel. Unbelled, the company of lepers drew him on.

Cook processed Bacon. He remembered and improved. 'Rubicund and definitely looked like an Englishman, except that I thought his eyes probed a little too far; further, in fact, than was good for them. He had a bottle of champagne beside him and was covered in splashes of paint.' When Cook used the word 'definitely', it was a poker player's tell. You knew he was winding back the material he thought you wanted to hear. He was a very generous interviewee, when someone was buying the drinks. He'd give you the complete history of a total stranger he met for the first time, that morning, in the Coach and Horses. For operators like Cook, trawling for bankable material, the dormant criminality of Tangier was a major attraction. The criminality of the Thames foreshore was lost in the past or hopelessly reputation-washed by offshore money launderers, part-time politicians and have-yacht oligarchs. He couldn't compete.

Bacon described Tangier as 'Muriel's club, on a large scale'. But there was also an embedded diaspora of international villains: semi-retired professionals from the Midlands and triple-agent safeblowers left over from various wars. The canny Soho face Billy Hill had come ashore, having escaped England unscathed, with biography intact. Bacon relished the atmosphere. He liked to imagine pleasurable retribution at the fists and belt of some obliging heavy: reality was less inviting. Hair in a boot-blacked helmet, Dalston-styled suit straining around thick shoulders, Ronnie Kray was an ideal (but never broached) model for one of the painter's sinister businessmen, pushing through drapes into the padded throne room.

According to Peppiatt, the Welsh actor/producer Stanley Baker – who made his reputation playing hardmen on both sides of the law, notably in Joseph Losey's prison drama, *The Criminal* – brought the Krays round to Bacon's gaff in Tangier. Baker enjoyed the West End clubland scene. He was a frequently photographed associate of Billy Hill and a business partner of Charlie Richardson in mining enterprises in South Africa. Peppiatt tries to untangle a labyrinthine narrative around the buying, selling and stealing of Bacon paintings. The point being that Bacon was attracted to the 'mad one', Ronnie; while Ronnie was attracted to a quick profit through flogging work he considered to be the kind of rubbish that solicited an immediate exorcism from the friendly local priest. From Broadmoor, he tried to put Bacon right, by sending him improving examples of his own oeuvre: 'soft landscapes with little cottages'.

Gangland memoirs are often concentrated around group photographs. But nobody remembers the name of the photographer. These men never put in an invoice. Criminals, in their over-tailored freemasonry, having a few drinks after a result, wanted evidence of access to show-biz royalty; to movie stars like George Raft, on whom they based the classic Bethnal Green Look. And an actor like Baker who had no objection to confirming his masculinity by getting a camelhair arm around the muddied shoulders of Sunday footballers, good Soho chaps like Frankie

Fraser. He was willing to pay his respects to the fellowship by donating a competitive wreath at the solemn interment of 'Italian' Albert Dimes.

The Beats, wrangled by Allen Ginsberg, their unofficial PR man and editor, behaved much like the London villains. They understood the value of a good group snapshot. But the model was not the night out at Winston's or the Kentucky Club. Ginsberg had studied the manipulations of the modernist canon, how collaborators massed around Wilfred Scawen Blunt, Ezra Pound and W. B. Yeats for an embarrassed garden encounter: thereby securing their own legacy. When it came to Tangier, Ginsberg was eager to assemble the established colonists alongside Beat tourists: Burroughs, Kerouac, Corso, Paul Bowles, Alan Ansen, Peter Orlovsky. The main shots were taken by Burroughs, for whom the camera was a notebook, and by Ginsberg himself. But the identity of the person charged with making the image was of no particular relevance. What mattered was the pictorial evidence: names, place, date. If there was no camera available, they squeezed into a photo kiosk with a ruffled curtain. In 1970 Ginsberg published *Scenes Along the Road: Photographs of the Desolation Angels, 1944–1960*. Niceties of framing and focus were not required. This was the true history of our gang.

Jack Kerouac, coming ashore from a Yugoslavian freighter, was photographed by Burroughs. He is wearing the oversize Irish cap that later turns up on the man himself, at the beach, now caught by Kerouac. Other Tangier frolics are recorded by Ginsberg. And there is a group portrait in the garden at Villa Muniria. Burroughs, in what looks very much like the telltale hat from the Deakin Socco Chico capture, has his finger on the shutter of his weaponised camera. Paul Bowles, in lightweight suit and striped tie, is the only one sitting on the floor. Kerouac is not there. He stands apart, a solo headshot taken by Burroughs, in the same grounds. He is lost: suspended, as he says, between 'lasciviousness, solipsism, self-indulgence, bullfights, drugs'. His tragic eyes are slits of pain, enduring a cruel exchange.

Good photographers hovered around the Beats, keeping the sub-culture diary: Robert Frank, Fred McDarrah. But there was no Beat equivalent for John Deakin, portraitist and pariah, always there or thereabouts, making mischief, abetting the art. On his return to the States, after years of travelling and seeking in Latin America, Japan, India, Europe, Ginsberg decided to organise a photographic collection for his archive. He gravitated towards a more considered form of portraiture with Robert Frank as his inspiration and mentor.

Allen Ginsberg Photographs, published in 1990, and printed in Japan, included reproduced holograph texts by the poet. This was the kind of book Deakin was never able to deliver. His Soho portraits are unadorned, bereft of facts or diary retrievals. The American poet's coffee-table production arrived with a brief justification: 'In recent years, Ginsberg has begun to catalogue and print his photographs, and to continue their visual history with a new series of portraits. Beneath each photograph the poet writes of remembered circumstances.'

'Allen always did possess a camera,' Corso recalled. 'What a foreseer he . . . At times a photographic sense caused me to suspect behind the faces the masks beneath them, seeing in my fellow mates a kind of hidden knowingness.'

In the Tangier Interzone, there was time for photography. For talking through the night. For the group editing of improvised chunks of William Burroughs prose. 'Routines' evolved, with the secretarial help of Ginsberg and Kerouac, into *The Naked Lunch*.

In a grey homburg hat, like his mysterious spirit double in the Deakin photograph, Burroughs poses for a wanted portrait by the garden wall of Villa Muniria, foreseeing botched Hollywood films.

Ginsberg challenges: 'Who are you an agent for?'

Frames of film tear in the gate. They flare and burn. Timothy Leary visits the set. 'We took psilocybin, Bill shut himself inside his gate . . . allergic, paranoid season.' Paul Bowles is caught, on the floor again, preparing mint tea. The group photograph in the garden at Villa Muniria, the equivalent of Deakin's Soho painters faking their Wheeler's lunch, is freighted by Ginsberg's recall. 'Burroughs thoughtful with hat to shade Mediterranean sun and camera . . . Paul Bowles squinting . . . all assembled outside Bill's single room, my Kodak Retina in Michael Portman's hands.'

Mikey Portman! His moment of fame forgotten by all. Getting to click the shutter because he isn't needed in the shot. Mikey was a Burroughs acolyte from a wealthy, landowning English family. The Burroughs biographer Barry Miles summarises him as: 'very selfish, greedy, and weak . . . He had never known what it was like to *do* anything.' Mikey was swept along towards destruction on a substantial trust fund. Ginsberg includes a sulky portrait of Portman in his book, cowlick and Mae West lips. 'Dorian Gray youth, he died in middle-age, alcohol and other dissipations.' Portman fades from the record. The characters who made it into the photograph in the garden at Villa Muniria, for which he was technically responsible, live on in glory. In archives and memoirs, they are ageless; still narrowing their eyes against the Mediterranean glare. The painters faking it in Wheeler's, shunted around by Deakin, define an era.

Desire lines tangle and knot. Bacon is fascinated by the Point Omega of suspended consciousness. He relishes the existential mastery of the abyss he locates in the conversation of Burroughs. Ginsberg, in his turn, is wowed by Bacon's savagery. He reports that the artist 'likes to be whipped and paints mad gorillas in grey hotel rooms'. Meeting Bacon in Tangier was like being granted access to a resuscitated Hieronymus Bosch hip to contemporary sexual mores. At which point, what actually happened in Tangier dissolves into stories that improve in every telling. What is sure is that Ginsberg offered himself as the model for a 'big pornographic picture', to be made while he was in rapturous congress with his lover, Peter Orlovsky. Respecting the way Bacon chose to work in solitude, he suggested that a photographer witness the performance. And pass the sequence on to the painter. The obvious man for the task, he had considerable form, was Deakin. And Deakin was in town. Such a session might have its appeal, in secondary rights, when Deakin flogged postcards back in London. Bacon told Peppiatt that Ginsberg presented him with a pack of photographs, the act thoroughly documented.

'The lover wasn't very interesting,' Bacon said, 'but there was something about this striped mattress and the way it spilled over the metal spindles that was so poignant and despairing that I've kept the photos of the bed and used them ever since.'

Photographer unknown. Lover inadequate. Bed immortal. The facilitator *might* have been Deakin. And if not, the mattress takes its place with other soiled and indented bedding ordered up by Bacon. In the pantheon of reclining figures, Henrietta Moraes is combined with Lucian Freud and now with Ginsberg. And the poet is assured of his position in the smear-and-splash tapestry of time.

There is official approval for the intimate connection between photo session and the resulting painting. In Martin Harrison's *Catalogue Raisonné* for Bacon, Volume III (1958–71), *Three Studies for a Crucifixion* is described as 'pivotal if not fully resolved'. It features a central panel of ripped and razor-scraped pink flesh and a snarling animal overbite. A soft skull disintegrates over a white pillow. The striped mattress and the metal spindles are lovingly rendered. Harrison was told by the critic John Richardson that the panel was based 'on a nude photograph of an American poet on a folding bed ... This was probably Allen Ginsberg, with whom Bacon had socialised in Tangier.'

Personal references behind his paintings are anathema to Bacon. The figure in the 1962 triptych both is and is not Ginsberg. Identification might be of interest to cultural historians; to Bacon it is an unnecessary distraction. The photographed mattress accepts many more couplings, many cannibal feasts and interspecies rapes. Ravished bedding is frequently associated with the figure of Henrietta Moraes, as supplied by Deakin. A naked woman punctured by the hypodermic syringe that Harrison associates with Bacon's first reading of the Olympia Press *Naked Lunch*.

The Bacon paintings that stayed with me from the period of the Tate retrospective in 1962, beyond the van Gogh series, were the ones that involved aspects of scorched Mediterranean littoral, from France and Africa. Now, with the retrospective editing in which we are free to indulge, I place the coupled figures on the mattress alongside the gestural sweeps and swerves of Bacon's attempt to paint *Landscape near Malaba-*

ta, Tangier (1963). Harrison calls up the spirit of Peter Lacy, a casualty of Tangier's narcotic indolence: the heat, the light, the vortices of hot, sand-heavy wind. He sees this painting as a lover's obituary wrenched from a specific place.

Deakin's Tangier file is substantial and militates against the brisk character assassination by Dan Farson in his magazine sketch 'An Insult in the Kasbah'. With humour and indulgence, Farson presents Deakin as a man in chaos, a parasite. The duplicitous journalist offers himself as a mere reporter. Without digressions, he tells the story. There is a jolly on offer and, obliging as ever, Deakin gets himself on the plane. He doesn't have a specific role, he's a minor court character: he's with Farson. Paw out for drink and ticket.

> 'We flew with Lady Rose MacLaren to Tangier where she was staying with her cousin, David Herbert. He met us at the airport and within ten minutes I was charging into the Atlantic surf at Robinson's Beach, followed by lunch in the simple open-air restaurant nearby, swilled down with quantities of chilled white wine.' The parties, the social visits and the Arab boys, would come later.

Deakin announces: 'This is my sort of life. *I* can understand it.' A sybarite, one of nature's aristocrats, he is returning to the comfortable existence he led with Arthur Jeffress. Sleeves of his white shirt rolled tight over the muscles he didn't have. Eyes shut. Lolling back. The smirk of contentment. His season as an ungrateful young artist, not painting, posing as some sort of Tennessee Williams rent-boy companion. *Sweet Bird of Youth*. The clarity of light in Tangier invoked days with the 8th Army in North Africa. Deakin survived the war, he thrived. He honed his craft as a photographer. He backed into a successful career. After the war, Jeffress killed his allowance. Deakin went to work, he grafted (after his own fashion). In Tangier, he was given a hotel room at the heart of the scene. Close to the cafés, close to the action. He declined to join Farson in his borrowed villa. 'I like to be in the thick of things, kiddo.'

But it's not true. Listen to the dead. If you can still talk, you lie. Evidence in the black album refutes Farson's slanted sketch: Deakin as dilettante, tolerated pariah trading an acid tongue for patronising hospitality. A dog of peace, a cur. Tongue out for any crusted fundament. Invigilator of nates. The album tells another story. Deakin walked. He watched. He waited. Farson's slim 'Kasbah' prose becomes a thick file of Deakin photographs; considered prints fit to exhibit alongside previous investigations in Paris, Rome, Athens, London. It doesn't matter how he got there, or how he behaved: he authored a mesmerising pictorial record. He left illustrations for the image-vine of William Burroughs, for Dan Farson's serpent strike, his celebrity gossip. And for this late and unreliable psychobiographical survey.

Darkly masked women on gravity-defying ledges outside padlocked and prison-grilled shops. 7 Up signs framed in a screeching thicket of language panels: French, Spanish, Arabic, American. Political hoardings peeling back to reveal the word GOYA. Street surveillance from café tables in Socco Chico. Children with punitive ice creams. Encounters between businessmen in European suits and gesturing accomplices in djellaba and fez. Mountain women. Women against barbed-wired walls on shadowed steps. Blocks of anonymous flats hoarding their secrets.

CAFÉ ARABE. MISSION OF CALIFORNIA.

A lone bicycle, unsecured, stashed on the kerb. Drinkers of mint tea regarding the camera with undeceived tolerance. A crowd of men, waiting for a work bus, sitting in the dirt outside a fortress building patched with film posters. And later, perhaps on Deakin's route back to the hotel, the same building, looking very different now, a miniature castle in a street of sheds. The men are gone, a miscellaneous woman is passing. A young girl, arms folded, endures under a film poster, in the shade of a lighting pole. Tangier, unlike Deakin's Poplar, is an occupied city, active in labour and leisure.

Deakin walks: out from the medina, out through warren estates to the secured walls and the invisibly tended status gardens of embassies and government offices. Women wait for buses. Overloaded donkeys wait with them. Deakin's tourism is persistent and persuasive. There are balconies, fruit sellers, and stalls trading franchised Coca-Cola. There is a profound lethargy: human hives, at a distance from a walled city with ancient towers, waiting. Watching.

Will you walk home and sleep safe among your fetishes, your prints? Is it already too late? *A la fin tu es las de ce monde ancien.*

Arches. Alleyways. The purity of light reminds Deakin of Malta. There are single shots, painstakingly composed, worthy of being removed from the flow, this crass cross-town pedestrianism, to stand alone. But that is not what the Tangier collection is about. It is about keeping well away from patrons, tramping miles until the zone lets him in on its mysteries. Lets him settle on his haunches like a native. Lets him attempt a new chapter, a new identity. Poet of the city, as effectively indolent as C. P. Cavafy in Alexandria. 'Standing absolutely motionless,' as E. M. Forster said, 'at a slight angle to the universe'.

DROGUERIA MODERNA. MIGUEL GARCIA. PINTURAS – CRISTALES – BARNICES.

A bearded, hooded figure we have seen before comes right at the raised fugitive camera. And the man who is not William Burroughs, but who dips his shoulders in the same way, and who wears the same sweat-ringed hat, goes crabbing towards the *farmacia* of his dreams. Like a white tropical suit with amoebic dysentery. Holding back encroaching waves of peristaltic crisis. 'In-between is visited by its many doubles,' said the poet J. H. Prynne. And he was right. There are more doubles in Deakin's Tangier Interzone than discrete identities marching proud in their selfhood. The photographs become a spinning carousel, with repeated persons and settings coming back in a different order.

'I can see why you thought it was Bill,' Miles told me. 'But the neck is too short, and the giveaway, the pockets are bulging and shabby and the hair looks strange. I'm sure it's not Bill. The hunched shoulders, elbows back and strange walk all look like Bill though.'

And Miles attaches a photograph of a lean, elegant, urbane figure: Burroughs in summer hat, in London, strolling through St James's, on immaculately polished shoes. He faces the photographer, in scandalised refutation of the skulking Deakin pretender.

Jim Pennington agreed with Miles. 'You are right about the look, the hat and the height (characteristic stoop) . . . as well as a purposeful striding toward the Farmacia indeed! But I just think the jacket is too ill-fitting, too broad across the shoulders. Great photo all the same.'

By their clothes you shall know them. By their chosen outfits, they ring the changes and disappear. The clubland Burroughs in London denies the past history of the scurrying Tangier man in the hat: all that was another life, another fiction. Tragic threads. I thought of the hunted Kolley Kibber, in the opening sequence of Graham Greene's *Brighton Rock*, as he shifts nervously, gulping gin and tonic, through pubs and promenades and piers. 'Kolley Kibber always played fair, always wore the same kind of hat as in the photograph.'

If this man was not William Burroughs, not his conjured double, his stand-in, his junk-collecting ka, what was he? What was his afterlife? Where did he fit into the story? Photographed, he was caught. His purpose unpurposed. His agency annulled. Badge handed back.

And what of the real Burroughs, on the run, trapped among the same Deakin figures from the Kasbah, bare head tilted forward, in the Allen Ginsberg photograph from 1957; the one chosen for the back cover of the Viking edition of *Interzone*? Burroughs is wearing a scruffy combat jacket; an Ugly American CIA-stringer, culture fixer, in Cambodia disguise. The jacket is as much a thrift-store purchase as the lumpy garment worn by Deakin's man in the hat.

Pennington offered, as consolation, a little gossip about Francis Bacon. 'Do you know the story about Ahmed Yacoubi and Bacon . . . someone commented on Yacoubi being in Bacon's studio while he was painting, saying they thought Bacon never wanted people in there when he was working . . . "Oh, he's just an Arab," was Bacon's response. I was told this by Paul Bowles in the early '70s. I think Bowles was being bitchy.'

Through the manifold possibilities of Deakin's Tangier, there was now a channel of communication opened into the past: how Burroughs, not yet an established literary star, was prepared to ship raw material, routines, to unknown correspondents.

'Breathing blue dawn on a dim luminous shore the crying of gulls his hand on my shoulder click of distant heels.' Burroughs tapped out a vision to be flown to old Dublin. Sandymount Strand. He sent his contribution to students setting up *Albatross*, a never-published magazine in that city. The clicking of the machine on which he beat out a steady percussion in a bare room strewn with sheets of dictation, ready to be assembled or screwed into an airmail envelope. 'Shadows from a distant postcard.' *Dead Fingers Talk*.

Pictures of men taped to a sweating wall. The windows won't open. The mirror is occupied. *The Process*. In a book by Brion Gysin, hidden on a London shelf, is one of the original Burroughs photographs; probably from Paris, rescued from an indigent traveller's suitcase. A sophisticated and dangerously occulted composition. Gysin, in shadow, facing whoever picks up this small print. Burroughs, his back to the open window, is duplicated, reduced, doubled. A young man, possibly Ian Sommerville, with raised camera hiding his face, is balanced against the insecure balcony rail. White shirt like young Deakin, sleeves rolled. And there is something sprawled across the open lap of the seated Burroughs. It looks like a man's hand, offering up a smooth-skinned rat. 'Yours in Present Time,' says the holograph inscription on the endpaper.

That was the Interzone milieu: bitching, getting wasted, retreating, honing the anecdotes for glacial revenge. The Deakin prints, loose and unregarded as Burroughs pages, have stolen light, smell, motion. If he did indeed take on the task of recording Ginsberg and Orlovsky on the striped mattress, his old mucker would surely have told Farson. And Farson would have used it in his journalism, instead of the tale of Deakin's disgrace at the palace of Barbara Hutton.

As well as making a record of the life of the streets and the port, Deakin paid his way by taking satiric portraits of the grandees on the mountain: the professionally enervated at their tables, posing against views they had done nothing to deserve. Souls crushed by the terrible responsibility of wealth. And how it was obtained. These sessions were the budget equivalent of Warhol's silkscreens of business folk, collectors and inheritors: they meant nothing in themselves, but cumulatively, and positioned alongside darker gleanings from the depths of cities, they made up a panoramic spread of the period in which the great hustler operated.

'Barbara Hutton and Deakin,' Farson wrote. 'Godzilla meets the Monster.' And they both played up to stereotype. 'I consider General Franco a great man,' Barbara Woolworth Hutton opened. Deakin, by Farson's account, then criticised her decor and furnishings. Crime of crimes! Hutton decided to cancel the ball on the roof of her Kasbah house until Deakin left Tangier. Lady Rose McLaren picked up the tab at Deakin's hotel. She settled the extras for broken telephone and burnt sheets. Returned to Wheeler's, Deakin lunched out on being called 'the second nastiest little man' Hutton had met in forty years. The killer Soho drinking game, thereafter, was identifying the first.

Good knockabout routines from Farson, but much less savage than the portraits Deakin took of the vampire grandees in their hollow palaces. If he were such a pariah, why would they let him in? The white-masked, bloodless women, flutes of fizz in hand, pose on their private terraces, while Deakin arranges unbecoming shadows, ugly plants spiking their exaggerated noses. The stitches in surgically enhanced profiles break loose. The masks crack. Old bones sculpt mummified ruin. Accompanying male dummies in Hawaiian shirts, calfskin feet on bar rail, are bored: sick with indulged perversions.

The grande dame in the castle, the one who changes costume, room to room, chamber to chamber, is alone. She can barely bring herself to acknowledge the photographer's nuisance: he is something more than a servant, something less than a guest. And he talks out of turn. She is musically flatulent, as Deakin delights in telling his Soho chums. She spreads an aromatic musk, kipperish and feline, between the gilded thrones and the plinths on which she has to lean.

The pariah keeps his distance, more interested in the tapestries, the blistered woodwork, the Hammer Films candlesticks, than the *Sunset*

Boulevard diva. The Tangier portraits are cruel as self-preening fiction. And just as true. When Deakin photographs the petulant Burroughs boy, Mikey Portman, he might be auditioning a corpse. Mikey looks like a lost child. This Denton Welch aspect must have appealed to Burroughs. But the black albums, unlike Ginsberg's published collections of photographs, carry no explanatory text.

Tangier was a place where it might once have been possible for Deakin to settle, to enjoy that other life. The travelling photographer made the shot and saved his chat for the bar. Burroughs, moving fast enough to swerve his persistent double, road-tested a more radical manifesto. Miles said that he spoke of 'dissolving the opposites and dualities that trap humanity in time and space'. He remembered how the man told Jeff Nuttall 'that he was interested in the newspaper format with its juxtaposition of columns, pictures, and headlines'. He was fascinated by the way the past invades the present through old photographs. Prints of dead people who refuse to die. What happens when you slice these distant faces with razors, tape them in random combinations on your working wall? Images breed like germ cultures in a petri dish. They develop active potentialities. And start to speak, to dictate their own terms. Photographers, Burroughs said, are neutral instruments, spoiled priests of a discredited culture.

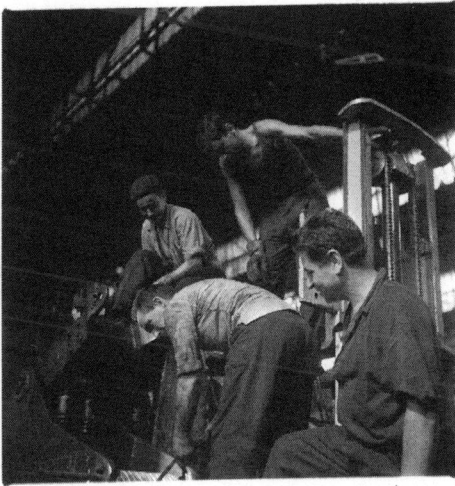

Voyage into Italy

Mussolini's Rome, with its operatic swagger and famed antiquarian detritus, its uniforms, spurious aristocrats and working thieves, admitted Deakin as walk-on companion to Arthur Jeffress. Confident in the bounty of their provisional relationship, Deakin advised Jeffress to go in for Soutine rather than Paul Delvaux. He was right. He had good selling taste for others. And Jeffress could afford to indulge his whims, before going his own way. Deakin was a purist, dedicated to self-destruction. He lacked the patience and the funds to be burdened with a serious collection. No stamina to waste valuable drinking time. That would be to invest in a past better left to snobs and aesthetes. Despite a show of muted enthusiasm for early Bacon, Jeffress backed Erica Brausen, the painter's determined dealer. His own holdings were extensive. Properties in

London, Hampshire and Venice featured works by Picasso, Modigliani, Balthus. And Soutine. His parties were a career. And transgressive habits a requirement: male guests as nuns. Jeffress, pearl-smothered and arsenic-white, appeared as Queen Elizabeth I. Gloriana among her gender-reversed courtiers. English newspapers were scandalised.

His wealthy benefactor took Deakin to Italy for a grand tour. In Venice, many years later, the fading and overweight Jeffress, offending local proprieties, became entangled in a traditional blackmail sting with gondolier, local police chief, his wife, and a thief. The episode sounded like the title of a film by Peter Greenaway. The gallerist retreated, hurt, to the comfortable Paris hotel where he killed himself in 1961. Deakin got nothing from the will.

Obliged to earn a crust, the photographer returned to Italy to harvest the images he needed as accompaniment for Christopher Kininmonth's book *Rome Alive*. Generously fired by *Vogue*, he blew a fuck-off gratuity on an Italian break. He found a perch at 6 via dei Greci. The resulting exhibition, *John Deakin's Rome*, at David Archer's Parton Gallery, opened on 18 September 1956. It was his last. Before the triumphant salvage at the Victoria and Albert Museum in 1984, after the archive rescue by Bruce Bernard and James Moores and the championship of Robin Muir.

Deakin's Rome was an orthodox iteration of 'abroad'. He recorded the usual sites from oblique angles. He showcased poverty and blight. *Rome Open City*. The rubble of war, exploited by Roberto Rossellini for a neo-realist fable (scripted in part by Federico Fellini), was still available. As a mood. A template. But it was just one graphic layer of the spectacular psychogeology surveyed by the escaping Londoner. His own director now, Deakin was storyboarding films that would never be made.

The cultural migrant is location hunting in a city where all the big productions are welcome. The Cinecittà Studios, founded by Mussolini and his son Vittorio in 1937, are thriving in the post-war years. The architecture of illusion has spread itself across ninety-nine acres of parkland. The former holding camp for displaced persons and refugees? The bomb damage of recent invasion? Forgotten. And forgiven. Tax-exempt Hollywood product co-exists with low-budget Italian genre quickies: white-telephone *giallo* horror thrillers alongside bodybuilder Steve Reeves in the Hercules cycle of sword-and-sandal *pepla*. Imported US headliners and natives, down the cast, with invented cod-Californian rebrands. Massage parlour marques.

The drifting Soho exile barters with the overwhelming heritage of previous Roman imagery. And he remains invisible. He is not really there. These photographs are taken without him. There are none of those Parisian reflections of the wandering operative caught in shop windows, asserting his own passage. Rome is arrogant, confident in its cultural status, locked in by civic monuments, by a million tourist snapshots of acclaimed ruins. By the black-on-white aesthetics of the Spanish Steps. The Trevi Fountain. The Protestant Cemetery. The flocks of wimpled nuns swooping around the Vatican.

After a few months, Deakin almost belongs in his present unbelonging. He tags along with the caravan of opportunistic Hollywood dealmakers, relocated leftists and border-jumping producers living on credit as they dive from one old fascist regime to another. One hotel of convenience for a better one. And, in just the way he faked those photo sessions with major movie stars, by shooting them from Soho screens, the slow-dying Deakin in his sorry Brighton bed pictures himself coming in triumph to Rome, in saturated colour, like Kirk Douglas in *Two Weeks in Another Town*. The Vincente Minnelli picture is about an attempted comeback: an alcoholic above-the-title actor, dropped by his studio, is wild to resurrect a burnt-out reputation. Not yet appreciating, like Scott Fitzgerald (or Deakin), that failure can be the supreme career move. The role promised to the Douglas character is withdrawn. It was just a handshake on the telephone. All that's on offer now is a dubbing gig. Until Kirk is obliged to take over the entire production and to mentor a smoother, younger, more pliable actor, played by George Hamilton.

Dying in a room by the sea is a special movie, or sequence of chemical highlights culled from everywhere, jump-cutting deliriously before settling on that same old German horror: the crematorium curtain, the oak table with the microphone. And the backview ape in the leather trench coat who turns out to be a bald Francis Bacon smoking a fat cigar in an ivory holder. Being dead, properly dead, is more comfortable. Being dead is universal silence with intertitles. Being dead is secure. Nobody talks back. Your confession is unbroken. It feels at first – while there is still a 'first' on offer – like a session grudging up those endless stairs to the Colony Room ward. Colonies of social lepers. The slow dead in a defunct hospital, a dumb cave of mortuary fridges where everybody is barred and nobody is getting away. And everybody sucks smoke into removed lungs. All the cocks are cunts now. Finger tips ring with frost and drop off. Wire beards continue to grow. Viscera scooped. Liver and lights. Hacksaw smoking against the bone cap before the jelly spills. You can hear voices screaming on the pier. High tide is swamping the toilet with refugees. Cold sick in buckets.

Kirk Douglas is not flying into Rome. He is putting a gun to his mouth in a field of crows. Auvers is ever again. Is Nevers. Soft grey with a river and amputated tree limbs. And a shaved woman on a bicycle. Hiroshima mon amour. 'It was horrible to be standing in that field,' Kirk said. 'It was the most painful film I ever made.' Bacon smiles. His decapitated head floats inside the monitor. Winking at Deakin. Who does not move a muscle. You saw nothing in Hiroshima. You saw nothing in Nevers. In Rome. In Malta. In Brighton. Head against the asylum wall. A white horse felled with jackhammers.

Port Sunlight! What a name. Soap powder snowfall to wash away the flaking skin of lepers. Sad precincts where the afflicted prowl. Another sea where foghorns wail and whales sing of distant shores. Ferry across the Mersey. Childheat of the birthroom swoon. The bathroom swim. His dream of life was no film. He was not yet himself. Or more himself than he would ever be again, in his motions, his disguise. He curled in hot wet shame. They stood around a barred cot, the congregation of the night. Misshapen things. Pillow toads. Gibbons and gargoyles. Half-humans lacking hair and hands. And the crew of belled lepers in brown rags seeking his kindness, not revenge. His birthright: a state of dread like some uncanny foretaste of bitter knowledge. The dead, all memory, do not remember, nothingness is their blessing. How surely and how far they come for the death beyond death. That *unreturnable gift of a bad fairy. Death, the articulate fly said, is what the living carry with them. To the last breath. The things of his mind are worse than any film.*

The comeback is an enticing concept. To come back you must once have been somewhere special: fame, fortune, darling of the gods. Minnelli's film was the lushest colour in grey Irish towns: widescreen, night drives with dramatic back projection. Provincial fleas gnawing at exposed ankles. It was more glamorous to come back from the oblivion of Hollywood drink and drugs, vengeful wives, than to be a tourist star of impeccable pedigree, such as Gregory Peck in *Roman Holiday*. Deakin relished his descent, the multiple sackings, the scorned benefactors: he was a natural child of malfate. If there was a way to fail better, he'd find it. Meanwhile, Rome was his dream city. His movie. City of images, repeatedly recorded, never exhausted.

A significant presence in William Wyler's *Roman Holiday* is the photographer played by Eddie Albert, a supporting act tasked with recording the escapades of fashion plate Audrey Hepburn against scenic backdrops. Even in 1953, the man with the camera was emerging as an accredited witness, charged with snappy wisecracks, cynicism as bulletproof morality. The photographer has become the chorus figure for a corrupted period.

George Hamilton, lean, tanned and available, was an archetype customised for Rome in the early Sixties. He once received a mocking birthday card, supposedly from 'Mum and Dad', decorated with a composite image of Tony Curtis and Anthony Perkins. Hamilton started well with *Crime and Punishment U.S.A.* for Denis Sanders, before settling for the high life, the Look and Italy. Real sunshine to burnish his perpetual sunbed tan. George strolled seamlessly from a connection with Lynda Bird Johnson, daughter of Lyndon, to social and financial entanglements with Imelda Marcos. Parties in a shoe-cupboard! Deakin nailed the Hamilton style in portraits he made of willowy young men in beautiful double-breasted suits and long coats, on call in flattering Roman shadows. He delighted in these idealised suitors-for-hire. His shots anticipating the role of the kept courtier from *The Roman Spring of Mrs. Stone*. Warren Beatty, grabbing his chance, was well cast as a Warren Beatty type in an adaptation of the first novel by Tennessee Williams. Vivien Leigh, in crisis mode, widowed in Rome, losing it again, was looking for the comfort of strangers. With Beatty as her lacklustre gigolo. Deakin's capable black-and-white prints of nameless actors do it better.

Rome is a cinema – *Rome Alive* – with Deakin swooping like Fellini's helicopter in the opening sequence of *La Dolce Vita*. Travelling at pace with camera primed, through fashionable bars, restaurants, tenements and ruins from the eras of Mussolini and Augustus, he shadows the paparazzi on their rat pack scooters. He scours Rome to provide visual ballast for the transcribed notebooks of Christopher Kininmonth. But these photographs are all his own, hoarded for a secret project independent of any writer.

He doesn't trail Marcello Mastroianni, the compliant and lethargic journalist in Fellini's film. He offers no social criticism and only hints at the Marxist underworld of pimps, rent boys and thieves informing *Accattone*, the first feature film by the poet Pier Paolo Pasolini. Deakin logs bombed cellars, catacombs and cemeteries. He makes repeated visits to the Cimitero dei protestanti at Testaccio. He photographs the gravestone of Shelley with its incised lines from *The Tempest*. And he salutes the pyschogeographic prompt of the Pyramid of Cestius at the Porta San Paolo. Concrete has been faced with white marble. A tomb with no exterior entrance.

As he came to know and appreciate Rome, Deakin shifted from neo-realism to a shared sexual dynamic with Pasolini, that fatal association with petty criminals. And dangerous wastegrounds. As well as prints that could have been frames from films, there were formal portraits of actors, writers and directors. Vittorio De Sica, in camelhair overcoat, is supercilious, hooded eyes looking down on the crouching photographer: an actor-director in his pomp, caught between *Bicycle Thieves* and *Umberto D*. Luchino Visconti, leftist and aristocrat, scowling at the intruder, endures a lengthy sequence in villa and garden, with sclerotic hauteur. Lesser figures from the neo-realist moment arrange their poses, ahead of Anita Ekberg, among the swollen statuary of the Trevi Fountain. The portrait of Gina Lollobrigida, in full bloom, in furs, a rose across her deep cleavage, was made in a smart bar in London.

Deakin loves his fellows, the street photographers at work. He looks for them in every city where he lodges. He searches out nuns. And sides of meat exhibited at Campo dei Fiori. He notices: postcards of muscle boys, cats, slum kids, processions, policemen and newspaper kiosks. He notices: disabled statues, tongueless marble heads. He notices: trams. He notices: beggars lying in the dirt and property barons bestowing a fraudulent blessing. The workers of Trastevere welcome his attention. Their women hold up babies. Street maps, lottery tickets, priests. The Tiber. Public buildings illuminated at night. Empty squares in the early morning. Street sweepers and covered market stalls. It is comprehensive, this documentation. But it is not enough. It is never enough. Deakin confirms his cocky alienation.

Returning from several months filming in Australia, still in demand, a Soho regular and not yet qualified to launch a comeback, Farson called on Deakin in Rome. Despite the awful burden of 'success', he felt a compulsion to renew his contact with the achieved disaster that was Deakin. That strange bat-eared homunculus, the pariah's pariah, had qualities that Farson knew he lacked: intensity, conviction, momentum and a willingness to accommodate all his demons. Deakin lived contentedly within the limits of his talent. He made the work and he set it aside. He trashed career prospects, betrayed patrons: he continued. Deakin thrived in managed misery with a marsupial's cheerfully annoying smirk. He was a self-mutilated veteran striking back. Dan laboured in vain to script the bits Deakin chose to leave undone. The nightmares unspoken. The celebrity publican couldn't help himself. He had to check on his friend and victim, every few months, to touch and sniff and probe, to be sure that the wayward photographer, star turn in a novel of fragments, was living down to the rank legend his boozy compadre was shaping for posterity. Deakin had his congregation of monsters, his night sweats. His warped genius for cruelty. Farson's worse moments came when he staggered against a spoiled mirror in a drinking club. And found no welcoming or devastating reflection. No portrait worthy of Bacon.

Two affectionate wounded and wounding strangers draped in an intimacy of cameras. Like speed-freak Hopper in *Apocalypse Now*. Farson hustling hard for *Picture Post* and Deakin cut loose by *Vogue*. Two unsteady rivals orbiting art world stars. Shared flights and train rides. Two pals disputing a gilt-edged freebie to the latest grand opening, some Bacon retrospective of retrospectives, with all the trimmings. Better to have the invitation snatched back and burnt than to see your best chum waiting on the platform, arms wide.

Without his shamed companion in mischief, Farson was never comfortable. He found Deakin quite at home in a rented Roman flat, the balcony loaded with flourishing plants in whitewashed tins. A reunion of betrayed conspirators. 'Deakin said it was like a release from prison.' They went out on the town, Deakin playing host.

He even found a hotel for Farson. And led him to the catacombs, where shelves of adamantine skulls were waiting to stare them out. They drank. With rapid and shuddering dedication. It was their bond. They found a table in an empty nightclub where 'the orchestra played luscious, sentimental Neapolitan songs'. Deakin broke the news. He was married. It was as if he had only agreed to undergo this shocking contract in order to have a yarn to entertain his friend, to draw him to Rome. The scene as Farson describes it – setting, musicians – is pure Fellini.

The Roman idyll had soured. Deakin tried living with a fashion designer, Gianni Baldini, in Genoa. He made a little change helping out with a collection, but fashion was never his bag. It brought out the residual venom in his veins. Italian family life stole his will to get out of bed. He made his escape. A well-presented but stateless Hungarian woman, living in Milan, needed a clean passport. They shared a fancy meal. She gave him five hundred dollars, which he used to replace his stolen Rolleiflex. And then there was a *Godfather* wedding breakfast for the entire Hungarian colony to endure. Envelopes were exchanged. Kisses aborted in favour of a hug or punch. In a slept-in pale blue suit, his worldly effects in a plastic TWA bag, Deakin returned to Rome.

New camera, renewed assault on the city. False friends. The Rollei was stolen again. This was the point, Farson reckons, when Deakin decided to abandon photography for painting. Nobody would steal his canvases. They had some camp interest. As usual, he found inspiration in postcards and junk gleanings, in dolls' heads and rolls of chicken wire. It was the art of the asylum, the get-out for old lags in well-deserved solitary. Farson acquired the portrait of himself lifted from the cover of the Australian *TV Times* and improved with a cauliflower wig. Lionel Bart and Joan Littlewood declined the self-consciously primitive confections Deakin named in their honour.

Among the unsorted assemblies for potential books, found in Berwick Street after Deakin's death, was a substantial set of prints made at a steel plant and tyre factory in Genoa. Heroic and engaged, here is one of the roaming photographer's finest pictorial essays. With the right accompanying text – Walter Benjamin, John Berger, Susan Sontag – the Genoa publication could have secured Deakin's posthumous reputation. It had the authenticity of neo-realist witness and the male-gaze eroticism of Visconti, from the period when the great director dramatised immigration to the industrial north in *Rocco and His Brothers*. Examples from Deakin's factory sequence are rarely reproduced. That this labour could have been undertaken when he was being housed by a fashion designer doesn't sit comfortably with the timbre of Farson's anecdotes. The industrial diary, followed through, has a unity not located in the other urban portfolios of wandering and portraiture. In Genoa, shortly before Deakin arranged for his latest camera to disappear, he proved to himself that he could execute, edit and deliver a story capable of standing alone. While remaining susceptible to interpretation.

The essay opens with arched black window slits among trashed white shells on which it is still possible to read the historic signage – NAZ – before plaster peels to bare brick, with the final letter lost. After a set of preliminary abstractions, chalked graffiti, torn posters with cinema faces choking beneath many layers of paper and paste, and after concrete ware-houses like execution sheds, Deakin presents his first worker. A happy man in a clean white vest arriving with a full satchel at his station on the factory floor. Groups, in oily undergarments and greasy caps, attend to massive machines. A futurist explosion of rolled-steel bales. And then a soviet panel of proud labour. Most of the men are smiling, smiling and smoking. They are proud to be in regular employment. Proud in their banter.

Established as an undemanding presence, and no snoop, Deakin focuses on individual portraits, men who look him in the face. As he trawls for suitable objects of desire: rude Renaissance angels, in the fashion of Pasolini, promoted from the streets into brief prominence as actors. After the parade of men, at labour and leisure, comes the poetry of architecture: the factory superstructure, circular storage tanks, pipes and improbably tall chimneys. Arcs of high-pressure spray. Cleansing water. A slice of sky through an open roof. Before Deakin pulls away, to the river, to the perimeter walls.

He sacrifices sharpness to the romance of mist and smoke. A solitary worker, face obscured, is holding a gushing hose with thick gloved hands. Men in the filthy white caps of their caste sit among the thermal fury of a volcanic eruption. The ground boils. Black boulders, the by-products of industrial process, melt. And congeal. Visored helmets of bare-chested welders make them into papal guards. Showers of sparks from the furnaces blaze against a night sky where galaxies are born. Deakin has lifted his report from the morning community of smiles and cigarettes to this nocturne of boiling vats, pressure hoses and erupting columns of steam. The point has been achieved where the relentless documentation of the black albums reconfigures as a dramatic narrative, a choral tragedy.

John Constable's late storms are rapidly scored through terror and grief. Paint bears the burden of loss and transfigures it. The immensity of the heavenly vault presses on a frosted band of winter sea. Those studies have the force to which Deakin now aspires, in this run of astounding impressions of mass and flame experienced through a diminishing perspective of railway lines. Through leakings and pourings. Through all the categories and conditions of light: natural, filtered, artificial. This Genoa factory album is a fully achieved sequence found nowhere else among Deakin's salvage.

And still he carries on: fortress blocks and stilted monstrosities, chimneys and angles, that ecology of industrial damnation depicted by Antonioni in *Red Desert*. But without the heightened sensibility, the soothing palette and the immaculately posed figures in catalogue coats. In Deakin's Genoa there are black dunes of toxic dust, hoists powerful enough to lift battleships. There is a wheelbarrow so crusted with ash that it might have been excavated in Pompeii. The open spaces are deserted. Human figures, tightly blocked on the factory stage, scrabble around the great machines, servicing their undiminished hunger. Until, at the end of a long shift, the workers can salve their thirsts, laughing around improvised tables. Bottle tops scatter in the dirt like cockleshells. Rough red wine in big-bellied receptacles. Vests and hard hats. Harder bread. Cuts of garlic sausage from their satchels.

Then back to the flames, the hoists, the railway tracks. The goggles and the leather aprons. Chalked calculations, hours worked. Targets achieved. The men put on white shirts and walk to the gates. Some are carrying briefcases. Deakin makes a final circuit when they are gone: an empty shower stall with political slogans. Crumpled sheets of corrugated iron. One last mapping of this terrible place.

Having successfully completed his commission, with no immediate prospect of publication, Deakin is done with the game. Back to Rome and Farson. Back to London. The old life, sickness with detergent chasers in a gay bar. Taxi rides out east with no cameras left to lose. If he ever travels again, it will be as an accessory, licensed to amuse, in company with his grudging patron, Francis Bacon.

Strangers on a Train

The Ticket That Exploded. A nightmare threesome in transit. A wealthy painter, exhausted from jousting with fame, in company with a reforgotten Soho photographer sliding backwards after sabotaging several promising careers and towing a gentle East London hardman with cleft palate; an alcoholic innocent open to the novelty of abroad. Bacon & Deakin & Dyer: a firm of City wine merchants entrained for a content-free TV travelogue. Rattling through – is that where we are now? – Yugoslavia. Deakin as chaperone. Soured joker and referee. Dousing the emotional conflagration between painter and impotent lover with a good gargle and rinse of petrol. Paying for his grudging *Orient Express* voucher, en route to Athens (yet again), John Deakin squeezes his elbows hard against brittle ribs, steadying his borrowed camera to make a memory prompt in the rocking restaurant car. This is what happened. Really. Does anybody care?

Things were not going well between Francis and George. There are only so many times you can pick up spare property – house on the Berkshire Downs, near Newbury racecourse, or studio flat in South Ken – before finding out that it is absolutely hopeless for work and giving it away. Investment portfolio thickened, in order to get shot of another inconvenient boyfriend. A good-looking, slope-shouldered gent who was, even after his inevitable and collaborative suicide (especially then), a compelling model. George had been expensively tailored on Bacon's tab. Another hotel suite. Bracered. In his undershorts. Slumped. Sick. At stool. Shitted out. Dribbling. Done.

With some encouragement and a cheque or two, George had achieved the Look, but not the temperament. The taste for physical retribution. Unbuckling a belt, bloodying knuckles was too much of a labour. Deakin, in his days as a hireling stalker, tracked George on commission from several masters. Heavy brows, hair helmet, proud beak. Jewish-Romany? Third-generation Paddy, digger of deepwater docks? Itinerant swede-basher with webbed feet? George had a sculpted profile that Bacon admired, lifted straight from *The Egyptian Book of the Dead: The Book of Going Forth by Day*. Classic hooter set by a brass ruler.

'That was the only straight thing about him,' Deakin muttered. Poor George! A stuttering statue full of maudlin complaints and indifferent table manners. But amiable and fit for a funny night out, anywhere, any time. George mumbled into his soup at Wheeler's or the White Tower. Deakin's Soho portraits set him up with special emphasis on the grip of the hands; two fingers nestling in a loose squeeze, part of some as yet uncracked courtship code. All Bacon's characters, nominated for shape and presence, were photographed by Deakin. Freud, Henrietta Moraes, Muriel Belcher, Isabel Rawsthorne, Peter Lacy, George Dyer: the petty gods of a minor necrophile cycle.

As George moves, or is moved, down Dean Street, Greek Street, Old Compton Street, Romilly Street, he doesn't appear to move at all: he strikes *precisely* the same attitude, paws over crotch, right hand flexed to absorb those two fingers. Scrubbed prehensile digits with no evidence of swollen boxer's mitts. Church-whipped fists like a lamp held against the darkness of the tight-buttoned suit. Always the hangman's knot of tie, the inverted V of the starched white collar.

George performs without shame: the Deakin snaps are a paper mirror he can understand. They are so unlike the grotesque malformations of Bacon. A surgeon deity of an old religion. Dyer is a bodybuilt mannequin, showered and shaved, repeating, on request, a formidably expressionless expression. He is transfixed, nailed to the spot, trapped in the roofless studio of the streets, while that familiar backdrop of wide boys and tourists, ever changing, is being dragged along behind him.

Deakin is feeding Bacon what he says he needs. What he has been instructed to feed him by the controllers, the explainers, those Secret State archivists with the publishing and museum connections. With the power of ennobling villains and enriching the right sort of criminal. But it is still a genuine and binding collaboration. Stronger than most marriages. The painter relies on the photographer for the source material with which to launch an important phase of his work. And he pays, unforgiving in generosity, with lunches, drink, insults and first-class travel.

George could be a bit of a nightmare, sending in the drug squad, moaning incessantly, ringing the bell at all hours, trashing Reece Mews. Abused by gifts, he was needy in his limited and modest compulsions. Tender hearted and sentimental, the emeritus bruiser was the wrong sort of nightmare for Bacon: Dyer was insufficiently motivated to dish out serious punishment. He couldn't impersonate Peter Lacy, Bacon's unstable and recurring lover; the sadist Deakin had posed among frozen beef carcasses on hooks in Smithfield Market. But clothed and coiled, not half-stripped like the arty Bacon version, made when Deakin knew his shot was just a staging post towards a serious painting. Lacy was the one who said he wanted to chain the painter to a wall and have him lie captive in straw and shit. The affair was always going to culminate in suicide, after renewed and unsatisfactory coupling, renewed rows among louche bars and pianos in Tangier. Lacy's bruised eyes and his silver-haired, black-browed rage, accurately channelled by Deakin, counterbalanced Dyer's bovine and self-admiring hopelessness. The open-necked check shirt of the spoiled pilot against the dark suit of the failed thief.

A cultivated decadent fighting for breath in the smoky dens of London, navigating the same dank alleys to the same cellars, panting up the same creaking stairs to the same man-cage of unfulfilled promises, to reek of the ape-house cocktail hour, Bacon needed to get away. Often. To dodge deadlines. To take a rest from his own myth. And in company of those he trusted to know their place: young Lucian Freud in Monte Carlo, Denis Wirth-Miller and Dicky Chopping motoring, with long lunches, to the Midi. Bacon could offset interpersonal disasters by taking to the road. In 1964, he visited Malta, Sicily and Naples. Without Deakin. The photographer was not required now, even in places where he could have been useful as guide and memory man, recalling wartime service around Valletta's Grand Harbour. The bars, the dives. The churches. The life before Bacon.

The 1965 excursion on the *Orient Express*, with Dyer and Deakin, was promoted as 'a journey to paradise'. There was an unrealistic expectation on Bacon's part that the sex rituals of his former arrangement with Dyer would be resurrected through leisured time travel. He hoped that jolting over the rails and crossing frontiers would inspire, when they had emptied enough bottles, antic couplings. Or, at worst, it would suspend for a few days the tedium of existence. The reality was more *Strangers on a Train* than the steel-blue, dining-car dalliance of *North by Northwest*. Bacon, as usual, was paying. Hoping for a little of the bondage and gangsterism of Alain Robbe-Grillet's *Trans-Europ-Express*, which was released in 1966, all he got, as they rattled through old Yugoslavia, was red wine, and George, whaling a steady stream of cigarettes, playing havoc with his blue-faced asthma attacks. Deakin, that ferret, rank with excitement, was in his element. The psychopolitics of the warring trio reflected the visible divisions of a conflicted landscape. But Deakin, the old pro, managed, as required, a composed two-shot: this macho bromance. With Baron Samedi, in top hat and tailcoat, smirking in the wings.

This may well have been the last relaxed and superficially benign photograph of George and Francis. Atypically, Dyer is in holiday mufti, a polo top with white T-shirt visible beneath. Heavy dark glasses, like Cary Grant in Hitchcock's film, disguise the effects of a couple of days and nights of hard drinking. George rests an arm behind the shoulders of Bacon, who is smiling broadly, in full flight, mid-monologue. Glass in hand. Bottles shuddering on table. Bon voyage! The restaurant car is abandoned to a remnant of the most dedicated drinkers.

There is limited documentation here. The terrible trip is not much exploited in standard anecdotage. It happened. It hurt. And it resolved nothing. The precise nature of the quarrels, furies fanned by Deakin, have to be imagined.

So imagine: waves of resentment, vanity and self-preservation, coming in hard, one after another, with no physical release. Another bottle! Another bridge, another frontier. Imagine Deakin, drawing on his own experience as a model for both painters, provoking George into saying that, all things considered, he *preferred* the two versions of himself painted by Freud to *any* of Bacon's rancorous distortions. Lucian was a gentleman. He took time over his work, offering George the opportunity to browse heavy art books and admire Frans Hals: a major discovery. He liked holding those beautiful and untainted objects, stroking thick paper. Then he washed his hands, repeatedly.

Freud's *Man in a Blue Shirt* humanises George: you can register the cleft palate and the choked elocution in the set of a twisted mouth. A misunderstood and melancholy man is spared the laundered white shirt and sharp collar of Deakin's Soho portraits. In Lawrence Gowing's 1982 book on Freud, Deakin and Dyer are linked, their portraits displayed, in monochrome, side by side: victims, rivals, accomplices. Twinned pariahs of the art market's brutal gangland.

As he struggled to steady his sea legs against the swaying motion of the train, Deakin pitched the outrageous theory that the naked and grappling figures, in that Bacon painting Soho called 'The Buggers', the one Freud owned and refused to lend to exhibitions, were the bitter rivals themselves, at the climax of their social friendship: Francis Bacon and Lucian Freud *at it*. The one on top, with arched back, did have something of the beaky sharpness of Freud, the amateur acrobat. While the round-faced submissive trapped beneath, lips peeled, bared teeth scoured with Vim, was Bacon. The grunting contest of wills between warriors was a murky Valentine.

'Balls!'

Bacon whinnied. Years before, when he was still with Peter Lacy in Henley, working in a shed that Freud described as 'a little medieval caravan', he produced *Two Figures*, the painting Freud acquired. William Feaver reports Bacon confessing to Freud that he sometimes thought he *was* indeed the figure of the smothered underdog. The dominant assailant would then be Lacy, driving down with the bestial force Bacon later transposed in *Study for Portrait of P. L., No. 2* (1957). Lacy's head is wet-fleshed, a memento mori. The sockets of his eyes have been scooped into black holes. Primal darkness swallowing the rest. Self-murder would be a kindly release.

'Friendship,' Bacon said, 'is where two people tear each other apart.' George Dyer was defenceless. It is left to Deakin to supply the voices. He has to keep the dialogue in play. Hold off the crisis of boredom for another few hours. Save these deadly companions from the horror of being left alone, alone together. Lovers, limp as last month's asparagus on railway booze, but still capable of wounding with words. Deakin's other role, delivering the images that the future ordained, was almost done.

One shot. Two men. Restaurant car of the *Orient Express*. Penitential liquid intermission between lunch and dinner. Bacon, chicken jowls choked by lightweight polo neck, sees the truth, the terrible prediction reflected in Dyer's dark lenses. The sheltering glasses of an ex-contender the morning after twelve hard rounds. The train is tilting away from them. George's arm steadies his companion. His unanchored rock. His tormentor. And he smiles.

Conversation, as proven drinkers know, lifts on a beat from an exchange of teasing insults to unforgivable accusations dredged from the depths of long-husbanded resentment. Never again to be forgotten or forgiven. Deakin and Bacon started to debate, to the utter bemusement of George, the *weight* of a human soul. Deakin read somewhere, or picked up in a bar, the legend that an American quack put a patient, at his last breath, on the scales. Then once more, immediately afterwards: believing that a soul had mass. Twenty-one immortal grams living through the fire.

'Tosh!'

Bacon sneezed. Papist mumbo-jumbo from a Scouse dwarf! Deakin referred him to a favoured authority, the old Egyptians again. Anubis trying the heart, in balance, against a feather representing Truth. The Greeks had more sense, the painter said, they knew the soul was breath itself, exhaled. Here and gone. The evident flaw in Bacon's theology was exposed in bodily metaphor, his asthma. His ka was maimed. He spoke where he couldn't work.

The only measurement that counted, Bacon asserted, was the heft of paint on the brush, the force of a stroke, and how effective it proved, on occasion, to leave the canvas unprimed and unviolated. How effective to destroy those examples of failed spontaneity.

Deakin said there was an equation to be formulated from the mass of photographs taken of an individual – Bacon, for example – and the necessary stripping away, layer by layer, of that subject's mortal span. The more photographs exposed, the greater fame, and the less *soul* left behind, intact. Take, if you will, Freud's superstitious reluctance to be snapped. Take the tragic price, willingly paid, for Deakin's self-portraits. Stations of alcoholic ruin. Dorian Gray prints, turned to the wall, are incrementally awful, raddled. While the subject is revealed to posterity as a barely animate corpse, a jackal wandering a burning wilderness.

'Oh god!' The painter groaned, before letting his head hit the rocky table, tipping and wasting half a glass of good red wine. George laughed. Mirthlessly. Like a razor scratch across a blue moon.

It was during the night of the third or fourth bardo, who's counting now, between reverie and punctured recollections never to be trusted, that the man born with a camera in place of a hand revived the plot to kill the painter and to push his body from the train. A plot hatched between fellow travellers deep in drink, to dispose of their only support in expectation of . . . what? Legacies, studio clearance, stories to tell? Forgiveness? It was the magic hour of spinal hallucination, the one reality. Rivers. Bridges. Village halts with names too fast to read. The twinned courtiers, respectful of mutual faults, tender with flaws, pooled their resources and talked of how best to rid themselves of their benefactor toad. Francis was staggering, smashing glasses, and holding fast to insecure doors. A catch gave. He fell. He tumbled out into air. Air becoming fire. White light. Radiance into imminence. The co-conspirators did not exchange a crime, they exchanged illusions. They were suicided, both, by the society they kept. Self-murder as a career choice. Sulphurous insemination. A world made up of warring elements no sooner destroyed than recomposed. The man on the Brighton bed, stiff as a stopped wave, resists the force of lies composed in his defence.

Which is no defence at all. No defence against the time-shredding genius of a painter able to predict the past and suborn the future. Francis adopts the railway assault that never happened. He revisions it, on his return home, into the central panel of a triptych inspired, so he says, by Eliot and Sweeney Agonistes. *Slaughter in a sleeper. The action poor George could not deliver. And Deakin failed to record. Meat and teeth. Saddles and horns. A fouled and bloody bed against half-drawn Mediterranean blinds. The anonymous detective, eavesdropping on this prodigious thrust and spill, is calling the cops. Before booking his own turn in the punishment cell.*

'And you wait for a knock and the turning of a lock.' And another Bacon painting from the same year. Isabel Rawsthorne's pink arm stretching back for the key. When the door of fate is already open and the person with the gold earring and the gouged face is hovering in the outer dark. What then?

They spent a few days in Athens, where Deakin had contacts. Bacon fancied, in his next life, achieving fluency in Classical Greek. He was adept at summoning the Furies to his Colony Room séances. He wanted the *Oresteia* of Aeschylus as source material, a thunder chorus in a pink world. The doomed trio lurched up the gangplank for the ferry to Crete, quarrelling, sick of soul, hugging the lifeboats; unfit for dark labyrinths and Picasso minotaurs.

And here, tracking a progression through Deakin's letters to Farson, and the gossip when he returned, the story becomes a spell, another posthumous dream. Weary of their own company, the three men perch in a 'pleasant old-fashioned' hotel on the harbour at Chania. The seats at the bar might be empty but you are not permitted to make a claim. The dance of light on the water never changes. The lighthouse continues to sweep its beams. Across the harbour, beyond the cafés with the touting waiters, the Scandinavian holiday groups, the exiled English painter John Craxton had his apartment. Deakin does not mention this fact. Young Craxton, fashionable in winter coat, was photographed for *Vogue* by Deakin in 1951. He was interrupted in the middle of packing his bags, before his departure for Crete.

The young painter, in the springtime of his success as illustrator and book designer, enjoyed cruising Piccadilly Circus for 'uniformed pick-ups', with whom he would spend the afternoon in the Pastoria Hotel, off Leicester Square. One of these obliging soldiers knew the Mediterranean, knew Malta and North Africa: this was John Deakin. Craxton was on terms with Bacon. He knew that his own friendship with Freud had faded. And it was not coming back. It soured into bitter recrimination after Lucian took up with Francis.

Chania, for many years, suited Craxton; he had his visitors, his followers and his sailors. But the Bacon party, it seems, made no attempt to contact their old associate. Craxton's 'open door', come-one-come-all hospitality, did not end well. One evening, his drink was spiked and his collection of paintings vanished, stripped from the walls: Miró, Ghika, Graham Sutherland, and a playful Matisse cut-out.

The Deakin snapshot, this fortunate accident in the restaurant car, holds time for an instant, before landscape, framed in the window, begins to stall and stretch. The plush carriages of the *Orient Express*, plunging into a tunnel blasted through resistant mountains, are still carrying the London excursionists towards Athens, but they emerge, blinking and disorientated, in Paris. The bemused trio are now joined by other Soho revenants and familiars – Muriel Belcher and Ian Board from the Colony Room, Roderigo Moynihan, Thea Porter – on their merry way to Bacon's greatest public triumph, the retrospective at the Grand Palais in 1971. Deakin, no longer requisitioned as collaborating portraitist, is brought along as minder or carer for George Dyer. Little credit in that. With the unspoken instruction to let him run free and wild, so long as he keeps well away from the showpiece dinners and dignitaries. And halts the drinking on the recoverable side of blackout. Poor George! Poor Deakin. Muriel wouldn't give him a glance. He would never be forgiven for his treatment of David Archer. One week after Archer's miserable death, his suicide, Deakin was on the ghost train for Paris.

George liked France. And would, with some encouragement from Bacon, have made an attempt at learning the language. The paintings for which he had been a consenting model were singing in their golden frames, secure behind protective glass. With his distorted image twice processed, twice damned, George was turned loose, unlanguaged, wads of froggy paper in pocket, to collude with rent boys and the night. Undiagnosed, his appointed nurse, John Deakin, was already a sick man. Sick in body and soul. A personalised carcinoma was comfortably lodged but not yet making a terminal nuisance of itself by ringing down for regular medication. Any excuse for opioid surrender. Later, the odd couple, squamous cell and failing lung, would become warring intimates: parasitic tenant and pickled host. Playing up as metaphors, they rubbed along. The photographer and his metastasising assassin were much like the old gang in the Caves de France. But this was to prove Deakin's final visit to the City of Light. The only exhibition of Deakin images still ahead, a show at which he would be both model and instigator, was a comprehensive hang of bad news X-rays, fouled with prophetic ectoplasm, and pegged up for unwelcome inspection by an audience of one.

The drama has been recounted many times in all its grim inevitability. Like the footsteps of bailiffs on the stairs. This horror synchronises so well with the death of Peter Lacy, on the eve of Bacon's Tate retrospective in 1962. Dyer was in constant pain. He had been spoiled with money, to such an extent that he had even acquired his own court of thirsty jackals and petty villains waiting in the Golden Lion. Bacon would dump George on some obliging follower, like the youthful writer and art editor Michael Peppiatt, before heading off to find livelier company. Whips and scorpions.

Now George is installed in Bacon's suite at the Hôtel des Saint-Pères in Saint Germain. In the afternoon, in company with Denis Wirth-Miller and Dicky Chopping, the painter strolls past the Grand Palais, to witness the preparations, the rolling out of the red carpet. He dines in a neighbourhood bistro, Le Petit Saint-Benoît, with Sonia Orwell and Marguerite Duras. Orwell has moved in on him, taking up his case: Farson says that she offered to find someone to kill George, to rid the great man of his troublesome lover. But Bacon had already forgiven the drugs bust landed on him by Dyer. Such things were quite fashionable at the time. It was just gossip, squabble and fuss. Nothing that Arnold Goodman, with his toadlike infallibility, his phone numbers, couldn't brush aside.

The death of Dyer hovers like a snuff movie, an optional extra for the DVD. A lurid tale cut and recut by a set of bored editors. Bacon returns from his triumphant outing to find George in the suite with an Arab rent boy. The painter's tightened breathing is offended by the rank smell of working feet: he decamps to share the room of Terry Danziger Miles, who has been sent over by the Marlborough Gallery, to assist the invaluable Valerie Beston.

Beston and Miles, on their way down to breakfast, meet on the stairs. *Where's George?* Bacon is uneasy. He asks Miles to check the suite. Dyer is slumped across the en suite lavatory, dead. Pick your own solution. Tuinal overdose? Accident? Contract killing? Preordained suicide timed to inflict maximum damage? These things can be arranged more smoothly in France. Suite locked. Party continues.

Michael Peppiatt, Denis Wirth-Miller, Dicky Chopping: they rendezvous by arrangement with Deakin at a café near the Gare de Lyon; before going on to the celebratory dinner at Le Train Bleu, an occasion hosted by Sonia Orwell and Michel and Zette Leiris. 'Word has clearly reached the whole Soho contingent that this is to be the pre-dinner meeting-point,' Peppiatt said. 'What a rabble' is Deakin's characteristic riposte. The terrible train ride to Athens, never ending, had reached its destination, decanting a tribe of spectral passengers at long linen-draped tables in the ultimate restaurant car.

This desperate feast, hysterical with eulogies, and waves of aftershock from whispered events at the Hôtel des Saint-Pères, is both a send-off for Dyer, most loved in his absence, and an obituary for the whole scene. They came as flotsam in the wake of Bacon's triumph and they left as phantoms, fated to feed on the crumbs of memory.

The great painter accepts the plaudits from friends and admirers. There are a number of uncredited photographs: Bacon on his feet, arms hanging loose, drinking the applause, the well-oiled huzzahs, the frantic clapping. He is framed against arched windows, vestal lamps, rococo decoration. Pairs of stern waiters in black bow ties. Men who know their business. And who might be asylum keepers in disguise. You can pick out Wirth-Miller, but not Deakin. The photographer was unweaponed, a condemned man.

Four days in Paris, in which to walk backwards to the point where the story began, finding a camera after a party, taking to the streets, exploring the avenues of Père Lachaise. Deakin was tramping to erase evidence held in the black albums. He wanted to summon the ones he had photographed before they lost their nerve; before they murdered themselves in order to remain a little longer, a little brighter in the archive of abandoned images.

From his hospital ward, back in London, Deakin recalled the misery of plodding, day and night, on a treadmill of paranoia and pursuit, street markets to Pigalle, churches to gardens. 'Mouth and throat full of pus, unable to eat, big toe oozing pus, itching blisters around my arse and my prick skinned and raw.'

In 1972, the year after Dyer's death, Bacon launched his own attempt to wind time back, to get a firmer fix on the horror, to open himself to the demons required for paintings made as revenge or restitution: in order to elevate mere happenstance into history. He returned to the Hôtel des Saint-Pères and asked for the suite in which Dyer's body had been found.

And hidden. Left alone. Locked away. Put aside until the party was over.

'He would sit on the loo where George died, sleep in the bed where George had lain with the rent boy with smelly feet,' Mark Stevens and Annalyn Swan report in their Bacon biography.

'Bacon, always a poor sleeper, left himself open, during this private ritual of expiation, to the night thoughts most people would do anything to avoid, enclosing himself in the ghostly room with only the vague hotel sounds to keep him company.'

Woozy and wool-headed with analgesics, in a redbrick Hackney hospital that was once an asylum for 'imbecile children', Deakin forgot how to sleep. But not how to dream. He hovered somewhere between image and essence. There were so many beds, peopled and unpeopled. So many pleas and moans in the night. 'I use the Homerton hospital,' Deakin said, 'like others use Aix-les-Bains.' When the shock of life has been transferred by chemical process into prints weighing less than a human soul, the image thief is redundant. The game is over, but not quite finished.

THE FRENCH HOUSE

Tarnished Angels

After so many months when the nagging presence of John Deakin – giving, withholding, sneering and revealing – dominated my locked-down existence, the voice of a dead man I never knew became the voice of London. Pungent vapour trails, Montecristo No. 4 and salt beef sandwiches, swept through deserted bars and shuttered restaurants, calling the vanished to rise from their sickbeds. And walk again. Old London, city of smoke and memory, was nothing but a stall of pillaged books and two great yellow boxes of photographs.

Then, suddenly and unexpectedly, with my halting tale almost told, everything opened up. Doors were unlocked. Neighbours nodded as they passed. Bushes, trees, birds. The city was taking a deep breath, shaking the ground. Vibrant colour returned to the cracks in the paving stones. One bright and frictionless morning I struck out, wide-eyed, with appointments to keep. Trains were running, major burrowing exercises were almost complete. Blind plasterboard enclosures removed their barriers to reveal revived permissions: the island labyrinth of Soho was touting for custom. Small enterprises were readying their caves. Fast-food stalls simmered and stirred. The polished windows of private dining rooms where aspirant bohemians drank and plotted in gleeful entitlement were visible on upper floors of Georgian properties. The entire zone was performative, straining to remember its ancient vices and visions. That shrug of winking wickedness navigated by Deakin. The thrashing of wild palms from posters displayed in the tactful windows of production houses. And the darker windows of offices without any declared purpose. The antic mysteries of forbidden entanglements are not accessible to the neurosis of digital capture. Without the alchemy of photographic negatives and positives, the heady chemical baths and red-bulb séances, there is no history worth retaining.

Blinking from swift Elizabeth Line transit, Whitechapel to Tottenham Court Road, and trembling like an arthritic old dog, I realised that I was already on Dean Street. It was such a smooth chute, right out of the respectable East End into once familiar and now convalescent haunts. Mythologised streets and pubs, and the moves sanctioned by Deakin on his compulsive circuits, were still there, still in play. Names and postal addresses present and visible, but gone in all other senses. Gone into the laminate of fading memorabilia. Specifics of London geography have been translated into predatory and unstable dimensions: snappy tweet tributes, drippingly affectionate blogs, graduate researchers with mendacious phone-cameras. We are way beyond dreary surveillance. In the days of Bernard Kops, Alexander Baron and David Litvinoff, in the amphetamine rush of *The Small World of Sammy Lee*, there was ground between Dean Street and Aldgate. There was a valid journey. A psychic causeway along which it was possible to contemplate what lay ahead and what was being left behind, home and family, the choke of respectability.

The first meet was set for Maison Bertaux, a patisserie with marble-topped tables where I would reconnect with a Hackney-domiciled couple, artists who had made their escape to Ireland. And found themselves seduced by the land of post-Brexit lotus-eaters, sweet-voiced Sirens and thirsty fiddlers; the country where so many of the finest counterculturalists of cancelled generations were now discovering affinities with a surviving network of hardcore exiles, embedded seekers and settlers from Trinity College and the communal Baggot Street attics and cellars of Dublin in the Sixties. The slightly stunned diaspora of Toners and Mc-Daids. Antiquarian booksellers, name authors, pub philosophers, wine importers, artisan carpenters and boat builders, new age restaurateurs, and dealers of every stripe: they shook the family trees of ancestral plantations for one splash of blood to trade against a fresh burgundy passport.

My re-rooted friends had established good terms with a near neighbour, John Minihan, that craftsman photojournalist with a penchant for literary figures, especially well-seasoned Irish poets. Their beards and broken veins honourably won in service of the muse. Some of them sheltered in London. They stuck close, through long afternoons, in superstitious fear of Dublin's suspended holy hour, to safe havens on Dean Street. Alternately letting rip on shows of public affability before miming boasted repentance by counting aloud the days since ardent spirits had passed their lips. Still very much active, if resolutely committed to the technology of a vanished analogue world, John was back in town, camera in hand, return ticket to Cork secure, for the annual gathering of former Fleet Street professionals. A few more empty seats each year but no let-up in reminiscence and proud fraternity.

The Hackney returnees, taking care of business, and plotting far ahead as ever, asked Minihan to snap a few shots of me, as a person struggling to make contact with Deakin in the days of Bacon. We couldn't find an inch of space in the pastry shop. It was rammed with Chinese, Japanese and South Korean visitors guided to this famously continental venue by their smartphones. Once inside, perch occupied, they picked at digital networks and published their location with carefully composed captures. And grinning emojis.

Our veteran troop straggled downstairs into a dim cellar. Minihan was with an old London compadre. He wanted to get the commission over. Within six minutes, six shots taken, we were back inside. Before the coffee arrived. We chatted. We marched to Brewer Street. 'Sit,' he said. An armchair left on the pavement. 'Last one.' Freeze for a moment outside the French House. 'Done.' Rejoin the company. The man with Minihan was Steve Walsh. He makes prints from the negatives. And he posts them back to Ireland. He also, so John told us, performed the service for Deakin and Harry Diamond. This was exactly what I needed at this point, my first chance in the newly opened city to talk to somebody with direct experience of the man. Steve gave me his number. We would arrange a meeting.

Things loosened up as soon as they walked through the door of the French House, cheered by the smoked gallery of anecdote-provoking portraits on the walls: old pals, old enemies, scores settled. Slights forgiven at the first swallow. 'Make it a bottle.'

I talked to John about the shots he made of Bacon on the steps of the Tate Gallery. That sequence with Bacon and Burroughs, busking on a Bloomsbury pavement, after another opening, felt like the job he'd done on me. Very efficient magazine reportage. Not using up valuable time for victim or photographer. With Bacon, Minihan made elaborate preparations. He was down there, hours ahead of the appointment the painter didn't keep. But he got the result he wanted: a designated and hierarchic informality.

There were good oak stools at the bar; photographer and printer warmed them for a catch-up conversation, laying down another layer to the mulch of Soho rumour and legend, before striking off for their Fleet Street lunch. Around a dogleg corner there was a prized table, round and roomy, out of general view, where projects flowered and died. My two Hackney-Irish friends, well schooled in territorial tactics, made their claim. And were now circling very gently around an improbable proposition that would require several bottles of smooth red wine.

'The liver seems to be the organic filter of the unconscious,' I heard the man say. A couple of large ones would help to channel the impassioned prose-poetry of Antonin Artaud. The terrifying voice of a madman who has seen the face of the absence of god in a hill of shoes. And brought it back to an audience of his Paris peers, shocked into confirming his ultimate damnation.

The Irish film pitch kicked off from the shamanic visionary's last great punt, before he disappeared into the tender care of the French asylum system, into drug therapy, drug addiction, and repeated electro-convulsive shocks. Achieved provocations for the linguistic delirium of Rodez. The letters and the lectures, so brilliant and so demented, so alien that they must have been transmitted from the dark side of the moon. 'They are raising all the whipcracks of my dead hand ... Nothing to stand as a barrier against the void.'

After Mexico, and that first death in the land of the Tarahumaras, Artaud scraped up the funds and contacts to carry the Bachall Isu, the Staff of St Patrick, to Inishmore. Left alone in his loud meditations in the rocky shelter of a broch, buffeted by Atlantic winds, the poet scribbled and yearned. I longed to hear the end of this story, to sit with the company while the day drifted, but I had other assignations to keep and people to see. When I got back, two hours later, nobody had stirred from the magic table. But now, the producer, down from the Midlands, train connections lost to no-speed rail chaos, told me his theory of Deakin's rise and fall. He had been brought up to speed on my project and was clearly looking for a tactful way to sidestep the Artaud gig.

'This was a pivotal year. World wars on the horizon. Revolution in the air. Artaud and Deakin, separately, in Mexico, at the point where the atmosphere was thinnest, red earth: "the periplum of the serpent." All unknowingly, spiritual quests were exchanged. And outsider status enforced. Like a scorpion tattoo on the eyeball. Transmigration of souls. Without a single word being spoken. No cameras were tolerated. On pain of death. Now *that's* your film.'

I let it rest for a couple of weeks, until I had finished my draft, then I got my wife to text Steve Walsh. His email was out, but he carried a phone. And checked it from time to time as he travelled back and forth to Ireland. After the excesses of the Deakin psychobiography, it was a requirement to grab this fortuitous opportunity, and to talk to the only person who could give me a flavour of the sacrificial pariah at the court of Bacon: the postponed suicide and his professional life.

The Minihan photographs from Soho had disappeared. They had slipped away into some dim place beyond recovery. And probably for the best. Trying to post a package to West Cork was insanity. There had been a suspected Russian cyber-attack on the postal system, Steve said, on just the worst day. Millions of pounds in blackmail payments were demanded to free the flow. Bureaucratic paperwork intervened. Phantom tariffs were imposed mid-ocean. It would have been cheaper to take a business-class flight with the box under his arm. Are these artworks? And, if so, what is their value at auction? Not much for the commissioned street snaps, but there were also portraits of Michael Longley, a respected Ulster poet.

Steve, a convivial man, occupied his favoured corner stool at the end of the curved bar at the French House. He was chatting to the landlady, a few drinks in, well positioned to keep an eye on the door. It was as if he had never moved after escaping from the Maison Bertaux basement. He raised himself in greeting as I approached. I have no memory for passing faces, but this one registered. Steve had something of the quality of the actor Roger Allam: he was believable. He was where he was, without gifting his essential being to some hungry digital device. He carried more hair than Allam; a time-travelled bohemian sweep over the collar, thinning a little at the scalp-line. He was settled into his denim shirt. After a warm handshake, and after Lesley Lewis, the obliging proprietor, vacated her stool, I moved in alongside. Steve did not look so much like Allam now, but he had the slow and steady shifts of that actor, when called on to play a veteran copper subsiding gently over a pint in an unimproved Oxford pub.

The printer was at home. This was his good place. The walls were papered with departed friends with whom he was still in conversation: the notable and the notorious, the posthumously tolerated. And those who were only included in the frieze because they had been around in the high days, the lost days, the weird days, and bought a bottle or two, contributing to the babble that never ceased. They conformed to non-conformity: the duty of attendance, holding steady or going under. The fraternity, and the strong women who were also good chaps, the ones who never thought their chat too serious to be thrown away on a shifting mob of life-artists buying into the consensus, the general contract of unspoken mortal creep.

Before we started on Deakin, his legend, I knew I would never get an inch closer to the man. Steve was too young to have done Deakin's printing in the days of *Vogue*. By the time Lesley, a cabaret performer who worked with a python, and who was later a Clerkenwell publican and strip club manager, took over the sinking French from Gaston Berlemont in 1989, Deakin had been dead for seventeen years.

There was a bit of a drama, tears, slaps, kisses, recriminations, kicking off at the other end of the bar, almost as if Lesley, who has been called a fragrant combination of Catherine Deneuve and Marie Lloyd, had arranged it: a demonstration of how the scene played when the Colony Room crowd warmed up for a session. I noticed the black beret hanging above the fracas like a vampire bat waiting to swoop on French wine spilled across resistant British oak.

'From Robin's head when he passed. I had it dry-cleaned.'

A potent memento. Everybody remembered the wake. Many of the faces along the wall had been on duty. Keeping ex-wives apart, greeting unexpected sons. Some never recovered. You could rely on a recycled Cook anecdote to establish your French House credentials.

'A very smart guy, Robin. Did the books for Bernie Silver,' Steve said. 'An Old Etonian, a toff, fiddling the accounts for a Jewish boy from Hackney! Bernie had complicated stuff going on with a bent Maltese traffic cop importing olive oil. There was all that and then the clubs, the girls. Somebody had to straighten the filth. And keep a record against a rainy day. Robin went through the ledger. He told Bernie there were legitimate expenses, a ton of straight cash left over from the porn squad. "Don't fuck about, son," Bernie told him. "A schneid fiver is worth ten of the kosher jobs. It's got form. Some cunt has given blood and sweat to earn it." Robin pissed off to his French vineyard right away. They love him over there. Chabrol films, the lot.'

Immediately behind us on the wall were two photographs. Cook, white shirt, leather jacket off, beret on, at his ease. He'd done a nice inscription for Lesley: 'Hugs & kisses!! Derek Raymond.' Book launch, *Dead Man Upright*? Lesley boasted how they could always round up the best journos, the cream of the cream, the freeloaders. Directly above Cook, cornered for interrogation, and terminally haunted, with no inscription or message from the other side: John Deakin. The porthole lamp on the wall obliterates my attempt to photograph the photographs. A sterile and gloating moon burning out detail, turning every conversation between the French House phantoms into a competitive interrogation. Faces without names. Names on their oak stools playing memory tapes that can no longer be punctuated by the reflex of firing another cigarette.

After Cook, Bacon. The yarns, the scandal. Round and round we go. Bacon implies Deakin. Deakin is ever-present. He is caught in the doorway, hovering, checking the clientele, primed for flight.

'I was fifteen or sixteen,' Steve said. 'First time.'

Working in advertising, in the zone, he was brought along to the Colony Room, as for an initiation, a rite of passage. If he said so himself – pushing against where he was now, what life had done – he was a good-looking boy. Not exactly Bacon's type. Apart from the leg irons, the orthopaedic device setting off his fresh stance. He could have been a proper painting. Like Deakin. Or Harry Diamond. But it didn't happen. He became a respected technician. He made the prints.

Deakin, the sodden apparition, will not step inside. He seems to be under a prohibition. He has left the photographs as his testimony. They are mute where the man was voluble, cutting and carving. On the run. But Harry was a friend. Harry, respecting and arguing the toss with his study partner, his partner in mischief, Mr John Deakin, was a French hound. He got along very well with Steve. They swapped favours. Steve was supposed to negotiate a print of Frank Auerbach, at the bar of the French, signed by the artist and returned to Lucian Freud. But it was too late, Freud queered the deal. He died before he could have another crack at Harry. The feisty East End photographer gave Steve a message to pass on. 'Tell Lucian to fuck off.' He couldn't take the way the painter squeezed him with the thumb of gravity, made it look as if his legs weren't fit to carry him home. And had Steve noticed – few did – the figure on the pavement outside? Lounging up against a wall. A watcher out of Fritz Lang. Beyond the thirsty plant, beyond the window, there was always a watcher. A witness. Without this angry husband or father, bookie's muscle, rent-boy spook, the painting doesn't work. Harry is on the loose. Harry is fucked. Look at that clenched right fist with the yellow finger. Harry is a piece of the street carrying messages. Threats.

When Robin Muir was assembling the Deakin prints for his 2014 collection *Under the Influence*, Steve went round to his house. He mentioned the Diamond shot of Deakin. In the doorway of the French. 'You can't see him, but he was talking to Bacon.' The pariah's head is on the tilt. He's quizzical. Alert. Paying attention. Or slewed, wasted. Gone.

'You actually *have* Harry's print?'

It went into the book as a frontispiece. And it fitted perfectly.

The bar at the French, acting as a camera obscura, swallowed light. With Steve as the resident magician. He worked, directly, with generations of photographers. But not with Deakin. Not in person. What Walsh printed, by way of Bruce Bernard and the Arnold Circus Archive, was the set of posthumous recoveries. The ones that I lived with for so many months. The ones that dictated the narrative of this book. Steve knew most of the Soho cast, but other captures remain mysterious and unidentified.

This was a dead end. Even with revived access to the old Soho haunts, I was no closer to the reality of whatever Deakin was, is, or had been in his pomp, in his slow sad post-photographic decline.

Wine glasses were refilled at regular intervals. Steve had a couple of house whites waiting for him. He was doing most of the talking, the heavy lifting. We drifted back to Ireland and the missing Minihan portraits. The patron of the Deakin archive, it appeared, had a magnificent house in the Burren. *The House on the Borderland!* One of the strangest geological platforms I have ever encountered. On a research trip with Chris Petit, who was auditioning the permeability of the landscape between Ulster and the Republic, psychic and physical, for *The Psalm Killer*, his novel of conspiracy and crisis, I identified, to my own satisfaction, the general location for that tale of cosmic horror by William Hope Hodgson, *The House on the Borderland*. Holidaying English outsiders, comfortable in their prejudices, blunder on an account of the heat-death of space, time and sanity, as rude swine creatures clamber from a smouldering pit.

As Steve described his working visits to this place, the gradual recovery of the confrontational and unquiet portraits from the negatives Deakin left behind, I couldn't help imagining those slavering beasts at the door of the interloper, Hodgson's Burren recluse: porcine horrors wearing masks made from Colony Room photographs. And as I tried to signal for another round, a trick Steve managed without lifting an eyebrow, Petit appeared at my side. A trigger word in Steve's discourse must have summoned him. In fashionable Connemara-knit rollneck and Malvern charity jacket, Chris was dressed for social infiltration of the kind that had public-school-educated special operatives taken out of village pubs in South Armagh at gunpoint. After a lengthy pause and inspection of the hissing Italian machinery, Petit accepted a small black coffee. 'On the wagon,' he said. And, after that, no more. Not a whisper. He stood. He lingered with intent. He looked around.

'Brighton' was the trigger word that drew him in. Steve was rounding off a yarn from a recent Irish return, some stranger in the village pub. They talked, they got on, an amiable fellow keeping it lively but giving nothing away. When this feller stepped outside for a smoke, a trusted regular told Steve your man was sound, a notorious bomber. He had done hard time for that Brighton business in the Grand: horrible deaths, collapsing ceilings, dust and devastation. A major contribution, as it turned out, to Margaret Thatcher's heroic legacy. The heavies got straight on to the bomber, kicked down his door, because of one careless element in an otherwise meticulously planned outrage. There was a fingerprint on the register card and the name given matched that of a person of interest in the security files. The name was Walsh.

Arriving without a ripple, after implying that he had always been there, Petit drifted away, around the blind corner to a table where, juggling his coffee cup and a double measure of whisky, he rejoined an unseen companion. Not having talked to my former collaborator in a couple of lockdown years, while he had been moving around – Berlin, Cape Town, Florida Keys, Rotterdam – I followed him to the inner sanctum. Petit had been responsible for one of the ripest accounts of Soho in the decades after Deakin's death. The book began as depth research so easy paced it had to be a front: second-hand bookshops, London Library, and rounds of cutting rooms and bars. Leisurely mornings, with small Dutch cigars and Ethiopian coffee, on the telephone. Solitary socialising of the suburbs. The project was commissioned as non-fiction but emerged as a novel of place. And persons: especially an avatar of Robin Cook.

'I wondered at the accuracy of Cookie's biography. Details could elude him,' Petit wrote. With his military upbringing, Chris was hot on detail. Even when dressed down for passing among the lowlife, his brogues were polished. The Soho fiction carried him to places on the far side of sessions in the great tradition. He never broke cover. 'I woke up in a porno cinema, with no memory of getting there.' This was a dangerous book coming out from the inside with alcohol-fuelled heat and momentum. Like the spontaneous combustion of Krook in *Bleak House*. Melting the meat envelope of the Dickens grotesque, an illiterate collector and surveyor of rubbish: fatty ash choked the London air, letters and legal papers were unscathed. Up the rickety stairs, small birds flapped against the bars of their cages.

Petit did not look up. He offered no introduction to the bulky figure with the impressive crown of silver hair; the one who was holding his glass to the light, checking it for colour or potential poison. The man made a great show of sniffing and swirling, being certain there was no contamination by cubes of ice. The gesture was finessed into a greeting. And, after this brief pause, the seasoned monologue rolled on. With the subtle punctuation of a vestigial stutter. The kind that builds tension in an audience.

They had been talking, as ever, about James Jesus Angleton, poet and conspiracy bureaucrat. A cracked emanation of the essential spirit of military-industrial paranoia, Angleton got the CIA slot that fellow Harvard man, William Burroughs, wanted. He was fated thereafter to live the madness, granting Burroughs time and obscurity in which to indulge and expose the evil machinery of state coercion and terror. The co-conspirators at the French were debating whether Deakin had bagged Angleton for his seventeen-volume portfolio: a face in the crowd at the White Tower or the Waterman's Arms? Or even here in the French? Could the super-spook be identified among the rogues' gallery of snapshots, party Polaroids and assorted Hammer Horror oil paintings displayed around the walls? More to the point, I thought, was the double-breasted chalk-stripe suit and the gold half-moon spectacles: the mocking clubland persona of Petit's thirsty guest. I had seen *him* in the Deakin albums. This man was caught at the head of the stairs in one of the sequences of film personalities, actors, producers, technicians and moneyman, assembled for a spiked broadsheet commission. One of the cultural ghosts I'd failed to name.

'Robinson,' the man said. With that reflex trick the best conmen employ, pretending to read your thoughts, one beat before you can do anything about it. And demonstrating an immediate recognition that I couldn't deal with the world in front of me, unless I referenced it to some book or film. Petit's garrulous guest, handler or controller, was enjoying himself, by playing at being a misplaced Harry Lime spectre emerging from the shadows at the corner of Manette Street. And letting a tomcat spray on his trousers.

'Did you know,' Robinson said, 'and Gaston's daughter swears to it, that Orson Welles and Errol Flynn were going through cases of rare wine down in the cellars right beneath our feet when de Gaulle was scribbling his famous 1940 speech, upstairs at the bar?'

I couldn't work out if Petit was punting a film to Robinson, or if the corpulent fixer was trying to reel him in, to get his name attached to a project that would never be completed, or even begun: spare funds from Finland, roubles that couldn't be taken out of Russia.

Asking if Robinson remembered Deakin was my mistake. Too blunt. Too direct. It set him off on yet another serpentine trajectory.

'After the war, we took time out in Rome. Hotels were terrible, but cheap. They were all there. All involved in the poetry racket, in property deals around derelict land and film studios waiting to be constructed from the ruins. Deakin? Oh yes. One of life's unfortunates. On the take in places with zipped wallets.'

Graham Greene and Angleton. They coincided in Rome. Petit perked up. Angleton was his special subject. He had a script that Christopher Walken wanted to do. If that was knocked back, he might turn it into a stage performance for Brussels. He told us how *The Third Man* came about. Greene was trying to hammer out a storyline for Carol Reed. Deakin did manage some sinister shots of *him*. Kim Philby had been involved with both men. Suspicion was deep-seated and mutual. Petit's story was that Angleton arranged for a bought woman to give Greene the clap. Greene sourced penicillin in Rome. It worked. And the episode inspired him to transfer the whole package to Vienna. He set up the speech that Welles claimed to have written for the sequence on the Ferris wheel, the Riesenrad in the Prater: Swiss neutrality and the culture of cuckoo clocks. An old joke of Robinson's, so he claimed. With a dismissive wave of an unlit Havana.

How old was this man? Welles would be 108 now. The storyteller in the suit, in a kind light, could have passed for sixty-five. But you almost believed him. He took possession of his anecdotes. In the French House, linear time is suspended. 'Boredom is the only crime here,' he said, 'tedious fact-checking has been annulled.'

Robinson conceded that there was something significant about the particular persons Deakin chose to photograph. Or to leave well alone. Carol Reed and Trevor Howard: in the file. No Greene. Stephen Ward: bagged and delivered. Not a trace of Philby or Angleton. Frank Norman and George Dyer: on Soho parade. With all the Bernard brothers and none of the Krays. On the occult side, Gerald Hamilton in place of Aleister Crowley. Robinson made it sound as if the catalogue of Deakin nominations had very little to do with the photographer himself and everything to do with shadowy interests in anonymous government buildings attempting to fix the narrative.

'Photographic prints are valves,' he said. 'They are fallible records of the moment of crisis. The hunter entrapped in the capture. The victim soliciting the assault. Portraits remove energy from source and transfer it to the possessor. Murder or suicide?'

Now the pressure of imagery on the tight walls of the French was too much. This exhibition of compulsory nostalgia. The godless theology of a discontinued past. The yearning hunger in those dead faces: the mugshots, surveillance frames, and wanted posters. Grids of former French House attendees become alcoves of grinning skulls in a Capuchin catacomb in Palermo. Flickering candles of extinguished consciousness. The undead in their patient undying.

'The quality that separates Deakin's snaps, printed by Mr Walsh, from an AI pastiche, is *spirit*. It would be facile to recreate your lost portrait taken outside this pub by Minihan. And it would be child's play to call up a simulacrum of your rather singular prose style. With a few words redacted, the book would write itself.'

'Why Brighton?' Petit asked.

'Where better? The place was always a marine euthanasia facility. Convalescents and concubines. Eros and Thanatos. Think of Deakin's list of associates and lovers, the tragic faces he managed to photograph. Arthur Jeffress: suicide. John Minton: suicide. David Archer: suicide. Stephen Ward: suicide. Peter Lacy and George Dyer: suicide. Dyer checked out in the same year as Diane Arbus, another prime facilitator of freaks. She went for the ritual in the bath. No remission. No second thoughts. Barbiturates *and* razor. Was Deakin suicided by the society he kept? Or by the conviction that his story had run out? The tape was finished. Was it a termination arranged by special interests, in order to boost a future market? The land of sleep is heavy with signs and shapes. There are no accidents.'

I fetched Robinson a drink. Petit had to leave, there were property matters to settle, agents to prod, he said. Lesley Lewis slid back onto the stool alongside Steve Walsh and picked up their original conversation. The French folded in on itself, its oral histories. The street outside was still there. It took years to reach it.

Somebody tapped my shoulder, while I was waiting to take my leave of the couple at the bar. He shoved a brown envelope into my hand. 'Sorry it's taken so long. John said this was the only picture of you that Deakin took. He never bothered to get it printed.'

I waited until I was back on the train and heading east. The portrait had been posed outside the French. And outside time. Here was the ultimate nightmare: a wattled corpse in a baseball cap. A revenge from some other place, conjured by AI oracle. The fiction of the posthumous Deakin print was too frightening to burn. Where could I properly dispose of the ashes? Poros? Brighton? I stuffed it into the book I was carrying. And left it on the Elizabeth Line seat.

NIGHTFISHING

'Here both murder and suicide are rituals, acts instantly transformed into legend, facts that in all their specificity transform everyday life into myth ... There is a constant war between the messengers of God and ghosts and demons, dancers and drinkers.'

– Greil Marcus, *The Old, Weird America*

I Fort We Wus Goin' to Brighton

Tipped forward without agency, a bedraggled and flightless gull, the post-operative survivor stretched out brittle raincoat wings, to hook his trembling remains over the top rail of the promenade. The saving obstacle cut deep into the butchered ruin of his belly. Even the speak-your-weight machine on the pier had been struck dumb by his request. Last coin wasted. There was a familiar surge of discomfort across his chest and into his throat. Nothing left to vomit. To dribble or spit. He pretended to look at the sea. An ancient novelty with no claim on his attention. Nothing to defend now. Nothing to hide away. Coloured bulbs fizzed and fused on their drooping string. Stars beyond counting are going out. The news they send back from light-years before his birth does not arrive.

Deakin tried to walk, not in the old way, but as rapidly as he could manage, going nowhere. Every miserable road in Brighton ended on the front. A pillowcase of stolen laundry he folded over the rail, gripping hard, as they'd encouraged him to do on that hideous frame in the spongy hospital corridor. A wheeled apparatus of Germanic pedigree that reminded him of the orthopaedic clutter in one of those daubs by Francis. A cage in which to display the latest humiliation of poor George.

He acted his part: a down-from-the-Smoke excursionist, chirpy convalescent out on the town. Deakin stared at puckered indentations in the foul grey conglomerate stretching to the water; a little less than stone, a little more than sand, a buffer between esplanade and exoskeleton of the illuminated pier. He willed summer holiday colour, not this muck. He willed the deep blue of a postcard from his island idyll. Not the blue of heaven, but the disnatured chemical blue of Swan Lake, that fun-fair puddle with the armada of plastic swan boats, down in Hastings, where he made loving-couple photographs for cigarette advertisements. A chill breeze stirred the thick surface membrane, staining the dull white flanks of the swans. A pungent and gritty blue squirted into the porcelain bowls of the adjoining Gents. He willed Piraeus, the ferry. The house on the harbour at Poros.

It was too easy to be lost in Brighton. It was worth murdering worlds to get here, to be primed for pleasure. Or pursuit.

For months, before Paris and after, Deakin was in and out of hospital. A curtain call with attendant privileges: waited on, hand and foot, by freckled Irish nurses, centre of attention, celebrity visitors bringing cake and champagne. Behave as badly as you dare. Compose letters to Dan, in the certain knowledge that he will preserve them, as archive, as evidence to flog to collectors and libraries, when the bailiffs and blackmailers come calling.

It is comforting to know that you have been accepted into the brotherhood of the damned, that you have passed over. You are a dead man out on licence. The quacks garbled the death sentence, dressed it up. *But he knew.* He read the pictures. No more interventions. Deakin followed a neurotic psycho-surgical transit across London: out from the homeopathic ward for tropical diseases at St John's Hospital for Diseases of the Skin, a grim colonial citadel from which he had already discharged himself to follow Bacon to Paris. Before returning to face the removal of a lung at the Westminster Hospital. And a stint, with two weeks left, clock ticking, at All Saints' Hospital in Austral Road, between the Elephant and Castle and the Imperial War Museum, old Bedlam. He was close enough on still nights, in cold fever, to hear the screams of generations of the lost. It was from the crisp sheets of that narrow bed, in the hospital of all the saints, that Deakin wrote to Farson, plotting a shimmering vision of Poros too beautiful to be realised.

'No chance of Poros for a couple of months . . . I have to learn to breathe again . . . Stairs & walking impossible . . . Alert & on the ball & yet physically so helpless . . . No plane would take me.'

He pictures, instead, tottering up another gangplank, eager to 'glide down the Adriatic in a white steamer to Piraeus to be met by Blackpatch & his matelot lover'.

Between worlds, post-mortem fantasies flood the system like a saline drip: remembered ports and projections of ports still to come; wealthy patrons, boys in uniform, and clips from afternoon films witnessed through a fug of Soho smoke. Bacon was impressed by Deakin's discipline, and how, after a punishing lunchtime session in the Golden Lion, a turn around the French, checking on who was in, he would remove himself to Berwick Street for a couple of hours of fretful kip, before the long evening began. *They have to locate Blackpatch.* But Blackpatch is a fiction out of Robert Louis Stevenson. He is Robert Newton and he is also a person with a passport, a person that nobody on Poros, when questioned in later times, can recall.

'A letter arrived two days ago offering me his home for the entire summer in Poros, on account of his being in love in Piraeus . . . He has a friend who can find me a balconied place on the harbour.'

Meanwhile, there is another staging post, courtesy of Bacon. 'Francis and Miss Beston arranging some place in Brighton for me.'

Miss Beston comes to Lambeth with caviar, champagne and the latest hardbacks. In 1970, for a new collected edition, Graham Greene was tweezering through the original pink-wrapped 1938 version of *Brighton Rock*, eliminating or disguising period racism, the reflex antisemitism inherited from T. S. Eliot, from 'Prufrock', 'Burbank with a Baedeker: Bleistein with a Cigar'. And *The Waste Land*.

Physically and morally spent, shuttled between hospital ward and Soho labyrinth, Deakin lost himself his own wasteland. Culverted sewage rivers flooding cellars of pornography. Feral pigeons on single legs hopping after sodden crusts. Preachers ranting in factories abandoned to insurance barbecues. Newspaper sellers doused in petrol. Medicated, dry-drunk and hallucinating, cursing the gift of pain, choosing where to rest, gagging on venom, the former photographer was more dead than alive. According to his circle of associates, friends primed to act like hyenas around any show of weakness, Deakin's cruelty to David Archer paralleled the sorry end of George Dyer. And Bacon's part in the official suicide. Deakin would not support his old lover and patron, but he surprised those who knew him by leaving sufficient funds in the bank to pay for his own funeral. He managed to squirrel away a few thousand pounds for a fantasy trip to sunnier climes. Paradise lost before limbo.

As he sat alongside the pool at the Oasis Baths in Endell Street, a secret of sorts, enclosed between Covent Garden and Bloomsbury, Deakin remembered Archer's daily swims in the Serpentine. Those accountant's spectacles, that fish-white body. The crow's eyes. Oasis traded up to its name. It had once been a place of assignation, a Turkish Bath, before fashion moved towards exercise and health: a strip of meagre cloud-reflecting water as an adjunct to gymnasium, squash courts and cafeteria. This captive substance, the ruffled chlorine, was like developing fluid for the transmission of future memories. Deakin registered the elongated rectangle with its duck-patrol lanes as a liquid print; faceless lovers were swimming back to him. He had found his spot for meditation and release from the neurosis of movement. Bardo yoga in Covent Garden.

Sometimes a drinking acquaintance from the Colony Room would adjust his *Dolce Vita* dark glasses, pinch running nostrils, and occupy the lounger alongside him, for quiet discourse; wishing there was a thicker glass to grip, ice cubes to poultice throbbing temples. Deakin glugged steadily from a jumbo water bottle, Adam's apple rising and falling: a ball of thyroid cartilage on a shooting gallery fountain. Cheerio!

One day, no camera to encumber him now, he was mesmerised by the spectacle of a man with artificial legs ploughing up and down the pool, length after length. Shoes and socks had been painted on the plastic limbs. Deakin confessed: 'I fancied him rotten.' He proffered the water bottle to his half-nude, rednecked friend: straight gin. Straight gin for bent gents. They drank, right out of it in London, watching a muscular amputee cleave unprotesting wavelets. Dark windows of surrounding offices. No telltale bulge among the incontinence pads. No leaks from zippered wounds.

Under pressure, Muriel Belcher relented. The Colony drinkers could be relied on for a show of sentiment over mortality. Crocodile tears plopping into the vodka. They liked a good funeral. Even better than the wake that followed. A Soho wake rubbed too hard against reality; too many festering crimes and insults would surface. Barred for life, after initiating the scurrilous and unfounded rumour that Muriel had helped herself to Christmas charity funds gathered to support children who were victims of thalidomide, Deakin was let back into the den for one inglorious exit binge, on a quiet Saturday afternoon. For years, after his expulsion, he had been a faithful attendee at the Salon des Refusés, a few yards down Dean Street, at the Caves de France. A drowned-brain's mushroom cellar with attendant waxworks and derelicts. He drank with the living and the dead, with the exiled and the reforgotten, with ticket o' leave visitors from former times. The street photographer gloried in sharing an insecure place in legend alongside the ones he had catalogued: Nina Hamnett, the two Roberts, Gerald Hamilton, Caitlin Thomas, Paul Potts, David Archer. And Dan Farson. On parole from Devon. Good old Dan.

A new crowd, performing bohemians, entropy tourists with investment portfolios remarked on Deakin's rank odour, the foxy trail from geriatric ward to booze pit, as he picked his way towards the bar of the Colony for the last time. He shuffled on hobbled sheep-feet across broken glass and smouldering unclaimed cigarette stubs. 'John Deakin, I adored,' said Colony regular Gerald McCann. 'He was tiny and smelly. You had to stand up-wind from him because he would wet himself and wear the same pants for days on end.'

Deakin was a sick man, waiting for a bed in the genitourinary unit at All Saints'. But he had to sustain, to the final breath, the double act with Bacon. He had to boast of his escape to Poros. 'You've never been south of Brighton,' Bacon sneered. A charitable expulsion was brewing. A plot. One more round and no reprieve.

There was a ritual element to Deakin's seasick jig to the communion rail at the Colony. He had some Liverpool left in him. Was he a Roman? That afternoon he was on the red wine, a steady transfusion. When he was done and his body clock told him that it was time for siesta in Berwick Street, curling in a ball on the bed over boxes of negatives, folders of abandoned projects, Muriel swooped on his licked glass. She carried it to the sink and smashed it. The gesture was interpreted by witnesses as a sign of 'abiding hatred'. But Muriel liked to honour a projected Portuguese Jewish descent and gestures had meaning. It could have been a moment of forgiveness, for both of them, for the lives they had led: a wedding vow with mistress death. Deakin was never coming back. With the gaunt woman, not so long for the world herself, intentionally breaking a glass marred with the print of a dying man's mouth: this was a divorce. In the court of history. Demons were appeased by the sound, the crunch of ice cubes crushed in steel jaws.

Before Paris, before Bacon's triumphant apotheosis: Hackney. Old grey labouring Hackney with its parks and politics. David Archer had been thrice denied. He had suicided. 'White curtains of tortured destinies,' said David Gascoyne, one of the Parton Press meteors, an Archer discovery. Deakin, after Athens and Crete, was given a bed inside this redbrick Hackney monster: a castle of manifold infirmity overlooking the Lea Valley. Fever and smallpox, sad children and desperate addicts: the plagues of the moment disappeared into the spiteful geometry of an enclosed asylum on Homerton High Street.

The rise from the marshes was madness. Some came running while they babbled, some naked as lizards. Some were stuck in freshly sprayed tar, melting like painted snowmen. The expelled, junksick with scorched temples, clustered at a bus shelter. Without ever taking a bus. Behind secure doors, the hospital was another country. Caste was enforced by separate dining rooms for doctors and surgeons, discrete wine lists. Nurses were considered fair game. The medics, to sustain their long nights of service, made free with the shelves of the pharmacy. Addicts treated addicts. It was a good staging post for Deakin. Hallucinogenic drugs were readily available. There was surgical spirit for the methsmen and the stokers at their ovens in the basement: winked-at booze on the wards, vintage clarets at white-cloth tables of brain-skewering lobotomy stars. Window slits pulsed and shuddered with aftershock of amphetamines and the thud of patients falling from the liquid cosh. The building hummed and sighed. Louder than a burning rookery.

'Consciousness,' Deakin read, 'tilts like a transparent ball over the numerical symmetry of the years.' He was a willing passenger again, floating and helpless, cord-fed, blissful, carried inside the mother he never mentioned. Falling vertically, through Mexico and Ireland and London, to the point where narrative becomes a balcony.

The major wound, a cutlass stroke across the back, necessary for the removal of a lung, was postponed until Deakin returned from Paris. There was a fallow period of signing on, as for hotel spa or smart addiction facility, then discharging himself, maimed but reinvigorated. At the Westminster Hospital, they gave him a temporary berth in the Marie Celeste Ward; a reference he appreciated, recalling a cut-up Burroughs text from Tangier.

'A man undressing his back caked with tide flat mud slow cold whisper in my throat and the words were mine once . . . The *Marie Celeste* out of Halifax . . . Who else so stretched and torn from the sea . . . Dying old friend. It's been good to know you . . . The second hand bookshop used to be right opposite the old cemetery . . . Standing there face luminous from the sea.'

Hospitalised, immobile, on his back, Deakin was guilty of everything. You name the doomed pathology, he had it. There was little point in assigning the sick man to any specific ward. He qualified for all of them. Bacon plotted Deakin's liberation from Austral Road with a lethal benevolence. Like the Kray Twins 'rescuing' Frank Mitchell, the Mad Axeman, from Dartmoor. Francis sent a comfortable motor to run the shivering photographer down to Brighton: he booked a room with a sea view in the Old Ship. It didn't end well for Frank. By rumour, he was butchered in the back of a white Transit, then netted as fishbait, and taken out on a North Sea trawler. While Deakin was left, shuddering at the shoreline, hooked over the chill rail, gathering his forces for a funny night out.

Blinded by full-beam headlights and unreadable signage, road miles provoke a fogged reverie. Hurting from knee to neck, unable to fit his bowed jockey's legs to a position that soothed the stabbing in his back, popping pills, any pills, glugging analgesics, sucking down recycled beads of pearly saliva, Deakin pressed his knuckles hard against the smothering curve of padded leather. His chauffeur, capless but uniformed in black like a moonlighting mortician, belonged with James Fox in *Performance*. The timing, 1972, was spot on. Villain-on-the-run smiling when he knows it is all over, when he is ferried to his ultimate dig-your-own-hole rendez-vous. It is like dozing in a hearse, eyes wide open, with the overwhelming stink of trumpet lilies. The person who is already dead does not have to endure this pain. There is still time in which to choose the most flattering expression for a wax-injected face. Which is no longer your own.

Nothing happens in Brixton. Or Streatham Hill. Nothing ever happens there. Deakin submits. He is not reading the country; ribbon-development suburbia, one endless street imposed over abdicated farmland, over churches, bits of parks. The period held at traffic lights stretches to infinity. Any stuttering forward momentum is a chance to switch off and doze. Deakin has lost interest in particulars. In the rectangle of the wing mirror, the future is always two hundred yards behind you. The past is lost in the Surrey Hills. But it cannot be redeemed. Deakin is drained of curiosity. He does not register that totemic figure, beloved by Francis Bacon: Vincent van Gogh, on the tramp, labouring with the instruments of his trade, shadow-stitched into the road. The young Dutch art dealer, on a whim, walked from Brixton, his lodgings in Hackford Road, without maps or guidance, to Brighton. He made no drawings of this adventure. He is always out there now, for those who are primed to see him.

Croydon is a necessary penance. They live there under compulsion. D. H. Lawrence served a brief sentence as a schoolmaster, crafting stories to purchase his freedom. Croydon is a furniture depository waiting to burn. It's the end of the line. Deakin slept. He snuffled and snorted like an old dog. Nobody stays awake, by choice, in Coulsdon and Purley. Land of dentists and freelance tax avoiders.

Sleep and the Brighton road. The reels are being projected in the wrong order. Francis liked to power-nap in afternoon cinemas, waiting for the night. Deakin went with him. He brought a camera and made

prints from the screen. One accurate thread in *Performance* is the requirement for any respectable criminal, one of the chaps, to demonstrate his
status by *always* having a wheelman, a willing stooge. And even if the
chosen one can't drive, he must honour the uniform: the cap, the Italian
suit, the dark glasses.

The first action in *Performance* involves splashing a Rolls-Royce
with acid and shaving the head of the unfortunate chauffeur played
by John Sterland. Johnny Shannon, who took the part of the bookie
and protection racketeer, Harry Flowers, was presented as an avatar of
Ronnie Kray. The former boxer was originally up for the minor role of
the victimised driver. The inner sanctum of the evil empire, Harry's office,
is transformed into a cloned Kenneth Anger pop video, a naked Bacon-
influenced animation.

Villain and *Get Carter*, both released in 1971, one year after *Performance*, one year before Deakin's ride to Brighton, sport with the same
archetypes, the same steals from the socio-cultural stew of the previous
decade. Ian Hendry in *Get Carter* is another in the line of sinister chauffeurs. Ian McShane in *Villain* is drawn from the legend of David Litvinoff, the Whitechapel-to-Chelsea gambler and joker, credited as 'Dialogue Coach and Technical Adviser' on *Performance*. Litvinoff had
experienced the brand of Kray retribution, over a gambling debt, or one
jibe too many, dished out by Fox in the film. Lucian Freud painted Litz
as 'The Procurer'. There was a period when Litvinoff shadowed Freud's favoured haunts, running up a tab, pretending to be the painter. Anecdotes
around the customised bad behaviour of characters like Deakin, Farson
and Litvinoff rub away any division between happenstance and myth.
Books solicit films. Films predict crimes. Criminals acquire paintings.
The homoerotic dance reels out from the East End to Soho, from Chelsea to Brighton, and back to Limehouse. Ghostwriters, in hock to professionals of violence, pen accidental originals. Deakin didn't care about
history, he hustled to survive. It was all performance, all true.

With his sailors and dockers, four chauffeurs and no motor, Dan Farson,
Deakin's truest friend and most treacherous biographer, removed himself

to the safety of his father's house in North Devon. A London car, packed with suited males, on the razzle, well out of their territory, arrived unannounced. In the tradition of Frank Mitchell's ride home from Dartmoor. In the tradition of so many films of the period. The status car waiting at the prison gates for Stanley Baker.

The boys from the Smoke, yawning and stretching, decanted at Farson's home, the Grey House, at eight o'clock in the morning. They had driven through the night, with regular stops along the way. The fellows, dressed for town, were aping forgotten films and inspiring future screenplays. When James Fox as Chas, hair dyed, on the run from his former associates, decides to change his mind and to hide out in Powis Square, Notting Hill, he was supposed to be heading to Barnstaple in Devon. All roads lead to the absence of Farson.

The last man out of the car at the Grey House, Putsborough Sands, shaking his heavy head, rolling his tired shoulders, was George Dyer, described by Farson as 'one of those lovable people who seem beyond redemption'. A road movie that had run out of road. Run into sand. Another cul-de-sac. George stared for a long moment at the Devon dunes. Marram grass. A solitary stalking dog. Unconvinced waves on a stub of rock. 'I fort we wus goin' to Brighton,' he said.

And you were, George. You were. They all were. Brighton is not just a name on the map, it is a death sentence. Elective amnesia with gin and vodka. The perfect destination for a long weekend when they've finished calling time on the last rites.

Burnt out and unshriven, at the end of his tether, navigating *The Lawless Roads*, on commission in 1939, Graham Greene wrote: 'I dreamed that I had returned from Mexico to Brighton for one day, and then had to sail again immediately for Veracruz. It was as if Mexico was something I couldn't shake off, like a state of mind.'

Like Brighton. And Poros. Like Deakin and Arthur Jeffress in white dinner jackets on their cruise liner. Coming into harbour. Making over a small portion of the coming Mexican nightmare as a film only accessible by poets and madmen. The snake dance. The dream of flight. Like the bardo of the Old Ship.

Brighton Rock

A hard moon hanging over the pier. Like the lost eye of a deranged cyclopean god. An illuminated chalk target. Out of range. And there are men up there, bouncing in the dust. Gathering scraps of moonrock with gloved hands. After this squalid picnic, lunar tourism will be suspended. Remember that moon over the Wirral golf course? Oil slicks and black seaweed and sewage. Boy from Birkenhead, turned out, on the loose in another port, New York City: *Lunar Caustic*. 'A man leaves a dockside tavern in the early morning, the smell of the sea in his nostrils, and a whisky bottle in his pocket.'

Malcolm Lowry, on a binge, is assaulted by tabloid headlines. As is his countryman, John Deakin, in 1972, in Brighton.

LAST MAN ON MOON. NIXON IN CHINA. BREAK-IN AT WATERGATE.

The world happens. But not to us. Not to the little people. That bowl of light in the hospital window is a substitute moon. Every walk now a confession of impotence. Shot knee. Butchered lung. When it goes, it all goes. A landslide. Hold that rail. Hang on. One more day.

Pursuit. Without volition or engagement. Pre-written. Contracted Spooks as remorseless as Jesuits. Why does nobody answer the telephone? Editors demanding revision. Where are the women? The officially exploited. Is this all fiction? He snacks on quotations. 'His manner cynical and nervous, anybody could tell he didn't belong.' The story has already been scripted to a conclusion that Deakin can do nothing to advance. Or avoid. He has to stick with the programme: Castle Square, Aquarium,

Palace Pier. A saunter along the front, check in at the Old Ship. *Be sure to lock that door. And pocket the key.* Precisely as Graham Greene laid it out in 1938. A hardback novel Deakin gifted to the nurses at the Hackney hospital. Now vanished into charity-shop curation on Kingsland Waste: the aerosol of death you can never mask. But the Greene itinerary remained with him.

'These were the limits of his absurd and widely advertised sentry-go.' The Soho convalescent couldn't march, he could barely crawl. Breath came hard, rasping. He spat a froth of yellow filth. From habit, he asked a respectable man in a hat, coming off the Palace Pier, for a cigarette. He put it to his dry mouth, but he couldn't smoke.

Did he ever do Greene? For *Vogue*? He thought not. Maybe Carol Reed? Who should have made that Brighton film with Dickie Attenborough. Attenborough delivered great psychopath, but he was wrong for Pinkie, the teenage killer, physically wrong. Greene's character was a poverty-bred starveling fixated on damnation. Rickety bones and feral sharpness. He was more like Deakin.

What he admired in Greene's prose was the managed corruption. The displaced confessions. Literary travelling shots, snaky sentences, following the pursuit of Hale, the man from the *Messenger* known as Kolley Kibber. Fate-stained paragraphs chunder down to Brighton on the train from London, shadowing the victim along a pre-arranged route, as he distributes his cards. Every sequence seems to finish at the Old Ship. Every walk nudges the plot. Topographical details become part of the motivation of the characters: the landscape of the wild hunt. Deakin understood. He left Greene's novel behind in the hospital. He got rid of it. He didn't want to know where the story ended. He was finished with Brighton long before he arrived.

Photographs leave the options open. They can be arranged in any order. Narratives can be revised. Unbroken travelling shots flow in just the way some mystics describe the river of time: no beginning, no end, past and present in overlapping layers. But the nonsense has to stop. The clockwork runs down, the battery fails. Time's up. He knows he is somewhere, but the devil knows where. And only the devil. It's like watching yourself sleep from inside a light bulb.

In the seventeen black albums there are prints invoking not only the atmosphere of Greene's Brighton, that mix of entertainers, still in vestiges of make-up, sclerotic drinkers and the pathologically convivial, but also poets, writers and filmmakers, responsible for promoting the mythology of a seaside town where everything is permitted, on a weekend basis.

The balance to Pinkie's shabby and virginal youth, with his misogyny and Catholic lust for hellfire, is the comfortably fleshed, easy-going and life-affirming Ida Arnold. The woman who pursues the pursuer and brings him down, restoring order to paradise. These are the contrary aspects of Brighton. Deakin gave his allegiance to the side of pleasure and booze and banter by committing a portrait of the woman who played Ida so effectively in the Boulting Brothers film: Hermione Baddeley. Off-stage, Baddeley ran the Gargoyle Club on the corner of Meard Street and Dean Street, in partnership with her husband, David Tennant. Deakin went there when they allowed him inside, in company with David Archer or Farson. Guy Burgess and Donald Maclean were members. Farson has a rather slurred snapshot, made from a kneeling position, of the approved Bacon exegete, David Sylvester, at the head of a table beside the famous Matisse mirrors.

Deakin's Baddeley, photographed in 1953, is closer to Greene's written Ida than the sanitised version in the film. Eyes shut, eyelashes cat-combed, Max Factor trowelled like mastic, Baddeley grips an empty glass with painted talons, and conducts her doting audience with a stub of cigarette in a black holder. She's laughing. A welcome to all: all the right ones, bohemians and aristocrats, spies and exiled royalty. She's the antithesis of Muriel Belcher. Baddeley is the embodiment of what Brighton ought to be.

Robin Muir, in *Under the Influence*, couples the Baddeley portrait with a memorandum to the commissioners at *Vogue* from 1954. 'I am very worried about John Deakin at the moment, since he is obviously a very sick man, and should not really be working at all . . . In his present condition he is finding it extremely difficult to wash, shave, etc., and I think that the whole business is beginning to get him down.'

When Hale, the man on the run from the razor gang, meets Ida Arnold in a bar, she says, 'in a friendly concerned way', that he looks a bit 'queer'. 'No,' he replies. 'I'm not sick.' And to prove it he carries on drinking. He can't eat but he tells Ida that he's hungry.

'Come and have a bite.'

'Where shall we go, Sir Horace? To the Old Ship?'

'Yes,' Hale said. 'If you like. The Old Ship.'

The Old Ship it is. Hale gets Ida into a taxi, but they don't come safely to the desired harbour. They are parted at the electrified arch of the Palace Pier. And Hale dies in what Greene paints as a sublimated rape; a heart attack induced by the thrust of a stick of pink Brighton rock down his affronted throat.

Brighton is where the ghosts expelled from London mingle with excursionists packed on trains. Crowds head for the beach, the racetrack, the bars and restaurants. And borrowed beds. Naughty weekenders and experimental couples of all sexual persuasions. Francis Bacon paid £20,000 to settle George Dyer in a property at the coast, somewhere out of the way. And he booked Deakin into the Old Ship. A room of his own. A room with a view of the pier. The photographer left his bag, unopened on the bed, and walked out across the road. 'He leant against the rail.' He had no camera. Closing one eye, as he used to do, he winked at the indifferent moon.

Hale marked his progress by leaving cards in hidden places as he moved from bar to bar, rinsing old hurts with gin and tonic. Deakin, on the rail, remembered certain commissions, that dreary encounter with Noël Coward, for example; when the great showman was appearing in Shaw's *The Apple Cart* and holding court in his dressing room. The fastidious Coward was horrified by Deakin's appearance, his cheeky enquiry after a mutual friend in West Africa. More acceptable dressing-room visitors, bearing tributes, were Laurence Harvey and Graham Greene. The author of *Brighton Rock*, back on ground he had thoroughly researched, crossed paths with the clown-faced Deakin. The jobbing photographer, ushered out, felt a lurch in his stomach. A decade ahead of reality, he was being chased by summoned forces into the anglicised voodoo of Greene's novel.

Deakin was accompanied by Dan Farson, on duty for *Picture Post*. Dan got the required shot of the 'Master' adjusting his bow tie – like an audition for Greene's perfumed gang boss, Colleoni, as he purses thin lips at the sordid company on the Palace Pier. 'A little wave of musk came over the room from the handkerchief in Mr Colleoni's breast-pocket.' Farson was granted full access. 'Coward was a professional to his manicured fingertips.'

The man from *Picture Post* ran his jaded victim, doing his gallant bit to promote a show, over most of the *Brighton Rock* locations: up on the Downs, out to the racetrack, pinball machines on the pier. And Greene in person. Farson also took, as was his habit, covering shots for his own history of the time as revealed through the misadventures of a minor character, John Deakin.

He snapped Deakin, spectacles on, peering intently at a light meter, with Coward, in a state of spray-on rigor mortis, waiting impatiently in full dress uniform. Gritting his teeth, but aware of social obligations, the actor/playwright said that Deakin would, when he was done, be permitted to watch the performance from the wings.

'No thanks,' the photographer replied. 'I'm taking Mr Farson to the theatre round the corner to see *Soldiers in Skirts*.' And then on, by implication, bar to bar, boy to boy, for another big night on the town.

Even for a person on the run, with scarcely strength to draw another breath, Deakin was slow to detach himself from the metal support. He was overtaken by the halt and lame. Nothing suited him better than the sentence running through his head: 'He leant against the rail near the Palace Pier.' Fifty yards from his cell. Two clean white shirts. A safety-stoppered bottle of green mouthwash: in reserve against night terrors, against the absence of a well-stocked minibar. One well-travelled bone hairbrush inherited from Ken Tynan. And an uncut French paperback. *Pour en finir avec le jugement de dieu*. He laid them all out with due reverence. Gris-gris stiff. Bones and cards and rags torn from the necks of lovers. He was comforted to know that they were waiting, up the tortuous stairs, on the bed in the Old Ship. He would avoid taking a decision of his own by following Hale, Greene's doomed pedestrian, down Old Steine towards the Royal Pavilion. Then he must double back through the gardens, Castle Square, East Street. Greene's pimply psycho covered plenty of ground, from the dark places of poverty and mischief behind the station to a bright harvest of electric light along the promenade. To plush hotels where he was shamed by his pauper's shoes. Pinkie was not a walker. Walking was for suckers, poor folk.

'I thought we were going to walk.'

Pinkie's dim but willing girl, Rose, is on a date, in the countryside, up on the Downs, out towards Peacehaven.

'This is walking . . . You don't think people really *walk*. Why – it's miles.'

A chap's invitation to walk means a free ride in the bus. With unspecified consequences.

Before he could clear his head for the night on the town with Rex Crutchfield, Deakin had to unmake photographs that held him in a captured past. He had to cancel faces, in order to free up memory. He began to imagine the outline of the thing that was chasing him. Suicides and Secret State spooks were calling in the contract that allowed him to put his name to those remarkable captures.

Spicer, Greene's *Brighton Rock* character, broken veteran of Pinkie's gang, gets away from the boarding house, striding out, going wherever his feet decide to carry him. He labours to avoid the moment when he will become a filed image for anyone to handle and interpret. A casualty of surveillance systems not yet in place.

'He passed into shadow under the pier, and a cheap photographer with a box camera snapped him as the shadow fell and pressed a paper into his hand.'

The action only confirms Spicer's conviction that there is no way out. He is done, too old for the seaside game. They had his likeness now. They pinned him to a board.

Pinkie, strolling with Rose, is too canny. 'Snap you together against the sea?' He throws up a hand, covers his face. And spots the photograph of the man on the run. Rose sees him too. 'The one you said was dead. *He's* not dead, though it almost looks . . . that he's afraid he will be if he doesn't hurry.'

HURRY UP PLEASE ITS TIME.

Graham Greene made a fetish out of letting it be known that his face was *never* to be seen when he was interviewed on film: a primitive superstition born of pride. And blind faith in the power of the unaccompanied word. Although Francis Bacon was much photographed, especially by his Colony Room pals, Deakin and Farson, he refused to appear in a posthumous 1991 Deakin documentary, *Salvage of a Soho Photographer*.

'Hardly knew him . . . He was not a particularly good photographer and photography itself is of no importance.' Bacon explained to the film's director, John Christie, that he had only commissioned those infamous Deakin snapshots as charity, a way to hand over a few pounds without shaming the poor man.

Neither Farson nor Deakin left a portrait of Rex Crutchfield. With that splendid 1930s name, Rex belongs in *Brighton Rock*. In Evelyn Waugh. Or some classic golden age murder mystery. Crutchfield was on the scene, but he managed to keep himself out of the thickets of reminiscence. He was a figure of the town, a good companion for the final binge. They met by arrangement, Deakin and Crutchfield; they talked, they hit the bars. Farson, who wasn't there (he was waiting for Deakin on Poros), said that the fading convalescent in the Old Ship scrubbed up quite nicely, happy to take on the part of a self-made man 'just down from the north'. Crutchfield was 'an old friend': a friend who is never mentioned in any of the books. Maybe they tarted up together as a pair of businessmen on the razzle. Sisters from Surbiton on the pull. Rex was the sort of person who turns up unexpectedly at a small private funeral. The one nobody can connect with the body in the box. The silent stranger without whom the ceremony fails.

On the fatal night, Rex was the chosen chum for a circuit of all the likely bars and clubs, through the Lanes towards the Pavilion, Steine

Gardens, and uphill to Kemptown. Nobody recorded their adventures. Deakin made it up the gangplank to the Old Ship. He woke, next day, around lunchtime, dry-throated, short of breath. He rang down for a pot of lukewarm hotel tea. Metal-tasting and improved, so it seemed, with salt instead of sugar. Rim of cup hot enough to burn the lips, yellow liquid filmy and cold.

At this point, with Deakin submerged in the pit of a black dreamless sleep, still booted, rigid on the unproven bed, tracking patterns of sourceless light across the dull cream ceiling, he called up the tiled balcony of the waiting house on Poros. Bougainvillea. Donkey shit. He remembered coming into Henekeys in Ship Street and being handed the black spot by an old queen. And watching that spot, on the lumpy palm of his sweating hand, break into a rout of copulating flies. Henekeys featured in *Brighton Rock* and in Patrick Hamilton's *Hangover Square*. Deakin understood those hard-won alcoholic blackouts experienced by Hamilton's George Harvey Bone.

'He was walking along the front at Brighton, in the sombre early dawn, in the deep blue, cloudy not-quite-night, and it had happened again . . . *Click!* . . . It was as though his head were a five-shilling Kodak camera, and someone had switched over the little trigger which makes the exposure . . . But instead of an exposure having been made the opposite had happened – an *inclosure* – a shutting down, a locking in.'

The coffin-cabin of Deakin's Brighton cell was another 'inclosure', swallowing shadows. A revelation of wild staring faces – Rawsthorne, Belcher, Dylan Thomas, David Archer – dragged back from the abyss and projected in a slideshow, *clickclickclick*, across the pitted ceiling of the Old Ship, every pore mercilessly exposed. *Clickclickclick*. The faces bubbled like stop-motion leprosy. A telephone rang somewhere under the pillow and a woman's voice, a drunken prankster from a lost weekend, said one word: 'Goodbye.'

How can you track a man who has left no itinerary, no prints of the final binge? A pursuer who had given up on the pursuit, I went to Brighton with a paperback reissue of Greene's novel and the account Farson gleaned at the Colony Room on his return from Poros. By then, the funeral was done. And the Soho crowd, caught in traffic, had missed it. I was chasing ghosts in a period of lockdown, when most of the witnesses were silenced. But I wanted to see if there were spoors left on the ground. To gather and evaluate evidence, before things opened up again, and we could use our own tickets to Poros.

The choice of English's Seafood Restaurant was a good one. A stalled venue dedicated to forgetting, after a couple of glasses of Deakin's favoured white wine (any wine), whatever storyline I was now trapped inside. And for keeping space at the table for Deakin and Crutchfield, if and when they choose to saunter through the door. To make a living return, thereby relegating me, as is right, to the role of literary ghost: ghostwriter of unstoppable prints.

The restaurant was not old-fashioned. It was traditional, French influenced, smoothly run and proudly shabby, with linen tablecloths and napkins, with cutlery and plates that did not draw attention to themselves. The food was reliable. It didn't demand a round of applause. The waiters had been there many years before Deakin and Crutchfield. They had waited on Graham Greene and given him no special service. In *A Gun for Sale*, the novelist described a businessman with an obvious 'private life': he lunched too often in places like this. 'One thought in his presence of comfortable beds and heavy meals and Brighton hotels.' If you wanted the atmosphere of Wheeler's in Old Compton Street, at the time when Deakin photographed that last supper with Bacon, Freud, Auerbach, Andrews and Behrens, this was the place to do it. This was where a big evening began slowly with the first dish of oysters ordered at lunchtime. With the first chalky sip.

Aimless abandonment settles around the ceremonial participants, around concentrated diners and creaking attendants in black coats that have aged to verdigris, a lovely green-blue patina. The senior man trembles like Wilfrid Lawson in *The Wrong Box*, but never spills a drop. Nothing is rushed. The solemn waiters are watchful, they do not hover and pour. Nobody interrupts your conversation, nobody appears to eavesdrop. If the room has absorbed traces of Deakin's last outing, it is saying nothing.

I had to invent the way the dying photographer moved down East Street towards the sea. The pier was still there but nobody was hooked over the railing, where I now paused. A young man was reading aloud to his unimpressed partner from a phone device.

'The gun fell away as he spun backward. The morphine ghost shrank, hiding away from the pain.'

The cropped boy laughed. 'For pity's sake!'

The Old Ship has been revised into an ice-cream block, a margarine-coloured profile studded with narrow blue apertures, vestigial balconies. When I lift the camera to make a dim documentary record, I see Deakin's shocked face in every window. But the original hotel is a little further to the west, at the end of the development, snaking around into Kings Road.

The East Street corner of the Old Ship has been retrofitted as a Memphis coffee shop and bar, with authentic jukeboxes, collectible Coca-Cola shields, blisteringly red gas pumps and leatherette booths. A museum load of auction room Americana with jaded English service; yawning locals, pale and pustular, in fancy-dress aprons and caps. Cheeseburgers and chips. Root beer. Mammary milkshakes. A necrophile iconography of Hollywood's satanic spawn clutters the wall: Tarzan and Jane, James Dean, Marlon Brando, Marilyn Monroe. A voodoo Elvis in autopsy paint has been plaster-modelled alongside a posse of generic TV gunfighters.

This is a perpetual Halloween and the seafront diner has attempted its own Mexican Day of the Dead by sticking black bats over the saltcaked window with a view of the pier. Grinning skeletons lounge against the gas pump. The fake highway sign pointing to my pink table says: DEAD END. Gentlemen, like the late lamented Mr Deakin, opting to relieve themselves in set-dressed old English facilities, can study the advice block printed over a steaming blue trough: STAND CLOSER, IT'S SHORTER THAN YOU THINK.

Deakin took to his bed. Outside the hired room, on the wall of the surviving part of the old hotel, plaster has flaked away. Deakin slept. Or lay perfectly still feigning sleep, while the room slept him. He was surrounded by voiceless others, previous occupants risen and disturbed. He snored. He snorted. They stepped back and scattered.

Now with the advancing footsteps, the creaking but unyielding door, comes the same terrible cycle of dreams that are not dreams. The poet rising from his grave, coughing dry leaves. Leaves made from burnt skin. Leaves printed with faces. David Archer nailing his hand to the ladder. Jeffress adjusting the sleeve of his dress. Henrietta Moraes patting the mattress, making room on the bed. That slow advance, crawling over sharp stones, towards the hill in Mexico.

He woke late, a single band of importunate sunlight across his pillow, his white face. He struggled to lift the iron weight of the telephone. He ordered a pot of tea. Hot, strong, sweet. It had been a night of mortal thirst. Of confession without penitence. The drugs that kept him going, more or less, kicked against the demands of his entire psychic being, every cell calling out for a jolt of gin. And nothing left but the green mouthwash. He cradled the plastic bottle like a sacrificial doll. He licked and sucked and forced his purple tongue into the rough aperture.

When Bruce Bernard made a call, checking on his friend, there was no answer. Had he gone out? Empty eyes were fixed on the door, trying to solve the riddle Crutchfield set. 'A man paints his door red on one side, green on the other. What colour is that door?' Something horrible. Like Bacon at his worst. The slippery bastard could paint both sides at once: he could paint hell from the inside out.

The maid with the tea knocked, steadied the slipping tray with her webbed hand, then let herself in with a pass key. Deakin was unmoving, hiding somewhere inside yesterday's suit. It was done, exit tailored to punchline like a humourless joke. He had long prepared for this moment, and its aftermath, which he intended to enjoy, well before it happened: he named Bacon as his next of kin, knowing that the painter would have to schlep to Brighton to make a formal identification. Farson imagined the scene. Sheet being lifted and Bacon remarking that the best of it was knowing that Deakin's 'trap' was definitively clamped for the first time. The painter, who said that he lived for surprises, was shocked to discover that he wouldn't be digging in his pocket to cover the funeral expenses.

The Colony crowd, invigorated by the last rites for one of their own, were astonished when the estate of John Deakin of 68 Berwick Street was published. The person dying with his boots on at the Old Ship Hotel, during the night, or early morning of 25 May 1972, had £2,383 squirrelled away in his bank account. Crafty pariah! Enough for the funeral nobody attended. Enough for a surprisingly small hole in honest Sussex ground. Farson, the unofficial biographer, rival and friend, was well away. Waiting on that balcony in Poros, swimming from the harbour and diving under, holding his breath as long as he could manage, to salt-scour head lice: he was alone. And unable to witness the final performance until it was over.

There were no photographs of record at the graveside. And none of the published accounts bother to record where precisely Deakin had been laid to rest. If the location was revealed, visitors might come. Sentimentalists. Scholars. They would keep his legend in play. The rescued prints, the more danced the better, command a decent market price. There are collectors and period enthusiasts. There are exhibitions and books. But no pilgrims that I noticed were travelling to Brighton, by road or train, to pay their respects.

Nobody knew that Deakin had caught the sound he'd been waiting for all his life. Like the slow creaking of rusted asylum gates, opening without visible agency. The lid of a cobwebbed granite sarcophagus pushed back by a desperate hand in a story by Poe. A paint-locked window some creature from outside is trying to force. It was the sound Malcolm Lowry, in his alcoholic delirium, described as 'a dithering crack'. A crack of protest felt across the crust of a slow-shattering skull: Deakin put his fingers in his ears, to block out the corridor and the stairs. He was hollowed of meaning, so far gone in drink and death that old sheets of newspaper floated from the floor like colourless birds. He felt the scratch of insult as flies shat their copious eggs into his ear.

'Once more,' Lowry wrote, 'with a dithering crack, the hospital door had shut behind him … He felt no sense of release, only inquietude. He kept gazing back with a sort of longing at the building that had been his home. It was really rather beautiful.'

Inquietude achieved. Fifty years from the photographer's Brighton abdication, my own release, to the last lockdown page. Like yours, my head is ringing now. With the enduring wonder of this man. His ghosted psychobiography in pictures is safe and stored. Ticking dangerously in its cardboard vault. There is no choice about it: I must book a room for the night. And draw the curtains against the view. Listen to the revellers and the ambulances. And ring down for a pot of tea that I have absolutely no intention of drinking.

List of Illustrations

Untitled I (photograph of Francis Bacon, 1967). © John Deakin. Courtesy of the John Deakin Archive.

Dylan Thomas in the graveyard, 1950. © John Deakin. Courtesy of the Dylan Thomas Literary File Photography Collection, P20, Harry Ransom Center, The University of Texas at Austin.

Untitled II (photograph of a darkroom in Malta, 1942). © John Deakin. Courtesy of the John Deakin Archive.

Untitled III (photograph of Jomo Kenyatta, 1945). © John Deakin. Courtesy of the John Deakin Archive.

Out in the Afternoon, 1957. © John Deakin. Courtesy of Conde Nast.

Untitled IV (photograph of the two Roberts, 1948). © John Deakin. Courtesy of the John Deakin Archive.

Untitled V (photograph of David Archer, 1952). © John Deakin. Courtesy of the John Deakin Archive.

Untitled VI (photograph of George Barker, 1952). © John Deakin. Courtesy of the John Deakin Archive.

Untitled VII (photograph of Bacon, Freud, Auerbach, Andrews and Behrens at Wheeler's, 1962). © John Deakin. Courtesy of the John Deakin Archive.

Untitled VIII (photograph of Stephan Ward). © John Deakin. Courtesy of the John Deakin Archive.

Untitled IX (photograph of Lucian Freud, 1964). © John Deakin. Courtesy of the John Deakin Archive.

Untitled X (photograph of Henrietta Moraes, 1961). © John Deakin. Courtesy of the John Deakin Archive.

Untitled XI (photograph of Francis Bacon, Daniel Farson and John Deakin at Charlie Brown's). © Daniel Farson. Courtesy of the Daniel Farson Estate.

Untitled XII (photograph of Daniel Farson at the Waterman's Arms). © John Deakin. Courtesy of the John Deakin Archive.

Untitled XIII (photograph of Paris optician). © John Deakin. Courtesy of the John Deakin Archive.

Untitled XIV (photograph of street in Tangier). © John Deakin. Courtesy of the John Deakin Archive.

Untitled XV (photograph of Genoa factory). © John Deakin. Courtesy of the John Deakin Archive.

Untitled XVI (photograph of Bacon and Dyer on a train, 1965). © John Deakin. Courtesy of the John Deakin Archive.

Acknowledgements

My thanks to Clare Conville and Harriet Vyner for their initial approach. That dangling Cheerio bulb definitely lit up at the mention of John Deakin. There was business outstanding since the Soho photographer and his drinking pal, Dan Farson, made their cameo appearances, under aliases, in my novel *Downriver*. The buried sequel within that story had been cooking, unacknowledged, for thirty years.

Reading a first draft of *Pariah Genius*, assembled during lockdown, Clare recognised something ominously close to fiction. An insight that gave me permission to trespass at the Brighton deathbed of Deakin. Fractured memories spun out from a bardo of posthumous seizures and reveries.

The facts and fables of a complicated psychobiography were derived in great part from prints showcased and contextualised in three groundbreaking books by Robin Muir: *John Deakin/Photographs* (1996), *A Maverick Eye: The Street Photography of John Deakin* (2002), *Under the Influence: John Deakin, Photography and the Lure of Soho* (2014). Muir's elegant pictorial curation helped me to navigate a path through the seventeen volumes of uncaptioned print generously loaned by James Moores and the Deakin Archive. My thanks to Jane Rankin Reid for hospitality and information on the Archive.

The headlong trajectory of the Soho legend was extracted from many sources, obvious and obscure. I owe my sense of period and persons to James Birch (Francis Bacon), Darren Coffield (Colony Room), Iain Collins (John Craxton), William Feaver (Lucian Freud), Martin Gayford (Freud), Geordie Greig (Freud), Gill Hedley (Arthur Jeffress), Carol Jacobi (Isabel Rawsthorne), Sarah Knights (Barbara

Ker-Seymer), Catherine Lampert (Frank Auerbach), Henrietta Moraes (Henrietta Moraes), Michael Peppiatt (Bacon), Nigel Richardson (Josh Averey), Servando Rocha, Andrew Sinclair (Bacon), Mark Stevens and Annalyn Swan (Bacon), John Lys Turner (Richard Chopping and Denis Wirth-Miller), Harriet Vyner ('Groovy Bob' Fraser and his circle). And Dan Farson, especially, for everything febrile and fabulous.

The parallel adventure of the *Pariah Genius* film, also commissioned by Cheerio, was made with Chris Petit, Emma Matthews, Susan Stenger and Anonymous Bosch. My particular thanks to all of them. And to the advice, gifts, corrections and inspiration of Nigel Burwood, David Erdos, Gareth Evans, Barry Miles, John Minihan, Jock McFadyen, Stephen McNeilly, Michael Moorcock, Alan Moore, Effie Paleologou, Jim Pennington, Jeff Towns, Steve Walsh, Duncan Wu. Thanks to Paul Smith for bringing me back, at the critical moment, to Antonin Artaud. And to Darren Biabowe Barnes, Maude Elms and everybody at Cheerio.